About the Author

Born in Derbyshire John Hassall qualified as a Quantity Surveyor and spent twenty years working in the construction industry before joining the staff of the University of Luton, spending twenty years there before becoming Head of English at a school in Dunstable. Since retirement he runs his own gardening and decorating business. A lay preacher, youth leader and church Elder in the United Reformed Church for over forty years, his main leisure interests are cycling, (having raced in more than seven hundred events since 1967), photography and model making. He has been married to Ann since 1967 and has two children Adam and Sarah and four grandchildren, Lewis, Ryan, Kezia and Isobel, (the most marvellous family one could possibly wish for).

Acknowledgements

Valerie Turner, Andrea Hyde, Marie Smith and Shelley Brown, for help in proof reading and suggestions concerning content.

John Hassall

RIDE THE RAINBOW

AUSTIN MACAULEY
PUBLISHERS LTD.

A CIP catalogue record for this title is available from the British
Library.

ISBN 9781784553715 (Paperback)
ISBN 9781784553739 (Hardback)
ISBN 9781784553722 (E-Book)

www.austinmacauley.com

First Published (2016)
Austin Macauley Publishers Ltd.
25 Canada Square
Canary Wharf
London
E14 5LB

PROLOGUE

The boy would always remember the eyes.

The rider was clearly in trouble. Zigzagging across the road whilst climbing, was not in itself unusual. Many riders did that, it lessened the angle of the slope thereby making the climb longer but easier. In this case however, the gradient of the climb didn't warrant the extreme effort that the rider was all too evidently wringing from his body. His pace was agonisingly slow. He was now barely making any progress up the white-capped extinct volcano that was the major battleground of this race. The boy at the roadside knew with absolute certainty that his hero was dreadfully close to breaking point. Suddenly and inevitably, the rider stalled and almost as if in slow motion, fell to the ground, his feet still fastened to his pedals by his toe-clips and straps. Spectators rushed to help the stricken rider who now even from some distance looked in a desperate state.

After what seemed an eternity to the boy but in reality was only a few seconds, the rider was helped to his feet and back onto his bike and started off again being given pushes by many willing hands.

"No, no, let him stop." The boy cried out, but, of course, no one took any notice. All riders in an event, like the Tour De France, have a bad patch now and again. They just had to be helped to get through it, finish the day's stage, get a good night's rest and hopefully be sufficiently recovered for the next day's stage. The boy knew that this was not going to be like that. He ran after the rider, now weaving even more crazily all over the road. The boy caught him up and looked into the agony etched on the rider's face. The boy knew that he must try and stop the cyclist, this was supposed to be sport.

"Allez! Allez! Allez!" He heard the cries from the predominantly French fans and the boy realised that there was nothing he could do. A few crazy yards further up the road and the one rider in the Tour De France that the boy had come to see, fell onto the road again. This time the rider did not move having slipped into unconsciousness. Fear gripped the boy and the other spectators also suddenly grasped the seriousness of the situation. Artificial respiration, the kiss of life, oxygen brought by the Tour doctor via helicopter always on hand for emergencies; all were tried.

The boy watched horrified and transfixed as each successive action failed to revive the motionless cyclist. After what seemed an age the helicopter lifted the rider, often described as the bravest rider in the world, off to hospital. In his heart, the boy knew that the rider would be lucky to live, let alone race on a bicycle again. He couldn't stop his tears.

The rider never regained consciousness and two hours after he first fell to the ground toe-strapped to his bike, he was pronounced dead. The repercussions of his death would reverberate through professional cycling for decades.

The boy would never forget the eyes.

CHAPTER ONE

"Bravo! Bravo!" the man next to her jumped to his feet applauding instantly the music finished and simultaneously shouted his approval. Although technically the performance had been good, she felt that it had lacked the fire necessary to bring out the best in the music. Shostakovich was one of her favourite composers and she had quickly accepted the invitation from the man now applauding beside her, when he had asked if she would like to come to the Royal Albert Hall, a few weeks ago, just before Christmas.

Now she was beginning to feel a little embarrassed. Her companion was going over the top to say the least. A few other people were standing but they weren't being anything like as demonstrative as her friend, and the audience, a big one, the Albert Hall being very nearly full, clearly agreed with her assessment of the performance. If her escort was trying to impress her, he was wasting his time. As an occasional date Dennis was fine, but only if the date included some interesting activity or was at a really good venue. As she saw more and more pairs of eyes turning on the still wildly applauding Dennis she decided that enough was enough.

"Sit down, Dennis, it wasn't that good." She spoke forcefully but without rancour in a rich modulated voice, which when she sang, was mezzo-soprano.

"Oh, I thought it was rather good." He sat down looking a little crestfallen and stopped clapping. She smiled gently.

"Rather good doesn't really warrant the ten-tenths applause, the bravos and the foot-stamping."

The applause was rapidly dying now, and the conductor, after being called back onto the stage for three bows, disappeared followed by the leader and the orchestra. They knew better than anyone that Shostakovich's tenth symphony had received better treatment in the past.

Dennis, recovering his humour manfully, entertained the girl very well for the remainder of the evening. An excellent meal in a fairly exclusive French restaurant just off Knightsbridge, during which conversation had remained platonic but amusing, had been followed by Dennis putting her into a taxi, thankfully alone. She was now cosily settled by the fire in her flat, in a very unglamourous nightie and dressing gown with an equally unglamourous cup of hot chocolate. It was just after 12:30 a.m. on Saturday morning and the weekend stretched ahead of her like a... like a what? She thought about the question and failed to come with a satisfactory answer.

She knew that from anyone else's point of view, she probably appeared to have it made. She was comfortably off, in fact very comfortably off, with an excellent flat in a much sought after neighbourhood of London and with a brilliant job that took her all over the world. Young, well fairly young, free and single, how much better could her life be? She knew differently. She knew with crystal clarity that she needed something in her life. Something or was it someone? The previous 'someones' she had definitely not needed. Too many like Dennis. There must be someone out there though, surely? Suddenly, she had felt unutterably sad. She put down her chocolate and went over to her phone. She dialled a number in America ignoring the time difference and waited after a few seconds she heard the only voice she really loved say, "Hello."

"Hi, Dad, it's me. I'm sorry about the time but I needed to talk to you."

***

Professional cycling is big business and generates a great deal of money quite legitimately. Not as much as in football, tennis or motor racing, for example, but still a very significant amount. However, as with most if not all sports, it could also be used to make money criminally. As Sarah was ringing her father, one man made rich by such a criminal use, was plotting to make even more money in the coming season, also criminally. Sitting in Club class in an A360 Airbus, high over the Atlantic on his way to London, the man's appearance and actions suggested big business and he exuded power. He was strikingly handsome but in an indefinable way. His good looks were somehow slightly disquieting. Just by looking at him, one felt instinctively that this man would have no time for the concept of equality, be it racial, sexual or of any other form. Women would be dominated by him and both love and hate it in equal measure.

He was not quite at the top of the very extensive criminal organisation of which he was a part, but only one step below it. He saw the new cycling season not only as his meal ticket but as a means of promotion.

At that moment one of the stewardesses approached him. The seat next to him was empty, he always booked two.

"Everything alright Sir?" She asked the standard question with professional brightness but it was less forced than usual. This man was impressive.

"Yes, fine thank you." A studied pause then, "I do have a small problem looming, however." In spite of the highly polished suavity, she knew that there was a line coming.

"Is it anything I could possibly help you with?"

11

"As I would imagine that you have a lot of contacts, perhaps you can. I have to attend a very important function this evening and my escort has been taken ill very suddenly. Do you know of anyone who would be willing to substitute for her? She would be well paid for her trouble, of course. She would need to be attractive, cultured and intelligent." Another studied pause. "Someone such as yourself, in fact." She pretended to be thinking for a few seconds.

"I can think of several of my friends who would be ideal, but I don't know if any of them would be available." This time the pause came from her. "However, I'm off-duty for three days after this flight. I know this sounds rather forward and not exactly cultured, but would I do?" His smile was as dazzling and charming as hers. She would, indeed, do. She would also regret it.

CHAPTER TWO

It is early January and three men are thinking about the same thing. The three men are different in many respects. They are roughly the same age, but that is their only similarity, except for the most important thing about them. They are all professional racing cyclists, more than that; they are all very good professional racing cyclists. All three are training, each within his own team and all are revelling in the satisfaction that hard physical effort always brings. Of different nationalities, one an American, one an Englishman and one an Italian, all three are hard at work at their teams' training camps. Southern Spain, the South of France, Majorca and various parts of America are the favoured locations for training camps and all three riders are very rapidly turning their pedals along various parts of the Cote d'Azur.

Now in the first week in January, the weather, by no means warm, was nevertheless sufficiently benign to encourage training rather than having the more discouraging effect that the weather in Northern Europe or North America would have brought. Roger Powell, the Englishman from Derbyshire, the Italian Giuseppi Vacchio from Sienna, and Bruce Connolly a Californian, were now working very hard to maintain as high a pace as possible in their respective teams, whilst thinking, when not having to concentrate entirely on their training, of one thing. That one thing was the World Professional Road Race Championship held in September. The winner of the World Championship is then entitled to wear the legendary "Rainbow Jersey" at every road race event in which he competes during the following twelve months.

Whilst winning the Tour De France had long been acknowledged as the greatest success a cyclist can achieve, being a three-week long stage race requires, apart from enormous quantities of all the essential individual cycling abilities, speed, strength, endurance, a very strong team. Many great cyclists have failed to win the Tour because of the lack of a strong enough team to support them.

The World Championship is different. Coming at the end of the season, it requires enormous reserves of power, stamina, speed and the ability to read a race very rapidly and respond accordingly. Whilst teamwork is important in winning the Rainbow Jersey it is much less so than in one of the major stage races. Powell, Vacchio and Connolly all had high hopes for the coming season. In addition to the rainbow Jersey, Connolly dearly wished to win the Tour De France, while the other two were targeting the single day "classics". All three would happily exchange all other victories to be able to don the Rainbow jersey. Irrespective of who won what, one thing was certain, the fans would have an exciting season to enjoy.

"In spite of all our efforts last season, Connolly shows no sign of being put off. I have received a number of reports that he and his team are training as enthusiastically as ever and that Connolly himself is extremely fit." The small blond man said the words without expression in his voice, but there was undeniable menace underlying the calm delivery. On meeting the man for the first time, many people were initially fooled by the somewhat effete prissy look of him. However, if they looked into his eyes they immediately changed their assessment of him. At the moment of eye contact, a chill ran through all who met him. Once in his employ, everyone obeyed his instructions implicitly and performed any task without question. The ten other men in the room knew that he was annoyed. Exactly how annoyed was impossible to gauge, but they all knew that the situation concerning Bruce Connolly would have to be resolved quickly. No one volunteered any comment.

"Is it the case that our initial assessment of the man was somewhat inaccurate, or is it incompetence within our own organisation which allows Connolly to continue to obstruct my plans? James do you have any opinion to offer us?"

James Dowling, the chairman of J.D. Textiles, cursed inwardly. The responsibility for this operation had been allocated to him. Sergio Induranna, Dowling's rival and the other number two in the organisation, saw Dowling as the only threat to him taking over as number one. He had proposed that Dowling be given the "Connolly Sanction" in the hope that Dowling would foul it up. On the downside, should Dowling be successful, he would leap ahead of Induranna in the pecking order. Induranna was therefore very pleased that things were not entirely going to plan. At the time, keen to improve his own standing, Dowling had happily taken on the responsibility for the 'total discouragement of Bruce Connolly' without appreciating the possible risks to his own position. He marshalled his thoughts into what he knew had to be a totally convincing explanation. Guided by an inner voice telling him to take the blame for misjudgement and see what happened from there, he began.

"I have to accept the blame..." There was a stifled but nonetheless audible gasp from some of the other men. Accepting blame usually meant a complete eclipse of standing and authority, if not a pair of concrete boots, "for the misjudgement of Connolly. He is proving to be far more resilient than expected apparently incorruptible and extraordinarily able. The course of action I suggested," he gestured to a document in front of the blond-haired man, "has been followed to the letter, and in every instance the operations have been carried out faultlessly. Similar courses of action have always achieved success in the past. Connolly is clearly made of sterner stuff."

Dowling waited for the response. His palms were wet and he felt sticky under his armpits. The tension in the room was palpable as the blond man steepled his fingers. Finally he spoke.

"Hmmm are you saying that that the man can neither be bought off nor frightened off? I presume that you have looked into the blackmail angle? There must be leverage somewhere."

"As far as being frightened off is concerned, no, I don't think he can be, certainly not in terms of his own safety anyway. As for bribery, money is clearly of very little importance to him. Until he came onto the cycling scene he is a complete mystery. We cannot find out anything about his family or even if he has one. As for blackmail it is difficult to see what with. We can't find anything even remotely criminal in his past that we could use against him. His supposed sexual exploits, none of which have ever been proven anyway, have been raked over repeatedly, and he obviously doesn't give a damn about the media."

The blond man looked thoughtful.

"Has anyone else any suggestions?" The silence stretched interminably, no one willing to put themselves on the spot. The man turned to Induranna.

"Have you no ideas, Sergio?" Dowling still uncomfortable himself was pleased to see his rival fail to respond.

"No? Then the matter rests with you, James. Come to me in forty-eight hours with further suggestions, and this time I will not accept such reasons for failure as you gave today, plausible though they were. Good day, gentlemen." He rose and left the room which immediately seemed bigger and less threatening. *What the hell do I do now?* Dowling thought to himself. Induranna was smiling pityingly at him.

"Don't worry, James, two days is a long time for a man of your talents. I'm sure you'll come up with something."

"Yes, I'm sure I shall."

"It appears essential to do so," Induranna purred.

"An absolute necessity," Dowling replied continuing the game.

"Don't hesitate to ask for any assistance, James."

"Thanks very much, I appreciate the offer, but I'm sure that I *shall* be able to manage."

Both of the men were aware that their conversation would be heard by their superior, the meeting room was bugged, and neither could allow any hint of their mutual dislike to enter into the conversation. Their smiles transmitted equally large amounts of malice and both men knew exactly where they were with each other. The remaining members of the group were now making their way towards the door and Dowling not wanting to appear indecisive strode past them all in order to be the first at the huge reception desk which was staffed by ten extremely attractive female personal assistants. In theory each girl was allocated to one of the group, but all were able to help when and where required. Each assistant's Christian name began with the same first letter of the surname of the man she worked for. Dowling's assistant's name was Deborah.

"I'd like you to get hold of these people and tell them to meet me at the Paris Hilton at 10:00 a.m. tomorrow. That is open. I would also like you to obtain the items on this list by 9:00 p.m. this evening. That is closed. Finally, book me on a flight to Paris arriving not later than 8:00.a.m. tomorrow." He smiled briefly but sincerely.

"Certainly, Mr. Dowling." Dowling's reference to open and closed indicated to Deborah that she could use any of the other assistants to contact the people on the first list but anything closed she must do herself. The same system was employed throughout the organisation and had failed only once. One assistant had passed a closed request to another girl. The first assistant had shortly after committed suicide by jumping into the Thames. Everyone within the organisation was well aware that the girl had been dead some time before her body had hit the river. Dowling didn't mind if others within the organisation, particularly Induranna, knew who he would be meeting in Paris, in fact he was counting on it.

Two minutes later, Dowling emerged from the rear exit of the rather sleazy nightclub which provided excellent cover for their organisation. With a conscious effort he pushed the icy tone of his superior's words, if not out of his mind, at least to the back of it, and made his way with a fairly light step towards Trafalgar Square. A couple of hours in the National Gallery would round the day off nicely. He was well aware that he was being followed, presumably by one of Induranna's men, but that didn't trouble him. His own minder wouldn't be very far away and he wanted Induranna to know his movements anyway.

Three hours later, the man who had been following Dowling was reporting to his employer, as Dowling had surmised, Sergio Induranna.

"I followed him to the National Gallery where he spent an hour and three-quarters, mostly in the Italian section, then took a taxi to his flat. He left in the same taxi three-quarters of an hour later for Heathrow, and the last I saw of him was in the Departure Lounge waiting for his flight to be called for his flight." The man looked tired but unworried.

"Did he stop anywhere on the way to the Gallery?"

"No."

"Do you think he knew you were tailing him?"

"If he did he made no effort to lose me." He had obviously had a long day but knew better than to ask if was done for the day.

"Okay, you can go. Report at the usual place, usual time, for instructions tomorrow."

"Goodnight, boss," he said, even though he knew he was talking to himself.

For a while after his underling had gone, Induranna did nothing. He had always thought that there was something not quite 'real' about Dowling. He had done his best to establish some connection between the man and the forces of law and order but entirely without success. Dowling's record of criminal activities, considered highly commendable within the organisation, but nefarious in the extreme, were second to none and much more impressive than his own. Induranna had killed people and had enjoyed doing so. Some of his extortion rackets were very productive and his standing within the criminal world was such that no one crossed Sergio Induranna. However, both the brutality and the scale of Dowling's criminal activities made Induranna's seem apprentice-like by comparison. And yet, and yet, the man himself did not exude the aura of someone as evil as his past activities suggested. Induranna had never voiced his doubts to anyone but contented himself with keeping watch on Dowling whenever possible and waiting for the opportunity that would surely come along to prove himself right.

At the same time that Induranna was worrying about Dowling, Dowling was worrying about Bruce Connolly. Travelling by plane was normally an enjoyable experience for him and usually helped to both relax and inspire him. His present flight to Paris was doing neither. Hopefully tomorrow morning's meeting would produce a result. Result. Something about that word triggered a switch somewhere. Result. Result. What was it about that word? Relax, let it come, he told himself. He allowed the sounds of the aircraft to permeate his being, knowing that the solution or at least a possible solution, would come to him eventually.

Dowling dozed briefly and then was wide awake, suddenly the answer was there! Result! Of course! They had been going about things the wrong way. You can't put off men like Connolly, they just dig their heels in more firmly. Connolly must be aware that he had been robbed of victories by unfair means, but it hadn't stopped him in the slightest. What if Dowling was able to affect the results so that Connolly won when he shouldn't? For all the man's apparent brashness, Connolly was an honourable man, of that Dowling was certain. For the American, success brought about by the machinations of others would have very little value. A few fake victories might well bring him to heel. Would the boss buy such a plan? There were a good many risks involved and the problems associated in bringing such a plan to fruition were considerable with a lot of expense involved, particularly as far as bribes were concerned. Connolly's team members were fiercely loyal, that was well known, and so to get at someone on the inside would be difficult. Nevertheless, there were always people looking for easy money, and to entice a few of them to his cause shouldn't prove too difficult. The political climate at the moment could also be brought into the picture to good effect. Feeling very much happier, Dowling settled back in his seat and had a pleasant sleep for the remaining thirty minutes of his flight to Paris.

***

The clouds were unbroken and a strong wind whipped the rain into the faces of the small group of riders like needles. The riders were strung out in an echelon across the road in an effort to gain a little shelter, but with only ten riders this was of limited value. In addition, the frequency of taking turns at the front, both as pacemaker and to bear the brunt of the wind, meant that the periods of shelter were fairly brief. At times like this the thought had crossed the minds of nine of the ten that maybe they should have found a job selling insurance or working in a bank. This was a far cry from the Cote d'Azur or Majorca even though that had only been just over a week ago. The group had been out for almost three hours and were saturated, the spray from the wheels in front combining with the incessant rain to thoroughly soak them. The dirt from the roads had also splashed up into their faces and their appearance would have terrified any young children and possibly some adults too who saw them. White socks had long since turned the colour of the darkest clouds above them and were full of grit from the roads. The mud-encrusted faces were virtually unrecognisable and their eyes were sore from the grit that had found its way into them. In rain as heavy as this, their sun/rain glasses couldn't be worn as visibility became a nightmare with the glasses on.

Alone amongst the ten, Roger Powell was enjoying himself. As a youngster he had read and reread lots of articles about the hard men of cycling, and in particular, the legendary Irishman Sean Kelly's apparent obliviousness to conditions which saw even the strongest riders looking to abandon races in which they still had some chance of success. Roger had made himself look at awful conditions in much the same way, an extension of the much overworked mantra, 'when the going gets tough, the tough get going'. Now Powell's mates were increasingly letting him spend longer at the front. All were praying that the halfway point of their ride would appear so that they could turn for home and have the murderous mistral at the backs blowing them home instead of into their faces.

After a few more minutes of purgatory, a small clump of poplar trees appeared on the horizon. From past experience the riders knew that here they would find their Directeur Sportif waiting for them and then they could turn for home. After another minute had passed, the shape of a car could be seen, and as they approached the car two men got out of it. Hunching themselves down into their overcoats, like a couple of latter-day Quasimodos, they watched impassively as the ten riders slowed, circled the two men, and accelerated away again. No words were said to the riders, but the older of the two men pressed the digital stopwatch in his hand, then nodded in apparent satisfaction and pointed to the watch. The other man also nodded, smiled and got back in the car closely followed by the older man.

After half an hour, the Directeur Sportif's car came up to the riders. A few words were exchanged between the group leader and the Directeur before the car sped off again. The clouds were still giving a passable impression of night-time and the rain was no less hard. The riders' eyes were still slits and getting increasingly sore by the minute but their pace was extremely rapid. So much so that after another half an hour the group leader held up his hand and passed on the welcome news that the boss was very pleased with their efforts and that what remained of the training ride could be taken at a slightly more relaxed pace. At this the riders formed themselves into five pairs and after regaining their breath began to chat to each other. Powell found himself next to Frederick Vachot, the team leader, whose English was much better than Powell's French.

"You were going very well there, my fren." Roger smiled politely.

"I felt pretty good."

"Ah-ah, not many riders feel good in this!" Vachot gestured to the skies.

"I've always been a Sean Kelly fan remember."

"Oui! 'E was truly 'ard that Kelly. That must be the difference. Neverless, 'ow do you say it?"

"Nevertheless," Roger corrected him.

"Ah, nevertheless, thank you. Nevertheless, you did much more than your share of the work today. All the others were impressed, I could tell. You made the training look easy today, you 'ave done well."

"Thank you". These words from a man Roger greatly respected increased his feeling of goodwill considerably. After some general conversation the outskirts of Fougeres came into view, and a few minutes later, the team's hotel swallowed up the riders and their bikes, and a very welcome shower, massage and rest preceded a substantial, if not particularly exciting meal. The Englishman went to bed very content with his lot.

CHAPTER THREE

His throat hurt, his legs felt leaden, his chest, arms, feet, hands and fingers were all screaming for mercy, and very slowly, inexorably, the rear wheel of the bike in front of him was inching away. He must not let a gap open. He had little enough strength left to hang on but he knew that once a gap opened, there would be no way that he would be able to catch the Italian and Frenchman in front of him a second time. The Frenchman flicked his elbow to indicate that Powell should go through to take his turn at the front. The slight slackening of the pace was enough to give him the briefest of relief and he took his time passing the other two on the inside. Once at the front he made sure that he kept the pace up but not quite as fast as had been the case. The other two quickly realised this and went past him again. The respite had been enough for Powell. Fixing his eyes on the Italian's rear wheel, he concentrated on conserving as much energy as possible whilst not letting a gap open. They had been in the break for just over an hour now. A quick glance at his route card told him what he already knew, that only twenty of the two hundred and ninety-eight kilometres remained of the first of cycling's 'monuments', the most important of the 'classic' races, Milan-San Remo, known as 'La Primavera'.

This was not Roger Powell's first continental classic race, but it was the first in which he had had a chance of victory. Last season had been a successful one, some would say, a very successful one, bearing in mind his age and experience. He had been a major player in quite a number of events, a fine fifth in the only Dutch classic, the Amstel Gold race, leading for almost two laps the World Professional Road Race, figuring in some decisive breaks in other classics and finishing tenth in his first continental stage race, Paris-Nice. He had also had five wins in less important but nevertheless fairly prestigious races. The manager of Powell's team PDZ-Light, Pierre Viclat had been highly delighted with his efforts, so had given him a much improved contract for the next two seasons and given him protected status within the team so that he could continue his success.

Roger knew that he had been lucky, not only in obvious things like being in the right break at the right time, avoiding too many punctures and mechanical trouble, but also in having received recognition, without being marked out as being a real threat to the established 'stars'. At the moment, he was certain that the Frenchman Delacroix, a previous winner of the Tour De France and winner of the World Championship two years ago; and Barronguardi, the current world champion, resplendent in his rainbow-striped jersey and a classics specialist, feared each other, but not him. Of the two, Barronguardi was the better sprinter but Delacroix looked the fresher. He had also contrived to do less of the pacemaking than the others. Although no mean sprinter himself, Roger knew that he was probably the most tired of the three but also that surprise was probably going to be his best weapon. He decided to hang on, do as little as possible at the front and hope that Delacroix wouldn't go for a long one anytime soon. They were now approaching the 'Cipressa', the penultimate climb in Milan-San Remo. Many winning moves had been launched on this famous hill and Roger knew he needed to very vigilant. Powell's team car came alongside.

"Bunch is at four-and-half minutes," said Albert Pope, the team's no-nonsense Yorkshire born Directeur Sportif, "So dunna mess."

Roger nodded and concentrated on his two companions.

Pope spoke again and this time with some urgency in his voice.

"The bunch 'aven't give up yet. Connolly and Martinez are at 'front goin' like trains." As the trio hit the bottom of the Cipressa, Barronguardi, surprisingly attacked. Delacroix launched himself after the Italian and Roger heaved himself out of the saddle in pursuit. For the next two minutes Powell was hanging on again as first one then the other of his fellow breakaways tried to get away. Fortunately for Roger as each mini-break was caught, there was an easing of the pace, and as the three reached the top of the Cipressa Roger heaved a sigh of relief as they speeded up down the other side. Only the Poggio, an even more crucial climb in past races than the Cipressa, remained. Powell did some rapid mental arithmetic. About ten kilometres to go at this pace meant about seventeen or eighteen minutes of racing. Could the bunch, towed along by the sound of it by Bruce Connolly, make up four minutes? With the Poggio slowing the trio down, yes it could, Powell realised. He went alongside the Frenchman. His French wasn't good, but his Italian was infinitely worse, and he passed on the intelligence. Delacroix gave him a doubtful look and shrugged his shoulders in the way that only a Frenchman can and waved Powell through. *What was that supposed to mean?* thought Powell. He looked to his left to see what the Italian was doing and in the blink of an eye both Barronguardi and Delacroix had gone past him on the right. Roger's heart lurched, he stood on the pedals, stamped down and went after them. If they didn't slow soon he knew wouldn't catch them. Pushing himself to his limit, Powell very slowly reduced the gap − thirty, twenty, ten, five yards and then he felt the slight lessening of the wind resistance as he gained the shelter of the two leaders. His heart still hammering, Powell slowly recovered desperately trying to hide from the others, how he felt. If either of them tried another break, he knew he would have to settle for third.

"Connolly and Martinez are now at one-and-a-half minutes." Poe's voice crackled in Roger's earpiece. That was definitely bad news. He moved to the front again to show that he wasn't finished yet, the three did bit-and-bit and to Powell's intense relief the other two didn't attempt an attack on the Poggio. *Maybe they're as stuffed as me?* Roger gained some confidence from this thought as they began the descent of the Poggio. More than once La Primavera had been won by demon descending so he had to be careful as well as rapid. It was now all over for the bunch. It would now be down to the final sprint. They were now travelling at well over forty kilometres an hour and accelerating. Powell felt a surge of elation, at least third in a Monument and possibly?... he dared think no further. The red kite banner which indicated one kilometre to the finish appeared ahead. Now it would normally be a cat and mouse game. Sure enough, there was an easing of the pace as the other two began to organise themselves for the final sprint. *Did he keep going at full blast and try and drop them, or play their game?*

He decided to let the pace slow a little more and then go for a long sprint. He no longer felt tired and he could vaguely hear the cheers of the enormous crowd lining the finishing straight. Slower and slower they went, eight hundred meters to go, and Powell was at the back in exactly the right place. Now! He jumped on the pedals and made one last supreme effort. Quicker and quicker he pedalled, his legs thrashing round, his heart thumping he flogged himself forward. He half-glanced behind to his left and he knew he had done it! Delacroix and Barronguardi were both beaten. He eased as the line approached, and for the first time looked at the crowd, preparing to lift his arms in the traditional victory salute. The spectators were going mad, but with intense alarm he realised that it wasn't with joy for him, but in alarm! Roger instantly reacted and surged again, fear and desperation clawing at him. The line was ten metres away and in those ten metres he was beaten by the width of a tyre!

Beaten by a man in the blue, green and white jersey of Brooklin. *Connolly, fucking, bloody Connolly .*

Bitter disappointment, anger, frustration then exhaustion all took turns to tear into him as he free-wheeled along the road to the team bus. *Suckered on the line by, of all people, Connolly. Bloody, bloody Connolly! Beaten by Delacroix, or Barronguardi, okay, but not by the American. Fuck it, fuck it, fuck it!* What made it worse for Roger was that the defeat was his own fault. He knew, as all riders knew, that you must keep going all the way to the line. How many times had he watched DVDs of Oscar Freire beating Eric Zabel and Mark Cavendish beating Heinrich Hausler at previous editions of Milan-San Remo, just because both Zabel and Hausler had thought they had the race won and were celebrating prematurely. All Powell's efforts wasted. He was still without a classic win.

At that moment Connolly came up to him and patted him on the back.

"Great ride, hard luck, you won't make that mistake twice. We've all done it. You'll win big soon, kid. See you on the podium." With that he was off. Apart from the slightly condescending 'kid', Roger was a little surprised at the American's words. He had always seemed a little arrogant and a bit brash at times but in that little speech there had definitely been some sincere commiseration. Connolly was something of an enigma. Absolutely brilliant on his day and a prolific winner up until the last couple of seasons, he still hadn't won either the Tour De France or the Rainbow jersey, races everyone thought he should have won long before now. He did seem to have more than his share of bad luck and had lost races he appeared to have won due to things beyond his control, sometimes due to collusion within the peloton. Every top rider experiences the ill-effects of combines working against them from time to time, but in Connolly's case they seemed to happen more frequently than to other riders. His successes and failures had little, if anything, to do with his popularity however.

Good-looking in a slightly knocked about kind of way, the word was that Bruce Connolly was attractive to women of all ages. He supposedly used the never-ending supply of female admirers in much the same way as he used bidons or racing tubular tyres − use them once and then throw them away. He had left many female hearts shattered around him, or so Roger had heard, seemingly believing it to always be the fault of others. In racing terms his value was enormous and his wins, like today's were almost always spectacular. His defeats, were, if anything, even more so. He had never been accused of cheating, in sprints he would always give as good as he got but never more than that. Virtually alone amongst team leaders, he refused to take any of his domestiques' bikes if he had a 'mechanical', preferring to wait for the ream car to bring him a spare bike. Woe betide the team car driver though if Connolly was left for any length of time stranded. His team members were devoted to him but exactly why no-one would say. The sponsors of the Brooklin team never allowed any of their riders to give interviews apart from Connolly himself and no rider on leaving the Brooklin team, itself a rare occurrence anyway, had ever been known to speak or write ill of the team, Connolly himself or any aspect of the team's organisation.

The blue, green and white clad riders, sponsored by a sweets manufacturer, always had the best of everything −hotels, equipment, training facilities etc., and yet the team collectively had never won anything like as many races as the Anquetil, Van Looy, Merckx and Armstrong led teams of the past. Several riders in the current peloton, Delacroix and Barronguardi to name two, had had more individual success in the past few seasons than Connolly. Nevertheless, Brooklin made it clear quite frequently that the racing team was an excellent investment for them and they would continue their sponsorship indefinitely. Bruce had certainly had his successes. He had won a number of the classics, Milan-san Remo, [twice now], the Tour of Flanders, Paris-Roubaix and the Tour of Lombardy, as well as stages in all the 'Grand Tours', and lots of other less prestigious races. In some strange way though, these successes were actually less than one thought he had achieved. In a sense he was a much more prolific winner in peoples' minds than in reality.

These thoughts passed through Roger's mind as he weaved his way through the various officials, soigneurs and mechanics towards the team bus. He received lots of 'hard luck' and 'too bad' comments and Powell, beginning to look on the bright side, realised that he had all but won a classic and that surely there must be better things to come. He began to think of the other Spring classics when he saw his manager Claude Viclat, running across to him with a huge smile on his face, gesticulating and shouting.

"Tres bien, tres bien, Roger." He grabbed Roger by the arm and dragged him towards the reporters who, in turn, were running towards Powell.

"You 'ave won, you 'ave won, magnifique." He then spoke in French far too quickly for Roger to understand. People began slapping Roger on the back and he searched for a face able to translate – his eyes picked out Pope.

"Albert, for Heaven's sake, what is going on?" Connolly beat me by half-a – wheel!"

"No 'e's been relegated to fourth for taking a tow from a car when e were trying to catch thee. Now get theself off t' dope control." A further set of emotions now took over Roger as realisation dawned. He gave a great 'whoop' of delight, before submitting himself to the ministrations of the dope control chaperone. A few minutes later, he was being ushered onto the podium, where a smiling Delacroix and a rueful- looking but not displeased Barronguardi both shook his hand.

"Congratulations my friend, now we know we will 'ave to watch you."

"Si," followed the Italian. "Now you will find ze next win even more difficult to come by."

"Don't let 'im put you off. When you 'ave won once, you can win again. 'E is cross because not only did he not

29

win, but also because I beat 'im in the sprint." All three riders laughed and Powell was grateful for their acceptance of his win in this very sporting manner.

Of Bruce Connolly there was no sign at all, and amid all the back-slapping, waving to the crowd, press interviews and kissing the podium girls, Roger began to feel sick, hungry, thirsty and desperately tired all at the same time. He was amazed to discover that over an hour had passed since he had crossed the line. As if reading his thoughts, Albert Pope and Dave Queen, the only other Englishman in Roger's team were by his side and in seconds had him in the bus and on the way back to the hotel. The short drive back was pleasant but not half as pleasant as the shower which followed. After the shower it was massage time.

The PDZ-Light team had a Canadian masseuse whose name was Francine. All the riders in the team lusted after the twenty-eight-year-old unmarried and currently unattached, hazel-eyed brunette. Within his team, Viclat had made it abundantly clear that Francine was untouchable. Whether this was because he wanted to ensure that no internal team rivalries occurred or because he wanted her for himself, no one knew. Certainly Francine was equally pleasant and conscientious with all the riders ,both as far as team matters were concerned and on social occasions. Her qualifications for her job were of the highest order. She had formerly been a soigneur on both the American and Olympic cycling squads and she had BSc degrees in physiology and psychology. Whilst with the Canadian squad she had also gained a Ph.D. studying the mental and physical effects of blood-doping on athletes. She had been a fairly promising cyclist herself until she had decided that 'thunder thighs belonged to guys', and had hung up her competitive wheels.

About her social background no one knew anything, or if they did they were keeping it to themselves. From occasional comments from Viclat, it had been inferred by the team members that there had been 'problems in the past'. Whether this was true or the product of over-fertile imaginations no one knew. Either way, Francine preferred to keep herself to herself. As Powell relaxed under practiced ministrations, their conversation drifted amicably, she making comments about the other teammates reactions to his win, (all positive and genuinely pleased), he telling her about the race. Not for the first time, Roger found it difficult to keep his mind off the fact that Francine was one of the most attractive women he had ever met. However, in the past he had not just won a major race. His euphoria and the endorphins running around were now overcoming his tiredness and horror of horrors, he began to feel then familiar stirring under the fairly skimpy towel. His growing erection showed itself immediately. Instantly alive to the changing situation and obviously ready for it, Francine spoke sharply.

"Forget it kid, I don't play with learners!" The harsh words had the desired effect, his hard-on subsided as quickly as it had arisen and Powell was left feeling distinctly foolish.

""Don't worry about it. That happens most times after a guy has won his first big race and I say the same thing every time. Now relax again and think about your next race."

"What do you think about Connolly?" Roger asked a few minutes later.

"As a rider, as a man, or in general?"

"I'm not sure, from any angle really. He seems to get a bad press and to listen to the gossip he doesn't seem to be the most popular bloke in the peloton. Yet none of the riders themselves have a bad word to say about him. His team will do anything for him, or so it seems and yet his reputation suggests that he is a supreme egotist who doesn't care about anyone but himself."

Francine spoke very carefully and deliberately.

"I have known Bruce Connolly a long time and I have never known him to do anybody down or do anything wrong. I too have heard a lot of malicious gossip but none of it has ever been proven, therefore I ignore it."

"But do you actually like him?" Roger persisted.

31

"I have never really got to know him well enough to either like or dislike him, but if I was pushed, I would have to say like rather than dislike." She added the last comment in a slightly surprised tone, as if only just realising the truth of what she had said.

"You don't like him much do you?" Francine asked.

"No, I don't," he hesitated, "well that is, I didn't, but to be honest, I don't know why. He's said a few slightly harsh things since I turned pro but no worse than lots of others, and at least he's been honest and said them to my face. Perhaps I've let myself be influenced by the comments of others."

The conversation lapsed and each quietly enjoyed the other's company until Powell's massage was finished. Francine was glad the conversation about Connolly had ended. Perhaps one day she could tell someone, perhaps even this dark-haired Englishman with the kind eyes who a few minutes ago, had awakened in her, desire suppressed for so long. Perhaps...

After his massage, Powell and Francine made their separate ways down to dinner. He was the hero of the hour, of course, whilst she was one of quite a large number of non-riding members of the team but both were treated in exactly the same way. Dinner was always used by Viclat (like most Directeurs Sportif), as the best opportunity to review the day. The order of things was always the same. During the first course any harsh words were dished out (there was almost always some). The main course would be used for discussion of the next few days racing, or the next stage if they were in the middle of a stage race and during dessert any due praise would be distributed.

Viclat tried to ensure that neither criticism nor praise were overdone, but the mood during this particular meal meant that the criticism was little more than a joke. Viclat tried to gently chide the team's chief mechanic for not having enough spare wheels to cope with all the punctures of the day. This rather died a death when Albert Pope politely reminded Viclat that it had been he who had decreed that the cars generally carried too many spares and to reduce the number. The boss took this very well and smiled as he reminded everyone that the format of the debrief must always remain the same, "otherwise you all would get the big 'ead, eh?" he joked.

Dave Queen, who always rode very unselfishly for the others in the team, nudged Roger and whispered.

"Even if we were at the Tour and we won the Yellow Jersey, the points, the mountains, the white jersey, all the sprints, the team prize and all the stages, he would still give us a bollocking for not winning the Lantern Rouge." Roger and Queen both laughed as did a few people who had heard the whisper.

"I 'eard that M'seur Queen, and you are quite right, I would give you the bollocking, as you say." This caused even more laughter. Queen, like Powell and all the other team members clearly held their boss in very high regard. Dinner passed very pleasantly and Powell had even more reason to be pleased as the evening wore on. Frederick Vachot, the leader of Roger's team, although very popular and highly respected, was having a poor season. Last season hadn't been great either, one stage win in the Giro d'Italia, only one other win of any consequence and a lowly, for him eighteenth in the Tour De France. These things suggested that, if not time for Frederick to hang up his wheels, it might be time for him to relinquish the role of team leader. Viclat, good at personnel management as he was, had suggested that Vachot should take a break from racing in order to prepare himself properly for the Tour in July. He would not ride either the Giro or the Tour of Switzerland. At the end of dinner announced that in Vachot's absence, Roger and Bruno Francesco would be co-leaders of PDZ-Light. The other riders were to work for both depending who was showing the best form and each was to work for the other when circumstances required it. Dave Queen would be Powell's 'super-domestique', and Claude Sancrent would do the same job for Francesco. This arrangement delighted

Powell and, it seemed Francesco too. Both recognised the ability of the other, and in spite of being potential sole team leader in the future and therefore in competition with each other, the men were friends. None of the other teams excepting Connolly's Brooklin squad had anything like as good a team spirit as that found at PDZ-Light.

For Roger the evening was one of the most pleasant he had ever experienced. His status in the team had obviously changed. He had certainly enjoyed lots of previous team dinners when members of the team, sometimes he himself of course, had won. Never, however, had he won something as prestigious as a 'monument'. Powell's manner as much as his obvious ability meant that not only were the other riders pleased for him, they recognised that that he would be both successful and a good leader to ride for. Not all the domestiques could count on the latter as one of their blessings. They felt that he would be generous to them as well as a strong but not overbearing leader. Stories abounded of previous greats – Anquetil, Merckx, Hinault et al handing over their prize money for winning the Tour to their teams for example. Powell, they believed was from the same mould. Even the staff in the hotel, enthusiastic about cycling as most Italians are, were distinctly more deferential to Roger than previously and one very attractive French waitress paid particular attention to him, spending longer than was strictly necessary around him when serving him and holding eye contact for slightly too long for the sake of courtesy.

Tiredness had again been creeping up on Roger and he realised that if he didn't get to bed soon, he would fall asleep at the table. He said his goodnights and made his weary way to his room. Unusually, the riders were not sharing rooms and Roger was grateful that there would be no teammate whose snoring or chatting might have kept him from falling into a dreamless sleep.

Tired though he was, he awoke some time later. He lay for a few seconds trying to work out what had woken him.

He suddenly felt the presence of someone else in the room. He lay perfectly still, trying to keep his breathing even and regular and tried to identify where the intruder was. Bruce Connolly's face flashed into his mind? Could the American be bent on vengeance? Was he that vindictive? Roger rejected the thought as quickly as it formed in his mind. Who else might intrude? It was by no means unknown for riders to be drugged without their knowledge. Not everyone would have been pleased by Powell's victory and the Italian fans, the tifosi, were notoriously patriotic, especially about their home races. Some would have been incensed that a non-Italian had won 'La Primavera'. Powell felt a frisson of fear. He could now make out a darker outline close to the bed and he tensed himself. A hand reached out to cover his mouth, a very small, definitely female hand.

"Sshh cher, it is me Domenique. I 'ave brought you another kind of reward for your success. Your masseuse, Francine, she tell me that you would, how you say, appreciate such a reward."

Roger relaxed and switched on the bedside light. Domenique was still dressed in her waitress uniform but had taken down her strawberry blonde hair. She slowly took off her blouse and skirt and stood in a black bra and G-string, fully aware of the effect she was having on him. Roger felt himself harden as she even more slowly took off her bra to reveal beautiful breasts, not overlarge but with the largest nipples he had ever seen, now hard with excitement and arousal. Neither spoke a word, conscious of the thinness of the walls. Roger tried to tell himself that this was a bad idea, he then gave up such thoughts as Domenique's expert fingers got to work. He was very conscious of her perfume and amid the tangle of delicious sensations and emotions coursing through him the thought that this is what could be called the sweet smell of success.

***

"And the winner of this year's Amstel Gold race is Roger Powell."

A huge cheer erupted, not only from the abnormally large contingent of British cycling fans present but also from the French, Dutch and Belgian fans. The young Englishman had obviously been taken to by the continental cycling fraternity. The kisses of the podium girls, the bouquets and the cheers were food and drink to Powell. Suddenly the P.A. system crackled into life again. Roger's French was not exactly fluent but he could pick up enough of the words to make him feel sick. "Proscribed substance... disqualification... enquiry." he had been disqualified for failing a drug test! He had never taken drugs in his life! Bizarrely, the first thought that crossed his mind after the initial shock was, why was it being broadcast? Drugs offences were never revealed until confirming tests had been taken and analysed and then only after the rider and his team had been told. There must have been some terrible mistake, a case of mistaken identity or something. Already people were moving away, not meeting his eye. He jumped off the podium and ran towards the Chief Commissaire.

"Excusez-moi, un moment s'il vous plait Monsieur." He looked at Powell and a contemptuous smile crossed his face.

"You are finished, Powell." He hissed and walked away.

"Finished Powell! Finished Powell." The crowd picked up his words and began to chant.

"No, no, there's been some dreadful mistake. You must believe me." Roger felt a hand on his arm.

"It's bad enough to do drugs, it's a damn sight worse to deny it." The voice belonged to Albert Pope. Roger stared in disbelief at Pope, the one person he had always felt he would be able to rely on.

"You don't believe this stuff do you?"

"The tests were positive, you must be on something." Pope said this with a slightly strange look on his face and an unusual note in his voice. With horror Roger suddenly made two and two equal five.

"You bastard! You set me up, you doctored my drinks!" His fury fuelled by disappointment, and the realisation that perhaps he hadn't won completely on his own merits after all, boiled over and he went for Pope. A right hook caught Pope squarely on the jaw and then a left made Pope's nose spurt with blood, before Roger was pulled away.

"You cheating swine, you'll pay for this!" shouted Pope, and Roger saw rather than felt punches from unseen assailants catch all over his body. Blows were raining on him and he realised that the mob were intent on disabling him at the very least.

"Help! Help! I've been set up!" he felt himself being shaken.

"Roger, Roger!" Someone was calling. He awoke to find Domenique leaning over him. His relief that he had only been dreaming was immense. The relief was swiftly followed by annoyance. The same nightmare again. When would he stop having these awful cycling dreams?

"Mon cheri, what ees wrong, you 'ave a nightmare, yes?"

"Yes, yes," mumbled Roger, "I'm sorry I woke you."

"Oh that is nothing, but it is getting light, it is better that I go." Roger looked at his watch. It was three-thirty. He looked at her and caught her eyes. He held them and then reached for her hand. When Domenique slipped out of the room half-an-hour later, the Englishman was sleeping like a baby and she felt very pleased.

"Who set me up?" Bruce Connolly didn't expect an answer from any of his teammates.

"I never took a tow. I don't play that way, everybody knows that. I won the fucking race fair and square. I mean to find the son of a bitch who did for me!"

"You reckon the Englishman had anything to do with it, Bruce?" Ron Morrow, another American in Connolly's team asked the question.

"Hell no. The guy's still wet behind the ears. He's a nice kid, mebbe too nice. Even after I took the piss a bit about beating him, he still said congratulations. He looked real sick but *still the English gentleman overcame all."* Connolly put on an upper-class English accent for the last few words which caused his teammates to laugh. Even Bruce managed a small smile.

"No Powell's got nothing to do with this. We all know that this isn't the first time that this kind of thing has happened, not by a long way. The same thing happened in Paris-Roubaix and the Giro last year and Powell didn't ride in either of them. No it's still the same old problem. Somebody hates Bruce Connolly real bad and I'd really like to find out who it is." He turned to John Ryan. "I need to talk to you later about this. I've been robbed of too many races I've damn well won and I don't intend to lose any more. I reckon I can win the Rainbow jersey and the Tour this year and no asshole with a chip on his shoulder is gonna fuck it up."

Connolly spoke to Ryan as if it was he who ran the team and not Ryan, the Directeur Sportif. The truth of the matter was that in essence Connolly didn't race for the money. He raced because he loved it. He didn't need the money, considerable though that was. Indeed, it was rumoured that it was his money that financed the team. Only a handful of people knew the truth, all but one of them, outside cycling. Ryan never found Connolly anything but completely agreeable to his suggestions and decisions about racing matters. Connolly never interfered in those aspects of Ryan's role. Even if Bruce disagreed with Ryan's ideas about the team's training and racing programme, or perhaps the tactics to be used in a race, he would always accept Ryan's view. Since Ryan was a very good D.S., success came to the team regularly, considerably more so than with many teams and would have been even more prolific had it not been for the peculiar circumstances concerning some of Bruce's results. However, it had been made clear to Ryan before he took on the D.S. role that as far as non-racing matters were concerned, Connolly was to be deferred to.

Unfortunately, the blight on Connolly had begun to spread to other members of his team. In the time trial stage of the previous year's Vuelta a Espana, one of Connolly's team member's urine sample had tested positive. Although the 'B' sample had tested negative, the rider therefore being cleared, the original result had caused enough of a fuss to embarrass the team and cast doubt on the rider in question. This had to stop.

CHAPTER FOUR

"A girl could get herself into trouble doing things like that."

"I was rather depending on that." The girl continued to slowly remove her dress. Connolly had walked into his New York hotel suite only a few minutes before and his sense of smell had immediately picked up an unfamiliar but extremely pleasant perfume. He followed the scent, discovering that the wearer of the perfume was in the kitchen area.

"Coffee?" she asked brightly.

"No thanks, I'll have a glass of orange juice, in the lounge."

"Wouldn't it be better in a glass?" *Ah-ha, a wit.* He thought to himself but smiled anyway.

"Not exactly original, but funny anyway," he said.

He sat down where he was able to study the girl as she made the coffee and poured the orange juice. The face was vaguely familiar. He put her age at late twenties, tallish at about 5 feet 7-8 inches, dark, almost black hair, not dyed. Her skin was a little dark for an English girl, for English she most definitely was and her face was very attractive if not strikingly beautiful. As for her figure, everything was in the right place and in exactly the right quantities as far as Bruce was concerned. No stick-thin supermodel this, but they did nothing for Bruce anyway. All in all therefore, a very presentable package. Connolly had been the object of a number of attempted pick-ups in the past and for the moment suspended judgement and waited. He didn't have long to wait and the approach, when it came, was disappointingly unoriginal and unsubtle. The girl had put down her coffee and started the striptease routine. Before she could finish taking off her dress, Connolly stopped her.

"Before you go any further sweetheart, stop. You're attractive but not unique. I'm not necessarily bothered about the love-at-first-sight thing but I'm sufficiently old-fashioned enough to want to choose my own lovers. A little of me is flattered but the rest of me is fucked metaphorically speaking. So finish your coffee and then run along to whoever sent you and tell them no dice." If Bruce expected her to be upset, he was disappointed. She stopped undressing but made no attempt to fasten her dress. Her expression was amused rather than anything else, with no trace of animosity in it.

"Is your reticence due to your state of health, your old-fashionedness or my lack of uniqueness?" She smiled.

"Look whoever you are, I've never had much time for games like this. You look too smart to be just a pick-up and good-looking enough to have no trouble getting men. There must be something else I guess, but to tell the truth, I'm too tired to care. Since you saw yourself in I guess you can see yourself out."

Instead of doing as Connolly had requested, the girl unhurriedly sat down and looked at Bruce. He stood up and looked down at the girl, feeling both annoyed at her staying and glad at the same time.

"You want me to leave but you also want me to stay." This wasn't a question, just a statement of fact. She slowly and deliberately finished her coffee, then got up and walked into the kitchen.

"I'll just make myself another coffee."

"What is it with you and who the hell are you anyway?"

41

"You really don't recognise me do you? I was afraid that you might."

"Would I ask the question if I did?"

"Sarah Curzon."

Of course! Now he knew why her face had been familiar. She was the eldest daughter of Jason Curzon – boss until a few years ago of Curzon Engineering, the parent company of Mercia Cycles. Mercia had provided all the equipment and a lot of the finance for the Mercia-McConnell pro cycling team. Initially highly successful in the English domestic cycling scene, the team's baptism into European cycling had not been similarly blessed. After a difficult first season, results began to come. A team victory in Paris-Nice, a few wins in the Classics and stage victories in all three Grand Tours made people take notice. As with all teams, riders came and went but the following two seasons were equally successful without any rider emerging as a clear leader. Then abruptly, with no reason being given, the Mercia-McConnell team ceased to be. All the riders were paid handsome 'redundancy' payments, something unheard of in cycling, and rumours abounded.

Inevitably drugs were mentioned, as was race fixing and other criminal activities. Because of his major involvement in the formation, running and control of the team, Jason's name figured prominently in the rumours. However, no criminal charges were ever brought against Curzon or anyone else for that matter, and both Mercia Cycles and Curzon Engineering continued to prosper.

Curzon had three daughters – Sarah by his first marriage, who was rarely seen in public, and Rebecca and Nicola, twins born eight years after his divorce from Sarah's mother, and four months after his marriage to their mother. Curzon's second wife had been killed in a swimming accident when the twins were seven years old. Sarah's mother, who had not remarried, had taken the twins under her wing until their sixteenth birthday. Nobody's wing would have been big enough, nor their temper patient enough to hold them any longer. They must be in their mid-twenties by now thought Connolly, so that must make Sarah hell about thirty-four or five, about ten years older than his estimate. She did it again.

"Yes, Mr. Connolly, I'm quite frequently told that I look younger than I am." She said it quite matter-of-factly without any boastfulness.

"How…?"

"Did I know what you were thinking? In broad terms I can usually tell what most people are thinking. It isn't a gift or anything, it's just that most people don't bother to try and look at things from the other person's point of view."

Bruce gave up, went over to the sofa and sat down.

"I know when I'm beat. Look if you're gonna stay and it sure seems that I've no say in that, would you at least do the dress up?" Her laugh was cheerfully triumphant.

"Ah-ha, so you are a man of some principle at least, because tired you most certainly are no longer, if ever you were, which frankly I doubt." She fastened her dress and then sat down again. Connolly, in spite of being more attracted to the girl by the minute, was still wary. He studied her for a few minutes before speaking again.

"So having established that I'm not all bad, would you care to tell me the reason for your visit and for the striptease routine for that matter."

"I've wanted to meet you for some time."

"Bullshit, lady. You could've met me any time, pretty much any place you wanted. You have a free ticket into cycling anywhere in the world."

"My father you mean?"

"He still has influence in cycling and in spite of let's say, past problems, is still one of the games most respected people."

"By whom?" she asked with a harsher edge to her voice.

"By those who matter."

"What do you know about my father?"

"Not a lot I guess, but I've heard enough from people who I trust and respect to be sure enough in my own mind that Jason Curzon, as far as cycling is concerned anyway, is alright."

"What about outside cycling?" Sarah ventured the question a little tentatively.

"I don't know anything about his world outside cycling. I can't even make a reasoned guess about your old man's standing but I figure he must be okay or else how come he remains as successful as ever, because successful he sure is and Mercia bikes are still up there with the very best." Sarah received his answer with a slight frown on her face.

"Do you know more than you're telling me?"

"Look, Sarah," she smiled at what she saw as a slight thawing in Connolly that the use of her first name indicated, "No one becomes as successful as Jason Curzon without upsetting a few people, maybe lots of people. Any chance they get, any of those guys will try to pay him back. So, sure I've heard a few things but they've been no worse than about any other major businessman. Now what is this all about? I'm not overexcited about the subject of this conversation, no offence you understand, but can we please change it?"

"Okay, what would *you* like to talk about?" Sarah smiled sweetly. Connolly sighed in exasperation.

"As I said a few minutes ago, I'd like you to tell me why you're here for Chrissakes!"

"Temper, temper, Mr. Connolly, now you're being boring."

"Aaagh! Maybe I'm being boring, but from where I'm at, I'm sure as hell entitled to some explanation, if you insist on staying that is." She looked at him very carefully for some seconds, any hint of amusement gone from her eyes.

"Have patience kind sir. It is simply a matter of trust. I have to be sure that I can trust you." Connolly smiled but said nothing. Sarah appeared to gather herself and clearly made a decision.

"In truth, I really have no alternative. I have to trust in someone and you are unquestionably the best bet that I have, in fact you are the only bet that I have."

"Go on, flattery will get you everywhere."

"This isn't funny."

"I never imagined that it was." Sarah took a deep breath and for the first time since Connolly had seen her looked slightly apprehensive.

"You must have thought at times during the past couple of seasons that you and your team, but especially you, have had some extraordinarily bad luck?" Inwardly, Connolly's heart twitched a little. *At last!* He thought to himself. He remained impassive however.

"Well, to be honest, no."

"No?" Sarah obviously had difficulty believing him.

"The happenings you are referring to had fuck all to do with luck, excuse me, Ma'am. We were stitched up."

"I thought for one awful second I'd made an enormous mistake. Can you prove it wasn't luck?" He gave her an old-fashioned look.

"Sorry, stupid thing to say. But how can you be so sure?"

It was now Connolly's turn to consider Sarah's discretion. She smiled her encouragement. Actually, he realised, it didn't really matter a great deal even if she reveal his opinions to the world at large.

She interrupted his thoughts.

"I'm not here to damage you. What I'm trying to do will help you if I'm successful."

"Okay." He paused, and then continued.

"When you've been a bike rider as long as I have, especially as a professional, you learn what is normal and that both good and bad luck tend to even themselves out. You learn to recognise when you've been deliberately taken out in a sprint and when it has just been a case of over-enthusiasm. I've been stitched up in a sprint by guys who are so desperate to win they couldn't give a damn about anyone or anything and I've also been switched just to bring me off my bike. There's a difference. It's the same difference as between some guy falling off in front of you because he's careless or knackered and bringing you down with him, and being brought down deliberately. You sense these things. With my 'problems' there have been times when other guys who've seen what's happened and thought something was a bit fishy, have asked me if I wanted them to speak up for me. I always tell them thanks but no thanks, I'll sort it out myself."

"Is that why you're not the most popular rider in the peloton?" Connolly laughed but without much humour.

"Who told you that?"

"It's pretty common knowledge isn't it?"

"I guess it's pretty common knowledge in the media, but how many riders have you talked to?"

"Well, none since you mention it."

"In the cycling media I'm a guy who is portrayed as somebody who nobody likes for some, possibly all of the following reasons. I'm American, or more particularly, not French, Italian, Belgian, Spanish or Dutch or even Swiss. I never ride a race just for the sake of it. I ride to win and that means I don't acknowledge any rider as the boss of the peloton the way other riders used to revere Eddy Merckx, Bernard Hinault or Lance Armstrong. Mind you, nowadays nobody is that good, but even if they were, I would still ride as I thought fit. Another thing is that some of the other team leaders think I give too much of my prize money to my team-mates. They see that as setting a precedent." He pronounced it *president,* Sarah noted with amusement. I've probably missed out a few but in there somewhere will be reason enough for some people, not to like me. However, I don't have any trouble with the guys in the bunch, except for maybe a couple of tight-assed team leaders because of my supposed generosity to my team." Talk to the other teams' riders."

"You didn't mention anything about your ability as a cyclist." The statement was really a question. Connolly half-smiled.

"Uh-hu. I guess a little bit of jealousy might just edge its way in somewhere but mostly riders respect other guys with ability. They may not actually like a guy who's got the edge but they won't dislike him either. Anyway last season my results weren't exactly world-shattering."

"The way I hear it, and from a good many people, you would have been pretty well unstoppable had you not had the 'bad luck' we were talking about earlier." Connolly shrugged and smiled again.

"We've kinda strayed off the point again."

"Not really, if you are so certain that you have been stitched up, why haven't you tried to do something about it?"

"What can I do? I've got no proof, neither have any of the guys in the team, and I, sure as hell, ain't goin' to look like a guy who can't take the rough with the smooth." Sarah pursed her lips.

"What if I said that some influential people in cycling happen to agree with your assessment of the situation and would like to help you?"

"That would depend on who they were, why they wanted to help me and what their angle was I guess." Connolly made no attempt to hide his scepticism.

"I can't tell you who they are, or what their 'angle', as you put it, is. Actually, I don't think there is an 'angle'." Connolly shrugged again.

"Forget it, I'm not playing games with shadows and I'm as sure as hell, nobody's patsy. I should have known there would be some crap somewhere but just for a while there I figured you for something better. Maybe your extra bit of

47

English class got in my peasant's eye. Well, sorry but it's been tried before and as you implied earlier, Bruce Connolly wins nothing in the popularity stakes. I'll call you a cab." Hurt, anger and disappointment were all evident in Connolly's face as he went to pick up the 'phone but before he could get there she called.

"Wait, please! Let me explain, at least enough to convince you that you are not being looked on as anyone's 'patsy'. Just relax a tiny bit before you tire me out." Her tone took away any possibility of offence in the words and combined with her smile was enough to bring Connolly back to her side.

"That's much better. So much for the tough-guy American, who doesn't care about anything." Connolly smiled somewhat ruefully. "Now I had better be brief as I should really be thinking about going." Connolly glanced at his watch and was amazed to see that it was past midnight. "Firstly and probably to you, most importantly, none of the influential people I mentioned earlier are in any way involved in any commercial organisation. Leaving aside for a moment the question of drugs in cycling, as well as in other sports, there are a number of aspects of the sport that are giving them cause for concern. They want someone on the inside as it were, to help them sort some of these things out."

"Leaving aside for a while the question of me trying to be world champion and not having a whole lot of time for much else, the big question is, why me? Also, why you?"

"The second question is easy. I'm one of the group of people for a start and it was felt that because of the type of person I am, someone who doesn't look like an 'official' if you like, I might have some chance of success." Connolly thought about his first sight of her and smiled.

"Official, you certainly don't look, especially with your dress half off. And the first question?"

"You got the vote for a number of reasons. Firstly, you and your team have suffered from the 'accidents' much more than any other team. Secondly, you are definitely not the archetypal continental cyclist and apart from when you are with your own teammates you tend to keep yourself to yourself and are clearly discreet. Thirdly," She paused and Connolly saw a twinkle of amusement in her eyes," It was left to me to decide who to approach from our 'shortlist'."

"Supposing for the moment, that I'm in on this, and I'm not sold yet by a long chalk, what would you want me to do?"

"Let's not run before we can walk. Give yourself a few days to think about what I've said. Think very carefully about things in races that shouldn't have happened and try to think of anything connecting them. Things that convinced you, that there was something not right about them and so on. I'll contact you in a few days to see if you have come to a decision. Now talking of decisions, I must go. As you said earlier, I found my way here so I can find my way home again." She rose, pressed Bruce's arm slightly and was gone.

What the hell, thought Connolly as he sat down on the armchair. *Is she for real?* Immediately, he knew that she was. Equally certainly he knew that he was very glad that Sarah and her friends were doing something positive. That certain things were wrong in international cycling and not just drug usage, had been hinted at by a number of people for some time. Now perhaps something would be done about it. Tiredness suddenly swept over Bruce and bed seemed to be the place he really needed to be. His last thought, before he fell into a dreamless sleep, was Miss Sarah Curzon still a Miss?

CHAPTER FIVE

Sarah Curzon tried to analyse her feelings about the evening she had just spent. Firstly, she realised how much she had been looking forward to meeting Connolly. Now that she was alone, she admitted to herself that that she wanted to see him again. Secondly, the object of the meeting seemed to have been achieved, even though Bruce had not actually agreed to her suggestion. She was convinced that he would help. He knew something was wrong and even more importantly, he was obviously completely innocent of any involvement in whatever villainy was afoot, except, of course, as a victim. She recalled her father's words when she told him of her decision to ask for Connolly's assistance.

This was just before she went to visit the American.

"Bruce Connolly? Not an obvious choice as a knight in shining armour, but you could do worse. At least he's honest, or as honest as anyone ever is." He had said this a little grudgingly but a little later he had chosen to elaborate.

"Thinking about this investigation of yours Sarah, the more I think about it the more I'm coming round to the view that not only is Connolly a good choice, he is the only choice."

"I thought you didn't like him?"

"It's not that I don't like him, Sarah, I don't know him well enough, apart from what I know of his cycling successes and so forth, to either like or dislike him. What I don't like are some of the stories I've heard about him."

"You mean the women?"

"Yes, I suppose so."

"You'd better go on, Dad." Curzon sighed.

"To be truthful all the talk I've heard about him has always been third or fourth hand, and I have to admit that had I been in his shoes I may well have been tempted to take advantage of, shall we say, the 'offers of entertainment'."

"Dad, I'm surprised at you." Her tone made it clear that she was not in the least bit surprised. "As far as you are aware though, the mud that has been thrown at Connolly has never linked him with drugs, bribes, extortion or anything associated with the actual racing itself?"

"No never, always exclusively about women." He paused. "That's what I've been thinking about since you mentioned him. You know in spite of absolutely appalling luck, Connolly always keeps his teammates. Even the likes of Van Looy, Merckx etc., tended to lose a few men when the teams didn't get the results, but Connolly never does. It seems that his men are utterly devoted to him." He paused frowning again.

"Are you suggesting that there is something," she struggled to find the right thing to say, "well, not quite above board about that?"

"No I'm certainly not saying that. Funnily enough, I'm convinced that pretty much everything about Connolly is straight, which is why it is so odd that his team and he in particular, should be subjected to such apparently vindictive action." It was the first time that Sarah's father had more or less admitted to her that there was some substance to the theory put forward by Sarah's group that there had been deliberate attempts to damage certain riders and teams, as well as affect the results of races.

"So you do believe that we are right?" Sarah exclaimed in triumph.

"Yes, reluctantly, I have to admit that it appears that something is woefully amiss in professional cycling at the moment, apart from whatever is, or is not going on, as far as drugs, EPO, etc. are concerned."

"You wouldn't care to advance any theories as to what, why and who are the problem, would you?" Curzon frowned again, concentrating on his answer.

"As to whom? Any ideas I might have, I'm keeping to myself, for the time being at least. As to the reason, ultimately everything comes down to money and I don't see this as being any different."

"But surely, any prize money, even in say the Tour de France, would be insufficient to make the conclusion you are implying, worthwhile?"

"Firstly, I'm not implying anything except that I'm fairly certain that money will be the reason behind the problem. Secondly, surely you cannot be so naïve that you believe that prize money is the only big money involved in sport! Far more money is won and lost at Royal Ascot through betting than is either won by owners or is taken at the turnstiles. The same applies to most other sports. Why should cycling be any different?" Sarah frowned, unconvinced.

"My group has looked at that side of things and although what you say, no doubt, has some truth in it, there are two aspects which don't add up. Firstly, why is there such a concentration on Connolly and his team?" She paused and waited for his response. He chose to hold his council for the moment.

"And the second?"

"Since the days of Merckx, there has never been a favourite for races as he was, and as there tends to be in most sports. Cycling is much more unpredictable. Okay, Indurain and even more so Armstrong were favourites for the Tours after they won a few, but they won relatively little else. Cipollini and later Cavendish won lots of sprints but they were beaten fairly frequently too. There have always been lots of riders capable of winning races and the situation today is even more open." Sarah waited for Curzon's response.

"Your point being?"

"It would be impossible to fix results, you would have to bribe too many riders."

"Okay, let's assume for the moment that I've got it wrong. What's the general view of your group as to the why?"

"We think either organised crime is behind it, whatever 'it' is. Other than that very broad area, which can apply pretty much anywhere to anything, we don't have much idea."

"I'm not really saying anything different really, organised crime has got to be the strongest possibility as to who, I just have no idea what they are achieving with this campaign against Connolly et al."

"Going back to your group for a moment, I can understand why you can't divulge their identities, but can't you at least give me some idea about who they represent and why they are trying so hard to clean things up? What's in it for them?" Sarah smiled a little wistfully.

"Is it not possible to believe that there are people associated with cycling who love the sport so much for its own sake that they just want it to be sorted out and be entirely clean?" She was obviously a little disappointed that her father seemed unable to see things in the same light as she did.

"No Sarah, to be honest I can't. I'm much more pragmatic than you. I'm sure Mr. Connolly will have a similar view. No one is more fond of cycling than I am, you must know that, and as far as cycling is concerned Bruce will be as keen as I am to keep it clean, but both of us have seen so much of the game that we would, for want of a better word, anticipate at the very least, some ulterior motive, not necessarily a dishonest one mind, on the part of at least some of your group members. Sorry, Sarah, but that's how I see it, and my bet would be that Bruce will see things much the same way. Remember that I've been hurt by cycling and so has Bruce, whereas you haven't.

"I can accept that, but can you not also see that your past experiences may be affecting your judgement?"

"Of course I can... If you can." Curzon smiled. Sarah pouted slightly, and then smiled herself.

"As usual, you're right of course." Curzon took his daughter's hands in his.

"I'm by no means certain that I'm right, I'm just suggesting that you should be perhaps a little more careful and a little less naïve, admirable characteristic though the latter is. Now, to more practical things. Firstly, is there anything that I can do to help?"

"Nothing for the moment, Dad, thanks, but I'll let you know as soon as there is. You said firstly, so presumably there's a secondly?" Curzon smiled a little mischievously

"Only for you to have a good time this evening."

Now as Sarah thought through both her conversations with both men, she realised with something of a jolt that there were many similarities between the two. She went to the bathroom, slowly undressed and turned on the shower. She looked at herself critically in the mirror. Whilst she knew that she was not a raving beauty, she knew that she was reasonably pretty. She also knew without being immodest that she had a good body. No children, although something she longed for, meant a still flat stomach. Firm and full breasts were accentuated by a narrow waist and what would definitely be referred to as childbearing hips, polite speak of course for a fairly big bottom, or as Bruce would no doubt say, ass. Never one to worry about things she could do little about, nevertheless when younger, Sarah had wished that she was a little smaller in both the upper and lower storeys. As she had grown older and hopefully wiser, she had learned that the majority of men she knew preferred a little too much rather than a bit too little. She was nowadays therefore glad about her tits and bum and that her shape was as good as ever. Considerable efforts in the gym and being an enthusiastic tennis player and horsewoman, [more than competent in both sports], had also helped. She also frequently blessed the Lord above, or whoever was responsible, for the fact that she could eat more or less what she liked without having to worry about her figure.

As the water poured over her, she let her thoughts drift somewhat dreamily over the time spent with Connolly. He was without doubt the most interesting man she had met in a long time. Actually, he was interesting and attractive, definitely attractive. What about that reputation of his though? It was a long time since she had been in a relationship and the sensuousness of the shower was beginning to get to her. *Stop it!* She told herself firmly, finished the shower as quickly as possible and went to bed. However, if going to bed, instead of staying in the shower was supposed to put thoughts of Connolly out of her mind, it didn't work. Romantic thoughts began to intertwine with thoughts of a much more physical nature. It had been too long and her hands went to her breasts. Sarah's nipples were very hard and she caressed herself luxuriously until the feelings between her legs demanded that that her fingers travelled further downwards. It didn't take much fantasising about Bruce before she brought herself to a shattering orgasm, the like of which she hadn't experienced, either with intercourse or masturbation, for a very long time.

Wow, what have I got myself into? She thought to herself, as she drifted off into a dream-filled sleep. The contents of the dreams she couldn't recall when she woke up, but she knew that they had been erotic to say the least.

After what seemed about half-an-hour but was in fact eight hours, she was awakened by the phone by her bed.

"Hello, Sarah Curzon," she mumbled.

"Morning Princess, how's my girl, this beautiful day?"

"Hi, Dad, I'm fine, but I'm firmly of the opinion that bed is a very nice place to be at the moment, so please don't say anything that will mean I have to get up yet." Curzon laughed.

"No nothing that you will have to work on until you feel like it and not necessarily even then. You might not think it worth following up."

"You obviously think so, so as the Americans would say, give."

"Well were you aware that your handsome American is a director of a company that has nothing to do with cycling?"

"Firstly, he is not my American as you put it, secondly, I don't think that he's particularly handsome..."

"The lady doth protest too much methinks." Jason interrupted her with a chuckle. Sarah ignored the interruption.

"And thirdly, you mean the architectural practice?"

"Oh you knew." Curzon sounded disappointed.

"We may not be the F.B.I. but we have done our homework. All we know though is that Bruce did some architectural training and became a qualified architect before he took up cycling for a living and that he likes to keep his hand in, so to speak. Do you know anything more?" Sarah realised that she was holding her breath and that her heart was thumping as she waited for Curzon's answer.

"No, not really, the chap who runs the practice, Henry Mitchell has a sound reputation, both as an architect and as a good guy. Both he and Connolly have won architectural awards for their designs too. I thought that a chat with Mitchell might be worthwhile." Sarah pictured the smile on her father's face.

"It can't do any harm can it? Do you have a phone number or an address, e-mail, or anything else useful?"

"Of course, this is your father, girl."

"Okay, oh mighty one, let's have it then." They both laughed and Curzon passed over the address and phone number. She rang room service and ordered breakfast in bed. She put on a negligee to cover her complete nakedness. She couldn't frighten the waiter to death, or give him ideas for that matter. She then picked up the book she was currently reading, a Dick Francis horse racing thriller, and waited for her breakfast. She quite liked staying in hotels, they could be impersonal but there were compensations, and breakfast in bed was one of them, especially when someone else was footing the bill.

After her deliciously lazy breakfast, followed by another luxurious shower, Sarah took up her father's suggestion. A phone call to Mitchell's practice might be prudent and in a matter of minutes she had made an appointment to see the architect that same afternoon.

Three hours later, the hotel porter called her a cab. Why she reflected did the Americans have to change so many things? Whatever was wrong with the word taxi?

Mitchell and Associates, had their offices in Greenwich Village, which in itself, said something about the practice. The drive from the hotel was an experience that Sarah was determined to make the most of. Being someone who enjoyed both the solitude of the countryside and the excitement of the city, Sarah loved both London and Paris, but found neither as exciting as New York. The inherent simplicity of the avenue and street system, to some people uninteresting, was to Sarah sensible and therefore to be commended. Although not as exclusive as the hotels on Fifth Avenue, Sarah's hotel on Madison was still extremely comfortable, relatively quiet and understated in its luxury. It was also fairly close to many of New York's museums and galleries, as well as to Central Park. Driving along in the cab, she looked critically at the architecture around her.

The height and number of the skyscrapers didn't intimidate her, even though no one could ever entirely push from their minds the 9/11 catastrophe. She wondered, not for the first time why American architects seemed able to produce sufficient variety in their skyscrapers without succumbing to the pandering to the extreme that one saw in London. Try as she may, she could see nothing of merit in London's 'Gherkin' for example, nor in what she considered, 'that ridiculous Shard'. Then again she found many of the exhibits in the Tate Modern obscene, pointless or both. Perhaps she was an art and architectural dinosaur? If she was, so be it. From her hotel, the taxi took her past the Guggenheim museum, along Fifth Avenue and past the Rockefeller centre. The gilded bronze statue of Prometheus by Paul Manchip standing in the Rockefeller Centre Plaza was not to everyone's taste, Sarah's included, but she had to admit that at six metres high it was certainly impressive.

She asked the cab driver to go down 42nd street, just for her to have a look at Times Square, then a couple of lefts brought them back onto Fifth Avenue. On the way to the Empire State building (something else she had always wanted to see, for whatever reason), the cab passed the New York Public Library in mid-town Manhattan, one of the world's great libraries, containing over six million volumes. Its classic lines contrasted sharply but well, with the surrounding, mostly early twentieth-century architecture. This contrast was even more marked when they passed St. Paul's chapel, the oldest church in New York, dating from 1776, which from certain viewpoints resembled St. Martin's-in-the-Fields on Trafalgar Square in London. The Empire State might not be anywhere near the tallest building in the world anymore, but in Sarah's view it remained the most impressive skyscraper anywhere in the World. Continuing down Fifth brought them to Washington Square, in the village itself. The Washington Arch, less imposing perhaps than Marble arch and certainly less majestic than The Arc de Triomphe, was preferred to both by Sarah.

Sarah's sightseeing tour over, the taxi dropped her in MacDougal Square, and in a matter of seconds she was seated in the reception area of Henry Mitchell's practice, making small talk with Mitchell's secretary. Her name tag indicated that her name was Mary and she was described as 'Secretary' not 'personal; assistant'. *How very English'* thought Sarah, fully approving.

After a few minutes chatting about the city, the weather and a little about past projects designed by the practice, the door to Mitchell's office opened and two men came out. Both men looked vaguely familiar. They shook hands, said goodbye and the visitor left, but not before staring rudely at Sarah. *'He recognized me but I can't place him',* she mused, a little disconcerted by the antagonism in the man's stare. Mitchell appeared not to notice the moment.

"You must be Sarah, delighted to meet you, come in." His handshake was firm and dry. "Tea or coffee?"

"Tea please."

"And cakes please, Mary."

Mitchell's office was extremely pleasant. It was tastefully furnished, of a size that was sensible and quietly impressive without being ostentatious. Just the right amount of paintings and photographs graced the walls. The large ebony desk had a working look about it with some drawings jostling for space with folders, books and various items of stationery. A drawing board stand with architectural sketches on it stood behind the desk. A table, three office chairs, a computer station, a bank of filing cabinets and a bookcase completed the business furniture, and at the other end of the room, two armchairs and a large sofa, all of dark red buttoned leather, were placed around a marble topped ebony framed coffee table. *Classy, like the man himself,* thought Sarah.

Sarah took in the furniture instantly but then the paintings and photographs began to register. Architecture was certainly represented, photographs of a number of Mitchell Associates projects sharing one wall with pictures of the Pompidou centre, the Hong Kong Shanghai Bank, Falling Water and other internationally famous buildings. All the other pictures came as a surprise. All of them were exclusively sport-orientated. Mitchell made no move to hurry Sarah so she wandered about the room looking at the pictures carefully. The pictures depicted cycling, motor racing and horse racing. A painting of Bernhard Hinault winning his epic Liege-Bastogne-Liege in 1979 hung alongside a painting of Bruce Connolly winning his first classic, The Tour of Lombardy. The motor racing paintings were of Gilles Villeneuve, Mario Andretti and Ayrton Senna, while the horse racing paintings were of Desert Orchid, Petite Ettoile, (Lester Piggott up), and Brigadier Gerard.

"Most people who come here hardly notice the pictures, and if they do, they only look at the architectural ones." There was a hint of a question in the voice. Sarah smiled. *What a lovely smile,* thought Mitchell.

"I suppose I'm more interested in sport than in architecture, although as I was coming here how much better architects here cope with the challenges of building skyscrapers, than do their London counterparts." Mitchell chuckled.

"I guess you're no great fan of the Shard then?" This time Sarah laughed.

"Exactly my thought as I passed the Empire State." At that moment a tap on the door announced the arrival of the tea and cakes.

"Thank you, Mary. Sit down, Sarah, and help yourself. You don't mind me calling you Sarah I hope? Please, call me Henry."

"No, not at all, thank you." She couldn't resist one of the delicious looking fresh cream cakes which tasted as good as it looked. Again Mitchell made no attempt to hurry Sarah and they tucked into their tea and cakes in a companionable silence.

"Before we talk about Bruce, would you mind telling me a little about why you want to know whatever it is you want me to tell you?" He smiled but Sarah could see the steel behind the eyes. For the second time she thought that there was something familiar about him. She had decided before she arrived that at least some degree of truth was going to be necessary in order for her to get anything useful out of Mitchell. She therefore gave him a potted version of the explanation she had given Connolly.

"Without wasting words, what you want to know is can Bruce be trusted and what is his connection with me?"

"Put like that it sounds a little presumptuous." Sarah looked embarrassed.

"It sure does. No matter. I've always had time for your old man and already I like you." He smiled as she raised her eyebrows at Mitchell's reference to her father. "You don't think I wouldn't check up on you just a little did you? A mysterious request from a Miss Curzon about Bruce Connolly racing cyclist was bound to get my interest. Relax, I take a keen interest in cycling, as you can see and I'm keen to help so no reason to apologise. Have some more tea and another of those cakes." Sarah helped herself, feeling very much at ease with this man.

"Okay, to Bruce then. I've known him for a very long time. Until he turned pro in the cycling game, he worked for me first off as a trainee, and then after he qualified, he became my senior assistant. He's kept his hand in whenever his racing has allowed, that hasn't been for a while now but we knew that would be the case. When he hangs up his wheels professionally, he'll come back as a full partner and hopefully take over the business when I retire. Not that he'll need the money. The thing is he likes architecture and he's as good an architect as he is a bike rider. He looks a hard case, which in some good ways he is, gets a bad press a lot of the time, especially over women, little if any of which is deserved, and is the most highly regarded team leader in the peloton. Regarding the women, I can tell you that he's been hurt more than he's caused hurt, and he takes a lot less than he gives in all walks of his life. I don't believe there's a more reliable man on God's earth, so help me. As far as biking is concerned, he's still got a lot to show the world and if it hadn't been for all the funny business he would be world number one right now." The words were forceful; the manner of delivery was not. The combination, utterly convincing. Sarah told herself that she was probably a little biased, nevertheless, she was more than happy to hear Mitchell's words.

"Wow! That's some recommendation. I would appear to have hit the jackpot in my search for a champion."

"You sure have, Sarah, you sure have." The conversation now broadened and they talked for another half-an-hour, each enjoying the other's company until a tap on the door heralded the entrance of Mary to remind her boss of his next appointment. With an invitation to visit him anytime she was in New York, Mitchell shook Sarah's hand, kissed her cheek and said a warm goodbye. Showing admirable efficiency, Mary had called a cab and Sarah returned to her hotel eager to see Bruce Connolly, racing cyclist and architect again.

CHAPTER SIX

"I've told you before, just because it looks clean doesn't mean that it is clean." John Ryan, Directeur Sportif and General Manager of Brooklyn, Bruce Connolly's team, made it clear to a newly recruited, still wet behind the ears mechanic, that the young man still had some things to learn.

"Excuse me, John, I'm sorry to trouble you, but I wonder if you could possibly do me, well, the team actually, a favour?" Ryan turned and smiled at the attractive woman now facing him.

"Judith isn't it? I'm afraid I don't know your second name."

"Taylor, Judith Taylor."

"Right, well what can I do for you, Judith?"

"This is very cheeky, but I was told that if I needed a favour you were the D.S. most likely to help me."

"Ah. Is that because I'm perceived to be a nice helpful bloke or because I can't resist a pretty face?"

"You've no need to flatter me, I'm the one asking the favour."

"Oh, I'm not flattering you, in fact probably the opposite, because you're definitely beautiful rather than pretty." This time Judith coloured and didn't quite know what to say next. Seeing her embarrassment, Ryan quickly continued.

"Sorry I didn't mean to embarrass you. So what's this cheeky favour then?"

"I know this is very unusual, but is there any possibility that you might have someone available to do a bit of soigneur work for us? All of ours have gone down with some bug. I know that it's asking a lot but I've tried all the usual channels and can't get anybody at such short notice."

Ryan was very surprised at the request to say the very least. Every team tended to keep itself very much to itself and jealously guarded its 'trade secrets' over things like massage, preparation, nutrition and the hundred-and-one things needed to keep a professional cycling team operating at maximum efficiency. Things must be really desperate in Judith's team to have to resort to such a measure. It was almost an open invitation to sneak. Seeing Ryan's expression, Judith quickly continued.

"Yes, I know it's a very unusual request."

"Unheard of I'd say," interrupted Ryan, but not unkindly.

"Yes quite, but it's not just that you are perceived to be a decent bloke, oh by the way, I haven't heard anything about the other aspect you mentioned", she smiled. "It's also that your team has been spoken of as probably the only one that wouldn't take advantage of the situation to gain some inside knowledge."

"Wow, we really are knights in shining armour, aren't we?"

"Now you're making fun of me."

"Only a little, and as you said, you're the one asking the favour. Anyway my immediate response would be yes but just let me have a word with Bruce. We try to clear all our decisions with each other. He's only in the bus, just hang on."

As John walked off, Judith's first thoughts were about Ryan himself. She had had no more or less contact with him than with any other member of a rival team, although it was slightly surprising that he said he didn't know her second name. Seemingly a person who kept himself to himself, he was said to be very good at his job, although that in itself was a bit of a mystery. He was certainly no ordinary Directeur Sportif. Actually he wasn't ordinary in any respect, thinking about him now as a man rather than as a fellow professional. He was a little over average height — he had a definite presence. She had never seen him with any women nor heard any talk about any, yet he was undeniably attractive. He was also clearly comfortable with women, the little opening exchange about her looks had clearly demonstrated that, and she had sensed that he had meant what he'd said. She would do a little discreet digging to see if there was any truth in the comment about him not being able to resist a pretty face. Hmmm. She then let her thoughts turn to her request. It was very unusual for the D.S. or Manager or whatever Ryan was, to defer to the team leader about anything other than racing matters, and in many teams not even then. It would appear that Bruce Connolly was rather more than just a team leader.

At that moment Ryan came out of the team bus with a smile on his face.

"That's fine with Bruce. I'll send over a couple of the lads in an hour or so. We think you can have them for today and tomorrow. How would that be?"

"That's fantastic, I was actually hoping for just one for one day."

"Well, keep them for the two days if you need them, send them back when you don't."

"Thanks. If there's anything I can do in return, just let me know."

Ryan's eyes twinkled with mischief, "Oh, I'm sure I'll be able to think of something given time."

Judith blushed again and quickly said goodbye. As she made her way back to her own team's bus, Ryan admired both her bottom and her walk. There and then he decided that his enforced bachelorhood had gone on for far too long. Judith Taylor may not be in the least bit interested in him, but he was certainly going to take steps to find out, both about that and about her own status. He sought out the two soigneurs he had decided to send over to Judith's team and then wrote a quick note, instructing them to give it to Ms Taylor as soon as they saw her. He then made a phone call. Half an hour later, Judith opened the note having sat down for a cup of tea in the team bus. She smiled as she read it.

You mentioned doing something for me. By agreeing to have lunch with me the day after tomorrow, you will enable me to avoid yet another cycle-talk fest. How about I pick you up at 12:30 p.m? You don't have to worry about your boss, he says you can have the afternoon off.

"Cheeky so-and-so," she said to herself, but smiled again.

The door of the bus opened and her own team's manager walked up the steps, he too was smiling. He pushed a bundle of Euros into Judith's hand.

"You buy the lunch and make sure you enjoy yourself. John Ryan is one of the best in this business." Judith thought back to her earlier conversation. Why not ask her boss?

"Can I ask you something about Ryan, Boss?"

"Sure, fire away."

"Is he something of a ladies' man?"

"John Ryan?" His tone bordered on the incredulous. "No, why do you ask?"

"When I went over to ask for the help, he said something about him only being asked because he couldn't resist a pretty face." This time her manager laughed out loud.

"Professional cycling is often talked about as being like a big family, you know that. It takes no time at all for gossip, information, rumours, call it what you will, to spread like wildfire amongst the teams. I've neither seen John with a woman, nor heard a 'genuine' word about 'l'amour' with anyone in the three years he's been with Brooklyn. But lots of less than genuine stories fly round about anyone who is seen as being a bit of a catch. I meant what I said when I called him one of the best in the business. That was both as a professional and as a bloke."

Judith smiled again. "Thanks, that's good to know."

"Anytime. Anyway, I'm off and I shan't see you until Friday, so as I said earlier, enjoy." He smiled again and left. Judith picked up the note, wrote on it, "Fine but on the condition that I, or rather, my team pay." Then she went off to give Ryan's mechanics the note.

CHAPTER SEVEN

The smell was somehow comforting, a reminder of the stability of life that had been all he had really wanted ever since he could remember. Not only was the smell comforting, so was the tingling sensation which would begin to feel almost like burning in a few seconds and then gradually diminish, leaving a warm glow to his skin. He was well aware that there were many newer forms of pre-ride skin preparation on the market, indeed, he had a sponsorship deal for one of them, but old-fashioned embrocation beloved by the old school of British time triallists was still his favourite and he used it whenever he was away from the scrutiny of the media. Although he was only preparing for a training ride, the application of the liquid still gave him pleasure.

Professional cycling had rewarded him far beyond his wildest expectations. Yet all the obvious signs of his success he considered as bonuses. All he had ever really wanted was to ride a bicycle as fast as possible. That the good Lord had given him that burning desire and had coupled that with sufficient ability to be outstandingly successful, made him continually wonder at his good fortune. That was why he was able to view the problems of the past season or so, more philosophically than most, if not all, of his peers. Before beginning this particular training ride, he took a long look around his house, as if to remind himself how fortunate he had been.

As a youngster his only real interest outside of cycling had been architecture. One day he had been taken by his father to Bear Run, Pennsylvania and whilst there they had visited Falling Water – Frank Lloyd Wright's most famous and well-loved building. Like many before him, Bruce had been hugely impressed by the extraordinary house. When his cycling had become the source of considerable income he decided that he would design a house for himself (and hoped – for future family), incorporating as much of Falling Water's design into it as he legally could. Combining the designing of the house with his busy racing and training schedule was not easy but that gave him time to very carefully consider where he wanted to build the house.

His father's house in the States was both big enough and welcoming enough to make a home of his own in America, unnecessary. Did he build his house in England, the country he probably enjoyed visiting the most, or France, Italy, Holland, Belgium or Spain, as they were all more sensible bases for his racing, even though the globalisation of cycle sport was expanding the perimeter of the cycle racing world? He'd always found the Dutch to be very pleasant people, Belgium was probably the most convenient, but the climate sucked and he found the scenery to be not much better. Both Italy and Spain had a number of plusses but he was not at his best in really hot weather. That left France. Admittedly, that could be hot too but not if he didn't locate too far south. Eventually, he found a delightful site a few kilometres south-west of the cathedral city of Chartres. The architectural treasures of Paris, Orleans, Rouen, Amiens and Beauvais were all fairly close as were the Channel ports. His second sporting interest was catered for at Le Mans and he had always preferred the Bretons and the Normans to their southern French compatriots. They were perhaps less friendly in general, but more reliable. Added to this was the fact that probably the two greatest French cyclists of all time, Jaques Anquetil and Bernhard Hinault, were both from northern France, Anquetil a Norman, Hinault a Breton.

The house was set in almost ten acres of land. Connolly had left most of the land virtually untouched, a large number of the trees on the site being retained. These allied with the undulating topography around the perimeter, provided Bruce and his teammates with an almost ready-made cyclo-cross course for winter training. When designing the house, Connolly had always borne in mind the fact that his present needs may be very different to those of the future. Five bedrooms, two en-suite, as well as another separate bathroom, a large study, a gym, a large kitchen/breakfast room, a dining room and a very generously proportioned and well appointed 'salon' enabled him to cater for most of the team when required with relative ease.

Happy with just himself for company, Connolly never felt the size of the house intimidating when alone, but of late he had sometimes wished for the sound of another human voice to listen to. The house was clearly occupied by a man, the pictures were predominantly male orientated, a number of cycling pictures including ones of Eddy Merckx, Anquetil and Hinault, one of a British steam locomotive, two motor racing paintings (of Ayrton Senna and Giles Villeneuve) and a splendid painting of a British Lightning jet fighter.

Lots of timber had been used in the living areas − walnut panelling, open tread stairs and a sycamore dado rail, together with a number of pine walnut coffee tables gave the room a comfortable warm feeling. The furniture was simple and unobtrusive, two large grey and maroon sofas, three matching easy chairs and a pair of pouffes catered for comfort. A relatively small table and six chairs indicated that eating was usually a fairly informal affair, hosting dinner parties not figuring in Connolly's diary. Indian rugs of various shapes and sizes, but all in browns, dark reds and greys matched the rest of the décor in the room being set off by the Canadian maple strip flooring. Bruce always felt considerable pleasure when returning to the house. He had taken a good deal of time in fitting out and furnishing the house, and there was little, if anything, that he would change.

The main entertainment medium was a very comprehensive music system. All the items had been very carefully selected, and that selection being determined by suitability, quality and value for money, rather than appearance or 'name'. Having said that, quality names were in evidence but by no means obtrusive and they rubbed shoulders with reliable but perhaps unfashionable items of equipment. It usually came as a surprise to visitors to Bruce's home to see both the size and variety of Connolly's music collection. He had kept his collection of well over a thousand vinyl L.Ps and now had a similar number of C.Ds. Within that collection could be found music from virtually every part of the music spectrum. His preferences within classical music were for Bruckner, Sibelius, Mahler and the other primarily romantic composers with Vaughan Williams, Elgar and Delius competing with the Russian masters, Shostakovich, Stravinsky and Rachmaninoff. Aaron Copland, George Gershwin and Samuel Barber were also amongst his favourites keeping the American faith as it were but modern composers such as Karl Jenkins were in his collection too. However, Connolly was just as much a fan of other branches of music, rock 'n roll, in the form of Presley, Jerry Lee Lewis, Eddy Cochran and their like as popular with Bruce as the Everly Brothers, Buddy Holly and Bob Seger and the masters of romantic popular music. He had a huge collection of 'Ol Blue Eyes' music, and plenty of Nat King Cole, Neil Diamond and Johnny Mathis. He also seriously rated Robert Plant, Bonnie Rait, and from the more classical arena, Alfie Boe, Kiri Te Kanawa, Kathryn Jenkins, Andrea Bocelli, Lesley Garrett and Russell Watson as well as the more established stars such as Pavarotti, Domingo, Callas and Tebaldi.

In addition, Connolly had collected a lot of discs of other artists in ones and twos simply because he liked the discs in question even if he wasn't particularly fond of those artists' music generally. Storage of this vast collection had been exercising Connolly's mind for some time, and he was not yet satisfied with what he had achieved so far but the problem provided an interesting diversion. Speakers were situated in the lounge, kitchen, master bedroom, gym and study as Bruce liked to listen to his music wherever he went into the house. The different acoustics in each room also created interesting differences in the sounds. Connolly had relatively few visitors apart from his teammates and their partners, but all who came, went away impressed with their impressions of the owner usually changed for the better.

The morning was clear and bright and the few miles from Bruce's house to the rendezvous with his training partners put Bruce in a good humour. France had many advantages over some other countries, (particularly the U.K.) for cyclists, not the least being the consideration shown to them by other drivers. More than once during those first few miles, lorries held back from overtaking rather than risk inconveniencing Connolly.

The training ride itself proved to both Bruce and his teammates, how well he was riding. His turns at the front were longer and faster than those of anybody else and he frequently moved away off the front slightly before slightly checking himself and easing the pace.

Pedro Colmos came up alongside his leader.

"You're killing us, boss, whatever you had for breakfast, we want lots of it tomorrow. You'll have to ease off a bit."

"Okay, Pedro, have I been busting it a bit?"

"Hear that, lads," called out Sean Brean, "Bruce asked if he'd been busting it a bit?"

A derisory cheer went up from the rest of the group and Connolly smiled. They had been riding for almost three hours now, and although Bruce still felt full of riding, it was clear that some, if not all of the rest of the team could do with a bit of a rest.

"Okay, we'll spin on the little ring for fifteen, take it easy to the turn, then gradually wind it up on the way back."

The traffic was beginning to build up now, and although still relatively light, the cyclists occasionally slowed the traffic now that their own pace had slackened. Everyone had to be a little more careful. Slower riding without a great deal of effort leads to a lessening of concentration and it is this, rather than riding quickly that results in the most accidents to cyclists. When Connolly changed up onto the big ring and bent his back just over fifteen minutes later, there were therefore mixed emotions within his teammates. Relief about the pace but a little concern too about the extra effort they knew the 'boss' would expect. They all had previous experience of what Connolly wanted when in this mood, work, work and then more work!

Over the past few days Connolly had been working everyone harder than usual. He had worked himself even harder. The good start to the season, in spite of the ever-present but never definable threat, had indicated to him that he had never ridden better. Could this finally be the year for him to lift the World Road Championship? Everyone in cycling dreamed of two things – winning the Tour De France and wearing the Rainbow Jersey of World Champion. Twice in the past he had looked a likely winner of the Tour until a bad day in the Pyrenees, in both years, had put paid to his chances of winning. He had also finished on the World championship podium several times but never quite judging his sprint perfectly. This will be my year, he thought to himself, and the little adrenalin rush resulted in a small gap opening up between himself and the rest. After a short while, he eased, looked around and was amazed at the distance he had put into his teammates. Brean and Colmos rode up to him as he free-wheeled, grinning between gasps and shaking their heads.

"If I didn't know who I was talking to, I'd swear you were on something, Bruce," Colmos eventually gasped out. By 'on something' he was, of course, referring to drug usage of some sort. It was well-known that of all the riders in the professional peloton, Connolly was as likely to use drugs as America was to turn communist.

"You're certainly going bloody well, boss, some of the Spring Classics must be yours this year," Brean chipped. By now the remainder of the riders had caught up.

"I've arranged to meet John at the house, so we'll head there now and talk about the classics, since you mentioned them, Sean, among other things." Every member of Connolly's team kept at least one spare set of casual clothes as well as team kit at Connolly's house, and an hour or so after finishing their training ride all had showered and changed and were tucking into a meal prepared by Connolly's housekeeper. John Ryan, the Directeur Sportif/ team Manager had arrived during the showering, and after the meal everyone gathered in the lounge to discuss the forthcoming 'Spring Classics' after the completion of Paris-Nice, the first important stage race of the season, and Milan-San Remo, the attention switched to Belgium, France and Holland. The Tour of Flanders, Paris-Roubaix, The Amstel Gold Race, The Fleche Wallone, Ghent-Wevelgem, and the oldest classic of them all, Liege-Bastogne-Liege, were hugely important events in the cycling calendar. Success in any one of these races pretty much guaranteed a rider's future. Conversely, lack of success by a team in the Classics made their sponsors twitchy, to say the least. The debacle of Milan-San Remo now behind them, the whole team sensed that success at the classics was there for the taking.

Ryan began by asking if Bruce had any preferences.

"I guess Paris-Roubaix and Liege are the two I most want to win. Of the two, Paris-Roubaix but we've got more chance in Liege though."

"Because?" the question came from Ryan.

"More tired legs after the other races," replied Connolly.

"Not if the conditions are lousy in the earlier races, and lots of guys climb off early and save themselves for Liege." This from Colmos.

"A fair point," responded Connolly, "but there's still more chance of tiredness in Liege than in Paris-Roubaix."

"The way you're riding at the moment, if you want to win, you will win." Brean smiled as he spoke, and there was a mumble of assent from the others.

"Maybe," Connolly also smiled, "but we all know how much luck comes into these things, especially Paris-Roubaix, and I mean ordinary luck, let alone the recently manufactured variety."

"So we go for more or less everything but especially Liege and hope to score well to take the pressure off before the Giro." Ryan's summing up was greeted with nods all round. Conversation then became general, and after another half an hour everyone except Connolly left.

Bruce went back to the lounge, put on a CD of Mozart piano concerti, made himself a coffee and sat down to relax. He had sensed for some time that this was going to be a make or break season. He was well aware that in spite of many successes he had not been the dominant rider in the mould of Merckx, or even Hinault or Anquetil that his early outstanding performances had suggested he would be. After two excellent seasons as a new professional, he had four seasons of less success. Good results, certainly, but no longer outstanding. A combination of poor management, naiveté, losing focus a little (a euphemism really for living the good life a little too much), and rank bad luck had conspired to disappoint both himself and his fans. Disillusionment with various team managers and Directeur Sportifs during those four seasons had resulted in Bruce deciding that to form his own team, select his own manager, and arrange the team sponsorship was much more likely to result in greater success than previously. It had taken a great deal of work, but the first season of his new team had shown that it could work. He had led in both the Tour de France and the Giro D'Italia before finishing fourth and sixth respectively. He had won the last classic of the season, The Tour of Lombardy and had been narrowly outsprinted in the World Championship Road Race winning the bronze medal.

The following season had begun brilliantly. He had won Paris-Nice — leading from start to finish, The Tour of Flanders, was third in the Amstel Gold race, and a puncture only two kilometres from the end of Paris-Roubaix when looking a certain winner, snatched that victory from his grasp. He had again been leading the Tour and in a very strong position when the first of the 'accidents' happened. For the remainder of the season, his successes had been significantly outnumbered by his near misses and he had come to be called the latest 'eternal second'. This year he was determined that things would be different. He now had some idea what he was up against, he was no longer without support (Sarah's group must be worth something, surely?), he had never felt fitter or stronger, he had never had as good a team as the current one and at long last his personal life had assumed some point.

CHAPTER EIGHT

The faces around him looked unnatural, he supposed that his was equally so – probably even more strained. This was not his first Classic but it was his first Paris-Roubaix, the 'Queen of the Classics'. Many of the aficionados of the sport considered that a victory in Paris-Roubaix was the equal of winning the World Championship. It had sometimes the case in the past that the World Championship had been won by a rider of relatively modest ability, Jean Stablinski, Benold Behect and Luc Leblanc being examples. Some of the courses had been so easy that too many riders were still there at the finish — meaning that the race was something of a lottery. In addition, the timing of the World Championships, near the end of the season had occasionally seen a field short of some of the best riders if they had already had a successful season. Other high class riders had perhaps been insufficiently hungry for success or were feeling tired. None of these aspects applied to Paris-Roubaix. The fact that the World championship was raced using national rather than commercially sponsored teams (the only race in the season competed for in this format), complicated the team rivalry situation with riders from one national team actually helping a rider from another country because they both rode for the same trade team during the rest of the season. Luck, of course, played a big part in all events but probably more so in Paris-Roubaix than in any other race. The cobbled sections called for great skill in bike handling and they frequently wreaked havoc with the field, and in addition, enormous amounts of courage and experience of reading races were required.

There had been a few, very few masters of this race. The most notable with four victories and a host of other high placings was Belgian Roger De Vlaeminck. Francesco Moser had won three in a row in the early eighties and 'The Emperor' Rik Van Looy had won three times in the sixties. No one had ever won Paris-Roubaix without having real class. Riders like these will be remembered for as long as there is cycle racing.

"Will anybody remember me?" thought Roger Powell as he looked at the faces of the riders waiting for the start. Winning Milan-San Remo, albeit in slightly unfortunate circumstances, had marked out the young Englishman as having talent, and importantly, luck. However subsequent less than outstanding performances in The Tour of Flanders and Ghent-Wevelgem had resulted in a lessening of interest in Powell by the media. A good showing today would certainly help restore his name and help to keep him in the limelight, always valuable to both riders and their sponsors. Powell felt a hand on his shoulder.

"Is it a good day for a young Italian or a young Englishman, my fren'?

Powell turned to see Giuseppi Vacchio smiling at him. He didn't know the Italian particularly well but he had liked what he had seen so far. He smiled back and then looked at Bruce Connolly.

"It might be a day for a not so young American."

Vacchio shrugged, looking the quintessential Italian as he did so.

"Yes, Connolly is looking as if he means business. Today I ride to learn, nobody wins this race at their first attempt however good they are, not in this day and age anyway."

"This could be the day to change that, Giuseppi." The Italian smiled again but said nothing.

"Look at the fear in the faces, this race must be all that it's said to be and more."

This time the Italian did respond.

"Yes, but fear of what? Of not winning? Of falling off? Of not finishing? These things are the same for every race. There must be something else. It must be the race itself. We shall soon know. Good luck, my fren'."

All the riders went to sign the start sheet and be introduced to the crowd. Then they made their way to the start itself. With more than two hundred riders in the race only a handful could be on the front row. Naturally, those riders were the team leaders. On the somewhat irregular row behind them, the 'protected' riders lined up. These were those who whilst not the team leaders were considered to be superior to the majority of the team members – the 'domestiques'. These are the riders whose job it is to do all they can to assist their leader to win. For many, this is a fairly thankless job as rarely do they have a chance to ride for themselves, and therefore win very rarely, if ever. Nevertheless, good domestiques have always been highly regarded and there have quite a few who have graduated to protected status over the years and a few who have eventually become leaders.

Powell, recognised as a potential star rider whilst still an amateur and then an 'espoir', had rapidly justified the faith in him. Now, whilst not yet a team leader, he enjoyed protected status. He knew that if he could make his mark early in the race, whilst not upsetting his own team leader, the other members of his team would work for him. Vacchio was in the same position in his team. Both thought that they had a chance in this epic race.

The Mayor of Paris dropped the flag and the riders slowly moved off. At the start proper at the end of the neutralised zone, the pace quickened but not much as the riders settled into a steady rhythm. In the first hour, only thirty-seven kilometres were covered – a very slow rate, indeed. Although the weather was fine with a very hazy sun occasionally peeking through the clouds, a lot of rain had fallen overnight and it was still cold. When they reached the cobbled sections the riders knew that the cobbles would be slippery. For all but a rare few the cobbled sections were always very uncomfortable, but wet cobbles were lethal. Water in the multitude of potholes, 'nids de poules' would mask the size and depth of the holes and crashes would be numerous.

After two hours of riding, the crowds along the course began to thicken as they reached the first section of cobbles. Powell had ridden cobbles fairly often in training and he thought himself reasonably well prepared. After only a few minutes, stark reality replaced this illusion – the pace, the mud, sometimes dust thrown up from the wheels in front, the appalling visibility and the dreadful jarring of every part of his body, threatened to overwhelm him. As stated by no less a person than Bernard Hinault, this was crazy! Hinault had pronounced the race madness, had ridden the race only once, had won it and had never returned. Powell tried to ride at the edge of the road where there were no cobbles, but instead found more mud, more holes and more riders looking for the easier option. Before this he could not remember being afraid on a bike, now he was. He briefly remembered his thoughts at the start and felt ashamed that, in his ignorance, he had been a little scornful of those riders failing to completely hide their fears. He could be an arrogant git sometimes!

The familiar sound of crashing bikes suddenly reached his ears, but before he could react, he was on top of the accident and unable to stop in time simply became part of the crash piling into the mass of bikes and bodies. Riders behind him followed suit and a succession of pains to various parts of his anatomy, indicated the impact of a pedal, handlebar, brake lever or saddle on some part of his body. Feeling winded, Roger waited for a few seconds before attempting to extricate himself from the melee and immediately realised that he had been lucky. The first riders to go down were still lying in the road and there was a fair amount of blood on their jerseys. He looked amongst the chaos for any of his team, saw none, checked his bike for damage and miraculously there was none, mounted and a little gingerly at first, rode off in pursuit of the leaders. Behind him team mechanics, the race doctor and spectators desperately tried to sort out the mess. Ahead Roger saw a group of six riders who had been a little quicker than him in getting going after crashing. Unusually the crash had happened right at the head of the race and few riders, seemed to have avoided it. He realised that this was a golden chance, and quickly increased his pace to try and catch the group ahead.

Gradually a group of nine riders came together – Adam Patston from Roger's own team, Brambani and Harnot from the Sansor team, two riders from the Bianchi team, whose names Roger couldn't remember, Claude Van Springel from Giuseppi Vacchio's team and almost inevitably thought Roger, Bruce Connolly and one of his lieutenants, Pedro Luis Colmos.

Having crashed once, rather paradoxically, Powell now felt free from the fear of falling again and put himself about to do his bit to keep the break going. Connolly clearly meant business and whenever he thought the pace not high enough he went back on the front and wound the speed up. With some relief all round they came to the end of this very long section of cobbles and immediately Connolly accelerated. There were still over a hundred kilometres to Roubaix and seven of the remaining eight looked at each other and clearly came to the conclusion that Connolly's move was that of a lunatic. Colmos merely smiled. Roger was at the back of the group when Connolly broke away and could do nothing anyway even if he had wanted to.

Colmos now did nothing to help the break going, indeed, his job was to now try and slow the group down to help Connolly to escape. Only Roger and Adam Patston made any real effort to catch Connolly, but they were getting nowhere. Two more sections of cobbles came and went without incident, and then another small group came up to Roger's group including Giuseppi Vacchio, who immediately came up to the two Englishmen.

"If we work together, the four of us can catch Connolly, 'e must be ver' tired now, e's been on 'is own for almost eighty kilometres."

"Okay, Giuseppi, Adam, you okay?"

"Sure, Roger, I'm in." Vacchio immediately said something to his teammate Van Springel who immediately upped the pace. Almost choked by dust where the mud had dried and then being occasionally soaked by water from the deeper puddles that had not yet dried out, the four thrashed on and on. Occasional reports through the race radios and from their team cars kept them in touch with what was going on in the race.

"Connolly is ahead by four minutes, and you have four minutes on the bunch." Later, "Connolly is now three minutes ahead, the bunch are eight minutes down on you, but another breakaway has gone off the front."

"That bloody American much be made of iron", Patston said to Roger. "He's got to be knackered by now, how's he doing it?"

"Don't give up, there's plenty of time left yet", was Roger's response.

With a little less than thirty kilometres left, Vacchio moved up to Roger's side.

"Claude 'as 'ad it I think."

Powell nodded and moved back to the front. He knew that Adam must be feeling the effort and he could also tell that Vacchio was slowing just a little, a sure sign that tiredness was creeping in. A few minutes later, Van Springel didn't come through to take his turn at the front, and after a few more minutes he lost contact with the other three. It would be a matter of minutes before he would be swept up by the bunch and almost immediately dropped by them like useless rubbish. The unfortunate Van Springel would end the day with nothing to show for his efforts but very tired muscles, cracked lips and a sore crutch. However, he would have the satisfaction of a job well done.

Five minute later, Patston too failed to come through and take his turn in the chain. "I'm sorry, Roger, I'm done, go for it."

"That's okay, Adam, great job, try not to get dropped by the bunch."

Now it was just the two of them. Perhaps surprisingly, the two taking turn and turnabout, began to go just a little bit faster, and with ten kilometres left to Roubaix, they caught their first glimpse of the American along a very long straight.

"We 'ave 'im now my fren'." Vacchio smiled as he spoke.

In spite of his tiredness, Roger felt a surge of elation as he realised that, barring accidents, he was going to be at worst, third in his first Paris-Roubaix and on the podium! As Vacchio had surmised, the pair caught Connolly within two kilometres, and as they came up to the still smooth-riding American, Roger wondered whether to try and go straight past him or wait a little and recover, albeit, only slightly. What would the Italian do? It quickly became obvious that Connolly was anything but all-in. Having been told that both were coming up to him he had probably eased a little, saving something for the last few kilometres. How tired was Connolly? From his expression, Roger could tell that Giuseppi was thinking along the same lines. Fortune favours the brave, thought Roger, and decided that he would go for a long one. At the same moment the American did the same. In spite of his tiredness, Powell flogged himself to keep with Connolly. For a hundred metres, two hundred, three hundred, the two seemingly tied together by a piece of string raced for all they were worth, and the Italian, just a little too slow to respond, couldn't get back to them.

With five kilometres to the finish, the two were hammering along at almost fifty kilometres an hour, but now, almost imperceptibly, Connolly was drawing away. Powell knew that unless the American faded, he was going to get away. With another hard push on the pedals Roger edged closer and closer to Connolly. Finally, he was level only for him to see The Brooklyn rider respond and start to draw away again. This time the young Englishman had nothing left. Feeling suddenly sick as well as shattered, Roger felt all his remaining strength drain away. He sensed the coming of Vacchio, but could do nothing to up his speed to try and hold the Italian. The last two kilometres to the finish were the hardest Roger had ever ridden. In that distance, the now very rapidly travelling much reduced peloton swept him up and spat him out the back. Sympathetic and sincere applause from the knowledgeable crowd accompanied Powell all the way to the finish. He found out later that he had eventually placed thirty-fifth. Connolly had won by over a minute from Vacchio who reached the line only ten seconds in front of the sprint for third place. In a state of virtual collapse at the finish, Roger was carried to the team bus, and on the drive back to the hotel, he realised just how much he still had to learn.

***

"Damn!" The last thing Roger wanted to do at that moment was to talk to anyone, but swearing at the phone achieved nothing of course, so after a few rings he picked up the instrument of annoyance. The caller was the hotel receptionist asking him if she should send his visitor up to his room or would he prefer to go down and collect them? Roger was puzzled to say the least. Generally riders were discouraged from having visitors, and Roger had certainly not made any appointments that he could recall.

"Visitor, I wasn't expecting any visitor. Ask him what he wants will you, please."

"It isn't a he, the visitor's name is Miss Green, will you come down?"

"Yes, okay, two minutes." He didn't know any females called Green or at least he didn't think he did. She was probably a bloody journalist. He quickly ran a comb through his hair, pulled on a pair of casual shoes, and thinking that he needed this like a hole in the head made his way down to the foyer. As there was only one person at reception and that person was female, guessing games were unnecessary.

"Miss Green?" She had been facing away from him, but when she turned, Roger decided that he wouldn't mind talking to this particular someone after all, even if she was a journalist. She was quite attractive.

"Mr. Powell, it's very good of you to see me without an appointment, and especially after a day such as you have had." Her voice was as attractive as the rest of her.

"That's quite alright, I wasn't doing anything important anyway and my teammate has gone out. Sorry, I didn't mean that the way it sounded." Roger shook her hand to hide his embarrassment. She laughed and Roger wondered if he had ever heard such a pleasant laugh before.

"I wasn't expecting you to be in conference with the Prime Minister or anything – if you had been I wouldn't have even got inside the hotel. Er, I don't suppose I could have my hand back now could I?"

Now feeling extremely foolish, Roger dropped her hand like a hot brick. He had suddenly become dry-mouthed and tongue-tied. He cleared his throat and sought refuge in formality.

"I'm so sorry, what can I do for you Miss Green?"

"Sally, please."

"Er, Sally. My name's Roger."

"Yes, I know, you're the cycling star remember." Her eyes twinkled, but seeing him embarrassed again she quickly continued. "As a small thank you for seeing me, I would be grateful if I could at least buy you a drink. Where's the bar around here?"

It's just around the corner to the left."

"Lead on Macduff."

Still feeling a little foolish, Powell led the way to the bar.

"Bacardi and coke, please and what would you like?"

"A straight tonic with ice and a slice, please."

"Racing and training and all that I suppose."

"Well, the boss is pretty hot on no alcohol, or at least, very little of it, but I actually like tonic. Anyway, you still haven't told me why you wanted to see me. Are you from the press?" They sat down and sipped their drinks. Now it was her turn to look a little flustered. She sipped her drink again and took a deep breath.

"No, I'm not from the press. In fact, to tell the truth, I now realise that I will sound very silly. In fact far too silly. I've made a mistake." She took a large gulp of her drink and then suddenly stood up.

"I'm sorry to have wasted your time but I must go. Goodbye." She began to walk towards the foyer. Roger sprang to his feet and grabbed hold of her arm.

"Hang on please. I'm sure it can't be that silly, and even if it is, I could do with something to laugh at today. Anyway, if you go now I'll have brushed my hair for nothing." This was received with a small smile. "Come, sit down and at least let's finish our drinks." He pulled her back to the chairs.

"Now silly or not, I demand to know why a struggling English cyclist is treated to a visit from the most beautiful English girl in the whole of... this hotel."

"I'm almost certainly the only English girl in this hotel."

"You see, I never tell lies."

The little joke did the trick and they both laughed and sat down. It was now as Sally's embarrassment subsided and

Roger's having disappeared that he was able to study her. Classically long almost black hair, that was dead straight and almost reached her waist at the back with a fringe at the front, framed a pretty rather than beautiful face with a wide generous mouth, she had quite wide set brown eyes with a smaller than average nose. A little eye make-up and bright red lipstick. She was wearing a simple white cotton short-sleeved dress with black piping around the neckline and hem and a matching black string belt. The skirt flared in what Roger thought was called dirndl style. Black patent sandals with about two inch heels completed the outfit apart from a black bolero-style top which she carried over her arm. Her figure, he thought would be described by so-called experts in such things, as petite or some such word. Whatever it was, in his view it was just about perfect. As he continued his survey he wondered why he hadn't really appreciated how attractive she was when he first saw her. Now as he concluded the tour, taking in her equally attractive legs and ankles, there was nothing he could fault.

"Do I pass muster then?" Her eyes twinkled again as she spoke and Roger realised that he had been less than gallant.

"Oh absolutely." He coloured again. "I mean, I'm sorry, oh hell! Look why don't we start again? What about a stroll and a bite to eat?"

Sally smiled but hesitated.

"What's the problem?"

"I know about the eating habits of professional cyclists, you must have had your enormous post-race meal earlier."

"I certainly have but that was hours ago and a snack for supper wouldn't be a chore I assure you. We could go Dutch, if that would make you feel better."

"Okay then that would be lovely." This time her smile lit up her face.

They stepped out of the hotel into what was a warm evening for early spring and a brisk pace kept them warm.

"Now are you going to tell me why you came to see me?"

"Only if you promise not to laugh."

"No, I shall not promise that because I laugh at lots of things. However, I will promise to try not to, how's that?"

"Okay it's a deal." She hesitated again, took a deep breath and then began.

"It sounds really silly now, but I felt so sorry for you at the end of the race today that I wanted you to know that not everyone who watches cycle racing is totally winner orientated. You rode an excellent race and you deserved to win. I've been a keen follower of cycling for some years, although I don't race, and I do know a bit about it. I'm not some bimbo ogling men in Lycra. You will definitely win again and win big as well as often, the Classics, Grand Tours, the Rainbow Jersey even, take my word for it!" The words came out in a rush, and when she had finished she took hold of one of Roger's hands and squeezed it hard.

He said nothing for so long that she began again.

"You see, I told you it was silly, you think I'm foolish."

"No, no I don't! I just couldn't think of the right thing to say." Now as he took hold of one of her hands the words from the aria from Madame Butterfly, 'Your tiny hand is frozen', came into his head. Her hands were, indeed, very small and beautifully formed, exquisite even.

"It wasn't silly at all. It was lovely. No one has ever said those sorts of things to me before. Coaches, managers, other cyclists have all said that I've got lots of talent and will be able to make the grade as a pro and all that sort of stuff. But nobody has ever said what you just did or with such belief, such passion!" They leaned towards each other. It was as if Roger's use of the word passion, had unlocked a door somewhere, or rather two doors.

Suddenly they were kissing urgently and deeply. Eventually, they came up for air and looked at each other as if seeing them for the first time. They began walking again, this time in silence, hand in hand. After half an hour, they turned into a small bistro where they enjoyed a meal, a meal that afterwards they couldn't remember a thing about, so engrossed were they in each other's company.

CHAPTER NINE

Surely nothing could stop him now – his first genuine Classics win. The triumph of Milan – San Remo was still in his mind; something of a clouded victory. Roger Powell was hammering his way towards the twin obstacles of La Redoute and the Cote de Forges in Liege – Bastogne – Liege. First contested in 1892, eleven years before the first Tour de France, Liege – Bastogne – Liege is the oldest of all the Classics, and although there have been a few boring editions of the race, there have been many memorable editions of 'La Doyenne' as the race is known. Who could ever forget the stupendous win by Bernard Hinault in 1980 in weather that kept all but the most foolhardy by their firesides. Counter-attacking on the Stockeau climb, Hinault rode through an horrendous snowstorm for ninety kilometres alone, arriving at the finish eight minutes clear of what remained of the ravaged field.

Powell had kept that image of Hinault on that day in his mind since he had crossed the start line. Weather-wise the day was an average one for March in Belgium, and for the first sixty kilometres the peloton had trundled along barely trying. A few breaks had briefly tried to get away but had been discouraged by the strong headwind. At sixty kilometres the pace increased slightly and just before Bastogne, a break led by Giuseppi Vacchio and containing eight other riders, the most notable of which was Guy Troussellier, the current French National Road Champion –

had 'made the difference', and after one hundred and twenty kilometres had a lead of six and a half minutes. Roger waited to see if the escapees showed signs of faltering, or if the peloton would pick up the pace again and chase down the breakaways or even see if anyone else would try to bridge the gap. The information from his team car was not of much help either. Powell decided to sit in for a little longer.

At the ascent of the 'Stockeau Wall', the gap had opened a little more and Roger decided that it was now or never. As the peloton recovered after the Stokeau climb, Roger powered away, and to his relief, four other riders decided that that to wait any longer would be folly. All four were powerful riders – Accacio Rodrigo, winner earlier in the week of The Fleche Wallone, (the Flemish Arrow), Mark Andrews, the leader of the American Ruff-Stuff Jeans team, Adrie Van Eyssen, currently second in the UCI World Tour rankings and Bruce Connolly. Momentarily Roger's heart went to his stomach. Connolly would really be trying and Powell couldn't help but remember his defeat at Connolly's hands in Paris-Roubaix. Putting that to the back of his mind, he concentrated on the 'here and now' and just rode. After twenty minutes Roger's team car came up to tell him that the breakaways were only two minutes ahead and the bunch now five minutes behind Roger's group. The additional information, that there was a problem with the radios was good news for Roger, he had never really liked the things. Fortunately, none of the riders in Roger's group had any teammates in the break, so it was in all their interests to work as hard as possible to catch it.

Up and through the climbs of Haute Levee, Rosiers and Maquisard, the five rode like men possessed until they saw their quarries only a handful of seconds ahead. Only Vacchio appeared to be working hard and at the top of the next climb the two groups came together. Sensing a slight easing by his fellow pursuers as the fugitives were swallowed up, Powell with adrenalin pumping, lifted his effort again and the combination of his acceleration and the slowing of the others catapulted him away. The other riders hesitated, looked at each other to see who would take up the chase and in that hesitation Powell was gone. Only the climbs of Thewe, La Redoute and the Cote De Forges remained before the very gradual descent into Liege and the finish. Could Roger stay away over those climbs and for the not inconsiderable distance involved? The twelve obviously thought not and concentrated on limiting Powell's lead and at the same time ensuring that they were not caught by the peloton.

The Belgian crowd, fanatical as always, had by this time decided that as all hope of a Belgian victory had long gone, none of the remaining twelve being a son of Belgium, it also being clear that the peloton was not going to catch the break, they would place themselves squarely behind the lone Englishman. Sooner a Briton than a Breton and sooner either than a Dutchman or an American.

Roger felt the support of the crowd as it got behind him along the roadside, and he made the last two climbs before the long descent in Liege much more easily than he would have believed possible. As he cleared the top of the Cote De Forges, his team car drew alongside.

"Connolly is at one-and-a-half minutes, the rest of the break another three behind him and the bunch nowhere."

So Connolly has decided to go it alone, Roger thought to himself. Don't try too hard and don't lose concentration, he kept telling himself. Stay calm and it's yours. He knew that all he had to do now was time trial to the finish. He had won numerous time trials as a top amateur in England, becoming National Champion at both 25 and 50 miles before he was twenty-one. He swooped down towards Liege, his tyres, impossibly narrow to the layman, hissing and humming depending on the type of road surface. The ten kilometre banner appeared just as Albert Pope leaned out of the team car window.

"Connolly's still a minute back, three others two minutes behind him the rest've been caught by the bunch. Tha's doin' fine, just keep thee cadence goin', he hasn't time to catch thee now." But Powell knew that Connolly did have time to catch him, or at least Connolly at his best did. 'Concentrate on time trialling, keep smooth, time trial, time trial, time trial.' The crowd was still urging him on.

"Powell, Powell, Powell, allez, allez, allez!" English supporters over for the race shouted "Dig 'em in" the time-honoured English time-triallist fans' favourite encouragement. His euphoria of a few kilometres earlier was gradually being replaced by the fear of the hunted. Try as he might, he knew that he was no longer as smooth and his rhythm was going. His shoulders were moving, betraying his tiredness. His legs began to feel like lead, and now he began to suffer as he never suffered on a bike before. Even the end of Paris-Roubaix hadn't been this hard. With five kilometres to go, the car drew alongside him again.

He's at forty seconds, keep it going up the Chaudfontaine and it's yours."

Even in his virtually exhausted state, Powell could see the strain and the pity in his Directeur Sportif's eyes. With the American at forty seconds, it would not be long before he caught Roger. Did he try once more to keep away, or rest slightly, let Connolly catch him and hope that he had saved something with which to hang on to the American and still take him in the sprint? Connolly must be as shattered as he was. Here was the last bloody hill. He ached as the climb bit into him. Cursing himself for doing it, Roger looked behind. It was almost always a sign of defeat. 'Don't do that again!' he cursed himself. The look back had confirmed his worst fears, he could see the American. The nightmare of Roubaix came back to him. 'That is sooo not happening again,' Powell told himself. He stamped on the pedals as motorcycles carrying the race photographers came by him. What are they seeing, winner or loser? he thought.

Suddenly he saw the red kite over the road indicating one kilometre to go. He pushed on the pedals again, and in spite of his warning to himself earlier, looked back at the American. Connolly's face was clear, the effort etched on his features. He's as knackered as me, Roger thought.

93

"Allez, Powell, allez, allez, allez. Come on, Bruce, allez, allez, allez! The crowd was going frantic, the noise deafening. Connolly kept coming, came alongside, and then edged ahead. From somewhere Roger found something and came back alongside then he kicked again. He was half a wheel ahead! Connolly did the same and made up the difference. Both riders were out of the saddle, lungs bursting, mouths agape, desperate for oxygen. Connolly inched ahead again, Powell threw his bike forward in a classic sprinter's lunge for the line and the white finish line flashed beneath the two front wheels!

The two riders both absolutely drained, freewheeled down the road, gasping for air, heads sunk, neither knowing whether he had won or lost. Connolly was the first to speak but his voice was hoarse.

"What do think, Roger, you or me?"

"I've no idea. You?"

"Same, I don't think you beat me but it sure was close."

"Ever been a dead heat in this?"

"No idea, but frankly I'm too tired to care", Connolly stopped, "No that's balls, I care a hell of a lot, but whatever happens, that was one hell of a ride you did there. I was sure I'd got rid of you at least three times and you still came back."

"Thanks, Bruce, but that makes two of us. See you on the podium." By now the two men had been grabbed by their soigneurs and were being helped off their bikes and into the team buses.

For the next fifteen minutes confusion reigned. Only the two riders most involved seemed unaffected by the bedlam that ensued after the desperately close finish. The organisation of most races in Belgium frequently bordered on the manic and no one appeared to know anything. Rumours abounded of course.

"Powell took the American's line, he'll be disqualified."

"Connolly has been disqualified, he switched Powell."

"Powell clearly won."

"Rubbish, Bruce won fair and square."

Both men went to the drugs control along with several other riders, put on clean gear, refusing to say anything to the press, in spite of being bombarded with questions, and made their way to the podium area and sat down in the holding area. Eventually after the usual round of sponsorship references and the introduction of various notables, the majority of whom the crowd didn't know, didn't want to know and would never remember again, the announcer came to the result.

"In third place, Mark Andrews." Andrews stepped forward to receive his award and the obligatory bunch of flowers, well aware that in most races, third was something of a consolation prize, but in this case, he might as well not have been there.

"In first place, Bruce Connolly", Roger's heart sank, "and Roger Powell!"

Seemingly all of Liege erupted! Never before had there been a dead heat in this, possibly the hardest of all the Classics to win, and it was ironic that the first ever tie was between riders from, in the professional cycling world, real Johnny-come-lately countries. The two riders, both smiling, embraced each other and then stepped back to receive their prizes. Both had tears in their eyes.

"I guess we got it about right."

"We sure did, Roger, we sure did."

CHAPTER TEN

"This is ridiculous." For perhaps the tenth time Bruce Connolly picked up his mobile phone. The number he needed to dial was in his other hand. 'What if?' questions again started to rebound about his brain, and then to his intense relief his phone began ringing.

"Bruce Connolly."

"Mr. Connolly, are you well?" It was her! Sweet Jesus.

"Miss Curzon, I'm very well, thank you. I was just going to ring you."

"You were?" There was a chuckle in her voice that told him without any doubt that she knew he had bottled ringing her. Even though he was alone he coloured up at the embarrassment. "What were you going to talk to me about?" He could still hear the amusement in her voice. He had suddenly gone dry.

"Er, well your, er, proposition."

"Oh dear and here was I hoping it might be something more interesting and entertaining." Oh my, he thought. He coughed to give himself time.

"Well we could combine our discussion with dinner, if you are free of course."

"Oh, I'm never less than expensive and never free, Mr. Connolly."

"I mean, er ..." He trailed off unable to think straight for the moment. This time the laugh down the phone was clear.

"Bruce, I'm ever so sorry for teasing you. Of course I'd love to have dinner with you."

"Great I'll pick you up at your hotel say eight p.m."

"I'll look forward to it, bye!" She was gone and he was trembling. God was he ill? It was still only mid-morning and eight o'clock seemed a lifetime away. There was only one thing to do. He made a few calls and quickly arranged an extra training ride with some of his teammates still in the States. That was going to be the only way he would be able to keep his mind off the subject of Miss Sarah Curzon.

On the other side of New York, Sarah, much less visibly affected than Connolly, nevertheless quietly planned her day to ensure that she didn't waste time thinking about her date. Date. Was it a date? She wasn't sure. It was obvious the American was attracted to her, in spite of the cool performance at his flat, but he did have that reputation, hmmm.

Nine hours later, Connolly looking immaculate in a light cream suit, presented himself at her door. He had given considerable thought to the question of flowers for her, eventually deciding that that was going too far. As Bruce looked at Sarah, he knew he'd made the right decision. No flowers could have added anything to her appearance. She wore a steel blue coloured silk dress with a flared skirt and square neckline which revealed nothing but somehow promised much. Dark blue patent open-toed shoes with, he guessed, three-four inch heels brought her up to within about three inches of Connolly's height and a pearl necklace, earrings and bangle completed an exceptionally attractive ensemble.

"Come in."

"Where would you like to go?" he asked slightly tentatively. He was right to be tentative. She frowned and his heart sank. Bad start, fuck!

"Connolly, you are a big disappointment to me. This big all-American superstar cyclist not only has to be practically asked out but then has no plan for the evening. Some lady-killer you are. How on earth did you get your reputation? Do you have some kind of substitute for your non-cycling activities?" Connolly, his heart still in his boots had no idea what to say and then Sarah smiled again and in that instant his heart went from his boots through the ceiling. Without a word, he picked up the hotel phone and dialled.

"Sam, it's me... Yeah great. Look I need a table for two in fifteen minutes. Send a car? Good, oh, and we'll have two of the usuals." He put the phone down.

"Who was that and where are we going?" A friend, and to his restaurant." She looked at her dress and Connolly smiled.

"Don't worry, you won't be overdressed, in fact you will be perfect, blue is Sam's favourite colour."

"What was the bit about the car?"

"He's sending one for us. It'll be about five more minutes I guess so we could talk about your proposition. I've thought about it and decided I'm in but then you pretty well knew that anyway. There will have to be one condition though − I'll have to bring John Ryan in on the deal, he's my Directeur Sportif. We clear everything with each other and have no secrets. I'll want you to meet him as soon as possible. Before you ask, there is no one on this earth I would trust more than John. That's a deal-breaker." Sarah smiled.

That's no problem at all, we've already checked Ryan out anyway and I'd be delighted to meet him." At that moment a car horn sounded.

"There's the car. Let's go." Sarah looked at her watch, five minutes exactly.

After a ten minute drive in a stretch limo no less, the car pulled up outside a restaurant with the word 'Felice' in blue over an understated entrance. As they approached the doors, they opened and a tall dark-haired impossibly handsome man in, Sarah judged, his early twenties, smiled, shook Connolly's hand, said, "It's good to see you, Mr. Connolly, welcome to Felice signorina," and gently ushered them inside. They walked through a dark blue carpeted lobby at the end of which was a smiling giant who Sarah judged to be Connolly's age but looked quintessentially Italian. He advanced towards them, took one of Sarah's hands in his, bent low over it and almost kissed it.

"Welcome to my 'umble café Signorina. It is truly an honour to 'ave such a beautiful English lady here tonight. You are wearing my favourite colour. You look divine." He released her hand and at last turned to Connolly and shook his hand. "We will talk later, my friend. Ramon will look after you." The young man who had welcomed them appeared again and they followed him to their table. Delight at the first few aspects of this evening, the limo, the efficiency, quickly gave way to astonishment, as they made their way to what was undoubtedly the best table in the house. Although not totally familiar with New York society, Sarah recognised a number of high profile film stars, directors and producers, at least two senators that she did recognise, a few very well-heeled, highly successful business people and a significant number of people whom she knew the faces of but not their names. Almost everyone in the restaurant paused to look at Sarah and Connolly as they passed.

As they sat, Ramon asked Sarah what she would like to drink. She asked for a small gin and tonic, he bowed and walked away.

"Do I presume that he knows what you will want to drink?" Connolly smiled a lop-sided smile and nodded. In seconds Sarah's gin and tonic and Connolly's plain tonic arrived. She took a sip and leaned back in her chair.

"Okay ace, how did you do it?"

"Do what?"

"This." Sarah waved her arm around. "This must be one of the most exclusive restaurants in New York. Senators, film people, business tycoons fight for space and you get the best table in the place with no booking, within fifteen minutes. The waiter knows who you are, the boss has clearly told him to look after us at the expense of everyone else and he automatically knows what you will want to drink. Give, Connolly."

"Sam and I go back a long way." He smiled again.

"That's it, that's all I get?"

"Yep." He hesitated. Well maybe a little more."

"Yes, come on I'm all ears."

"Felice is not Sam's name. Sam's name amazingly enough is Sam and he's not Italian. He's as American as I am." Sarah did notice, however, that Connolly always called his friend Felice whenever anyone else was in earshot. At that moment, Ramon brought a bottle of Chablis in an ice bucket and opened it. He didn't offer Connolly the opportunity to try the wine, just filled Connolly's glass. He then turned to Sarah.

"Signorina?"

"Yes, please."

"They, of course, knew you would want Chablis and you don't need to try it because you know it will be exactly right." Connolly smiled again and raised his glass to her.

"Let's eat." As if by magic Ramon appeared with two bowls of soup.

"Hey, Connolly, how do you know I'll like this? This is the twenty-first century, women have been considered as individuals for some time now." Connolly ignored the sarcasm.

"Okay, here's the deal. If you don't like this you can order anything on the menu, the same goes for the other courses. How's that?"

"Fine."

Connolly watched as Sarah tasted her soup.

"What is this? It's absolutely delicious."

"Soup."

"Yes, genius, I had worked that out. What sort of soup?"

"Soup. Sam doesn't ask me 'bout my racing secrets I don't ask 'bout cooking."

They dispatched the soup and the fish course which followed, a glorious concoction of poached eggs, smoked salmon and avocado, with alacrity and then Connolly stood up.

"How about dancing some room in our stomachs for the main course, signorina?"

"Connolly, you are full of surprises, but where do we dance, there's no floor and no band."

He took her hand and led her to one side and a very discreetly hidden floor appeared. As he led her onto it, a band began playing, a very good band of course. They first danced a foxtrot, then a quickstep and finally a waltz. She danced as well as she looked.

"How did you learn to dance so well, I can't remember a better dancing partner, but then every racing cyclist is an excellent dancer I suppose?" They both laughed at the absurdity of the suggestion as they walked back to the table. What the main course was called, Sarah didn't bother to ask, nor did she enquire what was in it. It was simply the finest food she had ever tasted.

"If we are gonna have some pudding, more dancing is required, signorina, and this time perhaps something a little more exciting perhaps?" Connolly looked behind him apparently at the blank wall and stood up.

"Oh absolutely!" Sarah practically jumped to her feet.

As they reached the floor the band moved into a tango, then some salsa and finally into a jive. Although a few other couples had moved onto the floor, after Sarah and Bruce had vacated it earlier, they moved away when it became obvious who the experts were. As the jive finished and they began to walk back to their table, applause rippled through the other diners. As they reached their table and sat down, Ramon appeared with their desert.

"This looks like an old-fashioned banana split."

"That's because it is." Connolly answered with another grin. "But not quite like your mother used to make."

"You're right again. It is old-fashioned and yet it isn't. There's no point asking what the difference is I suppose?"

"None whatsoever. Firstly, because I don't know, and secondly, Sam wouldn't tell you however may times you asked him." He paused, grinned then added, "Although he might if you pulled the striptease routine on him." Sarah bashed him with her handbag and giggled. Ramon now appeared with coffee and asked Sarah if she would like a liqueur. She declined. They drank their coffee in silence and then Sarah rose, took Connolly's hand and walked back onto the dance floor.

"A slow dance I think." As they arrived, the band abruptly changed from the quickstep they had been playing to a waltz.

"That wasn't a fluke, was it?"

"No, it wasn't, and if you're a very good girl sometime I'll tell you how I did it."

Sarah allowed their eyes to meet and she lost herself in his. She moved closer and told Connolly to hold her tight. He needed no second bidding. She looked ravishing and smelled gorgeous. He made no attempt to prevent the most obvious effect she was having on him and he allowed his hands to slip down to the bottom of her back and rest on the gentle curve of her bottom. As he did so she pressed herself to him a little more closely.

An exquisite combination of peace and desire seemed to have gripped him as they danced on and on. Connolly, almost as if in a dream, realised that Sarah had closed her eyes. There was only one thing to do, so he did it. Her lips were soft and warm and his whole being seemed to be suffused with intense happiness, freedom and sensuality, all at the same time. How long they remained like this he had no idea. When he eventually raised his head to look around him, the floor was deserted. The band played on but of either other customers or staff there was no sign. Connolly stopped, not that their movement had been very noticeable, and very shortly afterwards the band stopped playing. Bruce and Sarah applauded them as Bruce led the way back to their table. He then walked behind a screen, which Sarah had not noticed before, and reappeared a few seconds later. A few minutes later a beaming Felice came to their table.

"More coffee is on its way. Now then, Signorina Curzon, have you enjoyed your visit to my establishment?"

"Oh yes, very very much, indeed, but how did you know my name? Did?" She looked at Connolly.

"Oh no! Your father used to grace my café and I knew when your, er − friend here walked in with you, that I had seen your face before, if only in photographs. If this man brings someone here, something which happens only very infrequently I would add, they have to be very important to him, therefore they have to be connected in some way to the childish obsession of his. So I look back through some magazines and there you are − Signorina Sarah Curzon − although you look many times more beautiful than in the photographs. Bellissima!"

"Thanks, Sam, you've done my ego a whole heap of good there.

"Sarah, take no notice of this old fraud."

"I most certainly will. I take notice of anyone who says nice things about me." her eyes sparkled with mischief, and Bruce realised that much as he had thought these things, he had not yet paid her even the tiniest of compliments during either of their meetings. Again displaying her gift she turned to Connolly.

"No you haven't but, but hopefully you'll get around to it eventually." Her expression and tone of voice took away any possible hurt and she put her hand in Connolly's.

"Come on, cowboy, take me home." She raised her free hand to Sam's allowing him to almost kiss it again, said goodnight to him and then excused herself for the Ladies room. Connolly looked at his friend.

"This one is very definitely dangerous, my friend."

"Dangerous? Not the comment I expected."

"Oh yes. How long is it since you brought a woman here? I'll tell you, not since the rich bitch and then you weren't on this planet. Added to that both of you individually are undoubtedly attractive but not exceptionally so. But put the two of you together and wow! That is something else. When I saw you dancing I couldda cried, you were both so beautiful. Oh yes dangerous doesn't get close. A hundred bucks says you'll be married within a year."

"Get outa here, this is only our first date!"

"And you bought her here on your first date? I am so right about this! Five hundred bucks, no, a round thousand." He stuck his hand out just as Sarah reappeared.

"Okay, okay.!" He took Sam's hand.

"Bye, pal, and thanks for everything."

"My pleasure, hey come round for a beer and a couple a games of pool. The guys round here got no idea. I need to get the lowdown on the coming season as well."

"It's a promise." Sarah and Bruce walked outside and into the limo.

Once inside the car, Sarah took Connolly's hand in both of hers.

"That, Bruce Connolly, was the most enchanting evening I have ever spent. I cannot remember enjoying myself quite so much ever. Now we are both going to go to bed, you in your hotel room and I in mine, but," she raised a finger as she saw the disappointment cross Connolly's face, "I want to come and stay at your house in France, and sometime soon. Now here is your hotel, so out you go, I'm sure Felice will have primed the driver as to where I'm staying. In the morning you can ring me with dates for me to come to France, but only on the condition that the last thing you think about before you fall asleep and the first thing you think about when you wake, is me." She leaned across, kissed him full on the lips, allowed their tongues to meet for a tantalising few seconds, then pushed him away. She smiled and that smile was fixed in his brain forever. Connolly watched the car draw away, and then with a mile wide grin on his face made his way to his room. As he lay on his bed, his last fairly ridiculous thought was how would he know whether Sarah would be his last thought before he fell asleep?

Eight hours later, Sarah's hotel phone rang.

"Hi, handsome."

"Hi, beautiful. How does the week after next sound?"

"Actually it sounds like a long time away but I can live with it. Give me your e-mail address and I'll let you have my flight details as soon as I've sorted them. Now did you keep your promise?"

"Oh definitely, last thought, first thought and lots of thoughts in between."

"Oh do tell me, what sort of thoughts?"

"No way do I tell you those thoughts, or some of them anyway, over the phone."

"When I come to France then, please?"

"You might be shocked."

"Oh I sincerely hope so." She giggled again and Connolly was in agonies of desire again at the sound. They talked for another half an hour before making promises to ring again the following day. Connolly's admission to Sarah that he too had never enjoyed an evening as much as the previous one was as fervent as Sarah's and just as true.

CHAPTER ELEVEN

Sarah Curzon looked around her in some surprise. She had realised, as soon as she had met him, that there was more to Bruce Connolly than the general public, as well as she herself, had ever appreciated. Very much the brash, almost ignoble, typical all-American sporting hero in public, a much more thoughtful and gentle, sophisticated being lay beneath the surface. The beautiful home in which she now stood was further proof of Connolly's cultural depth. Whilst this was very much a man's home, there was nevertheless, a great deal of beauty here. Hung around the lounge, if that was what the enormous area in which she was standing was called, were numerous paintings, all individually lit. Half were in oil, the remainder were water-colours. Several paintings of cyclists – Fausto Coppi, Bernhard Hinault, Jaques Anquetil, and another surprise, Lance Armstrong, vied for attention with some railway paintings by Terence Cuneo, Chris Woods and Malcolm Root, and a couple of aircraft pictures by David Shepherd. Also expertly displayed and individually lit, were porcelain figurines of birds (mostly British, Sarah was delighted to note), and horses. All the display cabinets were recessed into the walls. The air of calm could almost be touched. Connolly had warned Sarah that he would probably not be at home when she arrived. His housekeeper had let her in, briefly showed her around and then disappeared.

Moving to inspect Connolly's home entertainment system, Sarah took in the breadth of the music collection with increasing pleasure. Very fond of the romantic composers herself, she was delighted to see that Bruckner, Mahler, Tchaikovsky and Sibelius were well represented as well as most of the 19th & 20th centuries' major composers. There was also a lot of British and Russian music right across the time span of classical music. Bruce's popular music taste was equally broad and extensive and mirrored hers, although some of the heavy rock in evidence was not exactly her cup of tea. She made her way into what was clearly the study and was confronted by an enormous number of books. The large number of sports books was no surprise and the paintings had prepared her for the collection of architectural, naval, aviation and warfare books on the shelves. What was something of a surprise was the large number of books on Art, Philosophy, Psychology and History. A considerable number of biographies and autobiographies were also in evidence. A complete absence of novels, however, made Sarah wonder if this extremely interesting new acquaintance was perhaps a little *too* serious minded.

"The fiction and the other lighter stuff are in the bedrooms." Connolly's voice made her jump and he smiled at her reaction. "The porn is in there as well." They laughed together as Sarah made a face.

"I was just wondering if, after misjudging you as crass and a bit thick in the past, you were going to turn out to be way too highbrow for me."

"Me, highbrow? The guys would die laughing if they heard you say that. Oh, and by the way, what do you mean, a bit thick?" They both laughed again.

"I'm sorry I wasn't here to meet you, but as you can see, I was at the office and couldn't rearrange things." He stood in Lycra cycling gear – multi-coloured team jersey, matching cycling shorts, track mitts and a cotton cap covering his by now unfastened crash hat. Socks and shoes were already off.

The tightly fitting jersey and shorts were like a second skin displaying a perfect cycling physique. Exceptionally well-defined leg muscles, powerful shoulders, by comparison, slim arms and not an ounce of fat to be seen. The slight sheen of perspiration covering his face and brow diminished his attractiveness not at all. He smiled again.

"How about you make us some coffee while I take a shower and make myself presentable? Oh I'm forgetting my manners. You see you were right, I am crass." He paused. "It's very nice to see you." He held her gaze for a long time before disappearing into the shower room. Sarah busied herself finding her way around the kitchen and produced some excellent smelling coffee just as Connolly reappeared, now dressed in beige slacks and a plain woollen sweater.

"What would you..."

"Did you have..."

They both laughed as almost inevitably in such situations, they began speaking at once.

You first." Sarah prompted.

"Okay, what would you like to eat, you must be hungry?"

"Yes, yes I am. Surprise me."

"Before that though, I guess you'd like to unpack and freshen up a little. You know where everything is I guess, except your room."

"Yes, to the first bit, and yes and no to the second. Your housekeeper gave me the lightning tour but didn't tell me where I'm sleeping. Before I change though, what are your plans for the rest of the day so that I know what to wear?"

"You too tired for a walk?"

"No, that would be fine, it's lovely around here."

Sarah's room overlooked a grassed area that could have been more accurately described as a clearing rather than a lawn. Surrounded by mainly deciduous trees, the clearing was bathed in dappled sunlight and looked peaceful and inviting. She quickly made use of the shower before putting on a pair of light green shorts and a matching halter top and a pair of sandals. She then turned to look at the bookshelves in the room. Here there were more surprises, although she should have been prepared for these. Connolly was clearly an avid reader. The books all appeared to have been read, indeed, some were quite dog-eared but it was not the quantity but the diversity that surprised her. She then reasoned to herself that it was only to be expected that someone with such catholic musical tastes as Bruce would be equally broad in his reading. There were all sorts here from Solzhenitzyn's August 1914 and Gulag Archipelago to the complete set of Patrick O'Brien's Captain Aubrey novels. War and Peace and Anna Karenina were on the shelf above Raymond Chandler and Boris Pasternak. The Iliad and Odyssey, The Lord of the Rings and a set of Neville Shute titles were alongside Hammond Innes, Dick Francis and Zane grey.

"Hey, Connolly, you weren't joking about the porn were you?" she called out, as her eyes alighted on some pornography magazines and books. She leafed through a few in which nothing was left to the imagination.

"No," shouted Bruce from the kitchen, "did you think I was?"

"I don't know, I'm just surprised that's all?"

"Surprised that they aren't hidden or surprised that I have them?"

"Hmmn?" The conversation was becoming a little uncomfortable for her and yet not altogether unenjoyable.

"You don't approve." It was a statement, not a question.

"It isn't that. I'm sure everybody or almost everybody looks at porn from time to time nowadays, especially with so much of it freely available on the internet. It's just that I'm surprised that you have them. I should have thought that someone in your situation wouldn't need something like this though." She waved a slim volume the cover of which showed a very attractive large-breasted girl clearly having sex with the guy standing behind her. Bruce laughed.

"There are quite a few points there. We could spend all evening talking about them, but for now I'll just say that, firstly, I'm not sure how many people who look at porn 'need' to, as distinct from 'want' to and secondly, I'm assuming that by 'my situation', you're referring to my reputation as a womanizer." He didn't give her chance to respond. "I don't 'need' porn any more than I 'need' any other type of book or film. Neither do I go out of my way to avoid it. Most of it is pretty crummy and the acting laughable, but some of it is okay. Just to complete the picture, yes, I admit that when the people in a porn movie are obviously enjoying themselves, are attractive and the action itself, arousing, I have found some of it quite a turn-on. As far as the womanizer bit is concerned, you've the first girl I've ever 'entertained' here, and when we went to Sam's, that was my first date for a couple of years. Hardly Casanova-like, wouldn't you say?" He said this with a smile which took away any offence or for that matter, defensiveness in his words. "Let me check on the paella while you think of your reply."

Well, Sarah thought, that was interesting to say the least. She had always thought of herself as being fairly worldly-wise but had hardly ever seen any pornography before. She had certainly never seen anything as explicit as some of the stuff in these books, nor for that matter had she been aware that some of the action depicted was practiced or even possible. Neither had she ever heard anyone speak so openly about the subject either. She could recall others, both male and female who had openly and vociferously expressed disapproval of pornography, but who Sarah had later discovered were into porn in a big way. Sarah herself had never really given the matter much thought. Clearly there were moral and ethical issues involved, but as she well knew there were many of the people who worked in the 'adult entertainment' industry who did so out of choice. Added to which she prided herself on being totally non-judgemental about others. Now as she leafed through some of the magazines she was certainly not repulsed by them and felt herself getting aroused. 'It's just been too long', she told herself attempting to justify the feelings beginning to build. She was interrupted by Bruce calling her to the table.

"The paella will be about five minutes so time for these first." 'These' were simple but delicious pink Florida grapefruit cocktails. Sarah felt ravenous. The grapefruit barely touched the sides and the paella she dispatched with great gusto. Connolly still had a third of his left when Sarah finished.

"That was, without doubt, the finest paella I've ever tasted. Where did you learn to cook like that?"

"Self-taught. I warn you though that apart from paella, the only other things I can cook are beans on toast, cheese on toast, and poached eggs on toast." They both laughed together.

"Phooey! Seriously, who taught you to cook?"

"I am being serious, I taught myself from cookbooks."

"I must borrow those books."

"Anytime. Now, what about some coffee?"

"Yes please."

Over coffee they exchanged small talk, her journey, his training ride, her father, his teammates until Bruce rose and took her hand.

"How about that walk now?"

"That would be lovely, lead on, MacDuff."

"MacDuff?"

"Don't worry about it."

For the next three hours they strolled through the woods behind Connolly's home. Lots of wild flowers, a wide variety of mostly deciduous trees, many of them unknown to Sarah and plenty of wildlife provided an idyllic combination.

"I now know what the word 'halcyon' really means." Sarah remarked. They had walked slowly, talking only occasionally, both revelling in the tranquillity of their surroundings and in the quiet comfort of the other's company. For half an hour they had sat by the small river that ran through the woods. Both had wanted to be touched, held, kissed and caressed by the other, yet were equally anxious not to break the spell woven by their surroundings. Eventually the sun, though still fairly high in the sky lost a little of its warmth and Bruce turned to Sarah.

"Maybe on this 'halcyon' day it's time we went back to Mount Olympus for some nectar and ambrosia?"

"That's fine by me, lead on, Mighty Zeus."

Connolly took Sarah's hand and they walked back to the house, both very conscious of their own expectations. By the time they reached the house, the early evening had assumed a silent all-encompassing ambiance which a clear still sky of deep cerulean blue, the merest hint of a breeze and absolute silence usually brings.

Sarah excused herself, went to her bedroom and changed into a favourite cashmere cat suit which she knew suited her. The relationship between Bruce and her had remained platonic by mutual consent. From the very first meeting, contrived though it was, she had been fairly certain that he had been attracted to her, possibly even very attracted to her. She was also even more certain that because Bruce was very concerned not to spoil their blossoming friendship, any move in physical terms would have to come from her. Not that that would be any hardship! She had admitted to herself some time ago that making love to Bruce was something she really wanted to do and the sooner the better. It was a very long time, if ever, since she had had the hots for someone quite as much as this. She looked in the mirror, just a little lipstick, a slight fluffing up of her hair and a few strategic squirts of Chanel No 5. Unfasten one more button on her top? Yes, still not too blatant but definitely promising. She nodded to herself in the mirror, smiled and walked into the lounge.

Bruce was pouring two glasses of Chablis. He smiled at her, his eyes appreciating every inch of her and handed her a glass.

"You look lovely. Here's to you." He raised his glass.

"Thanks, but I prefer, here's to us." They both took a few sips of the wine and stood in silence for a few seconds.

"This is very good. Now kiss me."

Bruce needed no further encouragement and their eyes closed as their lips met. Gradually the initial gentle touch became gradually more urgent. They pressed themselves against each other, Bruce's hands sliding down Sarah's back until they were on her bottom. Her response was immediate as she clenched her buttock muscles, slid her hands inside his shirt and then dug her fingers into his back. He felt her nipples harden through the cat suit and moved one hand to unfasten the remaining buttons of the suit. She began to moan softly and then gradually became louder. The door chimes sounded with the effect of a cannon going off. They sprang apart.

"Who the hell is that?" Bruce cursed under his breath. He went to the door as Sarah sat down. Still trembling slightly she re-fastened the buttons of her top. As Bruce opened the door he was engulfed by seemingly dozens of bodies.

"Hi, Bruce!"

"Evening, Boss."

"Hi, Captain."

"Hi, Bruce, sorry for barging in on you like this, but we wondered if you and Sarah might like to come out for a while, a kind of welcome, what do you say?"

The last words were shouted, as about a dozen people were all greeting Bruce more or less at the same time, by John Ryan, on whose arm Sarah saw Judith Taylor beaming at her like a long-lost friend, which in a way she was.

Hi, Sarah, long time no see. How are you?

"Fine, Judith, even better now I've seen you, it's been so long hasn't it." They hugged each other with genuine warmth, a fact not lost on the two men.

"I didn't know you two were er...?" Sarah trailed off. Judith laughed and turned to Ryan.

"Sarah is assuming we're an item. I came tonight because John thought it might be a little overpowering if you were the only girl. Thoughtful of him, wasn't it?"

"Very." Sarah replied but noted that there was a certain something in Ryan's eyes that suggested a hope that Judith would become something more than just a fill-in female.

"Hey, you guys, don't mind me but I do happen to live here. Do I have any say about what's going down?" Bruce sounded aggrieved but was smiling broadly. Eventually ten of the team plus Ryan and Judith were spread around the room. Connolly caught Sarah's eye and raised his eyebrows. Sarah smiled in genuine amusement. After everyone had downed a drink, it was suggested that they would go to a newly opened club not too far away. An hour later, they were all tucking into a more than passable meal and enjoying an extremely pleasant evening. Bruce and Sarah ate little but were able to relax. No doubt because of the relative seniority of Bruce and John, the rest of the teammates tended to leave the four of them to themselves after they had all eaten. The two women reminisced for a while and then moved to the present.

"How long have you known John?" Sarah asked.

"Professionally, as members of opposing teams, for quite a few years, but socially, not at all really. We've been out together twice professionally as it were, in the past two weeks, that's all. He told me this evening that you've been connected with cycling for years."

"I suppose so but not particularly closely. My father had a close involvement in the past and I have always had a reasonable knowledge of what's been going on in the sport:

who's going up, who's going down, that sort of thing, without ever really getting close to it."

"Until now?" Judith smiled and looked at Connolly.

"Is it that obvious?" Sarah felt herself colour.

"Well, as far as this lot are concerned," she gestured to the other riders, "you're probably just Bruce's latest, although having said that, it's a very long time since he's had a latest, in fact so long that I can't remember one, but I wouldn't mind betting a month's pay, that it's a lot more than that, and that our arrival, interrupted something, shall we say." It was a statement, not a question. Sarah laughed.

"Since we're on that subject, what about you and John?"

"Very early days, sometime I'd like to meet you in different circumstances so we can talk properly. Just for the moment let's say that I think I'm hoping."

The appeal in Judith's voice was unmistakable, but 'I think I'm hoping', seemed an odd thing to say.

"Sure, I'd like that very much. What about lunch sometime? You're much busier than me though, with all the racing just starting. Ring me when you've got a free day between races. Make it soon though, I haven't had a girly chat in ages."

"Fine I'll do that and thanks."

At that moment, John and Bruce returned with fresh drinks. A roll of drums heralded the beginning of the cabaret. A reasonably funny, not too blue comedian, a much better than average drag artist and two semi-striptease singers who were also talented and witty songwriters entertained them for an hour and a half. Nevertheless, Sarah would much rather have been back at Bruce's house and yes, in truth, in his bed. The frequent meeting of their eyes and their 'accidental' touches told her that Bruce's attention was elsewhere too. However, the other members of the group were obviously having a good time.

After the cabaret, Sarah was asked if she would like to dance by several of the team, which as they were all better than average dancers, was much more enjoyable than it might have been. Even so, the time began to drag as her desire to be alone with Bruce grew stronger. For only seconds at a time, did it seem that they were together and even then their conversation had to be shared with half the nightclub, or so it seemed. In spite of this she was still able to appreciate how popular and well-respected Bruce was, both by his team members and the locals in the nightclub. Clearly, to those who knew him well, this man was entirely different to the brash all-American, overbearing college-boy jock-strap hero portrayed by much of the media.

After what seemed an eternity, the party began to break up. Bruce and Sarah had been driven to the club by John and Judith so Sarah had resigned herself to a coffee-cum nightcap session to round things off. Connolly made the offer but Judith and John declined. Unfortunately for Sarah, most of the others accepted and they went back to the house. Bruce slipped an arm around Sarah's waist as they walked towards the door and then he suddenly stopped dead.

"Shhhh! Stay here."

He gently pushed the door and it slowly opened. Even in the darkness, and further back than Bruce, everyone could see that the inside of the house was a wreck.

Sarah felt sick and frightened and realised that she was trembling. Pete Weiss put his arm around her as went into the house. After a few minutes the lights came on and Connolly waved to them to go in. The scene that greeted them made them gasp. Wanton destruction didn't even come close. Broken glass everywhere, paint thrown all over the carpets, curtains and furniture which itself had then been smashed. Soft furnishings had been slashed. Connolly was moving slowly through the debris, his face impassive and Sarah marvelled at his self-control. Several of the others were also moving across the room. That was a mistake. In the same instant Sarah heard the sound of breaking glass and as time stood still, the sound of a gunshot. She screamed as Connolly dropped to the floor like a stone.

"Get down!" Weiss shouted and they all fell to the floor amid the sounds of cries and shouts. For a lifetime gunshots echoed through the night and Sarah, unable to move, was terrified that Bruce was dead. As quickly as the devastation had begun, it ended but no one moved Connolly lay where he had fallen and Sarah prayed.

"Stay down everybody. Are you all okay?" Connolly's voice sounded calm and Sarah wept.

"I think Vincent took a bullet, Boss." Sarah couldn't tell who had said it.

"Everybody stay down while I take a look at Vincent." Connolly slowly raised himself, then crawled across to his teammate and quickly checked him over. He then rang for an emergency ambulance and the police, then ran and came back with a very comprehensive first-aid kit. Vincent looked very pale and blood was running from a head wound. He'd also taken a bullet in his shoulder. Neither wound appeared to be life-threatening even though the head wound was messy, albeit superficial. The bullet to his shoulder had gone straight through. Nevertheless, Vincent had already lost a fair amount of blood and was in considerable pain as well as suffering from the onset of shock. With impressive expertise and even more impressive calmness Bruce dressed the wounds and eased Vincent's discomfort. Only then did he tell the others to get up.

Sarah pulling herself together, worked her way around the room checking how everyone was. The effects of the attack differed considerably from person to person. Some were clearly more or less in control of themselves, whilst others were in considerable shock. Bruce left Sarah to help the latter whilst he gathered together the least affected and they began the task of clearing up the carnage, bearing in mind the necessity of avoiding upsetting the police. Sarah was still amazed at Connolly's reaction. Still neither apparent anger, nor fear and certainly no signs of shock, although common sense told her that he must have experienced some degree of it. She would not have believed anyone could remain so phlegmatic under such stress, had she not seen it for herself. These thoughts were interrupted by the arrival of three ambulances and the police, and in seconds the place was inundated with uniforms. Vincent was carefully loaded into the first ambulance and all but three of the others were also taken to hospital. Quite a few were suffering from cuts sustained from broken glass when they dived to the floor when the gunfire began.

The police stayed a mercifully short time before leaving but only after Connolly promised that he and Sarah would make themselves available the following day for statements. Two very imposing guards were left behind however, presumably to discourage any repetition of the attack and/or vandalism, together with a couple of forensic experts who would be "here for several 'ours M'seur."

Sean Brean, Pete Weiss and Andy Palumbo, the three not needing hospital treatment, stayed to help clear up the mess as best they could, without hindering the forensic examination and for two hours the five of them worked steadily. Eventually the three riders agreed to leave, much against their will, but Connolly was becoming concerned about the amount of energy they were expending.

"At least the place can be lived and slept in now, you've done a great job so go home and get some sleep… and thanks."

"No sweat, boss, we'll be back in the mornin'." This from Sean, his rich Irish brogue and charming smile lifting the gloom that was threatening to engulf them. The other two smiled and waved goodbye.

Bruce saw them to the door and returned to the bedroom to find Sarah sitting on the bed clearly having difficulty preventing herself from crying. Bruce put his arm around her which, of course, opened the flood gates. She cried for a while and Connolly made no attempt to stop her.

"Oh, Bruce, when is it going to stop? We could all have been killed!"

"Hmm, yes but only by accident. If whoever it was, wanted to kill me or anybody else, I'm pretty sure they would have succeeded."

"So you're saying that Vincent was just unlucky?"

"Yeah, I guess so."

Sarah was incensed.

"Is that all you can say, he was unlucky! I thought before that it was amazing how calm you were. Now I realise that it was because you just didn't care!" She was shouting now and on the verge of hysteria. Connolly spoke very sharply to Sarah.

"Sarah, don't be stupid. Of course I care about the guys but I'm just facing facts. I'm certain that anybody with the weapons these guys had couldn't have missed, however bad their shooting was, if they had intended to kill or even just hit us. Now I sure as hell wasn't as rational as this while the shooting was going on, I was just as scared as everybody else." He smiled and pulled her close. She clung tightly for a few moments without speaking, then looked into his eyes and smiled a little wistfully.

"I'm sorry about that stupid comment about not caring, it's very obvious how much you do care. You are, of course, absolutely right." She paused for a few seconds. "Okay, wise guy, why the visit then?"

"Just a frightener I guess. What I don't get is what are, whoever they are, trying to frighten me away from? Nobody has ever approached me about anything, no threats, no 'do this or else', type scenes, no approaches to throw races, nothing − I just don't get it. One thing is certain, whoever is behind this has plenty of money and power, those guns weren't toys. He or she is a big operator."

"She?" Sarah was surprised.

"Why not? There are lots of high rolling women in business these days."

Sarah frowned, clearly unconvinced.

"You don't buy that?"

"No I don't. This business," she waved her hands around, "doesn't strike me as being at the instigation of a woman and neither do all the other incidents too. They are too..." she paused searched for the right word, "I don't like the word but I can't think of a better one, they're too macho. A woman would be more subtle."

"Okay, but how about a woman being behind the whole thing but all the various incidents being orchestrated by a man or men?"

"That's possible, but I think she would have to be in the dark about the actual incidents. I tell you, Bruce, these ideas would neither be thought up by a woman nor condoned by one, there's no finesse involved."

"Okay I get the message. Let's change the subject. What do you want to do now?"

"Well, I'm absolutely famished, so something to eat, something to drink and a shower, the order I'll leave to you."

The state of the house, their states of mind, the presence of the forensics team, and the visit to the police station the following morning made any continuation of their interrupted lovemaking out of the question, and Sarah returned home the following day after breakfast and the police station visit. Their mutual frustration was obvious to both when Bruce took Sarah to the airport to see her off but both realised that in the circumstances things would just have to be put on hold.

CHAPTER TWELVE

Stage victories in Paris-Nice (the so-called 'Race to the Sun'), the Tour of Romandy and the Giro d'Italia, as well as his excellent performances in the Spring Classics had enabled Roger Powell to hold second place in the year long successor to the old World cup, the ASO Challenge. As the Tour de France rapidly approached, Roger felt confident he would ride a good Tour, although it would be his first attempt at cycling's premier event. Roger's performances had resulted in him taking over the leadership of the team. Much to his delight and relief, the other possible leader of the team had happily accepted Roger's elevated status has he had not ridden particularly well thus far into the season and didn't relish the extra pressure that team leadership always brought with it. However, the decision would soon have to be made by the team's management as to what exactly were the team's ambitions in the Tour. Did they aim for the Yellow Jersey or concentrate on trying to win stages? Was winning the Green Jersey also a possibility? I'll let the big cheeses sort that out, thought Roger. For this evening at least his thoughts were on a different plane entirely.

As an amateur cyclist, Roger had always been aware that in order to break into the pro ranks, cycling had to be first, last and everything in between. Girlfriends had always had to fit in or around his cycling, be it racing, training, buying bikes and other cycling gear and even cleaning bikes. Unsurprisingly, few had remained very friendly for very long. At that time the relatively low esteem in which cycling was held in Britain didn't help either. Nowadays, with the superb performances of Bradley Wiggins, Chris Hoy, Vicky Pendleton et al on the track and the, if anything, even more admirable road successes of David Millar, Wiggins again, the amazing Mark Cavendish and Chris Froome, cycling was no longer the Cinderella sport it had been for decades in the U.K. Add to this the knighthoods of Dave Brailsford, Wiggins and Hoy and everybody in Britain now knew a fair bit about cycling. Even so, no sports enjoyed greater popularity on the continent than "La Cyclisme" and this, together with Powell's obvious potential had ensured that Roger had never been without female company whenever he wanted it.

To begin with, however, the problem had been that the vast majority of the girls had been either brainless bimbos or tramps on the make. Sally was different. For a start she had not been on the back row when the Lord had dished out intelligence. She was also genuinely interested in and knew a lot about cycling. She also seemed to know quite a lot about a great many other things, including Roger's other sporting love, cricket. She also liked to play chess and she and Roger were of roughly similar abilities. Add to this a sparkling personality, a very pretty if not exactly beautiful face, and a body exactly like Powell's fantasies and you have all that a man could possibly wish for, well this man anyway, thought Roger, smiling to himself.

The Tour was only two weeks away and Roger's directeur sportif had decreed that a little socialising was acceptable. Roger had immediately contacted Sally so that they could make the most of the evening.

As Powell finished dressing, Ritchie Moorcroft, his Australian roommate breezed in.

"Wow, who's the lucky lady tonight then, stud?"

Roger tried to sound cool and only vaguely interested.

"Oh er, only Sally again."

Richie's face split into his trademark grin.

"I spose sexy Sally is at this very minute saying to her best friend, oh it's only boring old Roger again."

"Yes probably."

"Yes probably balls. You've got the hots for pretty Sally, not that I blame you blue, and everybody can see it. And her for you, but what she can see in a dickhead like you I can't imagine. Been in her knickers yet?"

He ducked as Roger threw his aftershave bottle at him.

"Sally isn't like that." Roger protested.

"Sally might not be, though I wouldn't take bets, but you certainly are, you randy sod, Rocket Roger with his powerful pole."

He laughed and ducked again as a shoe hurtled across the room.

"Why don't you go and play with yourself?"

"That, me old mate, is all that I shall be able to play with, whereas you O Mighty One, will have all sexy Sally's toys to play with, and man I gotta say, she has some world class toys. Okay, okay, she's not like that, don't throw anything else, you're such a lousy shot you never hit me anyway and you might break a mirror or something. Seriously, Rog, are you sure she's not just another groupie?"

"Sure I'm sure and yes, Mum, I'll be careful."

"Where are the two of you going?"

"She's meeting me in the bar in…" he glanced at his watch. "Shit, five minutes ago, see you, ugly."

He punched Ritchie on the arm as he rushed out. His smiling teammate followed at a more leisurely pace. Roger took the stairs three at a time; lifts never came when you were in a hurry. To his relief, Sally came through the hotel entrance as he walked into the foyer from the opposite end.

She looks terrific, he thought to himself. She was wearing a bright red short-sleeved dress with a flounce at the hem which showed off her beautiful legs to perfection.

Round her shoulders she had a white silk stole and her white sandals accentuated her tanned legs. Matching pearl earrings and necklace and gold wrist and ankle bracelets completed the outfit which had instantly caught the attention of all the men and most of the women in the foyer.

As he waited for Sally to reach him, Ritchie came up and whispered in his ear,

"Red, hmm, that means she's in the mood for that beautiful body of yours, my son."

"Fuck off!" Hissed Powell.

Aren't you going to introduce me?"

"Not bloody likely, do I look that stupid?"

"The jury's out on that one."

As she reached him Sally kissed Roger on the cheek then took his hand.

"You look absolutely beautiful." Roger kissed her cheek.

"Thank you, I'm sorry I'm a bit late, the traffic was awful."

"That's okay I..." Roger was interrupted by Ritchie.

"Roger has only..." Powell's elbow caught him neatly in the ribs and he shut up abruptly.

"Sally, this is my teammate and general headache, Ritchie Moorcroft, Ritchie, this is Sally Hazel."

Ritchie moved to kiss her cheek, but she was too quick for him and held out her hand, which he took whilst smiling charmingly.

"I'm very pleased to meet you, Sally. Himself here has talked about nothing else but you for days. Now I can see why." How come no one as beautiful as you has ever crossed my path?"

Sally blushed a little. "I've no idea."

Powell, well-educated in the legendary womanizing ways of his teammate decided that enough was enough.

"Ritchie was just leaving, weren't you, Ritchie."

"Was I?" Another sharp dig in the ribs from Powell.

"Oh, yes, nearly forgot. Well bye, Sally. Don't forget what I said about being colourful, Roger. Have a good time both." He winked at Roger as he sauntered off.

"What was the bit about being colourful?"

"Oh nothing, Ritchie's a wally, a great mate, but still a wally. You do look absolutely stunning you know. Where would you like to go?"

"Anywhere, as long as it's with you." She put her arm through his and together they walked out of the hotel.

Half an hour later, they sat in a small restaurant recommended by Roger's team manager. As Sally leaned forward a little every so often, now minus her stole, Roger could see rather more of her. The suntan line indicated that the bikini bra or whatever she had worn when sunbathing had been very brief, indeed. If only he could have been there! Desire for her had all but made him speechless when she had first arrived and it had been mounting ever since. Dinner was going to be wonderfully difficult. He fervently hoped that Ritchie's words would turn out to be prophetic. He wanted this girl. God how he wanted her.

Later as Roger let himself into his room, a sleepy Ritchie heard Powell quietly humming to himself, 'Lady in Red.' Jackpot! Ritchie thought to himself as he drifted off to sleep. Roger's thoughts, although a little more romantic, were broadly along the same lines.

For her part, Sally felt very pleased with the evening. She had realised very quickly in their earlier dates that Powell was very attracted to her, the old-fashioned word 'smitten' came to mind. Her feelings for him were equally strong. Until tonight, however, he had behaved in an exemplary manner. He had been so keen not to cause her offence that she had had to stop herself laughing at his efforts to be the perfect gentleman more than once. Tonight she had decided that enough was enough as far as gentlemanly behaviour was concerned. She was as desperate for sex as he was. Back at her hotel after the meal she had given Powell no chance to become awkward. She closed the door and told Roger to sit down. She had then slowly undressed, not a striptease as such, that would have been too cheesy she had decided. She simply took off her stole, then her dress. She stood still, letting him take in her red bra, panties and suspender belt, still keeping her high-heeled sandals and stockings on. She then slowly unhooked her bra letting her ample breasts free, her nipples already extended with desire, then equally slowly pulled down her knickers revealing a luxuriant bush of dark pubic hair. She then walked over to Roger, pulled him to his feet, took hold of his hands and placed then on her breasts. He groaned. Slowly she undid his belt, removed his trousers and shirt and his shoes and socks. For the last two items she had to move away from him but she put his hands on her breasts again as soon as she moved in close. Finally, she put her lips on his and kissed him. It was gentle at first, and then as he kissed her back more forcefully, their tongues meeting and exploring, urgency took over. She now began to stroke his throbbing erection through his boxers causing Powell to make a sobbing sound.

"It's time we let this fellow have his freedom," Sally whispered in his ear, as she pulled his cock out of his shorts. They were the first words spoken by either of them since entering the room.

"Wow!" was the next thing she said, but that one word said it all.

"Much as I really really want you, Mr. Powell, I don't think you'd last very long if you put that beauty in me now, so let's make you comfortable first." With that she slipped to her knees, took his tool in her mouth, and sucked him for a few seconds. Then she took hold off his throbbing member and masturbated him for only a few more seconds before with a cry of release he shot off all over her superb breasts. She smiled in satisfaction as he ejaculated copiously over her.

"Oh, Sally, what an angel you are."

"Oh, I thought I made a rather good tart actually."

"Well yes you did…" his words tailed off as he saw her frown, "I mean, no I didn't mean…" he stopped again as she burst into laughter.

"All women are supposed to be part angel part whore if they want to keep their men interested aren't they? I played the tart, you think I'm an angel, I'm winning every which way as the Americans say. Now let's see if we can wake this mighty willy up again because my fanny is in serious need of an injection. Oh look he's waking up already. Now how would you like to inject me doctor? On my back, on my side, on all fours? Oh if it's all fours I think we should call it horse-style not doggy-style because there is no doubt about it you are definitely hung like a horse." Her words inflamed Powell, and needless to say, she got on all fours and he slipped into her in one delicious movement in spite of his size.

As she recalled what followed, Sally smiled to herself. Whilst neither of them was a virgin, it was obvious to both, that their previous sexual experiences had been poor introductions to this evening. She looked forward to the future with the highest expectations and she fell asleep blissfully content.

CHAPTER THIRTEEN

Not for the first time during the past few months, Jason Curzon found himself smiling wryly at the turn of events concerning his eldest daughter. Sarah's apparently empty personal life over the past few years had been a worry to him. Like many fathers in a similar position, his concern was merely that she may have been missing out on personal happiness. However that had never seemed to concern her. Now, unless he missed his guess, she was on course for an affair of some importance with Bruce Connolly.

Curzon had known Connolly for some years through their common involvement and interest in professional cycling. During the older man's management of his racing team, the two men's relationship had been only a professional one. However, Jason had formed a generally favourable opinion of the supposed brash American. He had never been affected by Connolly's non-racing activities and had therefore never concerned himself with them, although he had heard the rumours, of course. As his daughter was clearly very interested in the American, Jason had decided that to be fair to everybody, he would try to get some reliable information about Connolly's personal life. He had therefore detailed Michael Lewis, one of his most able and discreet lieutenants, to find out as much as he could about Bruce Franklin Connolly. Michal was now in front of his employer and after being settled with a drink, was asked for a progress report.

"It's all in here in detail, but I'll summarise verbally if you would like me to." Curzon nodded his assent. "I'll skip the cycling stuff because I'm sure you know most if not all of that, although it was more interesting than I thought it would be. Anyway the personal stuff. Connolly's reputation as a lady-killer is well known, but the more I looked into things the less I found out. Loads of people had 'heard' things about his exploits between the sheets, but it was all hearsay. 'Bruce Connolly, oh sure he's one for the ladies', 'Oh Connolly, he'll fuck anything', tended to be common responses but when I asked for names, only two were mentioned and they were fairly serious affairs. Apart from those two, no one could come up with even one girl's name, let alone the dozens he's 'reliably' supposed to have deflowered. What is fact is that he had a pretty disastrous marriage, which was effectively over three months after it began, although they stayed together for appearances' sake for more than a year. The only affairs that I could glean any reliable evidence for concern a fairly brief, and from time to time stormy, relationship with the English sports journalist, Valerie Cornell." Michael paused at this point and raised a questioning eyebrow. Curzon nodded for him to continue. "Both of them were on the rebound at the time. The affair ended amicably apparently and they remain firm friends, if fairly distant ones. Immediately before that and this is where the rebound came from in Connolly's case, and I surmise is where the bad press originates, he had an intense affair with that Italian actress-cum-singer Claudia Panatto."

"Ah yes, the rich bitch."

"That's the one. At the time, about eight years ago, Connolly was beginning to make his mark and then he fell for this girl very heavily. Everything was fine for a while and then Bruce began to lose form, not surprising really. Candle at both ends, in the middle and at least twice on any day with a 'y' in it. He realised the harm he was doing himself and pulled back a bit to give his career a chance. La Panatto didn't like this one little bit and suddenly Connolly was 'letting her down.' Then she accused him of cheating on her.

129

He refused to say anything at the time, which most people took to be a tacit admission of guilt. She dumped him. The Italian press did him no favours at all at the time, and for quite a while he didn't ride any events in Italy. Eventually it came out that the one cheating wasn't Connolly. If Bruce was on his bike and therefore unable to 'ride' Miss Panatto, so to speak, she made use of any other 'crossbar' that happened to be available at the time. Connolly was well aware of all this, was pretty cut up about the whole thing but has never said a word to anyone about her as far as I can tell. Miss Hot-Pants, however, has more or less constantly been revealing all of Bruce's imperfections and indiscretions to anyone who will listen. Nowadays nobody does of course because everybody now recognises her, somewhat belatedly of course, for the total trollope she is. One or two people who I rate as reliable say that eventually Connolly began to use the bad publicity for his own ends to some extent."

"To keep people at a distance?" Ventured Jason.

"Something like that. The same with the big bad macho old college boy image. I got a look around his house in France. It's very, very classy. He was charming as well, in a quiet kind of way and completely sincere, unless I'm a poor judge."

"Which you're not." Interjected Curzon.

"No way is the real Connolly any kind of yobbo. One funny thing though, boss."

"Funny peculiar presumably?"

"Well, I don't think it's funny ha-ha."

"Go On."

"Someone else has been on Connolly's trail, trying to dig up any dirt on him they can find. Now why should that be?"

I could hazard a guess, Curzon thought to himself, although it would be more than a guess, but instead he said.

"Don't worry about that for the moment. To be honest I knew pretty much all of what you've told me, but it was important for me to have it confirmed by somebody reliable. In your view Connolly is an all-right sort of bloke who has very unfairly suffered some bad press?"

"That's about it. One more thing though. Any woman I spoke to, and there were quite a few, made it very clear that they would have been his in an instant if he had so much as raised an eyebrow. A lot of them also added that they have in the past given him a very clear come-on with no response except for a very gentlemanly and tactful declining of said offer. In a nutshell, he could have had anybody and has had nobody."

"Hmm. And you think that the non-denying of the rumours is him just being a gentleman on the one hand and keeping people at a distance on the other?" Michael nodded assent.

"The only guys that he has as friends are his teammates and a few old pre-racing mates. They all say very little about him, but reading between the lines, I get the distinct impression that he's a private kind of chap and a bit of bad publicity on the personal front is useful in keeping unwanted admirers, especially female ones, at a distance. There is one other possible reason but this is only my guess."

"Go on."

"It's no secret that Connolly cares nothing for public opinion, except where it concerns his ability as a cyclist. That, he tends to fiercely defend when necessary. As regards other things it could simply be that it's just not worth the bother of denying the rumours."

"That, I'll happily go along with." Curzon smiled. After a few more minutes of general chit-chat, Curzon thanked Michael, and the younger man left. Jason was left with a kind of good news/bad news feeling. Obviously Bruce was not the wolf in wolf's clothing that he had always been painted to be, which confirmed his own opinion of the American. On the bad news side, how serious was the other muck-raking operation discovered by Michael? Deciding that he would have to leave that for a while, he picked up the phone and called Sarah.

CHAPTER FOURTEEN

"Have the police made any progress regarding the little incident at Connolly's house?" James Dowling looked at the three people, two men, one woman, in his hotel room.

"No, we've got it all buttoned up." The reply came from the weasel-faced man closest to Dowling.

"Good." He paused. "It would be good for Connolly to be, shall we say, unable to compete for a while, rather than for him to suffer from more racing accidents. People are beginning to think that he and his team have been just too unlucky." James Dowling looked at the three associates in the room.

"Any ideas?"

"I was going to suggest a training accident, but would that also be seen as too much bad luck, Boss?" The lack of expression in Dowling's associate's words mirrored the apparent lack of interest on his face but Dowling was well aware that there would be some fairly sound thinking behind the suggestion.

"Not necessarily. Training accidents are fairly common after all. It would have to be when he was out on his own, of course. I presume that you have some idea in mind?"

"I've got it on good authority that he's going to be England for a few days soon and his teammates aren't joining him until a few days later. He'll have to have some time out training before they come. That would be the ideal time. How long would you want him out of commission?"

"Ideally for a number of the pre-Tour preparation races, say two weeks."

"It's as good as done, Boss." As usual the use of the supposedly deferential term of 'Boss', didn't fool Dowling for a second. Dowling was, indeed, the man's employer as such but this was no master and servant relationship.

"Okay we're done here, let me know when you've made all the necessary arrangements for Connolly's 'leave of absence'. I've already cleared the expenses you'll no doubt incur. Jennifer please remain behind for a few moments." The other two associates rose from their chairs and left the room.

"You've done very well in your first month with me, Jennifer. Have you regretted leaving the airline job?"

"Oh no, not at all."

The now ex-stewardess had performed very well as Dowling's escort for the formal dinner, not realising that there was an ulterior motive behind his action. The expense of a complete outfit for the dinner was a small price to pay for her services, not all of which of course she had had explained to her. She was about to become a little more acquainted with what some of those additional services would be. To gain her confidence, Dowling had played upon the well-known but inaccurate reputation of Bruce Connolly and some inventive digital photography had further developed the picture of Connolly as being an egotistical predator from whom no woman was safe. Jennifer was now very keen to see the American get his come-uppance and the more she could do to help the better she liked it. She was also cute enough to realise that there could well be a lot in the arrangement for her if she played her cards right. What came next therefore was not really a surprise, although the degree of Dowling's 'requirements' would eventually go rather further than even she had expected.

"As I explained originally there will always be various services that I shall want you to perform for me, some like the dinner engagement will be necessary but probably quite boring for you, others will be much more personal but I hope rather more enjoyable, indeed, I hope that you will find them extremely enjoyable. However, before we go any further can I ask you if you have any 'reservations' shall we say as far as sexual activities are concerned?" He smiled what he knew of old, was a very charming and disarming smile.

Jennifer decided to play the game a little herself and put a little uncertainty in her voice.

"You mean kinky stuff?"

"Well, I suppose some people might think it kinky, I prefer to think of it as being more a case of enhancing our physical experiences as much as we can."

"What sort of experiences, group sex, things like that?"

"Well, yes occasionally perhaps but more like exploring each other's bodies as much as we can." Aha Jennifer thought to herself, so that's what floats his boat.

"I'm sure that I can enjoy that. You will look after me though won't you? I've done a bit of bondage and so on but being really hurt is not a turn-on at all."

"Of course I'll look after you. It will be my pleasure. Now, I would very much like to see you tomorrow evening so I'll send my car round for you at seven thirty. It would be a good idea to assume that you will be staying the night. You can have the rest of both today and tomorrow off because I'm sure lots of rest would be a good idea."

"Is there any dress code for tomorrow evening?"

"Oh no, we shall be staying in so use your imagination my dear."

Jennifer felt a flutter of excitement. It had been quite a while since she had had any real sex and enjoyable though pleasuring oneself with various toys was, it was in her opinion, nothing like the real thing. Dowling, she was sure would be very much the real thing. One thing she had never skimped on had been underwear and she was sure she could find something to please Dowling. She walked out of the room smiling.

***

Bruce Connolly hummed quietly to himself as he rode along the following morning. It was a day made for cycling. The sunshine was already warm even though it was only eight a.m. He was thinking that he didn't do what he was currently doing, simply riding for the pleasure of riding, enjoying the sights, sounds and scents all around him, anything like enough. Training was obviously very necessary and often quite enjoyable even if in a masochistic way. It was however always hard work and rarely, if ever, was there any opportunity to admire the scenery, drink in the scents of the hedgerows and just enjoy riding his bike for its own sake.

He became nostalgic as the perfumes of the springtime flowers caressed his senses. It had been the freedom of cycling that had first attracted him. His first bike, bought by well-meaning but ill-informed parents, had been a very high quality but completely un-sporty machine. Metal mudguards, steel wheels, 'Sturmey-Archer' three-speed hub gears, rod brakes, 'sit-up-and-beg' handlebars, painted blue and called a 'Space Rider'. It was made of 'gas-pipe' tubing, was as heavy as lead and he had loved it. He had always cleaned it after every ride and in spite of its completely non-racing image, he had seen himself as the Jaques Anquetil of South Street.

Much as he had loved his Space Rider, eventually the need for speed reared its head and he was given the chance to buy a second hand red drop handled bar 'racer'. Unfortunately, it was a racer in little more than the dropped handled bars, it had no gears and not even a fixed wheel. Nevertheless, this too had provided Bruce with an enormous amount of fun until he had been able to save up enough to buy a more or less properly equipped racing bike.

Where, he wondered, were the fifteen-year-old Bruce Connolly's of today? The history of bike racing was full of stories of the stars as youngsters, making do with second, third or even tenth-hand irons and by experiencing such hard apprenticeships, learning to suffer and then to become champions when able to use high quality equipment. These days, Connolly reflected ruefully, the moment a youngster shows an interest in riding a bike, his dad kits him or her out with the best of everything and gets them racing within a few months. Because the youngster has never experienced the fun of touring, riding around just for the hell of it and has never seen or smelt the abundant beauty of the countryside, he or she rapidly loses interest in cycling as soon as their racing efforts don't bring the kudos expected.

Dammit, Connolly thought to himself, as soon as this season is through, I'll take a tent and do some touring on the bike somewhere fairly warm. The more he thought about the idea the more it appealed to him. In his teens, cycle-camping had been almost a passion, either with his buddies or alone. His own company had always been sufficient for him and he realised that for far too long in recent years he had had too many people around him, numbing him almost, stultifying his thinking and reducing his world to one of racing, training, personalities, priorities and crises, and frequently other people's crises at that! He resolved to sort out some dates for what would be his first holiday in a dozen years.

Abruptly Sarah came into his mind. Was she a cyclist? Did she like the simplicity of camping? He thought that although it would probably a yes to the second, he wasn't so sure about the first. Her father had certainly been a cyclist and a good one. The cycle-camping would be so much better shared with Sarah, assuming, of course, that she would be happy to go. He began to think of possible difficulties and how to overcome them. Even if she was interested how would he approach the question of one or two tents? Would she think him quaint and old-fashioned if he suggested two, or pushy, graceless and crude if he assumed they would share? He realised that he would do all he could to avoid offending her in the slightest way and that the platonic approach was the way to go to begin with. The thought of what might have happened at his house had not John and the others arrived, brought a smile to his face and the beginnings of an uncomfortable swelling in his shorts. A beginning was all it would be however, Lycra racing shorts had no room for even half-formed erections! The striptease routine in his hotel had been a charade that was obvious now, although sometime soon he would have to ask her about that. What had really been her expectations? What would have been her reaction if he had behaved as his reputation suggested? In spite of all the pressure and his commitments, he had to see her again real soon. He must be able to sort something out easily, he was in England for crying out loud.

As his mind drifted along these very pleasant lines he noticed that his surroundings were improving all the time. The lanes he was now riding along had been his favourites since he first visited England. He loved the profusion of wild flowers − May blossom with its wonderful scent, a few early bluebells and rhododendrons. In the surrounding fields dandelions and buttercups were reflecting the bright morning sunshine. In others the glowing yellow of oil-seed rape flowers contrasted sharply with the brilliant blue sky. Whilst the scent of the rapeseed was not to everyone's liking, Bruce quite liked it and it certainly added to his sense of oneness with the world. The fact that he could smell it at all, something virtually impossible in a car, even with the windows down, was one of the joys of cycling and at this time in the morning, and for some inexplicable reason, especially in England, intensified his joy.

Connolly never tired of coming to England. Now of course, he had more reason than before but he was also pleased that the Brits had at last got their cycling act together. There had been numerous false starts, the Tour De France coming for a stage in 1974, what promised to be an explosion in cycling in the eighties and then again in the nineties, had all come to nothing and it wasn't until the successes on the track at the 2008 Olympics and the Grand

Depart of the Tour in London in the same year, following on from two successful stages in the 2004 Tour, that cycling in Britain really took hold of significant numbers of Britons. There was now a large number of Brits in the pro ranks and some of them were very good. They were almost always triers, even if a few were a bit small-minded. All that time-trialling, 'testing' as they called it in England. Connolly shook his head, thousands of guys and women too, once, twice, even three times a week, every week in the season from February to October riding only time trials! Jeez, they had to be a bit odd, to say the least. And what about those crazies in 24-hour time trials? 24 hours in the saddle, only stopping for a leak occasionally, just to see how far they could go! The current record he'd read somewhere was 540 miles, a quarter of the Tour in one day, all riding solo! Fuck that for a game of soldiers! This train of thought brought Connolly round to the official reason for his visit to England – an invitation two-stage single-day time trial. The morning stage was from Conway in North Wales to Llandudno followed by an afternoon hilly stage up the 'Great Orme', obviously some bitch of a hill, Bruce thought to himself. Most of the World Tour teams had received invitations to send teams of four, which with a sizeable home contingent, had resulted in a field of almost two hundred, considerably larger than the normal size field in a British time trial.

The event had generated a great deal of interest. The prize money had been put up by an unknown sponsor and the whole thing was being jointly organised by a consortium of British cycling organisations. It was still generally the case that for British riders to make it as professional cyclists they had to race primarily in France, Belgium, Italy, Spain and Holland. Increasingly, 'globalisation' of the sport had witnessed highly regarded events being promoted in America, Oman, Qatar, Canada, Australia and China, but the essence of the sport was still where it always had been, in continental Europe. As he rode along, Connolly reflected how much more quickly the U.S. cycling scene had developed than it had in England. As far back as 1965,

England had had a World professional road champion in the highly talented, immensely brave, and immensely popular but ill-fated Tom Simpson. The United States had to wait almost twenty more years before Greg Lemond became the first American wearer of the Rainbow jersey. In the next two decades Americans had won the Tour ten times through Lemond and the most successful Tour rider of all time, Lance Armstrong. The fact that Armstrong's name does not appear in the record books because of the use of blood doping is largely irrelevant as virtually all his fellow competitors at the time were doing the same thing. The British had to wait until 2012 until Bradley Wiggins won the Tour for Britain. Although cycling was no longer quite the minority sport it had been for so long in the United Kingdom, it was now almost as strong as the scene in America.

Connolly's thoughts were interrupted as he turned down a very narrow lane. Along the lane he saw that speed humps had been created since his last visit. The lane had always had a reputation for being something of an accident 'black spot' and these had obviously been put down as a traffic calming measure. Another of the minor joys of cycling was the fun to be had 'bunny-hopping' such obstacles, thereby being quicker than cars over them. Connolly smiled to himself as he pictured himself behaving as he always had as a kid. The first speed hump was only a few yards away and Bruce tensed himself. He lifted his front wheel... and found he was lying in the road. As if in a fog he gradually became aware of an intense pain from his neck and then very quickly he was hurting all over. He also became aware that he was half lying on his back being propped up by his bike or what had been his bike. He then began to feel a warm wet sensation down the right side of his face and there was definitely something wrong with his vision. He looked down at himself at the same time putting his hand up to the source of the intense excruciating pain in his head. Even through his blurred eyesight he could see that his mainly white training jersey was now turning red and his hand was covered in blood. Blood was coming down his face and dripping off his chin and he couldn't move. His last recollection before slipping into unconsciousness, was of the front wheel of his bike, apparently undamaged but separated from his bike, still spinning slowly round as if unwinding the final seconds of his life.

***

Several hours later Jennifer, the ex-air hostess, walked into the lounge of James Dowling's suite. The man himself was seated in a huge armchair dressed in a silk monogrammed dressing gown, with a half-full champagne flute in his hand?

"Champagne, my dear?"

"Oh yes, please."

He topped up his glass after passing one to Jennifer.

"To us." They both raised their glasses and toasted each other.

"Now thinking back to our conversation of yesterday afternoon is there anything specific sexually, that you would not be happy exploring?" Jennifer felt an exciting flutter gently ripple through her. She would need to play this carefully if she was going to get the best for herself.

"Well, as I said, I don't much like being hurt but I would also want to please you as long as I could be sure you wouldn't go too far." She thought that was a reasonable stance to take at this stage. 'Let's see what he's made of.' Jennifer thought to herself.

"Have you ever done anal, my dear?" He made it sound as commonplace as washing the dishes.

"No, but I've thought that I might like to try it sometime, with the right man of course, someone who is experienced and who would be careful with me. I understand that at least half the population has tried it at least once."

"Well, I'm sure I can be the right man and I'll certainly be careful. Paraphrasing whichever of the James Bond girls it was, I'll only hurt you gently. Come."

He rose from the chair, took her hand and led her into an exquisitely furnished bedroom. The satin sheets had been turned back and he sat down on the edge of the bed. Jennifer walked slowly over to him. Slowly, he undressed her down to her dark blue panties, bra, hold-up stockings and high-heeled shoes.

"I would be very grateful if you would walk around the room for a while so that I can both appreciate and anticipate your beautifully formed body." Dowling was not exaggerating, she was beautifully put together. Jennifer, of course, was aware that she had all the right bits in the right quantities and was more than happy to do as Dowling wished. After a few minutes he crooked his finger at her and she walked over and stood in front of him. She could now see the tenting in his trousers and without bidding began to remove his clothes. It soon became very obvious just how well-endowed this man was. A thrill rippled through her and for the first time Dowling's impassive expression slipped as she pulled off his boxers and wrapped her long slim fingers around his erection. She knelt down in front of him and began to slowly lick his frenum whilst holding his penis tightly and gently masturbated him.

"There's no way you will last long enough for my benefit if I allow you to enter me straight away, so relax, as you suggested we have all night."

Dowling's reply was a groan and Jennifer began licking the head of his penis a little more urgently. She now began to talk to him in very explicit terms and Dowling, always previously dominant in sex found himself extremely excited by the completely unexpected forcefulness of this angelic yet at the same time, sophisticated woman. He reached for her breasts as she continued the masturbation, but she slapped his hand away.

142

"Not until I'm ready and I'll tell you when. Now as well as being excited by the act of intercourse itself in as many forms as you can imagine, and probably then some, I really like to see a man spurt when I've masturbated him so let me see lots of your lovely cream. No not yet! Not until I'm ready!" She briefly let go of his member and watched as it twitched. She took the head in her mouth, sucked for a few seconds then took hold of his tool in her hand again. This time she immediately moved her hand very quickly up and down.

"Now, come now!" She squeezed his tool tightly and jerked him very hard. He groaned and bucked up and down on the bed.

"I want to see you shoot it all over me." She released her pressure and he spurted again and again as she kept saying, "Yeess baby, keep coming, keep coming, that's a huge load from a huge cock, yeesss!"

As Dowling finished his climax, Jennifer climbed onto the bed and lay down beside him. From somewhere she magicked a cool flannel and gently cleaned both of them. The flannel felt wonderful to Dowling.

"Now, in a little while when we've rested, I shall allow you to remove the rest of my clothes." At these words, he began to harden again. She slapped his penis with the flat of her hand, and he subsided with a muffled groan.

"I said in a little while. Then I shall require you to do the same for me as I've just done for you. I love cunninglingus, but if it isn't good enough, you won't get to put that great big tool in me, despite the fact that I do love big dicks." Naturally the salacious talk had the same effect again, which resulted in another slap.

"Not yet I said!"

Dowling didn't know what to do or say. He was completely floored. He had frequently been the dominant and had never had the slightest desire to be anything else. This girl was going to be the latest in a long line of submissives and yet without him realising it at the outset, she had now completely turned the tables on him and amazingly, he was loving it! He must have drifted off into a doze for a while. He was awakened by Jennifer's sultry yet still dominant voice.

"Okay, stud, now take off these clothes, then get down there, my fanny desperately needs some loving attention." He revelled both in stripping off her lingerie and then gazing at all now revealed. He then applied himself to her instructions

Normally whilst by no means averse to going down on a woman, in the past he had tended to do it as a means to an end. Now he found that he was both thoroughly enjoying the act and being excited by both Jennifer's and his own reactions. By the time she climaxed he was as stiff as a poker again. She now got onto all fours.

"Think of me as a mare on heat and I need your stallion's huge stiff cock now."

He couldn't remember when he had felt this horny. He entered her with a lunge, just like a stallion at stud and climaxed almost as quickly, but amazingly he was able to keep going, still stiff enough to give Jennifer her second blistering orgasm. They broke apart and without being aware of it Dowling was asleep immediately. Jennifer quickly followed suit, pleased so far with her carefully worked out strategy.

When he awoke it was to the sight and sound of the plasma T.V. He quickly looked at his watch, it was four hours since Jennifer had arrived.

"I've found something I like so you need to watch the screen and watch me. Another real turn-on for me is to pleasure myself while a man watches me and I watch porn, preferably men with big dicks being masturbated by their women. So watch and enjoy. Oh by the way, you can play with yourself by all means but don't you dare come, I'll want all the cream you've got left when I've finished doing myself."

She was lying beside him, one hand holding herself open whilst the other alternately rubbed her clitoris then putting two fingers into her vagina. Naturally Dowling became tumescent within seconds. Again watching a woman masturbate was not a new experience for the businessman, but always before it had been because he had told the women in question to do so. This was different and excitingly so. Was she doing this to turn him on, or doing it all for her benefit? That was an intriguing thought.

He had great difficulty not following the girl's example, so achingly stiff was he again, but he knew that once he took hold of himself he would have to continue to his climax.

"Suck my tits and put a finger up my bum until I come." He hastened to do so and was rewarded within a couple of minutes by Jennifer having another loud and unrestrained orgasm. She lay for a few seconds and then smiled lazily up at him.

"Now listen carefully, I want you to lie on your back and I'm going to mount you. You lie still, I'll do the riding or you'll spunk too soon. When I'm ready, I'll change and go reverse cowgirl until I'm ready to come again, by which time I'm certain you'll be more than ready to give me another big load. He did as he was told and she lowered herself slowly onto his French-stick like member. It felt absolutely heavenly to him. He concentrated on containing his climax as she slowly rose and lowered herself on his very impressive length. All the while she continued her sensual mewling sounds. She stopped as if sensing that he couldn't hold out much longer and turned around. Again she slowly lowered herself onto him.

"Now for a little while, I want you to fuck my bum with your finger, then we'll both come together." He inserted a finger into her well lubricated rectum and began working it in and out. Jennifer was clearly enjoying this, as was Dowling, but it couldn't last. She suddenly yelled, "Now!" and began bouncing up and down on him very quickly.

"AAARGH!" The cry of release was simultaneous. Dowling couldn't remember coming with such intensity ever before and for her part Jennifer knew that this was the way to keep this undoubtedly dangerous man, from growing tired of her. In truth, it had been no hardship, the sex had been as good as she had ever had and she was fairly certain that the same applied to him.

CHAPTER FIFTEEN

"Why won't that bloody goddam awful noise go away?"

"Ms rrcoonnny, rryoowaakemscoonny?

Gradually Bruce recognised the noise as a female voice. After a little while longer he made out what she was saying.

"Are you awake, Mr. Connolly?"

"Yes, I'm awake," Connolly said, but it came out in slow motion and sounded something like, "es, mwwck." He tried to open his eyes but found that his right eye didn't seem to respond and that the effort produced both a very blurred image of a white shape and an intense pain in his head. Gradually he became conscious of pains creeping over his whole being. Everything seemed to hurt but the right side of his head and face, his right arm and his neck were especially uncomfortable. He realised through a fog that the white shape was speaking again.

"Mr. Connolly, you have had a nasty accident and you will be in some considerable pain for some while. However, you were lucky and nothing really serious has happened. You did lose quite a lot of blood though and we did have to patch you up quite a bit. Would you like a drink of something?"

He tried to say, 'yes please', but he knew it didn't sound right, tried to nod his head but couldn't, so he raised his thumb. He opened his left eye again and this time his vision was much clearer. The white shape was, indeed, a nurse who was smiling at him. He was lying in, he supposed, a hospital bed. A multitude of recollections, thoughts and sensations suddenly flooded over him as the temporary memory block imposed by his subconscious was released. The narrow lane, the speed hump, the feeling of hopelessness when he realised that the wetness was blood and that he was possibly bleeding to death. At that moment, in spite of the pain he was experiencing, he was exceedingly glad to be alive. His thoughts then turned to cause. What had happened? Why had he come off for no apparent reason? He was noted as one of the best bike handlers in the peloton. He realised that what he wanted most, was to talk to John Ryan. He experimented with his mouth and found that by slowly and carefully forming his words beforehand, he could make sense.

"Nurse, John Ryan, please?"

He's visiting you at three o'clock, which is in about two hours' time. He couldn't get here any quicker if I rang him now, so you'll just have to be patient. Now get this drink down you and then some more sleep. Sleep really is the great healer you know."

She helped him with his drink and then left him. During the next two hours Connolly slept, occasionally surfacing for a few minutes during which he tried to find answers to the questions rushing around in his head. Ryan's entrance into his private ward woke Bruce.

"Good to see you, John." Connolly was relieved to discover that he could now speak reasonably clearly.

"And you, though no way could I say you look good."

"I'm fine really."

"If you say so but it's a peculiar looking fine as far as I'm concerned."

"Never mind all that. What happened? I don't fall off bikes dammit! And how did anyone know where I was? Who found me? Don't tell me it was an accident, because I'm not buying it." Ryan held up his hands.

"Steady, steady, you're supposed to be sedated."

"It musta wore off," Connolly retorted grumpily. "Now what's the score?"

Ryan forbore from telling Connolly that if he would be quiet he would tell him. Instead he said, "We think someone loosened your front quick release. While ever you kept the front wheel on the road you were fine but as soon as you lifted it to get over the sleeping policeman, sorry, speed hump, it dropped out. What we can't work out is why."

"How about, to do me some harm?"

"Sarcasm does not become you, young Connolly." Ryan smiled. "Why bother though? Even if you did come off, which couldn't be guaranteed, the most likely result would be some superficial injuries, which is exactly what happened. As racing cyclists tend to crash fairly regularly, they know how to fall and usually carry on racing. If you're right, whoever planned this wouldn't realise that and would expect you to be more seriously injured. Admittedly in this case you could be said to have been a bit unlucky, but it isn't very serious."

"If I'd come off in traffic, I could have been hit by a fucking great truck. That might've been a bit serious. Being dead is fairly serious wouldn't you say?"

Ryan smiled again at Connolly's outburst which sounded worse than it was, as they both well knew.

"Major injury was very unlikely. You never train on roads in towns if you can help it and the hotel is right in the country. Everyone knew that, or at least everyone in a position to be able to doctor your bike. Did you tell anybody your route this morning?"

Connolly thought for a little while.

"I mentioned where I was going at breakfast and there were a few of the guys there. I didn't try to keep my voice down or anything. Hell, John, half the people in the fucking hotel could've heard me if they'd been trying."

"Yes, that's more or less the conclusion we had come to?"

"We, who the fuck are the we? Oh yes, you still haven't told me how you found out about my off."

"John and I are the we and such language! I'd just about come to the conclusion that you had been suffering a bad press and weren't half as bad as people had been painting you. I can see that I may have to go back to my original view. As for the second question, you'll have to ask John."

The conversation had masked Sarah's arrival and Connolly's surprise at seeing her was only matched by his delight, quickly followed by embarrassment as her words registered. To his credit he blushed and became tongue-tied.

"Sarah, I... erm... didn't see you. Er, sorry."

"Evidently, however, the circumstances are a trifle unusual so just this once I'll forgive you." Her eyes sparkled. For his part Bruce had by now registered her appearance properly. Jeez, she sure looks good, he thought to himself. She was wearing a white dress of some kind of cotton, with black braid around the ends of the short sleeves, neckline and hem of her flared skirt. A black belt and a broad-brimmed black and white hat completed her ensemble. Fairly bright orange shade of red lipstick and beautifully made-up eyes added the finishing dazzling touches. She came across to his bed, kissed him on the forehead where there was an absence of dressings and frowned.

"You look absolutely awful."

"Gee thanks for that. You look absolutely wonderful, smell absolutely wonderful and now I feel absolutely wonderful."

"Huh! I thought Americans didn't use words like 'wonderful'?"

"This one does, anyway, how did you know about all this, I thought you were in Paris?"

"I was but I finished early, came home, and then remembered about the time trial so decided to have a couple of days by the sea. I'd also heard a rumour that some American handsome hot-shot racer was over here so came to get his autograph. Instead I find Frankenstein's monster. I arrived at the hotel just as John was told about the accident. I told John I was coming with him."

Connolly raised an eyebrow and looked at Ryan who shrugged.

"I wasn't going to argue. There's never any point getting into an argument you know you're going to lose. I'll leave you two and try to find out a bit more about the accident. I'll be back later."

Ryan's departure resulted in one of those silences between two people when both want to say a great deal, all of which they find difficult to put into words. As always in such cases, they both began at the same moment.

"I came because...,"

"It's great to see you, but why?" They both laughed. Another silence, both grinning. Sarah took off her hat.

"You first," said Bruce.

"This will sound corny and unoriginal but I came because I couldn't not come." The words came out in a rush and she looked away as she spoke.

"It might be corny and unoriginal, I wouldn't know, but it sure sounds fine to me."

He reached for her hand and she took his eagerly.

"How do you really feel, and leave out the hero bit."

"Stiff and sore in places but honestly I feel more or less okay now. I was pretty ropey when I woke up but much better now. Don't forget professional cyclists come off their bikes with boring regularity."

"What hurts the most?" He pointed to his head and the profusion of dressings and red painted skin.

According to the nurse, you have broken your nose, two ribs and have had about seventy stitches, mostly on your forehead and face. The remainder are on your shoulder and elbow."

"What's my bike like?"

"I've no idea and what's a bike anyway?"

"About ten thousand dollars, that's what." This was followed by another silence.

"I've missed you, Sarah."

"And I you." As she responded, her eyes began to fill with tears.

"Hey steady, honestly, I'm fine. I've come off my bike dozens of times and been in much worse messes than this!" He put his good arm around her shoulders and she put her head on his chest, not as gently as she might have done, treatment which Connolly's broken ribs did not respond kindly to. He winced so that Sarah shot upright again with an anguished cry.

"Sorry!"

"Connolly started to chuckle, winced again and grinned ruefully.

"Remind me not to laugh. Now come back where you were."

"Are you sure?"

"As eggs are eggs."

After a few minutes Sarah realised that Bruce was asleep and that she was beginning to feel uncomfortable. Very carefully she moved his arm, rose and silently left the room. She found Ryan in the hospital visitors' lounge drinking coffee and eating biscuits.

Sarah sat down.

"He's asleep. What now?"

"I'll find a nurse while you get yourself a drink. The coffee is very good, I'll have a refill if you don't mind, white with one sugar." Ryan disappeared.

As Sarah drank her coffee, (excellent as Ryan had said), she thought back to her arrival at Connolly's hotel. Her excitement and anticipation at seeing him again being swept away when she met a grim-faced Ryan in the hotel foyer. She shivered at the memory of John's first words.

"Sarah! I didn't expect to see you. I assume you've come to see Bruce. He's had an accident and I'm just off to the hospital to see him. I don't know how seriously he's been injured."

"I'm coming with you."

"It might be better if you didn't just yet."

"If you don't take me with you, I'll just follow you." No aggression, just a statement of fact. Faced with such an ultimatum Ryan just smiled briefly.

"In that case be my guest." Little was said during the journey. When they arrived Ryan insisted that he go in to see Bruce alone first. And Sarah readily agreed. As she nervously waited for him, she realised that John Ryan was another man in the cycling world who she could really get to like.

"Hello, Miss Curzon isn't it?" Ryan was now returning with a doctor who held out his hand. "I'm Doctor John Rowley. I've just been explaining to Mr. Ryan that although Mr. Connolly will be in some discomfort for some time and will be very stiff, no real harm has been done. I suggest that he stays here overnight and you can collect him in the morning. Make sure that he does plenty of deep breathing to help the broken ribs to heal. I will say goodbye then."

"Thank you!" They called to the fast disappearing white-coated back.

Ryan called Sarah back to the present.

"Right a quick look at Sleeping Beauty then back to the hotel to think out our strategy."

Back in Ryan's room, with yet more coffee, this time accompanied by a variety of delicious biscuits, Sarah began. "Do you think that that was a deliberate attempt on Bruce's life or just a warning?" Ryan could sense despite the calmness in her voice, a desire for reassurance as well as a fear of the truth. He however, had no difficulty being honest.

"The chances of Bruce being even seriously injured, let alone killed were virtually nil. He was always likely to hurt himself and the crash could possibly have caused enough damage to have ruined his season, but even that was very unlikely. No, my guess is that the result is about what the perpetrator, or perpetrators, intended. What concerns me much more is who could have done it. It can only be someone on the team, rider, soigneur, mechanic, masseur or a member of the support staff, or just possibly someone very close to the team, say a photographer. I've tried to think of some other conclusion but I can't."

Sarah looked a little shocked at this.

"Surely anyone could have gone by and loosened the quick-release when no one was looking?"

"Not according to how I've thought it through. No I'm sure that we have a traitor amongst us. Unfortunately, I have no idea who or how we can find that out."

"Surely that's a job for the police?"

"Maybe but I'd bet you a pound to a penny Bruce will not want the police involved, not yet anyway. One thing is certain though, from now on, Bruce must have at least two people with him at all times, unless he happens to be with you of course." Ryan smiled for the first time properly since Sarah had arrived.

"Or you," Sarah rejoined.

"How do you know it wasn't me? I had the opportunity."

"Don't be ridiculous!"

"Well, thanks for that vote of confidence but it makes the rule easier to enforce if I'm in the same position as everyone else. As far as you are concerned, I can't imagine anyone would want to play gooseberry." He smiled again and Sarah blushed slightly.

"Presumably you'll tell Bruce of these arrangements?"

"Yes, although it won't take him long to work it out for himself anyway. The real problem will be when he's racing. It's very obvious that there are quite a number of people involved in all this. It's pretty certain therefore that as well as at least one person within our own organization being a bad hat, there are almost certainly a rider, or more likely, riders, and in addition, a number of non-riding members of another team or teams playing the nasties as well. That is going to make life very difficult just before, during and after races."

"Is there anything I can do to help during the races?" Sarah asked. Ryan thought for a moment.

"How many people know of your... er... shall we say, attachment to Bruce?"

"Outside of the team, and I'm not sure if any of them have worked out how serious our relationship is, only my father, and he only has a suspicion that there might be something." Sarah blushed slightly again. "Oh and I suppose Judith might have an inkling?"

"I guess she might." Now it was Ryan's turn to colour up a little.

"Why, John Ryan, I do declare, you all might just be a little in love." Sarah said this in a very realistic southern drawl and after a couple of seconds Ryan's face split into a grin and they both fell about laughing.

"Am I that obvious?"

"Only to me I think, and I'm the world's best at keeping schtum. Anyway back to Bruce and I, other people may have seen us out together but we've only had three actual dates as such."

I'll try and check that out. For the moment I would suggest that you don't be too obvious about things. If the villains are unaware of your 'standing' with Bruce, you could be of use as an unconnected observer as it were." Sarah looked a bit doubtful.

"How do I explain my presence in the hotel, talking to you and being at the hospital?"

"Good point." Ryan frowned then brightened." How about this? You are doing some research for a book. Go to some of the other teams with a request to talk to some of the team members and so on. That can be the explanation of your time with us."

"Sounds good. Without wanting to sound like your average lovesick female, if there is such a thing, I do want to see Bruce again, and soon."

"Oh I don't think another visit to the sick would be out of order. Tell you what, I'll take Judith over to the hospital this evening and we'll pick you up on the way. How does seven-thirty sound?"

"It sounds way too late but I suppose it'll have to do." Her smile took the edge off her words.

"Don't worry, I'm sure Judith and I will need a long time-consuming drink sometime during the visit." They both smiled as Sarah squeezed Ryan's hand.

The evening visit to the hospital provided more time for the two of them to get to know each other better. They discovered a great deal about their respective backgrounds as they spent most of the time in conversation, nothing else being possible in the presence of John and Judith of course. The personal revelations of even the most trivial nature created the delight felt by a person seeing only the good in another. Bruce was amazed to realise that he now understood cricket; was certain that he would find his first visit to the Royal Albert Hall (whenever that turned out to be), absolutely splendid and became a confirmed fan of the Royal Family. For her part Sarah was now looking forward to her first visit to an American Football game, had revised her opinion of several American presidents and had decided that she must read some Ernest Hemingway, a writer she had never had any inclination to read whatsoever. Their topics of conversation ranged far and wide – most sports, politics, history, music, the Arts, their reminiscences of childhood, their hopes and aspirations for the future as well as all manner of trivialities. After a long conversation, John and Judith made an excuse to go and get something to eat and promised to return in half an hour. Sarah smiled at Bruce, then carefully leaned over him and kissed him deeply.

"I think that's enough talking for a while, don't you?" Bruce looked surprised.

"You're not going yet?"

"I was thinking more of something along the opposite lines." As she spoke she slipped a hand under the bedclothes.

"There are distinct advantages in being in a private ward aren't there?" She whispered and nibbled Bruce's ear. He realised what she meant at the same moment as her nimble fingers found his penis already somewhat engorged from the kiss. The realisation of Sarah's intention and the first ever physical contact from Sarah resulted in a staggeringly rapid erection. Whilst Sarah couldn't see Bruce's tool (pulling the bedclothes back was just a shade too risky), she could tell as he tumesced, that he was impressively endowed. He groaned as she alternately stroked, pulled and squeezed his now extremely stiff and hard erection. Connolly was now quietly moaning as she expertly played with his penis and balls whilst murmuring things in his ear. Slipping a towel over her hand she then kissed him, their tongues mingling and darting in and out.

"Oh my, what a big boy you are, Mr. Connolly, and so hard. I know I'm being a terrible slut but I just had to touch you properly. Now I'm sure you won't last very long, but it certainly feels like you have a lovely cock. I'm really, really looking forward to giving it a proper examination and thorough work out. I hope you can have sex with broken ribs because I need you big boy, as soon as possible. Oh, ohh, I'm coming, Bruce, come with me." With a somewhat despairing cry she masturbated him hard and fast as she felt her own orgasm break, at the same moment she felt Bruce spurt all over her hand and into the towel. Sarah gently rested her head on Bruce's good side as they recovered.

"Oh my God, that was unbelievable. Oh, Sarah, you are amazing."

"Now first of all, it wasn't unbelievable at all, couples masturbate each other all the time and secondly I'm not amazing. I was fairly selfish there, but hopefully you got something from it too. You'd better believe it though big boy, that I was not doing you any favours, I was doing myself one. I'm sure I'd be thrown out of here if the hospital staff found out." She grinned wickedly. "Oh and in case you're wondering, yes I've masturbated boyfriends before, but never anywhere like this and always before it's been for their benefit, not mine. Now it's sleep for you my lad and we'll come and get you out of here tomorrow."

After two days back at the hotel during which Bruce did much more physical activity than Sarah thought was wise, Ryan appeared at the hotel with Bruce's bike at which point Sarah's apprehension took a considerable hike upwards. However, much as he had enjoyed immensely Sarah's company during the past few days, both he and Ryan knew that it was essential that Bruce got back on his bike. The two of them followed Bruce in Ryan's car on a forty mile spin. On his return Bruce was tired but pleased, Sarah was hugely relieved and Ryan permitted himself a small smile. This ride, brief though it was, let both men know that Bruce could get back into serious training, something which they knew was vital. Sarah was equally well aware of the adverse effects both mental and physical, of a lay-off and resigned herself to the inevitable. Bruce arranged for Sarah to visit him again in France very soon and for he and John to return there immediately for some intensive training with just his minder. As Bruce and Sarah kissed at Heathrow before rider and mentor boarded the Air France Airbus, they were both anticipating Sarah's visit with light hearts. Notwithstanding his rapidly growing attachment to Sarah, Bruce was relieved to get back home and after a drink, a bite to eat and a little time for the food to have been properly absorbed, he was pleased to mount his turbo-trainer and put in a very hard hour's physical torture.

Meanwhile back in England, Sarah began the by no means unpleasant task of reading up on the subject of cycle racing. After her father's withdrawal from racing, Sarah's interest had waned a little and she had only had cause to look into whatever information she needed in connection with her involvement with the 'group'. It would be fun to find out exactly how successful her new beau was, where he sat in the pantheon of current racing cyclists and also where things had not gone quite as planned. It turned out to be a very interesting exercise, indeed.

CHAPTER SIXTEEN

It was a week since Connolly had been released from hospital, returned to France and resumed training. This morning's session had been hard but good and whatever edge he had briefly lost was rapidly returning. As with all top class athletes, Connolly's resting pulse rate was much lower than the average and was normally around forty-two beats per minute. This morning it had been forty-three so he knew he was almost there. Having showered, he dressed carefully. It was just less than an hour before he had to collect Sarah from the station. Whilst in hospital he had explained to Sarah the help the architectural practice was giving him in the detective field without elaborating. He had suggested that Sarah check on progress with her group as well as with Mitchell Associates and he was keen to find out what, if anything had been discovered. Even so, the anticipation regarding any investigative success had nothing to do with the butterflies in his stomach and the pleasantly disturbing ache which had been growing since first thing. The brief times alone with her at the hospital had keenly reminded him, not that reminders were needed, just how much he wanted her.

Pedro Louis Colmos, his minder for the morning, popped his head around the door of Bruce's bedroom.

"All set, Boss? French trains are usually on time and you don't want to keep a lady, especially such a high-class,

English lady, waiting, now do you?" Colmos had a smile across his face as wide as the Rio Grande.

"Go to hell, Pedro," Connolly good-naturedly rejoined.

"Why Pedro, I ask myself, is it that Mr. Supercool Bruce Connolly, is now telling his good friend Pedro to go to 'ell? Mr. Connolly is only telling Pedro to go to 'ell since a certain person appear. Is there a connection? Nooo, I answer myself. Mr. Supercool Connolly, man of the world, is too cool, too smart to 'ave woman trouble. It must be coincidence." Colmos' expression could best be described as being lugubrious.

"Pedro, I am truly sorry for telling you to go to hell as that is a very unfortunate end for anyone." Connolly paused. "I should not have said that. What I should have said was Pedro go fuck yourself." Colmos roared with laughter.

"I can't imagine what the women see in you, especially the very beautiful and classy English senorita. If I was as ugly as you, I would surely shoot myself. It must be that Miss Curzon is English, they are all loco." This time Connolly gave Colmos the finger and both laughed.

The half-hour drive to the airport passed very pleasantly. As soon as Sarah joined them, kissing both men lightly, Pedro excused himself. Small talk on the way to Bruce's house did nothing to help either of them relax and once in the house the tension increased. Fairly quickly Sarah realised that the lead would have to come from her. She raised a finger to Connolly's lips.

"Let me say it for you, because unless I miss my guess, we both want the same thing. You might expect me to be more romantic, a demure English rose or something. If so you're going to be disappointed. If you don't make love to me straight away, I'll go crazy. Lots of you Americans suffer from the delusion that we English girls expect and require to be treated with the utmost etiquette at all times. As far as this English rose is concerned, if you don't take me to bed now I shall have to conclude that I fancy you a lot more than you fancy me and I can't believe that I can be that wrong."

By the time she had finished speaking her face was an inch from his. The desire in his eyes was almost frightening, it was certainly very exciting. Their lips met. Bruce gripped Sarah's bottom with tremendous intensity but she revelled in his strength. She realised that it was very doubtful if she had ever had sex with anyone as fit and strong as Connolly. He breathed words rather than spoke them.

"Making love needs time, I just need to fuck you now, Sarah and then make love later, if you get my meaning." By way of assent she reached down and urgently rubbed the bulge in his jeans.

"This might shock you too, but it's a very long time since I went to bed with anyone and you wouldn't believe how many times I've thought about having you inside me in the past few days."

They had moved through the house as if by remote control. By the time they reached the bedroom, Bruce had only his jeans on and Sarah her bra and knickers. Sarah was delighted at Bruce's reaction. He was trembling. God he's desperate, she thought, as desperate as me. They had no time for finesse. In a frenzy of excitement they pulled off the remainder of their clothes.

"Quickly, Bruce, do me quickly, God I'm so horny."

Her words, combined with her fabulous body, gloriously full natural breasts, narrowing to a lovely slim waist then flaring out on beautiful rounded hips excited him more than he could ever remember. He felt as he did when a teenager. His penis ached and throbbed and he knew that he would climax very quickly after entering Sarah. She lay back and Bruce knew that she was ready for him. She reached for him and guided him into her in one deliberately urgent thrust. In spite of his size, which was even more impressive than she had thought when she had masturbated him in the hospital, it felt so so good. She had been celibate for so long, probably as long as for Bruce, and like him her most recent liaisons had been very forgettable affairs. Now she wanted him inside her forever. She had never felt so filled in every sense of the word. She gloried in the feel of him, part of her just wanting him to stay there. At the same time she was desperate for him to keep thrusting in and out of her. She dug her fingers into his impossibly hard and toned bottom as his lips kissed and sucked her distended nipples into a state of ecstatic tenderness. She felt him tense, felt the additional slight hardening and swelling of his penis and knew that he was coming. She had never experienced such power and strength. She was dimly aware of noises but as to who was making them she neither knew or cared.

Sarah felt Bruce begin to spurt inside her, something she could only remember experiencing once before and as if by magic she felt her own orgasm sweep through her as she lost control, her climax seeming to go on and on. It was the most satisfying, indeed shattering, sexual experience of her life. Somehow, she knew, without a shadow of a doubt, that it was the same for Bruce. Slowly she uncrossed her legs from behind his back and released him. Equally slowly he pulled himself away from her and then gently kissed all over the front of her arms, legs and body. Languorously, she turned over, all the time holding his hand. After kissing the backs of her legs, her back and her bottom, he felt her breathing deepen and then he too fell into a deep and untroubled sleep.

When Bruce awoke it was almost dark, the little light remaining giving the bedroom a deep royal blue, almost purple, hue. He felt a sense of peace such as he could never remember. He sat up very carefully and looked at the still-sleeping Sarah. The single sheet covering her from her lower back downwards had taken on the appearance of deep purple sand dunes, an impression which heightened his sense of tranquillity even more. After a few more minutes of silent contemplation it was so dark that he could no longer see her face clearly, yet he knew that he would be able to picture her face forever, wherever he was.

When he had first seen her in his apartment, he had thought her attractive, perhaps bordering on very attractive, but certainly not beautiful. How could it be that now he thought her the most beautiful woman in the world? Objectivity then entered his thinking. She hasn't suddenly become more beautiful numbskull, you're looking at her differently. The realisation that he had fallen in love with Sarah hit him like a high speed crash in a sprint. The intensity of his feeling for her was something else completely beyond his experience. He wanted to be able to touch her, smell her hair, feel her eyes on him and just look at her for as long as time itself. As far as the sex was concerned, brief though their first coupling had been, its explosiveness and sheer ecstasy had been so different to all his other sexual liaisons as to leave him amazed that anything could be so wonderful.

He realised that he was very thirsty. As silently as possible, he crept out of bed and went to the kitchen to make some tea. When he returned, the bedside lights were on and Sarah was half sitting up in bed. God she is so beautiful, thought Connolly.

"Tea, my lady?" He set the tray down at her bedside.

"Connolly, you are so old-fashioned. Who would have thought that this all-American boy would drink tea after sex?" Her eyes sparkled. "Not that I'm not grateful." She took a few sips of the tea. "In china cups of course, and it is very good tea. Mary and you are the only Americans I know who can make tea properly." She drank the rest of her tea and Connolly did the same. She now looked at Bruce and smiled.

"Now I'm just going to the bathroom and then you can give me the guided tour, well of the bedrooms anyway," she added archly and giggling ran into the en-suite. When she returned, Bruce took her hand and they went into the next bedroom.

"This is the main guest bedroom and therefore yours."

"I had better test the bed then hadn't I?"

Bruce took her in his arms and kissed her lips very gently. He then moved down to her throat moving his hand to the nape of her neck at the same time. She moaned slightly as he then equally gently kissed her ears as his hands caressed her back all the way from her neck to her beautifully shaped bottom. He moved his mouth to her breasts and began to kiss them gently, slowly circling her now erect nipples with his tongue. In Bruce's experience, girls with small breasts tended to have larger nipples than large breasted women. Not so with Sarah. After some sublime seconds of this their lips met again and each took hold of the other's bottom and gripped the instantly tensing muscles as hard as they could. Of course, by now Bruce's erection was straining and Sarah took hold of it and pulled Connolly onto the bed.

"Sarah," Bruce began but was interrupted.

"Yes, thank you for the compliment."

"I didn't say anything!"

"No, but you were about to tell me what excellent breasts or bottom or both I have, or more probably tits and arse, oh sorry it's ass in American isn't it?"

Although the use of her coarser language came as a bit of a surprise to Bruce, it pleased him hugely too.

"Well, yes I was."

"Good, I was sure you were and you have a lovely prick too, although again Americans prefer cock don't they?" Further surprises and words were halted by her kissing him. She pushed him down until he was lying on the bed. His penis ached and felt bigger than ever before. Sarah leaned over him then sat astride his stomach. The feel of her very moist luxuriant bush was very exciting. She reached own with one hand and took hold of Bruce's erection and then moved her whole body down his body until his penis was nestling against her now very open vagina. As she leaned over, her beautifully shaped pendulous breasts hung down, her nipples brushing the hairs on his chest. She then lifted herself a little so that she could masturbate him for a few seconds until it was now Connolly who was moaning. Then in a single glorious moment she lifted again and impaled herself on him. They both shuddered as he penetrated her. For what seemed like an eternity, neither of then moved, both loving the feeling of oneness. Eventually the urge to continue became too strong to resist and they began to rise and fall together. Sarah's breasts were alternately touching Bruce's chest then his lips as they moved up and down. Bruce's hands gripped her bottom again and halted her movement as he felt himself nearing ejaculation.

Sarah, also wanting to prolong the lovemaking, moved off Connolly and lay down herself. He raised himself and then began to kiss her feet, then her lower legs and then the inside of her thighs. All the while she was making little moaning sounds. Eventually he moved up to her mound. Gently parting her lips with one hand, he began to kiss and gently suck her engorged clitoris bringing her closer and closer to climax. Although Bruce had withdrawn early enough to prevent himself from coming too soon, he was very close himself and he knew that he would come as soon as he entered Sarah again. Her own movements were becoming more and more frenzied and he increased his own efforts with his tongue accordingly. His balls and tool felt so full and when he sensed that Sarah was almost at orgasm, he lifted his head, took hold of his penis and thrust it hard into her. Neither of them could have held back any longer even if they had wanted to. Sarah raised her legs and wrapped them around Bruce. His hands went under her and gripped her bottom again as his own tempo and urgency quickened.

"Now, Bruce, now oh please, yes ahhh, that's it, God, oh do it, yes do it, do me, yessss, ohhhh God!"

Almost there himself Sarah's words took him over the edge and he felt the rush from his balls up into Sarah. His power and fitness enabled him to continue the climax of their fuck to a point and intensity neither had ever experienced before. Both orgasms had been overwhelming and neither moved for several minutes. Eventually, Connolly rolled off Sarah and lay beside her. She took hold of his hand.

"Now aren't you supposed to go to sleep while I lie awake and wish you were talking to me. Isn't that the way it's supposed to be?"

"Well, if it is, it's not going to be the case tonight because I want to talk to you until morning, at least."

Sarah giggled. "Just talk, I thought you were a superstud?" She rolled over onto her stomach as Connolly laughed and gently swatted her bottom.

"I'm beginning to think, that I've been had and that I'm the innocent amateur and you're the one with all the experience, not, I would hasten to add, that I'm complaining."

"You don't know the half, buddy boy, you don't know the half."

After some gentle conversation they did drift off into sleep with Sarah snuggled up to Bruce as they lay together on their sides.

When Sarah awoke it was to feel something lying between the cheeks of her bottom. It took no time at all for her to realise what it was.

"Bruce?"

"Hmmm?"

"There's something hard and long and thick, a bit like a very big banana, seemingly wedged between my bum cheeks. Do you have any idea what it is? I can't sleep with it there, whatever it is. Can you think of somewhere else to put it?"

"Well, I can think of one place, perhaps I could try to put it there and you let me know what you think, how's that?"

"Sounds like a plan. Ohhh!... That's a really great place for it."

Sarah was already so moist with the little sex talk that Bruce was inside her all the way with one thrust and the force of the thrust made her gasp. After the initial penetration however, they made love slowly and gently.

'This time', Sarah thought to herself, 'this really is making love'. Her climax was however just as sweet as the previous one if not as explosive. Afterwards as they drifted off to sleep again, they both marvelled at how easy, uninhibited and unembarrassed they were together. The future looked very bright indeed to both of them.

CHAPTER SEVENTEEN

"Hi, Mary, it's Bruce, how's the most beautiful secretary in the world?"

"I wouldn't know, but I'm fine. How're you?"

"All the better for talking to you, It's almost as good as being in your gorgeous presence."

"Oh get off with you, you awful flirt. Did you know that we had a certain English lady here a little while ago? A little bird tells me you have been seen in her company. Is my little bird telling the truth and can I read anything into that if it is true?"

"I plead the Fifth Amendment."

"That's good enough for me." Mitchell's secretary chuckled. "About time too. I suppose you want to talk to Henry?"

"Sure do."

"Hi, Bruce, you get stitched up again?"

"Sure did and it's about that I'm calling. You had a visit from Sarah Curzon right?"

"What a delightful and beautiful girl."

"Yeah well, it seems we aren't the only ones anxious to get to the bottom of our problems. Sarah has friends in high places and they've asked me to get on board with their investigation. I said I would and that I'd try to help all I can.

Now I need a favour. You still got all the DVDs of my races?"

"Of course."

"Good. Now what I want is for Mary, if you can spare her for a while to carefully look through all the DVDs of the races where I had a problem and see if she can spot anything connecting them, or anything unusual, weird whatever."

"That's going to take some time, not to mention patience."

"I know that, that's why I said I need a favour. Think about it and let me know, if and when."

"No need to think about it, son, it's fine by me, but you'd better talk to Mary yourself." Connolly heard Mitchell call his secretary to the phone.

"Why do I think this is going to be bad news?" The voice held a slight chuckle in it. In a few sentences Bruce explained what he wanted.

"I presume Henry is okay with this? Yes, ignore that, he's smiling and nodding. Needless to say, this is going to cost you, lover boy."

"Whatever you desire, O beautiful one."

"You betcha. No doubt you wanted this information yesterday?"

"Fraid so, get back to me a soon as you can. Can you put Henry back on?"

"Yes, Bruce."

"In case you hear about it from somewhere, my house got trashed but it's sorted. I wouldn't want you to get too upset. Whatever the papers might say it was no big deal."

"If you say so." Mitchell didn't sound convinced.

"Okay, thanks, Dad, catch you later."

"Bye, son, and although I know I'm wasting my breath, take care."

"Sure, Dad. Bye."

After he'd put the phone down Connolly felt a little better. Fighting back always felt good he reflected. He knew Mary would do a good job. If there was something to find on those DVDs she'd find it.

CHAPTER EIGHTEEN

"Bruce, it's Mary, are you alone?"

"Yes, but I'll put the scrambler on if you like." Connolly smiled to himself.

"Oh very funny." Bruce's father's secretary was clearly not impressed by Connolly's levity.

"Is there any chance of you being able to get over here? Looking at your racing schedule, it looked to me as if you had a few days before your next big event. I'm certain you'll find it worthwhile coming over. I don't want to say any more over the 'phone."

Bruce thought quickly. Mary would not have suggested that he travel all the way to New York if it had not been important. He sighed. The prospect of a few days in the house with just Sarah for company had been very appealing. There was also the not inconsiderable matter of his racing preparation and training. The former would have to wait now until after the Tour De France and he would have to find some opportunities to train in New York.

"Okay, Mary, but I'll be bringing Sarah, if she's up for it. See you as soon as we can get a flight."

"Bless you, Bruce, see you soon."

"Jeez, 'Bless me', no less, it must be important." Connolly muttered to himself as he went to find Sarah.

Three hours later both of them were on the Airbus bound for New York. Whilst both had been to the 'Big Apple' many times, Bruce in particular, having worked there, they had obviously never spent time together there. When Bruce asked Sarah, she had been very keen to go. After the most enjoyable flight either of them could remember, which both attributed to the company, they were met at J.F.K. by Mary herself. Without preamble, Mary explained why she had called Bruce.

"I haven't had chance to actually look at the DVDs themselves yet, but I've given lots of thought to what you said about connecting factors, and I don't know how significant this is, but I've discovered one connecting factor between the races where there were 'incidents', or whatever you want to call them." She paused. "During the course of each race, more than one country was visited."

Bruce looked doubtful.

"Surely, there are lots of races that do that?"

"Yes, but more significantly, no 'incidents' took place in races where an official border wasn't crossed." Sarah now spoke for the first time since their arrival.

"Presumably you're suggesting that there is some sort of smuggling involved?"

"I'm not that certain, but it is the first thing I've found about the races in question which connects them. When we get to the office, you can have a look at all the info I've gathered and see the pattern for yourselves."

Mitchell wasn't in the office when they arrived but Mary had explained the situation to him and he would be joining them later. After organising coffee and cakes, Mary put a disc in her computer and began.

"Correct me if I'm wrong but the first event where you experienced an 'accident' was the Tour of Switzerland two years ago You were chopped in a sprint on stage four, yes?" Connolly nodded.

173

"That stage finished in Como, which is of course, just inside Italy."

"O.K. go on, Mary." Connolly remained non-committal.

"The Tour that year had its Grand Depart in Belgium. You were brought down, admittedly along with a lot of other riders but you were the worst affected, in the stage that started in Mons and ended in Valenciennes. Later in the same Tour you had a problem with accusations of receiving pushes on the stage that briefly went into Switzerland and finished in Geneva." Mary was now in full flow. "That season you also had problems in the Tour of Lombardy and in the G.P. de Nations, both of which, even if only briefly, crossed a border." She paused, almost triumphantly.

"Could these things be simple coincidences?" Connolly was clearly interested but was still looking a little doubtful.

"Of course they could all be coincidental, but before you turn me down look at the rest of the evidence I've put together." She turned back to her keyboard, punched a few keys and up on the screen came the first page of Mary's findings. It took some time for Bruce and Sarah to scroll through all the pages and assimilate the information.

"Brilliant stuff, Mary, you are definitely onto something here, well done, although exactly what that something is, I've no idea. You're right though, there is too much here for it to be just a whole heap of coincidences. What do you think, Sarah?"

"Yes, definitely but what happens now though? Although the circumstantial evidence seems pretty conclusive in that crossing a border has something to do with whatever is going on, exactly how do we work out exactly what *is* going on?

"Just a minute," interjected Bruce who had been studying the lists of events, "Milan-San Remo and Amstel Gold didn't cross any borders."

"Yes, I noticed that," replied Mary, I don't think that two out of so many, ruins the whole theory. Perhaps they were put in just to make it look as if the border theory wasn't the right one."

"Or perhaps," this from Sarah, "those two were genuine accidents, they do happen after all." Connolly nodded.

"The problem is, what do we do next?" this from Mary.

"Bruce, from what you know of the riders and the races themselves, how likely is it that there is smuggling going on? Sarah asked as Mary nodded clearly thinking along the same lines.

"As far as the guys themselves are concerned, who knows? Some of the domestiques in the less successful and poorly funded teams aren't very well paid, so the prospect of extra money would be a big pull I guess, provided that the money was big enough, of course. The problem is that with the exception of most of the top riders, hardly anybody can be certain of actually finishing a race, especially the classics like Paris – Roubaix or the Tour of Flanders. On the 'Grand Tours', elimination for being outside the time limit on the big mountain stages is not uncommon by any means. That's going to make anything which depends on a given rider finishing at a given time and place a bit risky to say the least. As far as moving stuff is concerned, you can forget drugs."

The two women didn't try to hide their surprise. "Why?"

"Too bulky, too heavy and too obvious. We are looking to take every ounce we can off the bikes. To make smuggling any kind of drug worth the risk, the quantity would be both way too heavy to carry for the distances involved and too big to be hidden."

"Okay," said Mary, "so no drugs. That leaves something like diamonds or other precious stones."

"That seems reasonable, but even if we are correct in that guess, we have no evidence and no idea as to who is involved in all of this, how whatever is done, is done, or even more baffling, why I'm involved in all of this?" Connolly sighed. Sarah turned to Mary.

"How much time can you spare to look further into this?"

"Henry has said that I can do whatever is necessary to get to the bottom of all this. If we need one, we'll hire a temp to do my everyday work." Bruce turned to Sarah.

"You obviously have a reason for asking?"

"I was thinking it may be worthwhile studying films of the events in question. I assume such things are available?"

"Sure, I've already asked Mary to carefully study the DVDs of the races where there have been problems for us. We often look at them to see what happened where and when, as a general aid in our training and preparation."

"Tell me again what I'm looking for exactly."

"I'm not sure, but anything unusual, anything that looks out of place, however trivial. Whatever is happening, we must be able to see it if we look carefully enough. I'm afraid you're likely to get very bored, Mary, but I'm sure it'll be worth it." Sarah looked at Mary sympathetically, as Connolly changed the subject.

"Now business over for the moment. Is Henry doing anything this evening, Mary?"

"I'm not sure, let me check his diary." She went into Mitchell's office and came back smiling. "No he's got a brief meeting with a client here at 4:00 p.m. then he appears to be free all evening for a change."

"Good. Second question. Are you free, Mary?"

"Er, yes, I don't go out much."

"Great, tell Henry when he gets back, that we're all going out for dinner and I'm buying. Dress up. We'll pick you both up at eight." He kissed Mary on the cheek and took Sarah's hand. "I feel like a walk back to the hotel, how about it, kiddo?"

Sarah smiled. "Suits me, but I've never ever been called kiddo before."

"Get used to it." The pair said goodbye to Mary and left hand in hand. When they reached the street Sarah became serious for a moment.

"Okay, hot shot, there's something I don't quite understand here."

"And what might that be, O fair one?"

"I'm thinking that here is an employer, apparently quite happy to let his secretary down tools, hire in extra staff to cover for her, so that she can spend God knows how long doing something that aforementioned employer knows little if anything about, for what is in effect, an ex-employee. To use a popular American term, I don't get it."

"Well, you see, I was a very good employee and Henry fully expects me to go back to the practice after I've finished racing. Simple as that. "

"If you think I'm buying that forget it. When you've finished racing you'll have no need of employment anyway. Of that I'm more than certain. So try again." Connolly sighed.

"If you're a very good girl I'll tell you the secret."

"That's the second time you've said that and I 'm still waiting for the first secret."

"That's because so far you've only been a good girl, not a very good girl."

"Humph!" Sarah scowled. Nevertheless she realised she wasn't going to get anywhere, so gave up. She looked at Connolly, he grinned back, she punched him on the shoulder and they both dissolved into fits of the giggles.

After the pair had left, Mary smiled at the recollection of the obvious attraction between the two. Wedding bells? She wondered. In spite of Bruce's well known and well recorded elusiveness, she sensed much more between the two than with any of Bruce's relationships that she had known about. As far as elusiveness was concerned, for Bruce read Henry, she thought wistfully. Until a few weeks ago, she had believed that Mitchell was becoming much friendlier towards her. Still professional in his dealings with her he had been more attentive and certainly much more complimentary about her appearance. Once there had even been flowers, supposedly a thank you for working late a couple of times, but she had worked harder and later previously without receiving any reward. Mary had found Mitchell extremely attractive from the moment she had met him and had begun to harbour hopes that the two of them might become an item, as current parlance put it. However, about four weeks ago Henry had become more businesslike again. Perfectly polite and never in the least bit unpleasant, there had been a lessening in the warmth which had been gradually building up. Mary sighed and completed her tidying of the office. Perhaps she might gauge the situation more accurately tonight. It would be the first time they had been out together for a very long time. She heard Mitchell arrive and began making him a cup of coffee. He smiled gratefully as he walked into the room and saw the cup.

"Well, Mary, did Bruce go along with your theory?"

"They both did."

"Both?"

"Sarah has come with Bruce."

"Oh has she? Is there something there do you think?"

"Think, there's no think about it. They have that look about them. You can see it a mile off." She smiled again as she thought of them together.

"I didn't think it was that obvious." Henry looked a little rueful. Mary chuckled.

"Not to you perhaps, but then you're only a man. Does the idea of Sarah being your daughter-in-law bother you?"

"Not in the least, in fact I couldn't think of anyone better, even though I hardly know her. However, a wedding?"

"Unless I miss my guess, that girl won't settle for anything less, nor should she. And the same applies to Bruce, or at least it should if he has any sense that is."

"Mmmm. I wonder how long it will be before Bruce tells her who his Dad is." Mary took her opportunity quickly.

"My guess would be this evening." Mitchell raised his eyebrows.

"Bruce has asked us out to dinner, they are picking us up here at eight."

"Sounds good to me. I'll just finish my coffee and then I'll give you a lift home. Give you plenty of time to relax and then get ready." Mary began to protest but Mitchell put up his hand.

"It's time you had it a little easier. Get your things together and yell when you're ready."

"You've got a meeting with Mr. Christy in ten minutes."

"Aw hell yes, so I do. Well I guess that means I'll have to get you a cab." He reached for the phone. Mary decided it was all or nothing and put her hand on his as he began to dial.

"There's no need for that," she paused and looked straight into his eyes. "I'd rather wait for you... if you don't mind of course." She held her breath, amazed at how much the answer was going to mean to her.

"No... no of course I don't mind." The timbre of his voice had changed and the two looked at each other for a long time. Indeed, time seemed to stand still. Mary could see that Mitchell was trying to say something but couldn't get the words out. It was a rare moment, indeed. Rarely if ever had she seen her boss at a loss for words. Then the 'phone went and the moment was lost.

"Mitchell Associate's, how may I help you?" As Mary took the call, Henry went into his office in a state of disappointment mixed with relief. Mary followed him in a few moments later.

"That was Mr. Christy, he will be a little late but he has to be away by five anyway." She smiled and for the umpteenth time Henry asked himself If he had ever seen a nicer smile. As always the answer was a resounding no.

"So you'd still like a lift?"

"Oh, yes please."

As they were driving to Mary's apartment forty-five minutes later, Henry surprised her again.

"That dark electric blue dress you wore at that Christmas party two years ago, do you still have it?"

"Yes, I don't think I've worn it since. I'm not entirely sure it suits me. You know the 'does my bum look big in this?' thing." Henry chuckled.

"Take this guy's word for it, it suits, believe it... I would be very pleased if you wore it tonight. I hope you don't mind my being so forward." For a moment Mary was too stunned to speak. Her silence threw Mitchell completely. "Forget it, you should never tell a woman how to dress, forget I said anything." He spoke quickly to hide his embarrassment. Mary realised that some urgent bridge-building was required.

"No, not at all. I was surprised that's all, not at the suggestion itself, but I can't remember you ever making any comment about my clothes before that's all. It's a lovely idea and I adore the dress. As I said, I've just wondered if there was just a little too much of me to put in it. After what you've just said I shall love wearing it." Henry smiled in delight and relief.

"Good, I'll pick you up at 7:45. Lovely, bye."

As she ran through her apartment, Mary felt like a teenager before her first prom. Henry had really said nothing but at long last she felt that her hopes might be realised.

Two hours later Mitchell and Mary were nursing drinks with Bruce and Sarah as the four of them were more or less silently considering the extensive and original menu at Felice's. The restaurant was full and yet there was an air of peacefulness around them. The use of split levels and the inclusion of an atrium near the centre of the restaurant and a smaller one towards the rear with the use of attractive yet deceptively strong screens created privacy and minimized the passage of sound. Sarah looked around her.

"The architect who designed this place certainly knew his business. It's even better on my second visit." The other three smiled to each other causing Sarah to look guardedly at them.

"Have I said something funny?"

"No no, my dear, it's just…" Mitchell was interrupted by the arrival of Sam at their table.

"Oh my friends, it is so good to see you again." He raised the hands of the two women and brought them almost to his lips, then shook hands with the two men.

"It's very good to be here Felice. This is Mary Opperman, my… Secretary." He made the introduction with an inflexion in his voice that made the others look at him in some surprise. Sam was the first to recover.

"If I may say so, Signora, the beauty of that exquisite dress is only eclipsed by your own beauty."

"Dammit, Felice, I should have said that," said Mitchell in mock annoyance.

"I am truly sorry, Signor Mitchell, but I have my reputation to maintain." They all laughed. "And you Signorina Curzon, if the only thing I could see for the rest of my life would be you, I would indeed be a happy man."

"You did again Sam. Why didn't I think of saying that?" Bruce exclaimed.

"Aha, you Americans. You need many lessons in how to talk to the ladies from us Italians." They all laughed again, Sam being aware that they all probably knew of his antecedents." Are you ready to order? I can recommend the lobster and the fillet steak or alternatively, the paella."

"Yours or Tony's?" Bruce asked. Sam put on his hurt look.

"As if I would leave these things to the 'ired 'elp with such guests. Connolly sighed in mock despair and continued the game.

"Well I guess yours is fairly good. I'll have a small portion of paella and then a lobster."

Mitchell followed suit and the two women ordered paella followed by a steak. Chablis and a St. Emilion claret were chosen by Henry and a raised eyebrow from Sam followed by a nod from Bruce ensured that dancing time would be available between courses. After a little comfortable conversation, Bruce asked Mary to dance.

"You look an absolute knockout tonight, Mary, that's not to say that you don't always look good but tonight you look kinda special."

"The dress wouldn't have anything to do with that would it?" She smiled a little mischievously.

"A little but only a little," Bruce replied.

"Henry asked me to wear it." Bruce raised his eyebrows. "Yes, I know. On another note, you're looking down my cleavage, not into my eyes as you're talking, Mr. Connolly."

"You bet," Bruce cheerfully admitted, "and there few better ones about, take it from an expert. I can't understand why the old man hasn't asked you to marry him long before now so that he can have a high old time with that beautiful body of yours." He grinned again and kissed her nose.

"Bruce Connolly, behave like the gentleman your father thinks you are. I'm old enough to be your mother." The admonishment was delivered with a smile.

"Maybe, but you sure don't look it. When we arrived, Sarah whispered to me, 'Doesn't Mary look absolutely ravishing?' So you see it's not only my opinion. This is absolutely straight up. I tell you if I didn't like you so much, if you weren't crazy about Dad and if he wasn't equally crazy about you, I'd have made a move on you long ago. You've got the greatest ass I ever saw." He moved his hands down and gave her bottom a playful squeeze.

"Bruce, will you behave!"

"Doubtful and you've got the looks to match." He squeezed her bum again.

"Will you stop it or I shall stop dancing."

"Okay, Maam." A few seconds later after dancing properly again, Mary kissed Bruce lightly on the cheek. "Did you mean all that?" She was suddenly serious.

"Of course I did. Honestly, I've always thought you were one of the classiest and tastiest broads, sorry ladies, I've ever seen. As far as age difference is concerned, what the hell and you really are very very attractive in looks, figure and personality. And seriously, your ass is to die for. You wouldn't believe the number of times I've thought about making it with you."

"No not that stuff, nice though it is to hear, although I'm not sure I should be hearing it, no, what you said about Henry."

"Mary, the guy is absolutely nuts about you, has been for years. He's just scared to make a move because he thinks you'll laugh at him. I've told him time and again, he's wrong but he won't listen."

"He's told you that?" Mary was incredulous.

"Not in so many words but he is my old man and we've talked a fair bit about you. Take my word for it, he is crazy about you."

"But what do I do? How do I play this? I shouldn't be saying this to you, his son I know, it isn't fair on you, but Bruce I want him so badly."

"Don't you worry about being unfair to me. I love you both, nothing would give me more pleasure than seeing you guys getting it together. Unless I miss my guess, it won't be long before he makes his move. Just hang on in there, relax and enjoy." The paella had appeared by this time so they made their way back to the table.

"Bruce, unless our eyes are deceiving us, Miss Curzon and I just saw you deliberately squeeze my secretary's bottom, twice!" As an attempt at chastisement, Mitchell's accusation was an abject failure.

"You sure did, and being such a great ass, any chance I get, I'll be there."

"Bruce, will you please behave!" Mary's attempt also failed as all four laughed, comfortable in their knowledge and confidence in each other.

After the delicious paella and excellent Chablis, Henry asked Sarah to dance and Mary excused herself and went to the ladies' room. Bruce seeing the obvious pleasure in the faces of the people most dear to him, felt an immense sense of well-being. It had been a long while since he had allowed himself the luxury of indulging in thoughts of the future beyond the next few races, but now he sensed that the problems of the past two years and the shallow relationships he had experienced since his disastrous marriage had ended, were perhaps about to become things of the past. It was strange, he reflected, that although it appeared that his own life was still in some sort of danger, it was good to feel concern about the well-being of others. Sure, he had always had a high regard for his father and therefore worried about him but he was nevertheless suddenly much more interested in the lives of other people than he could remember ever being before. Apart from Henry and of course Sarah, there was Mary, of whom he had always had a very high regard and not just for her attractiveness. He had however, never really thought about her happiness. He now realised that he was genuinely fond of her. Then there were his teammates and of course John Ryan, Sam, Frank Castillo and a number of other people. Why, he wondered, was he now thinking of these people in a different light? Had he always been self-centred and selfish? For a very long time past his thoughts had been more or less exclusively about cycling and yet the success that his dedication should have brought him had only been partially realised. Even before this present hate campaign, or whatever it was had begun, his results, good though they were, had included too few big wins and too many seconds and thirds, when taking into account his undoubted class and ability on a bike. Why? Why no World Champion's Rainbow jersey, no Yellow jersey, no Maglia

Rosa? He had had no one to win for but himself! The realisation hit him like a ton of bricks. He realised how much more he had been enjoying his racing this season, especially when Sarah had been watching. Of course that was it! His thoughts were interrupted by the return of Mary.

"From the look on your face, you look as if you've just proven Einstein wrong about the theory of relativity or something equally momentous."

"As far as I'm concerned, I think I probably have." He smiled beatifically.

"You're sure you're alright?" Mary asked with a slightly puzzled look on her face.

"Never better." They looked at each other, looked at the other two dancing, raise their eyebrows and nodded.

"Yep," Connolly said, "time to cut in."

As Bruce began dancing with Sarah, she asked him about the smile on his face when he had been sitting alone. He explained his thinking and his revelation.

"That's good, in fact it's very good because I very much like to watch you race, even though at times it can be agonising." For the remainder of the time until the arrival of the steaks and lobsters, they held each other tightly saying nothing. Although engrossed in each other's company they couldn't fail to notice that Henry and Mary were dancing much more closely together than a boss and his secretary would normally and they too seemed in little need of conversation.

Conversation during the disposal of the truly first class steaks and lobsters was minimal, the food deserving nothing less, but eventually the subject of the 'problem' came up. Mitchell was brought up to speed on the current situation and then with his customary directness he turned to Sarah.

"Do you think you could tell us who it is that you're working for, Sarah? I've put Mary at your disposal, more or less and I figure it's only fair that I know a little more about your people."

"I'm not sure that's entirely fair, Henry," Bruce interjected. "We offered to help Sarah without any promises from her that she would reveal identities."

"It's okay, Bruce, I'd already decided to tell you any way." Sarah smiled.

"Okay then, just before you do," Bruce again, "there is a factor which will help I'm sure, if you are still a little doubtful. For reasons which I shall explain when we have a little more time, the actual relationship between Henry and I, is one of the world's best kept secrets. In fact, you are about to become only the fifth person to be in the know. The other three are these two and Sam, as well as myself, of course. Taraaaah." Bruce made a drum roll noise on the table. They all smiled but Sarah's was slightly hesitant.

"Okay, so you've never actually worked for Henry at all have you?"

"Oh but I have, admittedly not for a while because of my racing, although I occasionally drop in and make some more or less useless suggestion. In fact the architect of this building you were praising earlier was *moi,* I'm afraid." Sarah looked slightly disappointed.

"Is that the big secret? I was expecting something more after the big build-up."

"Patience child, all will be revealed."

"You keep telling me you will tell me your secrets if I'm a very good girl, so no more have patience stuff hot-shot." The other three smiled conspiratorially.

"Henry, Mary, a little while ago, herself here asked why it was that a mere employer was seemingly doing so much for an employee, especially one who didn't seem to do much work for him." Mary now chimed in with a big smile on her face.

"The fact is, Sarah, that Hot-Shot here as you call him, is Henry's son." Sarah made no attempt to hide her considerable surprise.

"But why the secrecy?" Sarah now looked a little worried.

"Now don't throw the salt cellar at me, but as I said earlier, I'll explain all that when we have more time. However, that has nothing to do with what we are presently in the middle of, well at least I don't think it has. Henry, what do you think?"

"I can't see how. Anyway carry on, Bruce."

"As to why I didn't tell you before, I guess neither the opportunity nor the necessity came up before." He squeezed Sarah's hand. Mary now spoke again.

"It's a long story, Sarah, but you can take my word for it that there was and still is, to some extent, good reason for the secrecy." Mary's words overcame any lingering worries Sarah had. And she smiled.

"I'm sorry for being doubtful but I had no idea."

"That's good, if you follow me. Anyway, I promise you I'll tell you everything the first chance I get." He squeezed her hand again. After a few seconds Sarah cleared her throat.

"To get back to Henry's question, the members of my group all have a deep passion for cycling but have no financial interest in the sport at all." She then recited a list of eleven names, all of well-known and well respected people from several different countries and a wide variety of walks of life. Two top class cyclists of the fifties and sixties, a current English Cabinet Minister, a Dutch industrialist who sponsored many sporting events throughout the world but no cycling events, an Italian count and an American actor both known to have passion for cycling, two very wealthy members of Belgian aristocracy, the wife of an American senator of considerable standing, an ex-Olympic gold-medal winning decathlete and a now retired French politician.

"There are other members who are less well-known too," Sarah added.

It was now the turn of the other three to be lost for words. All three found their tongues at the same moment.

"How did such a group get together? How did you get involved? How long has the group been in existence? Why are they so interested in cycling? That's impressive, who's in charge?" Sarah laughed and held up her hands.

"When Bruce tells me his story, I'll tell him mine but just to answer those questions you just threw at me would take more than all night." Henry looked at Bruce.

"You better set aside quite some time for these discussions, son, you're gonna need it. Anyway enough business. Let's dance. Mary?"

"My pleasure."

As the older couple moved to the dance floor, Sarah turned to Bruce.

"Well, handsome, do we start our little talk now and finish it whenever, or do we dance?"

"We dance. We can talk anytime and anyway I want to watch all the other guys here see me dancing with you and watch them go green with envy." She punched him on the shoulder and then rose.

Everything she does, she does with such grace and elegance, Bruce thought to himself. Even little things like standing up she did in such a way as to make him tingle. Her dress was a deep crimson colour of some sort of silk. Connolly's knowledge of dress materials was on the dodgy side of sketchy. The dress was sleeveless with only narrow shoulder straps and a very low cut back. Relatively modest at the front by today's standards, only a little of Sarah's not inconsiderable cleavage was evident only when she leaned forward. The greatest impression was made by the close fitting nature of the dress. Altogether classy, elegant and downright sexy all at the same time. All her jewellery was made of pearls – a three strand choker, matching bangle on her right wrist and on her left wrist a watchstrap made largely of pearls. Earrings of five gradually increasing sized pearls completed her accessories. Sarah's long hair had been swept into ringlets which on many women would have looked childish but on Sarah looked just right. Dark red patent high heeled 'fuck-me' shoes completed an appearance that Connolly and every other man in the room considered absolutely stunning. They spoke little while dancing, content with the closeness of each other and happy to leave serious things to another day. Sarah did however remark that, "I rather like the idea of Henry being your dad."

"I kinda hoped you would. On that general subject, I really do like the idea of Mary as my stepmother."

"Me too, although as far as you're concerned, I hope that's not so you'll have lots of chances to grab her ass as you call it." She giggled.

"Oho, jealous are we?"

"Well, you did say that Mary's was 'the greatest ass I ever saw', I believe those were your exact words." Connolly grinned.

"Weelll," Connolly began.

"This had better be good," Sarah interrupted him with mock seriousness.

"There is a difference between greatest ass and sexiest ass. As far as what would be considered perfection in the ass department by the vast majority of guys, Mary's is just about perfect. Wait." He held up a hand as Sarah made to speak, "But the thing is I'm not your average Joe. Yours is slightly lower slung and ever so slightly bigger, both of which aspects are pluses for me, and without doubt, sexier."

"Not bad but how come this evening my 'ass' has remained unmolested whilst your father's secretary's has had several caresses. Furthermore, genius, if you are such an expert, what are our respective hip sizes?" Sarah was having difficulty containing her laughter.

"Piece of cake. Mary's 38 inches, yours 39! Bet you ten bucks I'm right. When we sit down ask her." Sarah laughed again.

"With you two sitting at the table? No way Jose."

"Okay, when you go to the ladies."

"Okay, you're on, ten dollars it is."

"One other thing, although Mary's are very good, your tits are even better, tits to die for in fact. Oh sorry, breasts," Connolly corrected as he saw what he thought was a frown but which was merely her becoming serious.

"No, don't apologise, she came even closer and whispered in his ear. "Tits is a much sexier word." Connolly went weak at the knees at these words.

During coffee and liqueurs (just coffee for Bruce), the four discussed the immediate future and in particular Bruce's racing. Clearly with the Tour now only days away there was nothing they could do until it had finished. They agreed to meet in four weeks' time. At a wink from Bruce, Sarah suggested that she and Mary went to the ladies' room and whilst alone Bruce was able to gently point out to Henry that, "Perhaps you've waited long enough, Dad."

"What do you mean?" was Henry's response. "You know very well what I mean. Women like Mary come around about as often as it snows in the Sahara. I would hate you to miss out. She absolutely adores you, can't think why. Oh, here they come."

As the two women reached the table Sarah surreptitiously slipped Bruce a ten dollar bill. Bruce hid a grin. The four made their goodbyes and Bruce and Sarah went back to their hotel while Henry drove Mary back to her apartment. For the first time all evening both felt slightly ill at ease as Henry drove his Trans-Am much more circumspectly than normal. The departure of Bruce and Sarah seemed to have allowed their discarded reserve to envelop them once more.

For her part Mary didn't know whether to ask Henry up for coffee. What if he refused? God it was so much easier in the past. She was hopeless. She knew she looked okay, as well as Bruce's worlds, bless him, she had had enough admiring glances during the evening to assure her of that.

But Henry is probably looking for a younger woman she thought, miserably, to herself. He looks so calm and collected and handsome as well. Oh God, please help, what do I do? Her apartment was only a few blocks away. Had she but known it Henry was in an equal agony of indecision.

What if she asks me up for coffee? Even worse what if she doesn't? He had also seen the looks guys, quite a few considerably younger than him, had been giving Mary in the restaurant. She's probably looking for some young stud anyway, although if Bruce was telling the truth, maybe I'm in with a shout. She looks so cool and relaxed and absolutely bloody gorgeous.

Henry pulled up at Mary's apartment with both still in agonies of indecision. Mary heard someone say "Would you like to come up for some coffee", and as if in a dream realised that it was her own voice. Until he heard the words Henry hadn't realised how much he had wanted to hear them.

"Yes, thank you that would be nice." Nice, nice, what kind of dumbass word is nice for Christ's sakes. Henry cursed himself but Mary didn't seem to notice.

While Mary busied herself making the coffee, he looked around the lounge of the apartment. Although he had been to the apartment before, after bringing Mary home from the office sometimes, he'd never been in the lounge. That the place belonged to a female was obvious even though there was nothing overly feminine in the room.

Most of the furniture was fairly new, even pristine, yet the room oozed a welcome. There was a sense that a visitor would be expected to take their ease and make themselves at home without being asked. Yet much of the room was almost masculine. Bold colours, strong prints on the walls and on a sideboard an architectural model of Mitchell's most successful designs, and one of his favourites. He'd had no idea that Mary had the model and the revelation delighted him. He was looking at it when Mary arrived with the coffee.

"Oh, I'd forgotten that. I never asked your permission to bring it home. I hope you don't mind." What on earth was she doing apologising for paying him a compliment, he thought. He'd never bothered to question what had happened to models not required by the building's owners, another example he realised of taking his secretary for granted.

"Mind, how could I mind? I'm just sorry I never asked what happened to the other models over the years. Do you have any others?" Mary shook her head. "A few of the better ones are in the storeroom, the others I either threw away or gave to anyone who asked for them". They both smiled. The conversation remained light but much more relaxed than in the car and then during the brandy that followed, sitting together, the scent of her perfume, the warmth of her presence and her evident pleasure in his company suddenly combined in a single moment to galvanise Henry into action.

Without any preamble, he turned her face towards him then took her hands in his. He looked deeply into her eyes; they were the deepest blue he had ever seen. He felt an enormous peace envelop him as finally their lips met. Perhaps it was because of the time since either had had any romantic involvement but the kiss was exquisite. It wasn't long, however, before Henry's peace was supplanted by burning desire. The initially soft and gentle kiss rapidly became urgent and full of passion. Of course the kiss was the hors d'ouvres for the lovemaking that followed.

Initially, in spite of the desire, both were a little tentative, so anxious to please and believing that they were no longer as physically attractive as they once had been. They soon discarded their inhibitions when the pleasure they were giving each other became evident. Henry certainly appreciated that under the stunning blue dress, Mary had worn equally stunning blue underwear. Asking him to take it off had heightened Henry's desire even further and beneath it her body was unbelievably beautiful to him. Still firm and full breasts and a relatively flat stomach, matched, if not bettered by, as Bruce had observed, a superb bottom.

Henry was no disappointment to Mary either. Frequent exercise, a healthy diet and an abhorrence of corpulence had ensured that his weight had remained constant for the past twenty-five years. As for his fitness, few men half his age were in better condition. After making love as exquisitely as to be beyond words, they fell asleep both thinking how true was the expression that love was wasted on the young.

CHAPTER NINETEEN

"I read your report, James, and although I have slight reservations here and there, I generally concur with your thinking and proposals. With hindsight it would appear that both of us were in error in our assessment of Connolly, but as is too frequently said, hindsight is a wonderful thing." The blonde-haired man paused and looked first at Dowling and then at Sergio Induranna. Dowling allowed himself a moment's slight relaxation. "You have read James' report; do you have anything to add, Sergio?"

Induranna was desperately trying to work out what the 'reservations' might be but couldn't, so he had no option but to simply add, "No, Sir".

"Good, in that case, I accept that, whilst the income from your work is up with your forecasts, James, the time is now right to put pressure back on Connolly. As with previous incidents, he was clearly unfazed by the 'accident' in England, so, as James proposes, we need to be rather more persuasive this time. Now as far as income is concerned, will both of you bring me up to date on your various operations? You first, Sergio, as it is a while since I received your last written report."

Dowling surreptitiously glanced at his colleague and was surprised to see that Induranna suddenly didn't look quite as cool as he usually did. "Oh-ho, something's not quite right and the boss knows it, perhaps that's why he soft-pedalled a little with me."

"I'm afraid the forecasts for the income from the Cuban franchise turned out to be a little optimistic however." The interruption was quiet but as cold as ice.

"How little is little, Sergio?"

"Just over three million." This time Induranna waited.

"So we made just over four million?"

"That's right, four point two million, in fact."

"Do you think that three million out of just over seven million is little, Sergio?"

"No, sir, I guess not".

"Forty per cent, Sergio, forty per cent. Under no circumstances can that kind of percentage be considered little. Now you of all people, Sergio, must be aware that I much prefer an initial underestimation of potential profit, to one based on over optimism. If I recall, I was a little, and I mean little in this case, doubtful about how much your operation might produce. Quite a number of the other board members, including James here (at this point Dowling had the sense to keep looking straight at the boss) voiced similar doubts. Your words, however, were that 'this estimate has been deliberately reduced to ensure that there is no possibility of underachieving'. Your exact words I believe?" There was still no emotion but the menace in the delivery was immense. Induranna was now sweating.

"Yes, boss."

"It was only on your assurance that you had under-estimated the profit that the scheme was approved. I expect that you will have put into place those measures necessary to recoup the lost profit. I also expect that the lost profit will be recovered by the end of the month". All three men knew that there was no possibility of that being achieve.

"You can go." Induranna left the room as silently as he could.

"Whilst I am not entirely happy that the Connolly sanction has not been successful, it does not appear to have had any adverse effects upon the operation as a whole and, from a financial point of view, the results are better than anticipated. However, you have no doubt wondered why I instructed you to concentrate on Connolly quite so much?" Dowling was clearly expected to answer. "Be very careful" a voice in his head whispered.

"The thought had crossed my mind." The boss smiled. This was such a rare occurrence that Dowling almost smiled but stopped himself in time.

"I would have been disappointed had it not done so. Did your thoughts extend to hazarding a guess as to why there was the concentration on Connolly?"

"I assumed that you had your reasons and would explain what they were if and when you considered it necessary".

"Hmm." A hint of a smile again. "Tell me has the financial situation changed this report?"

"Up by a hundred thousand, as anticipated."

"Good. Continue as suggested." He looked down. Dowling left as silently as Induranna had done but wearing a hint of a smile himself. When he reached the secretaries' level he saw that Induranna appeared to be waiting for him. Induranna raised an eyebrow. Dowling nodded very discreetly and Induranna left. After a short conversation with his secretary Dowling followed Induranna out of the building. The man clearly wanted to talk and Dowling didn't need to be a genius to work out about what. How did he play this? It appeared that Induranna's star was waning but the boss was not above providing little tests for his operatives, especially his senior ones. To refuse to help could be interpreted as a refusal to help the 'company'. On the other hand, it could be perceived that Dowling was insufficiently ruthless if he did go to Indurrana's aid. He decided for the moment to back both horses and just see what Sergio had in mind.

He walked over to where the other man was waiting...

CHAPTER TWENTY

John Ryan just out of bed, heard a sound at his hotel room door. As he padded to the door in his bare feet he saw a large thick envelope on the carpet. There was only the word 'RYAN' on the front. Somewhat puzzled and at the same time feeling distinctly uneasy, he tore open the letter and instantly felt sick. The cause was the contents of the envelope. Ryan was by no means naïve and he had certainly been around the block a few times. He had had his share of dealing with the world's low life but he had never before received a poison pen letter.

Since the time of the visit to Connolly's house in France when Judith had given Ryan cause to believe that she might feel something for him, she had been cool towards him. Now he knew why she had been a little less enthusiastic about furthering their relationship than he had hoped. He had wondered if there had been something in her past that she was ashamed of. The letter appeared to confirm this. The revelations in the letter, even if they were true, didn't overly concern him. He was far from innocent himself and had strayed outside the law more than once. The cause of his disgust was the accompanying comments attached to the unsurprising photographs and equally unsurprising diary of Judith's indiscretions. Whoever had sent the little present was nursing considerable hate towards Judith or himself, or perhaps both of them. Gradually anger replaced the disgust and then clear thinking took over. What was the best thing to do now?

Showing Judith was certainly not the thing to do. Nothing would be as cruel. However, he knew that she would never let him into her life while she feared that he might somehow find out about her past. Somehow he had to find a way of letting her know that he knew about her past and didn't care.

The letter had been compiled using letters and words cut very carefully from newspapers and revealed nothing. Perhaps the police would be able to get something from the letter but Ryan couldn't and he certainly wasn't going to the police, at least, not yet. He turned to the photographs. Most of them were coloured and of a high quality. They showed a younger Judith in a variety of poses, most of them of her in the nude. They were he guessed, from the more expensive men's magazines, Playboy, Penthouse etc. For the type of thing they were, they were quite tasteful and Judith certainly looked very attractive. However, the remaining photographs were entirely different in character, all pornographic, some showing Judith with both men and women. Nothing was left to the imagination. The photographs were also much poorer in quality. He looked at all the photographs for a little longer and in spite of the circumstances, began to feel the stirrings of arousal. Suddenly, somewhat ashamed of himself he pushed the photographs away. As he did so his eye was caught by one of the men in several of the sleazy pictures. He picked one up and looked at it very carefully. There was something about the man's face. After a few more moments of study, he suddenly smiled and picked up the phone. He made two calls, the second one being to Judith. When she answered, he made himself sound light and cheerful.

"Hi, Judith, it's John, how are you?"

"Oh hi, John, I'm fine thanks how are you?" Her voice was courteous and careful.

"I'm pretty good too. Look I very much want to see you again. Something has come up which we need to talk about. It's not just personal. When are you free?"

"Well, I'm pretty busy all the time, you know what it's like at this point in the season." Whilst this was true, they both knew that there were bits of time between races.

"Please, Judith, it's important." He was still cheerful but firm. While she hesitated he took his chance.

"Look I'm free all morning. Can I pop around now?"

She wasn't quick enough with a reason to say no. Straight away he was in again.

"That's fine then. I'll be at your hotel in say twenty minutes. Bye." He put the phone down and quickly showered and dressed. As he finished dressing, the phone rang. The conversation was brief but at the end of it, Ryan was smiling. He then made another call, this time to Bruce Connolly.

"Bruce, it's John. I think I might have a lead on our troubles. I'm saying nothing on the phone. Meet me at seven. I'll pick you up. Okay? Thanks, bye."

Fifteen minutes later he was at Judith's hotel room door, holding a bunch of red roses. He had decided that valour was the better part of discretion. As she opened the door he pushed the flowers into her hand. With both his hands now free he took her face between them and kissed her. Very lightly at first, then when she didn't resist and allowed her lips to soften and began to kiss him back, he gradually increased the pressure. The urgency of their kiss increased, their tongues darting in and out of each other's mouths until suddenly Judith pulled herself away from him.

"Stop, John, please stop. You said you wanted to see me about something. I said last time that you had to give me some time." He took her hands in his and she didn't try to pull them away.

"I think events have rather overtaken you. Sit down please. I promise that I won't try to kiss you or even touch

200

you again until you want me to. Now you must let me finish what I'm about to say. It will take some time, but you must hear me out, promise?"

She nodded looking a little nervous. She bent down and picked up the roses.

"I know that though we have been *acquainted*, let's say for quite a while, we have only really known each other a short time. I also now know that I love you. I say now because I only recognised that fact this morning. I've been telling myself that although you were very nice, I was going to keep my distance. But I was trying to fool myself and I failed. I love you and want to spend the rest of my life with you." He held up his hand as she started to speak. "You promised to let me finish and I've barely started." He paused drinking in her beauty. He realised that in all probability, his objectivity in this respect had long since disappeared, but he didn't care.

"I know all about your past, or at least, those parts that you were probably most afraid of being discovered." He saw the pain in her eyes. "There is no reason at all to worry. A *friend* of either yours or mine saw to it that I received some, shall we say, compromising information about you."

"Photographs?" She whispered the question with her eyes looking at the floor.

"Yes. What the fool didn't realise was that in the first place I have never ever been judgemental and other people's behavior is, as far as I'm concerned, their affair. Secondly, this attempt to poison our relationship has done just the opposite. When I saw what was written and looked at the photographs, I wanted only to get to you to protect you. It was at that moment that I knew that I loved you." He judged that this was not the moment to declare how erotic he had found the photographs.

"After my initial anger had given way to logical thought, I looked more carefully at the photographs. Then I made a couple of phone calls as I thought that I recognised one of the men in the photographs."

201

"Men?" Judith looked sharply at Ryan with a look of complete surprise on her face. Ryan smiled.

"I thought that might be your reaction. Now think back about fifteen years I would guess."

Judith still looked puzzled.

"Your sister?" Ryan prompted.

"My sister, how did you know I had a sister and what has she to do with this?"

"Exactly what, I don't know yet. As to the first question, I have quite a few useful contacts in a number of police forces around the world. Now do you know what happened to Jessica after your act folded?"

"Not really, we didn't keep in touch very much I'm afraid." Again there was hurt in her eyes.

"Well, as far as I can establish, a little after your act broke up, Jessica's luck and money both ran out and she had a stab at pretty much anything which paid her well enough for her to be able to maintain her high style of living. Eventually this included 'modeling' for pornographic books and appearing in porn films as well. These are stills from some of the films. This is her isn't it?" He handed her the poorer quality photos. She nodded as she looked at them.

"It looks awfully like me doesn't it?"

"Indeed, it does, which is of course, what our poison pen friend was depending on. These, however," throwing across the better quality prints, "are of you, are they not?"

Again she nodded looking very forlorn. He thought he might risk a little lightening of the mood.

"If I was a woman who looked as good as that with nothing on, I would be profoundly grateful to my maker, not be sitting there looking like a wet weekend." She smiled a little smile.

"Had I not looked at the man in this photograph who I thought I recognised, and then looked a little more carefully at the photograph as a whole, I wouldn't have sorted out the truth. You are too much alike not to be twins but there is one distinguishing feature isn't there?"

"Yes, the mole."

"Exactly. No mole in the porn photos, but clear in the Playboy ones, or whatever it was."

"Playboy, Penthouse and Mayfair actually," she added this abstractedly, still looking miserable.

"Hmm, I must have missed those issues, worse luck. "This brought another little smile.

"Did you buy those things then?" she asked this in a surprised voice.

"I would have thought that you would have been aware that most, if not all men look at, if not buy, those things, as you put it. The hypocrites don't admit it that's all. Anyway, in the glamour shots you can see your mole just below your navel and there is no sign of it in the porn ones. Airbrushing might have happened the other way around but nobody bothers that much with porn shots. A few phone calls established that the two of you had a successful dance act, after which Jessica had a brief period with a few escort agencies and then under a different name became a well-known porn star. As for you at the end of the dance act you were a bit of a naughty girl for a while, some nude modelling, a bit of soliciting and then you disappeared altogether. I also found out where a lot of your money went. Whatever you think about yourself, I know my past is worse, so don't look so glum." With these words Judith began to sob and John put his arm around her.

"Now I have many skills but coping with crying women has never been one of them. What about some tea?" She nodded and he picked up the phone and ordered tea and sandwiches from room service.

"Come on you can't let the waiter see you crying, he'll probably try to throw me out for molesting you."

The joke was feeble but it produced another small smile. They sat quietly until the tea and sandwiches arrived, which were very good. By the time they had devoured them, Judith eating more than John, he was pleased to note, she was much more perky and eventually admitted to being vastly relieved that she didn't have to hide her past any more from John.

"I am relieved but still feel hugely ashamed of what I've done."

"Whatever for?"

"Oh come on. It's no good you trying to say that my past activities were of the same order as any nine to five typist or a school teacher, or shop assistant."

"Well, for a start that rather depends on what the typist, teacher and shop assistant do in their spare time. I would suggest that there is more honesty in being a prostitute than in being one of the many wives who use sex as nothing more than a weapon to blackmail their husbands or boyfriends with. No more nookie 'til you buy me a new three-piece suite etc. Added to which you certainly made a brilliant job of the modelling."

She looked steadily at him clearly trying to assess his likely reaction to what she was about to say.

"Would you be shocked if I said that I enjoyed the glamour shoots, even the nude ones?" Ryan smiled before answering.

"You would not have looked anything like as good as you did if you hadn't been enjoying it."

"Hmmm. Okay, although that doesn't really answer my question. What if I said that more often than not, I enjoyed the sex when was I was on the game. Does that not shock you?"

This time Ryan laughed, taking hold of her hand again as he did so.

"Certainly not. The same applies there as to the glamour work. You wouldn't have been very good if you hadn't enjoyed it or at least some of it, and your clients wouldn't have kept coming back, which I presume they did?"

"Oh yes, most of them."

"There you are then. Look, Judith, perhaps it might help a little if I give you what I'm pretty sure is most men's view of prostitution. Very few men, even those who haven't been to a prostitute, have nothing against them and lots of those men would love to go to one if they had the spare cash, the bottle and the confidence. Even those men who are happily married with a full and interesting sex life would like to give it a try."

"I hadn't thought of it like that, although I must confess at the time I wasn't particularly ashamed of what I was doing, even though I knew it was wrong in the world's eyes."

"So if you weren't ashamed then, why are you now?"

"What about being, as they say, damaged goods?"

"Oh I see. So every girl I've had sex with was a virgin before I had my wicked way with her were they? I don't think I've ever had sex with a virgin thinking about it."

"That's not the same."

"Oh but it is it's exactly the same. At least one of my ex-girlfriends had had umpteen lovers by the time she met me. What difference does being paid for it make?"

"You make it sound so simple. No one has ever said this kind of thing to me, even the other working girls. I must be sure though, you aren't just saying this to make me feel better?"

"I mean it with all my heart. Incidentally, tell me why did you stop?"

"For two reasons really. Firstly, I began to get frightened. A few of the girls got beaten up. Secondly, I thought that I could do something more demanding and fulfilling with my life, so I decided to quit."

Ryan had picked up the Playboy photographs.

"You look really really gorgeous in these you know. You have a fabulous body as well as a lovely face. How old are these?"

"I packed up modelling about ten years ago and these were among the last I did." She paused, suddenly the atmosphere had changed, and tension hung electric in the air. "Even though it's ten years older, wouldn't you rather see the real thing than the photographs of it?" Her voice trembled a little and had gone a little deeper. As if in a dream, Ryan heard himself say, "Yes please, oh yes please, I can't think of a single thing I would like more." He had been uncomfortable for some time and it had been a long time since he had had sex. Judith led him into the bedroom, then held his arms by his sides as she kissed him.

"Now I'm going to undress you and then I shall undress but you mustn't attempt to touch me until I tell you to." Ryan nodded as she skilfully took his clothes off somehow managing to avoid touching any part of him, even his, by now fully erect penis.

"Now just in case you start thinking about my past experience, just to reassure you, you are at least the equal of all I've experienced." She looked at him with hooded eyes as she spoke. Ryan had been aware, ever since masturbating sessions with the other boys in the showers in his upper school that he had not been on the back row when the Lord had been dispensing male genitalia, nevertheless Judith's words added to his excitement. He was also aware that she was going to use all her sexual skills for his pleasure in order to exorcise the guilt that she still clearly felt about her past. Judith now pushed him down on to the bed and very gently ran her tongue along his considerable length from root to bell-end. He could hardly stand the intensity of both the desire and the pleasure.

Judith now straightened up and began undressing. Unhurriedly, erotically but never lewdly she undressed down to her deep red bra, panties, suspender belt and stockings. He couldn't remember ever seeing anything quite so alluring. Her voice was soft and husky.

"You can take off the rest."

Even through her bra Ryan could see that her nipples on her deliciously heavy breasts were distended and he reached to touch them.

"Not until you have undressed me completely." Her voice was still gentle yet somehow masterful, a very erotic combination. He took off the remaining slips of silk and satin, trembling all the time, until she took his penis in one hand while taking his hand with her other and placing it on her breast.

"Now before I take advantage of this gorgeous thing," she squeezed his erection, "I need you to caress me all over. I've always loved having my nipples kissed, nibbled and sucked and my breasts played with, but slowly and gently to begin with."

For the next ten minutes, which were indescribably pleasurable to Ryan, she told him exactly what to do to please her. There was no domination involved, merely the making of suggestions to a very willing pupil. By the end of the ten minutes, by which time he had covered her body with kisses and had gently caressed gently and sometimes not so gently, her legs, her stomach, her neck, hands, feet, her bottom and her breasts, she moved slightly away from him, took one of his hands and placed it on her vagina.

"If you entered me now, you would come straight away, so we'll wait for that for a little while. For the moment I'll play with yours while you play with mine."

She took his penis and began to masturbate him, slowly but firmly while he slipped first one finger and then two into her extremely moist hole and gently stimulated both the walls of her vagina and her clitoris. Judith moaned.

"Oh that's so good, you are so good at that, don't stop." As she felt her orgasm coming she increased her masturbating sensing that Ryan was very close too. They exploded together both crying and moaning as they did so. John seemed to be spurting forever and Judith experienced the most tremendous orgasm she had had for years, if ever. As their passion subsided, they turned to each other and kissed for a very long time.

After kissing they lay side by side each barely able to believe their good fortune. Judith then reached for John's hand and placed it on her breast again. With her other hand she stroked the inside of his leg, gradually moving upwards to play with his balls. As she did this, he took one of her nipples in his mouth and circled it with his tongue, from time to time sucking it while still fondling her other breast with his other hand. She moved slightly so that she was half on her side and half lying on her back. John took hold of her right thigh and lifted it up. Divining his intention, she now wiggled her bottom a little until she was presenting her by now fully open vagina to his penis.

Although only a matter of minutes since she had so expertly masturbated him to such a glorious climax, his balls felt full again and his tool felt so hard it hurt. He felt himself at her entrance and trembling again, for the first blissful time thrust himself into Judith. She gasped and then moaned, first at his size and then at the intensity of her pleasure. For a few seconds he moved in and out of her with feverish power. The angle of his entry and how they were both lying enabled Ryan to see both Judith's extremely sexy bottom and his tool pumping in and out of her. This of course added to the excitement. For her part, Judith was experiencing more pleasure than she had ever dreamed possible. Sensing that John was not far from climaxing again, she whispered to him.

"Steady, just lie still inside me for a little while, I want this to last forever." Although his desire to continue thrusting in and out was enormous, John did as he was asked. After a short period, Judith now guided John's hand onto her highly stimulated and enlarged clitoris and whispered to him to gently stroke it. This he did, gradually increasing the speed and pressure until Judith was continually moaning and talking to him in a totally abandoned way. As he frigged her, he began to move slowly in and out of her again, knowing that to move any more quickly would instantly bring on his own climax. However, neither of them could stem the increasing power of their oncoming orgasms however much they wanted to prolong the delight being experienced. With a loud cry, Judith started to come, clamping her legs together and tightly gripping John's penis inside her. As her orgasm hit, John felt her love juices begin to flow and this took him over the edge too. His gentle strokes turned into urgent frantic powerful ones and as Judith's orgasm continued unabated, so he spurted into her, further prolonging her own climax. When they eventually stopped they were completely spent. Without a word but still coupled together they fell asleep. After several hours of dreamless slumber, Ryan woke and with a start realised that he would have to leave immediately if he was not to be late for his appointment with Bruce. Leaving a note, he kissed the still sleeping Judith on the forehead and silently slipped away.

CHAPTER TWENTY-ONE

Connolly was already in the lobby when Ryan arrived.

"You sounded a little short on the 'phone, John, something up?"

"Yeah I think so. Let's find somewhere really quiet and private."

Connolly led the way to a small bar at the rear of the hotel. Apart from the barman it was deserted. Oak panelling, red plush upholstery and velvet curtains gave the bar a feeling of old world opulence that was both relaxing and surprising as it differed completely from the rest of the hotel. As Connolly well knew from past experience, everyone who used the bar could not help but feel at ease. Armed with drinks, soft in Bruce's case, the two men wasted no time in pleasantries.

"Without going into great detail now, I'm pretty certain that probably unknowingly and certainly innocently, Judith is somehow involved in our 'problems'."

"Judith?" Connolly was surprised to say the least.

"Yes. I've been certain for some time that something has been bothering her and today I discovered what." Connolly said nothing and waited for Ryan to take a drink.

"This morning an indirect attempt was made, or more accurately, the first stage of a blackmail attempt was made on both Judith and myself. Or at least, that is what I think will happen."

"Photographs?" This time it was Ryan's turn to be surprised.

"How did you guess?"

"I didn't. To be honest, I thought that I recognised Judith when she first came into my orbit as it were, in cycling. Remember, I've done my fair share of girl-watching in my time and like most guys, had my share of horny men's mags. I was pretty certain that either Judith or someone very much like her had been in some of them." He smiled.

"You never said anything." It wasn't a question, merely a statement. Connolly drank some of his fruit juice.

"Why should I?" Even if you think that someone who poses naked for a girlie magazine is a bit suspect, which I don't anyway, that was a long time ago. Hell, it's being bloody hypocritical to get pleasure from looking at porn and then have a down on those people doing the stuff, don't you think?"

"I've never really thought about that last point, but yeah I guess you're right."

"Anyway I like Judith and I think she's okay, although I guess I'm a bit worried that you now think she's mixed up in all of our 'business'," he paused and they both sipped their drinks. Ryan passed across the magazine photographs.

"You having said all that makes me feel a whole lot better. Are these the photos you remember?" Connolly looked carefully then smiled.

"Don't take this the wrong way, buddy, but I have to say that you sure do have great taste. This is one gorgeous girl. If I wasn't fixed up myself I'd be seriously thinking of moving in on you." Ryan smiled.

"Down, boy. Before we go any further, look at these." He passed the other pictures across to Connolly. The American's face fell immediately.

"Jeez, John. I didn't realise. These are way beyond Playboy. I didn't peg Judith for this sort of thing. I'm sorry." To Connolly's surprise, Ryan smiled.

"No need to be sorry. Look carefully at both sets of photographs." Connolly did so but after a while he raised his head looking puzzled.

"It isn't Judith in the hardcore shots. Look very carefully." After a few more moments of study, Connolly whistled.

"You're right by God. So who is the second girl?" Ryan brushed aside the question.

"Look carefully again but this time at the guys in the porn shots and think." The light in the bar was not the best for careful study of relatively dark photographs and it too Bruce a while before he snapped his fingers.

"Yes, got it!" He was now excited. "So who's the girl?"

"Before we talk about the girl I was hoping that you would say that you'd seen at least one of the men at some cycling event or other."

"Yes, I 'm pretty sure I have but don't ask me where or in what specific connection but at least two of the faces are familiar. Now, for the third time, what's with the girl? If it isn't Judith who is it?"

"Okay, tiger, fair enough. It's Judith's twin sister who she hasn't seen for some years. They used to have a successful dance act. Judith doesn't know anything about the hardcore pictures but the fact that the bad guys are targeting her is a bit of a worry."

"Maybe they're not after Judith at all. Maybe the blackmail, when it comes, if it comes, will be aimed at you." Ryan pondered on Connolly's words for a while, and then slowly shook his head.

"The more I think about this, the more I think this isn't a blackmail thing after all. Okay I'm very taken with Judith, to say the very least, but the extent of my affection is as yet known to no one. You didn't know?" Connolly shook his head, "And you're as close to me as anybody. People might guess but that's not enough to risk on a blackmail scam. No, this is another message to let us know, us being the team, that these bastards will use anything to ruin us. But why for heaven's sake?"

"I don't have the slightest idea but somehow I think that this" he gestured to the photographs, "was a mistake on their part, I'm not sure why but I just feel it. How much does Judith know about all of this?"

"All of it. I went round to see her earlier and after the initial upset and clearly feeling pretty ashamed of herself, we had a long talk and she's okay now. In fact she has been afraid for ages that these photographs would come into my orbit sooner or later, which is why she was very cool towards me. I have to thank the bad guys for removing all of that." Ryan couldn't help a big grin spreading across his face.

"Does that stupid grin mean what I think it means?"

"I suppose so."

"Attaboy, it couldn't happen to a nicer guy, I'm really pleased for you, fella." Connolly put his arm around Ryan and gave him a hug. It was a pleasant moment for both but the seriousness of the situation quickly brought them back to practicalities. Bruce was the first to speak.

"How do you feel about letting Sarah in on this?"

"Well I know that she is understanding and compassionate, and in the best sense of the word has been around, but I'm not sure what value there would be in bringing her in." Connolly sat back in his chair and steepled his fingers before replying.

"There is something you need to know about Sarah. I haven't told you before because I wanted you to be as focused on the racing as much as possible. However, after this little episode, you need to be fully in the picture." As succinctly as possible Connolly explained Sarah's role and a little about the organisation she represented without revealing names. Ryan whistled then smiled.

"What's so amusing?"

"It isn't amusement it's more relief. At least we have some good guys in our corner and we aren't the only ones who think we are being shafted. Obviously we have to tell Sarah about this immediately." Connolly smiled again.

"One other good thing is that Sarah and Judith like each other."

For the next half an hour the two men talked and planned. They parted feeling that at least they were beginning to get on equal terms with the opposition. Back in his hotel room Connolly first phoned Sarah and explained the gist of his conversation with Ryan, and then he talked to his father and had a quick chat with Mary briefly explaining the situation to both.

Feeling a little jaded now Connolly knew from past experience that what he needed now was some simple physical exercise. A session on his turbo trainer should do the trick. He always took it with him when travelling because riding a turbo trainer was much more akin to riding on the road than an exercise was. A warm-up, half an hour's concentrated effort and a long warm down followed by a stretching routine reduced Connolly to a sweat covered automaton and it was with some relief that he took a shower. After the shower, feeling much better he settled down to think armed with a large glass of recovery drink. He had loaded the cartridge of his CD player with Sibelius's second symphony, some Bruce Hornsby, Bob Seger, Neil Diamond and Frank Sinatra. His last selection was Bruckner's eighth symphony. He first spent some time thinking about the current season and the next one. 'The problem' could wait for a while. He noted down his main objectives again and what he had achieved so far this season. He compared this with his original objectives set out before the season began. There had been some successes, but the failures there rankled, not because he was a sore loser, but because he knew that he had been robbed in some of those races, if not in all of them.

Bruce now considered his personal life. As he did so, he recollected the moment he had realised that now he actually had a personal life. There was no doubt that he was in love with Sarah and he was sure the feeling was mutual. What was to follow? Fortunately, Sarah understood cycling and was therefore familiar with the life of a top class cyclist and the pressures such a life brought with it. She also clearly enjoyed the sport. How long would she tolerate the eternal merry-go-round, the frequent separations, or the living out of a suitcase if she chose to go with him racing? What would follow for him when he did eventually hang up his wheels? As an architect? He didn't really see himself as a full-time architect — not exciting enough. Aim for high political office? He laughed at that thought. Be a farmer like Bernard Hinault or Sean Kelly? That hadn't totally satisfied them and he didn't think it would satisfy him either. Of course he already had more than enough money not to have to find gainful employment, but a life of idle indulgence was infinitely worse than any of the earlier options he had been thinking about.

Getting nowhere fast with the thoughts about his future, he moved to 'The problem'. He wrote down what he and his associates knew, then what they had surmised. Then a list of possible motives and a list of the people they knew were involved. None of the lists were very long. As far as motives were concerned, part of the motive could well be smuggling, that seemed the best bet, and smuggling of gems also the most likely. By whom? A big zero there. What had the smuggling to with the Brooklyn team? Another equally big zero. Who might stand to gain? Other teams to some extent, but not to a huge extent. Who were the big losers? So far, only he and his team. Who had been losers in the past? Connolly suddenly sat up in his chair. Who had lost in the past? Of course why hadn't he thought of it before? Jason Curzon was one big loser. Of course! He would pay a visit to Jason. It was time he paid his respects anyway. After all he was spending quite a lot of time with the guy's daughter, some of it in bed.

In two days' time, the Tour of Switzerland would begin, one of the traditional aperitifs to the Tour De France. Normally a good guide to form, The Tour De Suisse was an event Connolly wanted to do well in and now having sorted out his mind to some extent, he went to bed, leaving Nat king Cole singing to himself. As usual these nights, his last thoughts, as he went to sleep, were of Sarah.

CHAPTER TWENTY-TWO

Giuseppi Vacchio had begun to believe that even in this, his first complete season as a professional cyclist, he was capable of winning at least one of cycling's major titles. His early success in the Giro and good placings in the Spring Classics had caused him to be noticed and his fellow professionals now afforded him the respect his performances merited. Realistically, the Tour de France was beyond him, even if his team decided to let him ride it, but the Autumn Classics, the newly re-introduced legendary Grand Prix De Nations time trial were, he believed, within his reach. He also felt that, assuming of course that he would be selected to ride for the Italian team, the World Championship road race was a possibility, even if only a slight one as the Rainbow Jersey was notoriously difficult to win.

Now he sat alone in his hotel room mentally preparing himself for the time trial stage of the Tour of Switzerland. One of the traditional preparation races for the Tour, the Tour De La Suisse, to give it its correct title, had had many distinguished winners in the past. Although success in the Swiss race by no means guaranteed Tour De France success, it was certainly the case that many winners had, indeed, done the double and it was very rare that a good performance here was not followed by similar success in 'Le Grand Boucle'. A good performance here also instilled a certain amount of fear in one's competitors.

Giuseppi was currently third on general classification, just over a minute down on the leader and a good time trial performance today could put him in the leader's jersey. This was day six of a nine day tour and opportunities for him to take the lead after today were very thin on the ground. Today was the day.

Although a very good time triallist and still improving, Giuseppi felt nervous. 'The Race of Truth' as a time trial is called, is feared by all but the very best at the discipline and even they are well aware of just how hard time trials are. Even those masters of the time trial: Bernard Hinault, Miguel Indurain, Eddy Merckx, Lance Armstrong and perhaps the greatest of them all Jaques Anquetil, all admitted to pre-race nerves before a time trial. It is unremittingly hard and lonely with no shelter at all. All cycling races are hard, many mountain stages particularly so, but in every road racing stage there are usually opportunities for brief semi-rests. Riders can take shelter from other riders and a good deal of sharing of the pace-setting and bearing the brunt of head-winds is the norm. In the early part of a stage the pace is usually more modest than later on and riders can sometimes even free-wheel a little. None of those things apply in a time trial. For those riders looking for success not only in the time trial itself but in the overall race must give one hundred per cent all the way. He must measure his effort so that at the end he has nothing left and it is in this measurement of effort where the real skill lies. Even for the very best time triallists, this means a great deal of pain. If and when a rider hits a bad patch, he is on his own, there are no teammates to help him and the only thoughts in his mind are wanting the pain to stop on the one hand and the fear of being caught by the rider behind him on the other.

Now Vacchio could almost feel the presence of a pursuiting rider about to overtake him, a feeling dreaded by all, even as he sat in his hotel room. He knew he was expected to do well today. At breakfast the directeur sportif had made it clear that he expected Giuseppi to be in the lead in the overall race after the time trial. That was pressure he could well do without. It was the first time in his professional career that he had understood what the weight of expectation really meant. Nevertheless, the nervousness was balanced by a feeling of quiet confidence. He had ridden quite a lot of the course that morning and he felt that there was nothing there to really trouble him. The distance, a little under fifty kilometres, was a lot for this race but meant that it was long enough for the good time triallists to gain significant amounts of time on less able riders at the discipline. The two riders ahead on general classification were competent riders against the watch but not of his ability. Encouraged by these thoughts Giuseppi began to get ready. As third overall in the race at the moment, he would start third from last, only Giles Duclat and Patrick Martens behind him. The riders started at one minute intervals except for the last ten riders, who started at two minute intervals. The objectives, apart from riding the course in the shortest possible time was to catch as many riders as possible who had started before you and avoid being caught by the riders who had started after you.

With time trials, the selection of equipment was left to each rider even more than with general road stages. After carefully considering the weather forecasts, Giuseppi had asked his mechanic to put deep rim wheels front and rear. A strong wind was forecast for some parts of the course and he felt a rear disc wheel would be too unstable if the wind did get up. This pleased him anyway as he had never been a fan of disc wheels, their clanking noise not helping his concentration.

Half an hour later, having thoroughly warmed up on a turbo trainer, Giuseppi made his way to the start house. Only a few riders were left. Amongst the early finishers, Sarro, Brean and Rodrigo had produced the best times. Heading the leader board Sarro's time of one hour sixteen minutes and three seconds was thirteen seconds faster than Brean's time. Reports from the course had Roger Powell almost half a minute up on Sarro's time with ten kilometres to go. Bruce Connolly was also making up for a fairly undistinguished

219

Swiss tour thus far and was only fifteen seconds down on Powell at both the thirty and forty kilometre checkpoints.

Giuseppi watched the rider immediately in front of him go down the starting ramp, then rode up onto the rear of the start platform himself. He settled on his saddle, fitted his shoes into the clipless pedals and waited for the countdown. Two minutes! The wait seemed interminable. He began breathing deeply, getting as much oxygen into his lungs as possible. "One minute," droned the timekeeper. More deep breaths; a quick prayer; thirty seconds; more breaths; twenty seconds, ten seconds, five, four, three, two, one, go! He launched himself down the ramp, pushing hard but being careful not to overstrain, more than one rider had fallen off a starting ramp before! Moving smoothly now and powerfully, he moved up a gear and after a few more seconds, up another. He settled down to concentrate, willing himself to concentrate as never before. Efficiency of movement and power were the keys to success. Crowds lined the whole of the route cheering on all the riders but Giuseppi saw none of them. He felt good, or as good as one ever can in this most cruel of all races. Just after twenty kilometres he caught his minute man, not a noted time triallist admittedly but certainly a competent one and Giuseppi knew that he must be going well to have caught him so quickly. Much sooner than he had expected, in itself another good sign, he began climbing the Susten Pass just as his four minute man came into his sight. Through his radio earpiece his directeur sportif was telling him that he had been a few seconds up on Powell at the thirty kilometre checkpoint. More importantly, he was up on both Duclat and Martens by enough to take the lead if the time gaps remained the same.

Now however the effort began to hurt. As both the gradient and the wind strength increased, so the effort began to tell on the young Italian. To encourage himself he started to count his pedal revolutions. When this palled he turned to his favourite self-motivating trick. He imagined that he was his cycling hero Felice Gimondi. In a biography of the winner of the 1965 Tour De France at his first attempt, multiple Giro winner and World Road champion there was a photograph of the handsome Italian riding in the most revered of all time trials, the Grand Prix de Nations. The caption to the photograph said, "Gimondi, always superb against the watch." The trick worked. Vacchio was now Gimondi. Today he too had to be superb against the watch. He concentrated on keeping his style as smooth and fluid as possible and almost imperceptibly the riding became just a little bit easier and just a tiny bit faster. He was now desperately dry but didn't want to break his rhythm to take his bottle. He flashed under the red kite indication one kilometre to the finish which caused an adrenaline rush.

Vacchio's directeur sportif was now yelling in his earpiece that he was now almost half a minute up on Powell and had increased his lead over Duclat and Martens. All he had to do was keep going for one more kilometre and he would be leading the Tour of Switzerland! He put all he had left into the last kilo. The crowd was cheering wildly, if they couldn't have a Swiss victory an Italian one was the next best thing. Suddenly Giuiseppi had nothing left. His legs were dead, his breathing became a series of laboured rasps and his body swayed from side to side as his style left him entirely. Mercifully, there, only just ahead was the finish. He stood on his pedals, willing himself to keep his cadence going and then he was over the line and free-wheeling to a halt, completely spent. His mechanic and other helpers caught him as he fell off his bike.

"Super ride, Beppi, magnificent. Better than we could have hoped for, brilliant stuff." This came from his directeur sportif. Other congratulations from teammates, race officials and riders from other teams made Vacchio really feel on top of the world, which in cycling terms of course, he was. His D. S. spoke again.

"You're in the lead by nearly two minutes, Martens had a poor ride and you beat him by almost four and a half minutes. Duclat did better, you beat him by three minutes and he leapfrogged over Martens into second."

Giuseppi had never felt so good. In the Giro his temporary tenure of the Maglia Rosa had only really come about because other riders had not been too keen to push themselves in the early stages of the race. When they decided to put the hammer down he had had no answer. Here in Switzerland he now held the race leader's jersey by right and he felt confident that, barring accidents, he could hold it to the finish. His soigneur interrupted his thoughts.

"Oh by the way, Beppi, you were also second on the stage, well done again."

"Second?" His surprise and his disappointment were obvious. "But I thought I was well up on Powell as well as the others. Surely I didn't fade that much at the end?"

"No you easily beat him," the soigneur had a resigned look on his face, "But Connolly beat you by nine seconds. He really pulled out all the stops in the second half and to be honest, we weren't really paying too much attention to him."

For a second or two the disappointment welled up inside Vacchio but he soon dispelled it. Connolly was the best around even if he hadn't appeared to be trying too hard in this race so far. In actual fact, a nine second beating by the classy American when Connolly was really trying put Giuseppi's ride really into perspective. Anyway reflected the young Italian as he was being driven back to the hotel in the team bus after the hugely pleasing podium ceremony, "It is I Giuseppi Vacchio who is wearing the jersey of the leader of the Tour de la Suisse, not Bruce Connolly."

Four days later the situation was more or less the same. Connolly rode better and better as the race progressed, as did Roger Powell, but neither were in a position to threaten Vacchio's overall lead. Both overtook Duclat and Martens illustrating that both would be contenders for the Tour De France. Vacchio's victory in a tour only one step down from the three 'Grand Tours' was hailed as enthusiastically as Andy Hampsten's win in 1986. Now the journalists, particularly the Italian ones, were beginning to ask if Vacchio could be the new 'Campionissimo' the successor to

Giradengo, Bartali, Coppi, Gimondi, Moser, Saronni and, Bugno. Being young and impressionable, Vacchio found it difficult not to believe them. Could he now win the Tour De France? He asked himself. There was no reason why not, he answered.

CHAPTER TWENTY-THREE

Words like incredible, unbelievable and amazing were
certainly used carelessly, inaccurately and all too frequently
by sports commentators, Roger Powell reflected wryly, but
he could think of no other words with which to describe the
scenes before him and of which he was apart for the first
time. The Tour De France! Ever since he had been able to
ride a bike properly, this annual event, the world's greatest
annual sporting event without question, had been the centre
of his life. As a young man he had travelled on the cross-
channel ferry to watch a few stages and he had always read
all he could, to keep in touch with the institution that the
Tour had become. Now he was about to begin realising his
greatest ambition. He was about to start the Prologue time
trial in 'Le Grand Boucle'. He tingled all over with
excitement. Fear, joy, awe and tremendous respect for his
peers, some of whom, not so long ago, had been his idols, all
combined to produce a feeling of unreality. No other race,
not the other "Grand Tours", The Giro and the Vuelta, nor
the "Monuments" in the sport, as they were called, Milan-
San Remo, The Tour of Flanders, Paris – Roubaix, Liege -
Bastogne – Liege and The Tour of Lombardy, bore
comparison with this. To add to the wonder of all of this, he
was reckoned to have a good chance of a top ten placing and
perhaps winning a stage. His reverie was interrupted by a
clap on the shoulder.

"Well, Roger, how is England's number one rider feeling, pretty good I guess?" Roger smiled as he answered.

"Hi, Bruce, yes I feel great I must admit. Scared to death though in a way, as well. Did you feel like that before your first tour?"

"What do you mean first tour? I don't suppose I feel much different to you right now."

"You?" Roger was surprised. Connolly was not as unfeeling as stories about him suggested, Roger knew that by now. Nevertheless the American was still Mr. Supercool and it always looked as if this very fit-looking ultra-confident individual didn't have a nerve in his body.

"Sure it never really gets any different, well not for me anyhow. I still get a bit twitchy before just about every race, not just the Tour. But this," he waved his arm across the scene in front of them, "this is something else. You've just gotta go out there and enjoy it as much as you can. Course it'll hurt, hurt like hell at times, but just keep asking yourself, would you rather be hurting in the greatest sporting event in the world, or not riding at all."

"Put like that, I suppose you're right." Powell still sounded less than totally convinced. Connolly continued.

"Just look around you." He waved an all-encompassing arm. "Can you think of anywhere else you'd rather be? All these guys are bloody good bike riders but not that many of 'em have got what you and me and a few others have got." He unobtrusively pointed out a dozen riders. "A real love of the game and that bit of extra talent, ability − call it what you will. For some of these guys this is just a job, maybe just a little bit more than that. But for me and I'm guessing, for you as well, it's a whole lot more than that. Enjoy and you'll end up winning sooner or later. Forget how to enjoy and you'll never win again." Connolly held out his hand. "Good luck."

Powell took his hand, similarly wished the American well and watched him walk away. Bruce was most people's favourite to win the Tour in spite of the troubles that had been dogging him. Recently he had been riding very well and the word was out that he was hungrier than ever to win his first Tour De France. Even though Connolly was favourite it was not by very much and this year's Tour was considered to be a very open affair. Powell knew that as always there was bound to be a fair amount of alliances struck up between riders for self-protection and advancement but he knew that his directeur sportif would keep his ear to the ground over such things.

The day was what Roger had always thought of as a French day. A dazzlingly blue totally cloudless sky with heat that even at nine a.m. was never experienced in England. As was frequently the case with the Tour, the first day's racing was a short prologue time trial used only to decide who would be the first wearer of the yellow jersey this year. Roger was off at number sixty-five which quite pleased him, not too obvious at the beginning but not leaving him to wait too long. Rheims was the location of the 'Grand Depart' this year and the prologue wound its way through some of its streets. The course was a fairly 'technical' one, which is cycling speak for a course having lots of twists and turns calling for good bike handling skills. It also included a couple of short climbs. Roger had been an excellent 'tester' as time-triallists in England were quite often called, winning a number of National Championships and felt reasonably confident that he could do well today.

After his warm-up on the turbo-trainer, Roger quietly rode around the start area to keep his concentration as high as possible and his muscles warm. With two minutes to go he presented himself at the start house and then found himself being held up by his pusher-off waiting to be launched into his greatest yet cycling experience. He concentrated like never before as he waited for the last five seconds of the countdown.

Suddenly he was off. He charged down the start ramp and gave everything he had for the next ten minutes. As he crossed the finish line he felt that he could not have pushed himself for another metre. It was a strange thing, he reflected as he recovered after the seven kilometre ride, that a rider could feel as exhausted after a short prologue like this as he did after a two hundred kilometre road stage. Nevertheless he felt good and knew that he had ridden well. How well he would find out after another two hours or so.

He rode slowly over to the team bus to towel down and await official confirmation of his time. Around nine minutes fifteen seconds according to his own computer. Extremely nervous before the start, that nervousness had completely disappeared by the time he did start but it now returned with a vengeance. As he handed his bike to his mechanic, he looked at the leader board. Jean-Pierre Danguillente, a noted French time-triallist, headed it with nine minutes twenty-six seconds. The Frenchman had been many of the pundits' tip to win today so if his computer was anything like accurate he would have done very well indeed. Still sweating, Roger was drinking some deliciously cool mineral water, courtesy of one of the Tour's sponsors when Albert Pope spotted Roger and rushed over with a whoop of exultation.

"Nine minutes eighteen seconds, lad! A peach, an absolute peach of a ride. Tha's top o' leader board and that could stay there wi any luck." Albert's Yorkshire accent became much more pronounced when he became excited.

"Steady, Albert, there's more than a hundred riders to come in yet." Nevertheless he felt very elated and was a great deal more excited than he appeared. He became aware that Albert was still talking to him and that his directeur sportif, Pierre Viclat was shaking his hand.

"Did thee 'ear wot I said, lad?"

"Sorry, Albert."

"I said thy time'l tek sum beatin'. Colmos, Vachot and Sarro are slower. That only leaves the eye-talian kid Vacchio, Connolly an' Rodrigo as serious challengers, wi p'raps Andrews from Ruff-Stuff or some real surprise outsider who could beat thee."

Roger smiled and was about to reply when Viclat pointed to the board.

"Well Connolly's not going to beat you, he's moved into second, five seconds slower." Viclat's smile was very warm.

In spite of his cautious words earlier, Roger had great difficulty in remaining calm. 'It's only the prologue', he reminded himself, but it was of considerable prestige nonetheless. As the minutes passed, Roger now seated in the seat of the current leader with Connolly next to him and Danguillente next to Connolly, gradually allowed his hopes to rise. Giuseppi Vacchio had taken fifth so far and Connolly's teammate Colmos fourth. The general consensus was that of the remaining riders, only Mark Andrews posed a threat to the top three.

Roger watched on the TV monitor as Andrews left the starting ramp. He certainly wasn't hanging about as he disappeared around the first bend. From then on it was simply a matter of waiting. Time-checks were made around the course and these were relayed on the TV screens. Riders' reactions varied from joy to disappointment amongst those hoping to do well, to indifference on the part of the large number of riders for whom any time trial even a short prologue was just a necessary evil. Pope came hurrying across.

"Unofficially, after two kilometres he was one second up on thee." Viclat shrugged his shoulders, nobody else said anything. Two more minutes went by and Pope reported that Andrews was now three seconds up. Powell's heart began to sink. Unexpectedly, Connolly who thus far had looked merely calm, if interested, suddenly smiled.

"Relax, Rog." (Not 'kid' anymore Roger thought to himself), "We're okay, he might get third." Roger raised his eyebrows questioningly. "He'll fade, he always does. Not a lot but enough for you and me." In spite of these words from the American, Roger couldn't relax. Albert hove into view again to report that with one-and-a-half kilometres left he was just a single second up and beginning to struggle.

By Roger's calculations Andrews must be just about coming into view on the finishing straight. They all looked at the TV monitor. Sure enough cheers and applause greeted the American as he came onto the straight. Roger looked at watch for the umpteenth time. To win Andrews had eighteen seconds to finish. As Powell watched Andrews seemed to be moving in slow motion but so did the timing clock. They could see the American's face; the intense effort he was making clearly visible. Suddenly, Pope clouted Roger on the shoulder as the Englishman saw that Andrews had some metres to go and Roger's time had passed. At the finish Andrews was eight seconds slower than Roger and therefore had taken third place. Connolly smiled at Powell and winked.

"He faded, he always does."

Relief and delight coursed through Roger's veins as Bruce and the others congratulated him. A Tour De France on the first stage at his very first attempt! Another Brit, David Millar had also done that but that was a long time ago. Could life get any sweeter? In a matter of seconds he was besieged by reporters, some of them none too gentle. Fortunately, both Viclat and Pope had had plenty of experience at this kind of thing and with apparently no effort (although in fact it took a great deal), they spirited Powell away to the podium. Although Andrews was not the last to finish, the intermediate times of the remaining riders on the course were already indicating that they would all be well outside the top six.

Connolly, apparently very happy with second, was already at the podium and a few seconds later they were joined by Andrews, clearly rather less happy with third place. As Roger pulled on his first Tour de France Maillot Jaune, surrounded by the podium girls and was presented with obligatory bunch of flowers, he felt absolutely fantastic. As his eyes swept the crowd, he caught sight of Sally waving at him, wearing a smile a mile wide. He had the distinct feeling that the prizes in his hands weren't going to be the only rewards he would receive on this very special day.

CHAPTER TWENTY-FOUR

It was now almost six months since John and Judith had allowed their hitherto superficial acquaintance to begin to develop into a much deeper relationship. As each day passed, Judith gradually allowed herself to hope that in spite of her past, permanency in their relationship would be the ultimate result. For his part, John was convinced that Judith was the one person with whom he wanted to share the rest of his life. However, the continuing problems surrounding both unfortunately prevented their relationship developing as firmly as they would both have liked.

Judith, being an inherently modest person, perhaps surprising considering her past, doubted that her own feelings could possibly shared by another and with so many similar relationships foundering in the past, she didn't have the confidence to throw caution to the winds and declare the total depth of her feelings towards John. She was equally certain that John Ryan was the man for her future but she was allowing doubts about her sister to cloud her thinking. She was still not absolutely certain that her past didn't matter to John and she was still worried about her sister for a number of reasons. Although having lost touch with her years ago, she was aware that Jessica was still a prostitute, albeit a high-class, highly paid one. Judith was half-expecting her to appear at any time. Ryan was also worried about Jessica but not for reasons of propriety. He genuinely didn't care about her lifestyle or morals, or rather her apparent lack of them, but he was bothered about whether knowingly or unknowingly or possibly against her will, she was in some way involved in the smuggling business. How though could he say anything to Judith? Both were aware that there was a lack of openness about their relationship and the strain was beginning to tell as well as to be obvious to both of them.

Ryan was on his way to check out one of the Tour's stages. Connolly was also due to ride a post-Tour criterium in that area too. The day matched John's troubled mind. One minute, dark clouds scudding across the sky, bringing equally showers, the next, the clouds breaking, changing into masses of white candyfloss, whipped into fantastic shapes, changing as rapidly as they formed, allowing bright sunlight bounce off puddles in the road, making driving sometimes dangerous and always difficult. As he squinted against the brightness, Ryan felt the beginnings of a headache and he decided to pull in for a break as soon as he saw somewhere suitable. He came to the next village which was virtually deserted and drove slowly through. He spotted a boulangerie with a café and pulled into the small parking area alongside. His French was passable and well aware that everyone is expected to make an attempt to speak French when in Northern France, he made a reasonable job of ordering a latte and a delicious looking creation of choux pastry, chocolate, fresh cream and strawberries, which tasted as good as it looked. His arrival and fairly obvious Englishness aroused a certain amount of attention from the other customers but he buried himself in the recently purchased programme of the forthcoming criterium in Dunkirk.

Halfway through the coffee, having finished the pastry, he suddenly stared intently at the photograph on the back of the programme and almost dropped his coffee cup in surprise. The photograph was of the previous year's edition of the race. In the middle of the crowd next to a very eminent figure, was either Judith or her sister. At that distance it was obviously impossible for Ryan to tell them apart. Judith shouldn't have been there, she should have been with her

Directeur Sportif, ready for the arrival of her team's riders, so it was almost certainly *her* sister. On the face of things, innocent enough, but Judith had never intimated that Jessica was even remotely interested in cycle racing. However, what was much more significant was the person next to Jessica. If they were together, as distinct from merely standing next to each other that would really be of interest to Bruce. And the others! He jumped to his feet, threw enough money on the table to more than adequately cover the bill and rushed out. The other customers merely shrugged their shoulders and resumed their reading. Back in his car he phoned Bruce who was of course in his hotel after the day's Tour's stage.

"Bruce, it's John, I'm in Dunkirk and I've got something really important to show you. It will be worth staying up for if you aren't too tired." As a Directeur Sportif Ryan knew how important sleep was to the riders in a stage race, especially the Tour, but fortunately tomorrow's stage was due to start later than usual as it was a very short one.

"Okay. I've got Sarah with me, is it worth her looking at this information?"

"Actually it's even better that Sarah's there. Keep her there till I arrive. She'll be very interested in what I've got to show you as well. See you soon." It would take Ryan several hours to get back to Bruce and Sarah. Plenty of time to ring Judith. It was time, he decided, that everything was out in the open.

"Hi, Judith, it's me. Look I've got to talk to you as quickly as possible." Judith's thoughts had paralleled his.

"I was thinking exactly the same thing. Where and when? To be honest, in a minute's time wouldn't be too soon." John felt elated to hear these words.

"Same for me but it will be a bit longer than that. I'm in Dunkirk at the moment. I'll call for you at your hotel when I get back. No, better still go to Bruce's hotel room. Sarah will be there. I've got something important to show you all."

"Okay, bye." She sounded a little unsure.

"Everything will be fine I promise. Remember… I love you."

"You too. Take care."

This would be the perfect opportunity to bring everything out into the open with Judith. The music playing on the radio, some French singer in the Edith Piaf mould hardly suited his mood, so he put in a CD of Billy Joel which fitted perfectly his now lifted spirits. Even the day seemed brighter although it was now late afternoon. He smiled as he thought of all the love songs with lyrics about love turning grey skies into blue, turning rain to sunshine and so on, and he realised that at the wrong side of forty he had finally properly fallen in love. These and other thoughts concerning Judith and his imagined future with her occupied his mind for the remainder of the drive. Every village he drove through seemed attractive, even though he knew from past experience that they weren't particularly so, the trees seemed somehow greener and more majestic, and the fields reminded him of the more pleasant aspects of his childhood. He remembered walking through cornfields such as these, picking the ears of corn and eating them as he and his mates ambled along. Later in his teens, the same fields were the silent witnesses of his first attempts at the gentle art of seduction. A few kisses, the occasional fondling of a still developing breast and if he was really lucky, the reciprocal stroking of his throbbing tool and the almost immediate ejaculation with its attendant relief. These memories flitted in and out of Ryan's mind adding further to the improvement in his temper. The drive had taken him through countryside which was much more beautiful than he had remembered it being on the outward drive to Dunkirk. Tall trees of various species lined many of the roads and at one point the road ran parallel to a small river, its name unknown to Ryan. Several times flashes of bright blue puzzled John until he realised that kingfishers were the cause of the mystery.

When he reached Connolly's hotel, Ryan made his way to Bruce's room. He was pleased to see Judith there already and asked if he could talk to her alone for a few minutes before all four got together. Connolly and Sarah quickly left and went down to the hotel lounge. Immediately Ryan launched into his more or less prepared speech.

"Judith, it's time I stopped messing about. It doesn't matter what has happened in the past, or for that matter, what might happen in the future. It is of absolutely no importance to me how much or how little involvement in Bruce's problems, either you or your sister have had or are having, either knowingly or unknowingly." Judith opened her mouth to speak but Ryan held up his hand. "There are times when reason can say one thing but the emotions throw that kind of reason out of the window. I just want to spend the rest of life with you. I've said it before, I'm no angel so whatever is in your past, apart from what I know about already, if anything, will be no worse than mine. Marry me, Judith, stay with me today, tonight forever." he took a deep breath. "That's it, I've done, your turn." Judith was silent for a while clearly marshalling her thoughts.

"Oh dear, dear, wonderful, John, if only it was that simple. It would be so very easy to fall into your arms, swear undying love and rush off and get married. But, I don't want to sound pessimistic but how do you think I would feel if another attack on Bruce was successful and it turned out that my sister had had a hand in it?" Ryan shook his head.

"In the first place, how long is it since you had any influence at all on her? To paraphrase the good book, are you your sister's keeper? Secondly, how you feel, isn't going to change how I feel. Thirdly, even if your pessimism turns out to be justified, which I'm convinced won't be the case, us being together or apart won't make any difference how you will feel anyway."

"How do you know I haven't had some involvement anyway?"

"I don't. But you haven't said that you have and I think that you would have had to tell me by now. You could have been laughing at me all the time but my money says you're straight. I won't pretend that things don't look a bit bad for Jessica but if and when the reckoning comes for her, I'd like to be around to help. If there's something relevant about yourself that you haven't told me, for both our sakes, perhaps you should. As I've said, I don't give a damn."

"There is nothing you don't know about my past." He put his hands in hers and they kissed for a long time. Eventually the reason for the meeting came back into their thoughts.

"Look at this picture and tell me if that's you." He felt very pleased that she was obviously having difficulty deciding.

"I would say no, but to be honest, more because I don't recognise the surroundings than anything else. I don't remember ever being there, so I would say it's Jessica."

"What about this chap, do you recognise him?"

"No, definitely not, do you?"

"Oh yes, well I'm pretty certain who it is, but I want Bruce to have a look."

"Where is the place on the photograph?" He passed across the brochure of Dunkirk he had picked up.

"Look at this." Judith looked through the brochure and then back at the photograph. Recognition dawned.

"This photograph was taken at Dunkirk." Ryan nodded affirmation.

"In that case it can't be me, I've never been to Dunkirk, I've always been at other races when the team has raced there." A discreet knock on the door sounded and it slowly opened. After kisses all round and everybody had sat down Ryan handed the photograph to Connolly and Sarah.

"Judith?" Bruce queried.

"Nope, her sister," said Sarah with absolute certainty. The other three looked at her with varying degrees of surprise.

"How can you be so sure?" Ryan said. "Even Judith wasn't that certain."

"Easy. Firstly, look at the make-up, totally different to Judith's. Secondly, look at the expression on her face. Have you ever seen that sort of expression on this one? No. Thirdly, as I keep telling *you*," she emphasised the 'you' and jabbed Connolly in the ribs, "I've been around more than you give me credit for."

"So?" Connolly's question was mimicked by the other two.

"It was you, O mighty one, who told me that Judith had a virtual lookalike sister. However, I know this girl as Joanne Turner. Actually she's an extremely..." Sarah suddenly realised she was on possibly dangerous ground.

"It's okay, Sarah, I know what she is. Thank you for trying to spare my blushes, but there won't be any." Sarah smiled gratefully and continued.

"High-class prostitute and socialite. She's very expensive with some very high-powered clients. The chap she is with is one of her fairly frequent escorts, Gareth Raisen."

"The singer? It never is." Ryan pointed to the man on the girl's left.

"No, not him," said Sarah, "this chap." She pointed to the man on Jessica's right. As she did so, she let her glance fall on the man known to Ryan.

"Oh my God." Sarah instinctively put her hand to her mouth. She pointed out the man to Connolly, whose equally surprised response was to whistle.

"Are they together?" Sarah asked. Ryan turned the page of the programme. Overleaf were a number of smaller photos taken at about half-second intervals, of the same race finish. It was difficult to see the faces clearly. What was clear was that Jessica/Joanne was in conversation, not with her singer friend, but with the other man. In one of the shots he had his arm around her shoulders.

"Jackpot." Bruce said quietly.

CHAPTER TWENTY-FIVE

Bang! The report was all the more startling because of the relative silence all around him. The only sounds were the hum of the tyres on the road and the whirring of the chains and sprockets on the bikes. The puncture was instantaneous and Connolly was riding on the rim of his wheel almost immediately. He cursed and raised his hand. Fortunately, he had been vaguely aware of the presence of the neutral service car just behind him for some time and it was only a matter of seconds before the car pulled up behind him. Two of Bruce's teammates had heard the puncture and were now waiting just up the road ready to pace him back to the bunch as soon as he had a new wheel.

The first mechanic jumped out of the car already holding a replacement wheel. The driver also leapt out of the car and came towards Connolly. Why? Bruce thought to himself, the driver never gets out. In a split second Connolly registered a number of things: the face of the driver, although vaguely familiar it was not the face of any of the regular drivers of the service vehicles; the look of surprise and then alarm on the face of the mechanic and unbelievably, the gun in the driver's hand. As these thoughts registered, Bruce acted. Fortuitously a drainage channel ran along the edge of the road and this was Bruce's only hope. He took a dive into the trough as he saw the driver raise his arm. A searing pain in Connolly's upper left arm was accompanied by the sound of a gunshot. He heard two more shots as he landed in the channel. As he lay gasping and hurting, he heard shouts, another shot, more shouts rapidly followed by the squeal of tyres and the sound of a car being driven off at high speed. Seconds later, more squealing, this time of brakes and seconds later Bruce was being lifted out of the channel. The Tour doctor had arrived and immediately took charge.

"The wound looks much worse than it is. The bullet just grazed you. The shock will be more of a problem than the physical damage. How do you feel?" The doctor was carrying out running repairs as he talked. Bruce remounted his bike, a new wheel having been put in.

"Okay I guess, no different to an ordinary crash."

"You will get some reaction in a little while. You should really abandon. In such circumstances it is the only sensible thing to do. However, I don't suppose for a moment that you're going to are you?"

"No chance! I mean to win the Tour this year Doc. Do me a favour will you? Keep the fuzz off my back until after the end of today's stage." The doctor nodded. "Thanks. How much time have I lost?" John Ryan had arrived at the scene less than a minute after the shooting and he now spoke up.

"You had a lead of almost six minutes when you flatted. They can only be two minutes behind now and they're eyeballs out. Don't push it, let them catch you while you recover and then..." He stopped in mid-sentence simply because Bruce had gone and was now rejoining his still bemused teammates who had halted a little up the road when they heard the bang of the puncture.

"With luck we can still stay away. You guys take it in turn for a while and then I'll get stuck in."

"Okay, Bruce, you're the boss." They knew better than to argue when Connolly had that look in his eye. Ten minutes of seriously fast riding with Bruce at the rear brought Ryan up in the team car. He was smiling.

"Your lead has gone up a little and you now have just over three minutes. How do you feel?"

"Fine-ish." He had, indeed, felt fine until about two minutes earlier when he had suddenly felt himself shake and seemingly crumple up inside. Fortunately, Joe Colmos, the closest of Bruce's teammates had noticed him suddenly go pale and had instantly slowed so as to be behind Connolly, yelling at Jean-Luc, his other teammate to slow down, at the same time. Bruce knew that this was only the doctor's prediction coming true but he also knew that if the reaction didn't wear off quickly, not only would they be caught by the peloton they would be dropped by it too. He gritted his teeth and tried to concentrate on his riding and used all the techniques he knew of to help his concentration but all to no avail. He felt as bad as he could ever remember in all his riding. He felt a hand at the bottom of his back and looked to see Joe at his side.

"Dig in, boss, don't give in." Suddenly Connolly thought of Sarah and after a few moments of daydreaming, he began to feel just a little better. Whether it was simply the reaction wearing off, or the thought of Sarah taking his mind off the pain, he neither knew nor cared. Jean-Luc sensed the change more quickly than Joe.

"You're looking better, boss, but don't start pushing again yet. Leave it to the two of us for a while." Connolly nodded and managed a smile. He was now feeling decidedly better. After another five minutes, the team car which had been following the trio virtually all of the time now pulled alongside again. Ryan leaned out of the window.

"The gap is now down to just over a minute and there's twenty kilometres to the finish. How about it, Bruce?"

For an answer, Connolly merely grinned pressed down on the pedals a bit harder and moved to the front. For the next thirty minutes Connolly rode like a man possessed. In all his years in cycling Ryan had never seen anything like it. Jean-Luc and Joe could barely hang on to his back wheel. Very rarely could either of them take a turn at the front and when they did it was only for a few seconds before Bruce was back in the lead turning the screw. In twenty-five minutes the trio covered eighteen kilometres which included a couple of stiff, if short climbs and put the stage out of reach of the peloton. In that time the lead went from one minute to almost five. As the trio went under the 'Flamme Rouge', marking one kilometre to go, Connolly sat up.

"Okay you guys, the sprint's between you two now."

"No way, Bruce," rejoined Joe. "You did most of the work today, especially in that last twenty K."

"Without you two, I'd have been nowhere back there. My Tour would've been over and we all know it. I'm in yellow now, thanks to you two and I mean to stay that way. Now I'll lead out the sprint but the rest is up to you, no argument."

Jean-Luc and Joe looked at each other and shrugged. With three hundred metres to go, the huge crowd lining the finishing straight screaming with excitement, Connolly launched a fairly convincing but not quite all-out sprint for the line. He could sense the other two just behind him waiting for the right moment. Word of Connolly's trouble had somehow reached the spectators and they were urging him on like dervishes. With seventy-five metres to go, Bruce eased and pulled a little to the left to allow the other two through more easily. Of the two Joe was the better short distance sprinter but Jean-Luc better on a long one. As these thoughts flashed through Bruce's mind he glanced back to see who was going to win the stage. What he saw astounded him. They were both twenty metres behind him, both virtually free-wheeling, sitting upright, applauding and grinning hugely. Before he could do anything he had crossed the line, the stage winner. A huge lump came into his throat and he could feel the tears beginning. The crowd went wild, although not a European, there was no doubting Connolly's popularity.

Before he could get to his teammates, Connolly was mobbed by his soigneur, Ryan, Frank Castillo and dozens of reporters. Every stage finish on the Tour tends to resemble a rugby scrum as reporters besiege the stage winner but this was even more frenzied than usual.

"Can you tell us what happened when you punctured?"

"Did you recognise the man who shot you?"

"Do you have any idea, Bruce, why the gunman tried to kill you?"

"Do you think this attack has any connection with your run of bad luck?"

These and many other questions were being hurled at Bruce and his teammates by different groups of reporters. In a matter of seconds, Ryan, Castillo and all the available mechanics and soigneurs from the Brooklin team had placed themselves between the three riders and the reporters. Ryan raised his hands and waited for the noise to quiet.

"In view of the seriousness of the situation and the unresolved nature of the crime, a press conference, which will be attended by the police, will be held in two hours' time. Until then neither the riders nor any of the Brooklin team officials will have any announcements to make whatsoever. Good afternoon."

As with reporters the world over, Ryan's announcement did absolutely nothing to stem the flow of questions but very efficiently, John and Frank assisted by a significant number of police officers escorted Bruce, Joe and Jean-Luc first to the doping control and thence to the podium, where the crowd went wild again. For Bruce the stage winner's presentation, delightful though it was just a taster before the enormous thrill of having the maillot jaune on his back. It wasn't the first time it had happened but somehow it felt better, 'the greatest moment in my cycling career', he said afterwards and no one doubted it. Because of the circumstances the podium ceremony was completed in almost indecent haste, then it was back to the team bus. Once everyone was on the bus, Ryan spoke.

"It goes without saying what a phenomenal performance you all produced today. What Joe, Jean-Luc and Bruce produced today was beyond anything I've ever seen and as you all know I've been around the block a few times. But the rest of you guys did a brilliant job controlling the bunch. So, a huge well done all round. Unfortunately the celebrations will have to be put on hold for a while. After showers and massages and whatever else you can do in the time, meet me in the hotel lobby in an hour-and-a-half." With that Ryan left the bus and went to find the police.

As soon as John had left, Connolly tried to give a bollocking to his two teammates but he was clearly wasting his breath. They just smiled and said, 'Yes boss', and proceeded to pull his leg for ten minutes. During Bruce's massage, an extremely anxious Sarah came on the phone but Bruce reassured her that he was fine.

"I must be fine, mustn't I? I won the stage and I'm in yellow by a reasonable margin." Sarah wasn't entirely convinced by Bruce's explanations but she had to give up when he had to present himself at the press conference. She was a little more convinced after several of Connolly's team-mates also had a chat with her. By this time it was time to assemble in the hotel conference suite.

The main room was packed with reporters. As many newspaper editors considered the story to be much more newsworthy than cycling stories usually were, even though the sport as a whole was much more high-profile than it used to be, even if the race in question was the Tour de France, there were many more reporters than anyone had anticipated. Standing room only was the order of the day. An expectant hush gradually settled over the room as Ryan, Tour Director Jean Giradot and the three riders filed into the room and sat down. Giradot then spoke in French then in English.

"Ladies and gentlemen I shall read a short statement and then you may ask questions of any of us."

The statement simply stated that during the day's stage. Members of the Brooklin-AJ team had been fired on by an as yet unidentified gunman who had so far eluded the police. Slight injuries had been sustained by Bruce Connolly but

Jean-Luc Bernhardt and Joe Colmos were uninjured. It was believed that the mechanic in the gunman's car had also been shot but how seriously was not known. As he finished dozens of questions were all asked at once, all by the non-cycling reporters, the regulars knew better, all of which were unintelligible because of the din. Giradot raised his hands and made it clear that nothing further would be said by any of the group until silence returned again.

"If you have a question, please raise your hand."

The Tour Director then selected the journalists known to him as Tour regulars, rather than the Johnny-come-lately types who were only there for the scoop and almost certainly, not be seen again. After thirty minutes of questions most of which were predictably aimed at and fielded by Giradot and Connolly, the tour Director stood up and announced that enough was enough. He thanked the press with the utmost courtesy and then escorted the other four out. After having assured himself of Bruce's welfare he excused himself and left. Back in Ryan's room the four got themselves some coffee and sat down to talk through the incident. Ryan began.

"Do we all agree that today's episode was another part of the same overall campaign, whatever that campaign may be?" Two nodded their heads but Connolly didn't. "Bruce you obviously don't buy that idea?"

"I wouldn't go that far I'm just... I don't know, there was something not quite right about the whole thing but carry on."

"Okay, but regardless of that, do we agree that as far as the police are concerned, we are of the opinion that the gunman was some kind of nutjob with a grievance?" This time three assertive nods. "Now did any of you recognise either the driver or the mechanic?" Connolly spoke up.

"The gunman seemed familiar, in fact I've definitely seen his face somewhere before but no way can I remember where or in what kind of circumstances. Jean-Luc, Joe?" this time Joe responded.

"Ditto for me, but I get the feeling that I'll remember where eventually, probably when I'm not trying to, you know what it's like." Ryan nodded and turned to Bernhardt.

"Jean-Luc any ideas?" The Frenchman shook his head.

"Well, we'll have to hope that one of you remembers where you've seen matey with the gun. Is there anything else that any of you can recall which sticks in your mind?"

"The mechanic didn't have any idea what was going on." This came from Bruce in a flat no-argument tone of voice.

"How can you be so sure?" Ryan questioned.

"There was blank amazement in the guy's eyes when the loony-tune jumped out the car and pulled the gun. My guess is, he was a new mechanic who our boy had picked out because he was a bit wet behind the ears. Unless I'm very much mistaken, he'll have been dumped by now and lying by the roadside somewhere, very dead, poor bastard." Joe now spoke up.

"I don't suppose there's been any kind of lead from the service car people?" From his tone of voice it was obvious he held out very little hope. He wasn't wrong.

"No the car was a genuine neutral service car but the real driver had a message late last night saying that the stage was being shortened and the start time would be two hours later than scheduled. Then this morning the people who organise the neutral cars received a message saying that the driver was sick but that his brother was standing in for him today."

"Security allowed this to 'appen!" Jean-Luc was incredulous and incensed at the same time. Ryan sounded apologetic, although he had nothing to apologise for.

"I'm afraid no one thought to verify the story, everybody is supposedly too busy." It was obvious that Ryan also thought the whole business a shambles which ninety-nine times out of a hundred would have resulted in a fatality. He continued.

"Let's just roll this on for a while. Is there any doubt in your mind, Bruce, that matey was trying to kill you?"

"He sure scared the hell outa me. I certainly thought he was aiming to kill me and if I hadn't dived, I'd be dead. I don't think he was just trying to knock bits off me."

"Okay, that's my of it reading too, what about you two?" Joe and Jen-Luc nodded. "In that case, two things. Firstly, that being so, this marks a distinctly different approach. Before this all the previous incidents were not designed to kill. At your house Bruce, any kind of marksman would have had no trouble dropping you. As for the front wheel business, that was only ever going to hurt not kill. Secondly, there was no attempt to make this look like an accident, whereas all the previous racing incidents have looked like they were accidental and that's how they still look to everybody else."

"Are you suggesting anything particular here, John?"

"No not really, Joe, just thinking aloud really." Connolly spoke.

"I hesitate to say this for obvious reasons, but maybe before they were just trying to scare me, is it that now they really mean business?" Ryan slowly shook his head.

"It's possible I suppose, but if we go back to the beginning, you weren't the only rider who was involved in the 'accidents', so why home in on you so very specifically now?" Jean-Luc who had been quiet since his earlier outburst now leaned forward in his chair and spoke again.

"Earlier we were fairly sure that this incident was part of the overall scheme?" The others nodded although earlier Connolly hadn't been sure. Jean-Luc continued.

"What if that was not the case? What if this was a one-off? I 'ave been listening to all you 'ave been saying and the whole thing is strange. Bruce called the man a loony-tune, John has pointed out how different this was to the other incidents. We 'ave all agreed that there must be a large organisation behind the whole campaign yet today's business does not look like the work of such an organisation. It was not professional enough. Would today's attack 'ave been left to one man? I think not. I think this is a different kind of thing altogether. Both Bruce and Joe think they 'ave seen the gunman before. Our 'friends' would surely not take risks like that. Think about enemies, Bruce, individual enemies you 'ave made. That is the key, I am sure." Jean-Luc leaned back. An untypical Frenchman in that he was known for his brevity of speech had broken all known records with the length of this contribution. There was silence for a while as his words were digested, broken eventually by Connolly.

"Powerful stuff, Jean-Luc, powerful stuff. I guess you've put into words the doubts I had earlier." Ryan nodded and then spoke.

"Okay, I think we've talked enough and we've got a Tour de France to try and put out of everybody else's reach tomorrow. Everybody will be expecting you to have some reaction, Bruce and all the other big hitters will be after you so all three of you need as much rest and sleep as you can get."

The four said their goodnights and made for their beds. Bruce's only thoughts as he drifted off into a surprisingly restful night's sleep were only about the following day's stage. If he could keep the yellow jersey with most if not all of his lead intact tomorrow, the Tour should be his.

CHAPTER TWENTY-SIX

Ercole Santana looked across at the man he had always thought of as 'Sad Sam'. For the first time that he could remember, he did not feel fear in the gaunt man's presence.

"Well, Ercole, where do you reckon we can do the move tomorrow?" The two men were talking in a secluded meeting room in Santana's hotel on the evening of the third from last stage of the Tour de France. It was the first time the men had met since the Tour of Switzerland. Santana smiled a little wistfully.

"I do not think there will be a move this time."

The other man's eyes narrowed and he looked even more sorrowful than usual.

"Oh and why's that then, Ercole? I mean the boss is dependin' on us. Without us 'e's goin' to be outa pocket, so to speak. 'E's not goin' to be 'appy 'bout that, Ercole. Know wot I mean?"

Santana still a little charged up, was feeling fairly confident and answered firmly.

"I 'ave 'ad enough. What you get from me, it is worth ten times what you pay me and anyway I want to get back to the top." Sam sneered.

"You, on top o the 'eap again? Don't make me laugh. You're an 'as-been, worse, you're an 'as-been who's a junkie as well. You never were at the very top and now you're finished. Make some more bread with me now while you can." The scorn in Sam's voice was matched by the cruelty in his eyes.

"I will kick the drugs."

"Oh yeah? Even if you could, which I very much doubt, you're far too fuckin' weak a rider without'em. 'Ow you goin' to keep from gettin' dropped when the bunch begin to wind it up a bit?"

Santana could feel the effects of his last shot wearing off and he no longer felt as confident. Still he battled on.

"I'll take the off-season away to get sorted." Sam leapt out of his chair and before he had grasped what was happening Santana had been punched viciously in the stomach and he collapsed gasping on the floor. Sad Sam got hold of Santana's still sweat-soaked racing jersey and yanked him to his feet.

"Now listen loser and listen good. Forget all this crap. You're in and in for good. Geddit?" He slapped Santana hard across the face twice, drawing blood. He pulled out a map and made a mark on it.

"This is where we make the move tomorrow. Be there or you're a dead man!"

He threw the map on the floor, pushed Santana hard against the wall back-handed him across the face and strode out of the room. Santana sank down onto a chair and sat for a while with his head in his hands. Eventually he sat up and walked a little unsteadily over to the phone. There was the slightest of grim smiles on his face as he picked up the phone. He asked to be connected to the Brooklin team hotel. Once through he asked for Bruce Connolly's room. He realised that he was still shaking and prayed that Connolly would be there. He was in luck.

"Bruce, this is Ercole Santana. I'm sorry to bother you but I need to see you as soon as possible. I 'ave a proposition which I think will 'elp us both. Can I come over now? Good. I'll be there in ten minutes. Oh, please don't say anything about this to anyone — not even Ryan, at least until I 'ave seen you. Thanks." As he put the phone down, Santana felt drained but also vastly relieved.

At the same moment, Connolly was very surprised by the call from the leader of the Sansor-JD team. He had heard occasional rumours about 'questionable preparation' on the part of the Spaniard but he had always made it a rule never to believe anything without absolute proof. Nevertheless the phone call itself was strange and why all the cloak-and-dagger stuff? As with the vast majority of riders in the professional peloton, Connolly had enjoyed a reasonably friendly relationship with Santana without ever being particularly friendly. A good rider who was probably a bit past his best, would have been Bruce's assessment of him, had he been asked, but as he thought, he realised that Santana was the same age as himself. While waiting for his visitor, he made a phone call to New York.

"Hi, Mary, it's Bruce, look I can't chat now, but can you find out all you can about Ercole Santana for me. I'll call again tomorrow and explain then. Thanks, bye."

Santana arrived a few minutes later. While settling him in, Connolly took the opportunity to unobtrusively study the undeniably handsome Sansor leader. He certainly looked older than his years but that might have been because of the stress he was all too clearly under. Tall for a cyclist at 6' 2'', Bruce could see why Ercole had never lacked for women. Long black hair, a pencil moustache and slightly darker skin than Connolly's did nothing to minimize his Latin origins. He was dressed in a pair of dark blue mohair trousers, a T-shirt and a cream-coloured jacket which should have clashed but somehow didn't. It had been some time since Bruce had been close to the Spaniard for more than a few seconds but now it was certainly the case that the man didn't ooze joi-de-vivre. Under the suntan, his face was strained and his body language betrayed the fact that he was tense and nervous. Connolly was impatient to discover the reason for this very unusual visit but he spent some time trying to put the visitor at his ease. Santana obviously had something important to tell him but Bruce sensed that he could easily be frightened off. With big sigh Santana eventually began.

"I'm not sure where to start but I need time to explain everything."

"Tomorrow's stage is short so we've a fairly late start Ercole and we have a few hours before bed so take your time."

"I'll start at the end and work backwards." This is going to be good, Connolly thought to himself. However, Santana's next words came as a complete surprise.

"Bruce, I need a job on your team." Connolly couldn't hide his surprise.

"You, but I thought…"

"Let me explain everything first, then you can ask me as many questions as you like." Connolly nodded assent. "I need a job with another team and it 'as to be your team. I need to be able to explain everything and feel confident that it will go no further. I will ride for the prize money only and do whatever you ask. I am in big trouble and it is no exaggeration to say that my life is at stake. 'Owever I'm not the only one in danger. I know a lot about the cause of the problems you 'ave been 'aving, in fact to my shame, I've been involved in the whole awful business for some time. I can 'elp you get the rotten business finished with and the bastards be'ind it all in jail where they belong, 'opefully for a very long time. Before I continue I need to know whether or not I'm wasting my time." Connolly pursed his lips.

"Well I'll need to know a lot more than you have told me but before we go any further there is one big question I have to ask." The Spaniard interrupted.

"I can guess what it is and the answer is," he hesitated, "yes, I have done drugs in some events for some time, but I swear I'll kick it."

"Sorry, Ercole, no deal. Whatever mess you're into, there's no way anybody riding for me isn't one hundred percent clean. Sorry." Anguish filled the handsome face.

"Bruce, I need protection. Viclat is going to push me if I don't jump first and once out of the big races I'm a dead man. You 'ave go' to 'elp me. You might be 'ard but you are straight, everybody knows that. If you can't help me, I don't think anybody can. Bruce, I'm begging you." Connolly knew enough about the tall Spaniard to have some idea how much this pleading must have been costing Santana as far as his pride was concerned. This must be something really serious.

"Look, I'm not promising anything but you'd better tell me everything and then, maybe, just maybe, we can work something out. It won't include riding for me though, at least not until we know you're clean." Santana nodded the relief, even with Bruce's provisos, making it impossible to speak. After Bruce had made both of them a coffee, Santana told Bruce all he knew, his involvement with drugs, his part in the recent operations and as far as he knew them, the names of the other people involved. He made it clear to Bruce that he didn't know who the top man or men were. Nevertheless, it was the breakthrough Bruce had prayed for. Connolly looked at the notes he had been taking.

"What about the shooting?"

"Nothing to do with the operation I am sure. The guy I work for, the one I call Sad Sam, 'e said 'is boss was furious about it because it would bring in the police and make everybody even more careful."

"Hmm, we guessed as much, well some of us did anyway. So I can blame you for my accidents eh, Ercole? I could have been killed. You cost me a lot of good results, not to mention a fair bit of loot. The same applies to my teammates. Can you give me one good reason why I shouldn't hand you over to the police?"

Santana groaned inwardly as he realised that he had been counting his chickens much too soon. He shook his head and almost whispered, "No I cannot."

Connolly let the silence hang in the air. He thought about his own situation and that of this devastated man in front of him. There but for the grace of God... He had never thought of himself as being soft but he knew that Santana was not only a pawn in all this, but also that Bruce now owed him something, something that may well turn out to be a great deal. After what seemed an eternity to the Spanish rider Connolly spoke.

"That answer was the only one that was going to do you any good, Ercole." He now smiled and Santana began to let a ray of hope grow again.

"I think we can probably sort something out but I'll have to talk all this through with a few people. You'll have to trust me on that. We shall have to be very careful. Were you followed here?"

"I'm certain I wasn't. Sad Sam was sure 'e 'ad frightened me too much. To be sure though, I doubled back on myself several times on the way here."

"One more question. I'm fairly certain that there's a mole in my team, presumably put there by your bosses. Can you confirm that and if so what do you know about him or her?"

"You're right, there is. I don't know who it is but I do know it isn't a rider and I've no idea whether it's male or female."

"It's good they're not a rider. Okay, this is how we'll play it. Finish the Tour. I'll get my lads to help you as well as they can for the rest of it, bearing in mind our priority is to win the thing." He grinned. "Carry out your planned activity tomorrow, we'll make sure the bad guys don't realise that we're onto it but we'll make sure we don't get hurt. Don't take a charge, we'll nurse you through. I mean that I have my own testing procedure and my doctor will test you after each of the last three stages. If you think I don't trust you, that's too bad. Then just before the World Championships resign from Sansor-JD and we'll get you away to straighten yourself out before anybody knows you're gone. Next season you can ride for us legit with a proper decent contract. It won't pay as much as you've been getting. But I guess that won't be too big a deal for you to cope with." He grinned again.

Santana's relief and gratitude made it impossible for him to speak and after a while he left in a taxi feeling, if not exactly happy, at least more at peace than he had for many months. Bruce took some time to digest everything that Santana had told him. Having more or less decided what to do, he rang John Ryan to arrange a quick get-together of the team in the hotel lounge in half-an-hours' time. He then spent that half an hour talking on the phone to Sarah.

On the other side of town, Sad Sam, whose real name had disappeared long ago under a mass of aliases was detailing his conversation with Santana to Matthews.

"Okay, so he's shit scared of you but all we need to know at this moment is whether or not he can be trusted tomorrow?"

"You're the boss, you tell me." Matthews sighed heavily, not for the first time in his dealings with this unwanted but vitally necessary associate and spoke to him as if he was a child.

"In your opinion from your meeting tonight, can he be trusted for tomorrow?"

"I guess so." Matthew didn't like 'guesses' but he realised that that was the best he was going to get.

CHAPTER TWENTY-SEVEN

The atmosphere was exactly as she remembered, and yet, in some indefinable way, much more so. Her father's interest in cycling, both as a sport and as part of his business dealings, had meant frequent and sometimes quite extended trips to those continental countries where cycling was one of, if not the, most popular sports, Belgium, Italy, Holland and of course France. Sarah supposed that she must have been to all of the classic races but it was always 'Le Tour' which she remembered as being the most exciting and the source of her most vivid memories. She would always remember, even though only a toddler, her father's grief when the enormously brave Tom Simpson died while trying his heart out, literally as it happened, to win the Tour. The first Englishman to wear the Yellow jersey, his death affected her father deeply. Her clearest memories as a little girl were of the dominance in the eighties of French cyclists, in particular the hugely talented and some would say the equally arrogant Bernard Hinault, but France also had Laurent Fignon, Charlie Mottet and Jean-Francois Bernard among others to cheer. Not since the golden age of French cycling with Jaques Anquetil, Louison Bobet and Raphael Geminiani had France had so much success. Sarah regretted never having witnessed the dominance of the greatest ever cyclist, Eddy Merckx, or the grace and beauty of the Italian idol Felice Gimondi, but she lost touch with the world of cycling after the Hinault and Lemond years, before being attracted back by the group with whom she was now working.

The Tour had always been larger than life, had held enormous interest for her and appealed to that side of her nature which was attracted by sporting success achieved by commitment and determination rather than simply by natural ability. Millions of people throughout the world ride bikes, a fairly small percentage of them quite quickly. Many top sportsmen from all types of sport could probably do quite well in some cycling events, but only a miniscule percentage would ever gain selection for, let alone finish the three and a half thousand kilometre epic that is the Tour de France.

Sarah now delighted in the sights, sounds and aromas of the Tour. That Bruce was now leading the Tour and should win it unless disaster befell him in the few remaining stages, certainly added spice to the experience. Of course the shooting incident and his narrow escape had alarmed her and she could never quite rid her mind of the fear of further trouble. Nevertheless, the spectacle of the Tour, the colours of the bikes and the jerseys and shorts (and/or skinsuits), the noise and bustle prior to the start of each day's stage all combined to weave a cocoon of excitement around her. All the riders were now being introduced to the huge crowd at the daily signing-in and it was now Bruce's turn for the big build-up, resplendent in the maillot jaune. He had already kissed her goodbye for the day but now caught her eye and held for a few seconds. They still felt it prudent not to advertise a relationship which had by now progressed well beyond the stage reached by either in relationships for many years.

Connolly certainly had an aura about him. It was obvious that the riders had considerable respect for him and not a few, genuine liking, in spite of his sometimes brusque and taciturn manner. As the wearer of the yellow jersey, he was the target for all the riders aspiring to victory but as each day passed with him in possession of the 'golden fleece', his quiet confidence seemed to grow. Now it seemed that it belonged to him. When talking to Sarah each night on the phone he had always been circumspect and had never anticipated easy days or overall victory in advance. Everyone could remember that in the closest ever Tour finish Greg Lemond had wrested victory from Laurent Fignon in the final day's time trial by the almost unbelievably slender margin of eight seconds. Bruce had never been one to count his chickens anyway so he took every day as it came. As the riders moved to the 'Depart' for the day, Sarah made her way to the official car provided by the director of the Tour after lengthy consultations with members of Sarah's group. For the remainder of the day's stage she would only get glimpses of Bruce, yet to be in such an advantageous position made her feel immeasurably more comfortable about his safety than when she was away from races.

The day's stage was a fairly long one of almost 240 kilometres including three big climbs and a number of smaller but still significant ones. Connolly was reasonably confident of victory in Paris if he could withstand all attacks today. After this stage all that remained were flat stages, one of which was a time trial, which of course was one of his strengths. None of the other noted time-triallists were close enough on the general classification to trouble him even if they did manage to put time into him in the time trial. Everything depended on today in the mountains.

The famous publicity caravan of garishly painted vehicles which had left the 'depart' some time before, had taken Sarah back in time and yet the cavalcade was now even more extraordinary than she recalled. There were still the famous 'Michelin Men' riding motorbikes standing up and steering them with their feet or standing on their heads as they rode, but each year there were more and more vehicles advertising more and more products and services. Banking, water, building, carpets, bubble gum, aircraft and everything between seemed to be being carried by vans, lorries, caravans, motorbikes, some vehicles which defied categorisation and floats which could have been mounted on any form of transport. People dressed in all manner of clothing including clown costumes, animal suits, skimpy bikinis and some, amazingly enough, in normal clothing, were distributing hats, catalogues, sweets, magazines, goody-bags and a multitude of other promotional items to the enormous and wildly enthusiastic crowd. All these things added up to what has been described many times as 'the greatest show on earth.'

This particular town which had hosted the start or finish of many stages in previous Tours, like every other start or finish town, except for all the various types of catering and service establishments, closed down for the visit of the Tour. France without the Tour was unthinkable. Sarah, as English as it was possible to be, was, as in the past, entranced, transfixed and enraptured by the whole thing. That the Tour had become a commercial as much as a sporting affair, bothered her not at all. In this day and age one could not have one without the other. It was no more commercial than the Olympic Games and in her eyes at least, much more honest about its commercial necessity. One other huge difference was that at the Tour, no one paid to watch. The humour and gaiety which accompanied the Tour was infectious. Everywhere she looked, except perhaps in the faces of many of the riders, Sarah saw delight, excitement, eager anticipation and sheer joy in the eyes simply at being there. Her heart was already light and now as the stage began it lifted even higher. 'Thank you Lord', Sarah prayed, 'for allowing me to be here.'

By taking a number of shortcuts, Sarah's driver reached a point on the route of the stage just before the publicity caravan passed by. They waited as the vibrantly coloured cavalcade went past, taking some while to do so. This was followed some minutes later by the first of the motorcycle outriders, then, various official cars followed before the peloton came into view. Bruce was somewhere in the first twenty or so riders surrounded by some of his Brooklin team-mates, looking comfortable as the complete peloton swept past in a prolonged burst of colour, a whirring of wheels and a humming of tyres. Of the two hundred plus riders who had started the Tour almost three weeks earlier, less than a hundred and forty remained, the very high temperatures and high humidity having eliminated more riders from this year's race than in most recent tours. Those critics who had been talking of the Tour having gone soft in recent times had been silenced this year.

There were many tired legs and bodies in the peloton. Every rider was well aware that with only two flat stages and a flattish time trial, today was the last real chance anyone had of usurping Bruce Connolly's leadership. Today's stage had been recognised from the unveiling of the Tour route the previous October, as the 'queen' stage. Two second category climbs were now just ahead of the peloton followed after twenty kilometres by a first category climb immediately followed by a technical descent and a 'hors' category mountain. A long descent preceded the last climb of the day another of 'hors' category severity. With just one flat kilometre after the summit to the finish there would be no time to recover time lost on the mountain in that final kilometre.

At the signing on, Connolly had looked composed as well as fit and strong, but neither he nor his closest challengers thought that the Tour was his quite yet. Before the start some of the Tour's past champions had been presented to the crowd. Five times winners Eddy Merckx, Bernard Hinault and Miguel Indurain, seven times winner Lance Armstrong, a very elegant and still handsome Felice Gimondi, winner at his first attempt in 1965. Frederico Bahamontes, 'The Eagle of Toledo', winner once but King of the Mountains six times and one non-winner, 'The Eternal second', Raymond Poulidor in spite of never winning the Tour, possibly France's favourite cyclist, were also present. All these celebrities made efforts to talk to their successors and it was obvious that they had a high regard for many of the present peloton including Andrews, Miguel Velasquez, Antoine Delacroix, Powell, Santana, Vacchio and Connolly. For the riders, however, this little bit of public relations was something they would gladly have done without and it was with considerable relief that the riders eventually rode away. Since the shooting incident security had been significantly increased but once on the road worries of that nature, amongst the riders at least, were forgotten. Everyone seemed to sense that today's stage would be special.

In brilliant sunshine the riders rode over the two second category climbs with relative ease, although the sprinters were shelled out the back but not by very much and managed to regain the peloton on the second descent. Two lowly placed domestiques attacked on the second descent but the bunch let them go reasoning, accurately, that they would be picked up again on the climb of the Telegraphe, the first category mountain. The Brooklin riders were very vigilant although very tired. Ryan's team briefing that morning had formulated a no-risk policy for the day, the objective being to merely counter any attacks that looked dangerous. However, the day was made for heroic deeds and three of the actors in this day's play decided that it was their day to take centre stage. Thus it was that this, the eighteen stage of the Tour would be one of those stages which would be talked about ever after.

With everything to lose and nothing to gain by attacking, Bruce Connolly nevertheless decided that the best form of defence was attack. As this was completely opposite to the day's plan he went to the team car to explain his thinking to Ryan. This done he had a quiet word with a few members of his team.

A few minutes later, at the foot of the Forclaz climb, he nodded to Pete Weiss the teammate nearest to him. Surprise showed briefly in Weiss's face. "Already?" he silently mouthed, raising his eyebrows at the same time. Connolly just grinned and began to slowly make his way to the front of the peloton. The yellow jersey is always a marked man and as Bruce moved through the peloton, the riders in the teams of his closest challengers moved with him. However, once Connolly got to the front, he merely stayed there with Weiss at his side. The bunch relaxed again, their thinking clearly being 'No way is Connolly stupid enough to attack so far from the finish with all the big climbs to come. He's obviously gone to the front just to keep out of trouble.' It was certainly cycling folklore that crashes tend to happen at the back end rather than the front end of a peloton. Bruce moved slightly closer to Pete. As Connolly rode along he pointed to things by the roadside as if discussing the scenery.

"Get Joe and Sean up here as unobtrusively as you can. When you're all here, one of you follow me while the other two block. Keep the others in reserve." Weiss nodded and slowly slipped back through the bunch. Equally slowly Weiss collected his reinforcements who one by one rode up to be fairly close to their leader. By the time the Brooklin foursome was in place, about two thirds of the Forclaz had been climbed. Sure of his tactics, with a clear idea of just what was left in the stage and feeling confident, Connolly launched his attack. Very reminiscent of Pedro Delgado's blistering attacks in the 1987 and '88 Tours and those of Lance Armstrong, Connolly's effort left everyone but Weiss stranded. Connolly pounded up the climb with Weiss being very hard-pressed to keep up with his leader. Back in the bunch chaos reigned. Initially indecision prevented the organisation of any chase and the two Brooklin riders at the front of the peloton slowed things down as much as they could. By the top of the Forclaz the escapees had over a minute's lead and were still going away.

Eventually Adam Padston of Roger Powell's PDZ-Light team, Miguel Velasquez, team captain of Giuseppi Vacchio's Bianchi-Jerez team, Amoroso Sarro, Vacchio and Powell launched a counterattack. To protect Connolly's interest Jean-Luc Bernhardt and Sean Brean latched onto the group. They would not work to bring the other two back, everyone knew that. They were only there to help Connolly if the escape was caught. Both Vacchio and Powell were worried. This wasn't supposed to happen for God's sake! They were supposed to be attacking the yellow jersey, not the other way around!

At that moment the second player to seize his moment, caught up with the pursuing group. Antoine Delacroix, leader of the Citrive-Minerva team, one of a number of older riders in the twilight of their careers, 'made the difference'. He pulled himself up to Powell's group and then after a brief respite, stamped on his pedals and accelerated away from the group like a man possessed. Rapid though the progress of the Brooklin duo undoubtedly was, Delacroix made them look almost pedestrian as he swept by the spectators lining the climb of the Telegraphe, they stood awed by his speed. Days which the fans of Delacroix remembered from some time back, sprang back suddenly to the forefront of their minds as the tall blonde Frenchman powered along.

Up ahead, Connolly and Weiss, themselves still riding powerfully learnt of the Frenchman's progress from Dragonard and Ryan in the Brooklin car.

"He will catch you just after you cross the summit of the Telegraphe at his current rate. It makes sense for you to let him get up to you as long as you don't slow down and then try and ride to the finish as a three-up. An extra man up the two hors cats has got to be worth having, added to which he's no threat on general classification." The advice made sense so without slowing appreciably Bruce and Pete didn't resist being caught. By the time Delacroix had caught them their gap back to the chasers had grown to almost four minutes. Truth to tell, Pete was glad of the slight easing of the pace and he could clearly see that the arrival of the Frenchman was of considerable benefit. Three of them stood a better chance of staying away than two. For his part Bruce cared little one way or the other. The form of Delacroix was something of a surprise but his own form was holding up very well and so it appeared, was that of Pete. As he saw it, only mechanical trouble or a crash could deny him a result today. The time gap ought to be enough for them to stay away and first, second or third would give him a time bonus too. That should put the Tour out of reach of his rivals. He smiled inwardly, revelling in his own physical power and in the enjoyment that that power was bringing.

Back in the chasing group, Powell, Vacchio and their respective teammates could now only hope was that Connolly would tire, not unreasonable in the circumstances, but hardly a proactive approach. They were pushing as hard as they knew how but the trio ahead was still increasing its lead. A time-check from a motorcycle outrider confirmed their fears as they descended the Telegraphe. The lead was now at five and a half minutes.

As there are the favoured few in the peloton who are awesome sprinters, and another equally small band who are exceptional climbers, so there probably an even smaller numbers of riders whose descending ability is simply staggering. Adam Padston was one such demon descender. He was the third rider to seize the moment and with an apparent complete absence of fear he dropped like a stone down the descent full of hairpins and potentially murderous precipices as if on rails. The third actor to take centre stage had made his move. Padston, another rider who thus far had had a quiet Tour, saw this as his chance to shine. Although in the same team as Roger Powell, his status was such that he was not under strict team orders to only help his fellow Englishman. He had therefore moved up to Roger a few moments before and let him know his feelings.

"I feel like having a dig, Rog, O.K?"

"Sure."

Roger's answer was instant. He had nothing to lose anyway and since he didn't have any spare energy with which to accelerate, there would be no means of attacking Connolly even if he caught him. Padston was also a very good time-triallist, another ex-National time trial champion in England and his considerable skill against the watch now came to his aid. It is always against the odds for a single rider, irrespective of his ability, to catch three riders sharing the workload and themselves trying hard. But on this extraordinary day, that is exactly what Padston did in the next twenty-five minutes. He joined the other three as they reached the bottom of the mighty Galibier climb. This year, the top of this truly iconic mountain effectively marked the end of the day's stage, the finish being less than two kilometres beyond the summit. There was now enacted one of those sporting sagas which live for years in the memories of all who witness it and for ever in the memories of those who were the actors in the truly heroic exploit.

By the time a third of the climb had been covered, the fearsome pace of the quartet had made the efforts of the chasers mere token gestures. They were now over seven minutes down and the remnants of the peloton another seven minutes behind the chasing group. Behind the peloton there were riders all over the road, some an hour behind the leaders. There was no doubt already that there were going to be many riders outside the time limit for the day and would thus be eliminated from the Tour.

At the front, the four worked as a four-up team time trial, each taking a turn at the front, swinging off and being replaced by another. Very common on flat stages and relatively easy to do, it was much more difficult to do when climbing as few riders share the same climbing style, cadence and pace. Nevertheless, these four made it seem easy. For the moment, that they were from three different teams was forgotten. The common aim was to put as much time between themselves and their pursuers. Halfway up the climb, the four became three. Inevitably, Weiss signalled to Connolly that he was spent and he slipped out of the back. All he could do now was wait to be caught by the chasers, try to recover a little whilst doing so and then try and keep with them to the finish. The demise of Weiss encouraged Delacroix and Padston of course and Connolly sensing this, pushed the pedals a little bit harder and daylight opened up between the American and the other two. With total concentration they inexorably closed the gap until the status quo was restored.

Back in the chasing bunch, Powell and Vacchio were desperately trying to limit their losses and keep their positions on the overall leader board. At the beginning of the day, both Delacroix and Padston were outside the top ten and seemingly out of contention. They were both more than ten minutes behind the young Italian and nine minutes down on Powell in third. The riders between Powell and Delacroix in eleventh place were well out of the picture and had not succeeded in making it across to the chasing group. Unless Roger and Giuseppi recovered some of current time gap, they would slip to fourth and fifth and off the podium.

As for the three leaders, their thinking now began to change. They were now aware that they were not going to be caught and would finish well ahead of the rest. The only thought on their minds was winning the day's stage. The yellow jersey was now Bruce's. The other two, although knowing that getting on the podium in Paris was now a distinct possibility didn't know exactly the present time gap and weren't worrying about it. Connolly's last effort when Weiss had dropped back, had taken its toll. With five kilometres to go Padston tried to break the other two. Connolly couldn't instantly respond and neither could the Frenchman. Adam had a thirty metre lead before Connolly found something to respond with and he began to claw back his quarry. Delacroix, also finding some energy from somewhere, came up to and then slowly passed Bruce. Turn and turn about the duo slowly caught up with the Englishman. It was now inevitable that that the three would need to "ride to recover" for a few minutes. It was now a case of whoever recovered quickest being the winner. With now only a kilometre to the summit, therefore less than three from the finish, the crowds were immense and cheering madly. All cycling fans love to see the yellow jersey attacking and whatever happened at the finish Connolly had made many fans by not sitting and defending but illustrating that the best form of defence was attack. It had been a long while since the fans had seen this. Many recent Tours had been won by virtue of dominant time-trialling backed up by more than adequate, but still defensive performances in the mountains. Here the American was showing everybody how it should be done and the crowd was loving him for it.

Naturally enough, the French fans being in the majority, lining the route in their tens of thousands were shouting for Delacroix, but this performance by le maillot jaune was a la' Coppi, Merckx and Hinault.

Connolly desperately tired after being in the break for so long wondered for the umpteenth time how tired the other two were. Antoine had been with him longer but he hadn't had such a hard chase as Adam. All three knew that Connolly was the best sprinter and Bruce knew therefore that one of the others would almost certainly go for a long one just before the summit. With less than half a kilometre of the climb left it was Padston who made the move. The gradient here was relatively benign and Padston went down the inside of the other two just as Connolly moved alongside Delacroix. As both the American and the Frenchman hesitated Padston gained ten then twenty, then thirty bike lengths. Connolly heaved himself out of the saddle and went after the Englishman, Delacroix followed. As Padston went under the red kite he had five seconds on the others. He desperately looked back and saw that although he had the lead he knew it wasn't enough. He visibly sagged back onto his saddle bowing to the inevitable, utterly spent. As the other two passed him, not yet sprinting but going fast enough to make him look as if he was standing still, Connolly managed the smallest of commiserating smiles. Padston had ridden magnificently. Now there was half a kilometre to the line. The longer Bruce left the sprint, the better his chances. Connolly now feeling confident waited for the jump from Antoine. When it came he was ready. The surge from Delacroix took him six or seven metres ahead of the American before Bruce, changing up a gear, got into his stride. The gap became five, then three, now one metre, and then Connolly was in front! Bang! The puncture was instant. Fifty metres from the line and suddenly Connolly felt like he was riding in sand. The American watched helplessly as Delacroix rode away from him as if turbo-powered. Connolly swore and thumped the handlebars in frustration. As he crossed the line barely moving, he was caught by

Ryan, Sarah, a couple of mechanics and seemingly several million other people with overwhelming enthusiasm.

"You've lost the stage, Bruce, but won the Tour with the greatest ride I and lots of other people have ever seen. It was truly awesome!" Ryan had tears in his eyes as he spoke.

"That was nothing short of magnificent, Bruce, you were absolutely wonderful." Sarah kissed him as she spoke, oblivious of the sweat, the dirt and the salt-rimmed eyes of her lover. Connolly, still amid much back-slapping and surrounded as always at such moments by journalists thrusting microphones in his face, now found himself face-to-face with the smiling Delacroix.

"Ma foi, my fren', what a ride! That was terrible bad luck but I'm not complaining. I would 'ave won anyway, No?" Both riders knew very well, as did the crowd who would have won but for the puncture. Connolly good-naturedly punched the Frenchman on the arm.

"No, yes, who cares, you deserved the stage, congratulations."

"And to you, my fren', you 'ave surely won le Tour today."

"I sure hope so, I'm beat." Connolly realised that although he had really wanted to win the stage, his prize was much the greater one and he had, indeed, put the Tour well beyond the reach of anyone else. An epic ride indeed, probably, no certainly, his best ever ride. As he took liberal gulps of mineral water he saw a somewhat dejected Adam Padston finish the stage. He had lost almost a minute on the other two but still many minutes ahead of the chasers who were still to reach the summit of the Galibier. Connolly walked over to the Englishman.

"That was a hell of a ride, Adam, you've done yourself a heap of good today, the rest are still nowhere." Padston looked slightly surprised and raised his eyebrows questioningly.

"Yeah, you and Antoine have made the podium by enough to keep you there."

"Really? My earpiece packed up and I didn't really know how much time we had." He brightened considerably.

"Who won? With a ride like that and your sprint, you must've done. You sure deserved to."

"Thanks but I punctured fifty metres from the line just as I'd got past Antoine." Connolly shrugged. "But that's life, I'm sure as hell not complaining." The two shook hands and Bruce then surrendered himself to the reporters, the doping control and the podium presentation.

Two days later, Bruce Connolly safely finished the Tour de France in the middle of the peloton surrounded by his Brooklin teammates in time-honoured fashion, in beautiful weather on surely the best finishing straight in cycling, the Champs Elysees. The last two stages had been largely uneventful but Connolly had duly won the time trial. His winning margin was over thirteen minutes, a huge gap for a modern Grand Tour. The damage done on the Galibier stage had been enormous. The superb rides by Delacroix and Padston, backed up by excellent rides in the time trial, especially by Adam, second to Connolly by less than a minute had indeed brought them onto the podium in second and third respectively. Roger Powell and Giuseppi Vacchio were the big losers, their efforts in trying to limit their losses on the final climb and thereby keep their top three places, had had the opposite effect, both cracking halfway up the Galibier. Both had lost almost fifteen minutes on the day and they only just kept in the top ten, Roger ninth, Giuseppi tenth. What they had learned would stand them in good stead in the future, however. Thirty-one riders had been outside the time limit and should have been eliminated but they were reinstated due to the extraordinary nature of the stage and the very high speed of the winning trio. Connolly had not only won the Tour but had also taken the polka dot jersey of the King of the Mountains. His ride would pass into the annals of cycling lore as one of the greatest ever Tour rides.

CHAPTER TWENTY-EIGHT

She looked at his hands. The hands of the winner of the Tour de France! She was being caressed by the hands of the yellow jersey winner. It sounded impressive. How she loved those hands! Strong and big and so accomplished. Why she wondered, had so few of her other lovers discovered how much she had been aroused by caresses? Most women enjoy being caressed but with her it was much more than that. It was virtually a prerequisite for sexual gratification as far as she was concerned. She couldn't remember ever having climaxed properly without first being massaged, stroked or caressed at some length. Now her whole body tingled with anticipation. She was lying face downwards as those lovely hands alternately squeezed then rubbed her bottom, then very gently moved up to caress the whole of her back and then moving back down again to her behind.

He was astride her and as he reached forward to rub her shoulders she could feel his erect penis rubbing up and down the cleavage between her buttocks. For some minutes now she had felt the delicious damp feeling between her thighs but she knew better than to rush him for both their sakes. He possessed excellent self-control and he knew exactly what to do and when to do it to get the most out of sex for them both. He continued this alternating process for several more blissful minutes, her excitement gradually mounting exquisitely. He now moved back a little and then slid his hands down her sides and onto her hips, lifting her very gently as he did so. Responding to his unspoken suggestion she raised her bottom and he was thus able to slide into her very easily but powerfully. Prolonged caressing followed by instant and full entry never failed to bring her to an almost immediate orgasm. As he held himself absolutely still inside her, she let herself go and in seconds he felt her climax and open inside, her juices covering his erection as she cried and almost whimpered in ecstasy. After a few moments with him still firmly up inside her, she fell forward and then rolled over onto her back.

She was full-breasted and had the largest nipples he had ever seen. Especially exciting for him was that her nipples were dark for a woman who had not yet born children. He now moved forward still straddling her, cupping her breasts and then pushing his still glistening penis between them. With a gentle circling motion he rubbed her breasts whilst moving his tool up and down her cleavage. In spite of his excellent control he had now been erect for a long time and she could feel him begin to tense. She could feel the hardness of his balls as he slid up and down and she tried to divine what he would enjoy the most. She raised her head ready to take his glans in her mouth but he shook his head. Stopping his movement apart from still caressing her breasts, he now took her nipples in his mouth in turn and sucked on then hard. She gasped in a mixture of pleasure and pain then felt him turn her half over until she was lying on her side. He had by now moved to be lying behind her and she lifted her right leg, completely exposing her fully open vagina. He now thrust himself into her again as hard as he could. When she was as open and aroused as she was now, entering her this way gave her the greatest fulfilment. Not on the back row in the penis department, very near the front in fact, he was nevertheless taken quite easily by her in any position when she was like this. Lying like this, he felt bigger and particularly thicker than in any other position. Reaching for her clitoris he now began to stimulate it while moving in and out of her at a gradually increasing tempo. After only a few seconds she was murmuring, sighing and making little incoherent noises one moment and speaking lustfully the next.

"God you feel enormous tonight." Her words were thick with desire.

"You are so beautifully open I thought you might not be able to feel me as much as usual."

She shook her head. As he spoke he thrust a little harder and she groaned again. She pulled her knees up a little higher in response to his harder thrusts and as she did so he moved his hand up to her right breast and strummed her nipple. She began to gyrate her behind as he moved in and out of her at different angles with each stroke.

"Oh my God that is sooo good, please don't come yet, I want you to keep going like that forever. I love having your huge cock up me this way. When I'm really ready, I'll get on all fours and you can take me like the fucking horse you are."

Controlling himself with considerable effort, her crude words inflaming him even more, he thought of anything other than what he was doing, to try and stem the tide of his climax. He made sure he didn't look at her superb bottom as he continued to pound in and out of her until she moved to get on her hands and knees. Slipping out of her momentarily helped to stave off his ejaculation and she now presented the most erotic sight imaginable. With her voluptuous breasts hanging down, her nipples erect, her behind raised slightly with her legs parted to reveal her vagina and erect clitoris, she looked magnificent. She moaned again as he entered her and after only a few very powerful thrusts, accompanied by explicit language from both of them, they came virtually simultaneously, their mutual sense of release intense. He spurted again and again into her as she used her vaginal muscles to grip and then release his penis as he kept ejaculating until they were both utterly spent. They collapsed on the bed and fell asleep.

Their sleep was, however, brief. The earlier prolonged foreplay had built up their desire to such heights that their orgasms, superb as they had been, had only temporarily assuaged their desire. He woke first and his penis began to harden, lengthen and thicken immediately. As if by telepathy, she too began to stir and instinctively she moved her body towards his. In a state of virtual somnambulance she reached down and took hold of tool and began to gently pull it up and down. This, of course, quickly completed the erection process. By opening her legs and easing him between them she now began to use his completely rigid member as a dildo to stimulate her clitoris. From a previous lovemaking session they both knew that prolonging this particular activity heightened the ultimate pleasure considerably. She was now aching for him to enter her as he was similarly desperate to quench the desire manifesting itself in his raging hard-on. Yet both continued with this almost painful pleasure, moaning softly and talking lewdly to each other all the time. In addition to pleasuring herself, from time to time she would gently rake the underside of his member, starting with his balls, moving up to the root of his penis and then continuing up his considerable length, delaying at his glans and rubbing the frenum until now plum-coloured knob was swollen and throbbing almost unbearably.

It couldn't last. When she felt that she couldn't wait another second, she whispered, "Now?" He gave a gasping assent. He took a very firm hold of her breasts, now feeling beautifully heavy and pendulous, his left hand under her left arm and she opened herself up with one hand and placed his tool at her glistening opening. The moment he felt himself there he pushed himself into her with all his strength. She grunted with satisfaction and he, with almost frenzied intensity thrust in and out as she sighed her pleasure at every stroke. His tool felt as if it was going in and out of a pot of melted butter only better. He had never experienced sex anything like as marvellous as with this woman. Their second climax came very swiftly and it was as glorious as the first. Her climax crested over her, building sublimely and he was not far behind. She was crying, "Yes, yes do me, harder, fuck me, oh keep fucking me, yes, yes, yes!" She screamed in ecstasy and with a roar he shot off into her. Her orgasm seemed to take a long time to subside and then she cuddled against him and they both fell into a long deep sleep.

It was dark by the time that Connolly stirred. Lying looking at Sarah still asleep, the rightness of her for him struck him so forcefully that he wondered why he had not realised it with such certainty before. Their relationship had been developing in spite of the various problems and Sarah's imperturbability in the face of the difficulties plaguing Bruce, had impressed him enormously. He had never had much time for histrionics and he had always highly valued what he called sensible courage. Sarah appeared to have plenty of it. Their blissfully exciting sexual compatibility had been very evident from the start and their subsequent lovemaking had just got better and better.

Only the somewhat dangerous situation in which he still found himself was holding him back from asking her to marry him. Was he risking losing her if he didn't soon make his intentions known to her? They hadn't known each other very long it was true but he had already worked out that Sarah was someone would not be messed about with. Was there any way in which in which he could assure her of his ultimate aspirations without making promises which he could not be sure he could keep? She was such a wonderfully suitable mate and so lovely that he must not lose her. In all his thoughts of the future now, she was automatically there. Some of his ideas may not be to her liking of course but nothing entered his head without Sarah figuring very largely in it.

He suddenly realised how thirsty he was. He knew that Sarah would also be ready for a drink when she woke up. He carefully slipped out of bed and switched on the kettle. He could have called Room Service but decided that he would let Sarah sleep for as long as possible. As quietly as he could he made some tea and took the cups back to the bedroom. As he put a cup on the bedside unit, Sarah stirred. She sat up and smiled dreamily at Connolly.

"Thank you." She took hold of Bruce's hand and then suddenly giggled. Oh how he loved that sound!

"What was that for?"

"I was just thinking, looking at you in your birthday suit, what an enormous contrast there is between an aroused man and one for whom sex is the furthest thing from his mind." She giggled again. "In your yellow jersey, which I have to say suits you to a 't', you look magnificent. But now in the nude I look at your willy and I have to giggle. There it hangs so limp, inoffensive and almost comical, and yet as soon as the merest suggestion of anything sexual enters your consciousness, it rears up, becomes so much bigger, so much harder and so impressive, that it's not in the least bit comical. It is fascinating and so horny to watch it grow, especially when it's as big as yours." Sarah was smiling broadly now and of course Connolly's tool had been growing as she had been speaking.

"Look at it, just a few words and it comes to attention and look how it sticks up and out. And do you know, it's the strangest thing, but there is a special place where you can put that monster, now that it has woken up completely. It's a tiny cave which also grows in size when it knows the monster is approaching." They were both smiling broadly now and Connolly was experiencing the delightful feeling which accompanies a growing hard-on. Sarah had thrown off the duvet as she had been speaking and was now lying in a blatantly provocative pose with her legs wide open as she idly played with herself. The smile left her face to be replaced by a look of simple intense desire.

"Come on, stud, I need you, now, a quickie, race you."

Connolly, by now full and throbbing, needed no second bidding. He entered her with a rush and neither wanted to wait a second. Sarah climaxed almost immediately and Bruce a split second later both orgasms long and intense. The spontaneity and urgency of their lovemaking more than

275

made up for any lack of perfection. Lying back smiling at Bruce, Sarah hesitated only briefly before plunging into what she knew might ruin everything.

"Bruce, I want to say something which I think must be said sooner or later and unless I miss my guess, which as you now know isn't often, is something you were also thinking about before I just raped you."

"I thought I raped you."

"Foolish boy, you never had a chance. Now, you were I believe, thinking something along the following lines. You are worried that the danger you are still in makes it a little foolish for you to make any commitments. However, if you didn't have to worry about that," she paused, then continued on in a voice, which for all the confidence suggested by the words, was laced by fear, "you would ask me to marry you. You were also thinking that if you didn't say something, you would lose me. Oh ye of little faith." Having got this far, there was no retreat.

"Well, if I am right, as arrogant as I probably sound, don't let anything stop you." She rushed the last sentence and stopped abruptly. For a while there was silence as Connolly drank in the earnestness, the exquisite beauty and the love in the eyes of his object of adoration.

"Not only are you, wonderful and so lovely, you are absolutely priceless." He got off the bed and knelt on the floor.

"Sarah, will you marry me?"

Sarah giggled again as relief and joy flowed through her.

"Of course, of course, of course!"

The kiss that followed was long and infinitely tender. The tea had long since gone cold.

CHAPTER TWENTY-NINE

Giuseppi Vacchio had never had much trouble attracting the opposite sex. Ever since he could remember, girls had seemed to want to be in his company. For his part he had always been equally happy to spend time with them. He had always been fortunate in that all his relationships had been exactly as he had wanted them to be. There had been a few girls who had meant quite a lot to him and others who had meant very little at all. As yet, however, there had been no one whom he had felt himself to be in love with, whatever that feeling was supposed to be like. As far as he could judge, the girls had felt more or less the same and there had never been any of the 'famous final scene' situations where profuse amounts of tears tend to flow.

As he had gained some success in cycling and had become increasingly well-known, his status had grown and his appeal had similarly increased. Not for the first time did he reflect that everything in his garden was growing very nicely. Already in his first season as an elite rider, he was being hailed by some as the new 'campionissimo', (champion of champions), following in the footsteps of Constante Giradengo, Alfredo Bibda, Gino Bartali, Fausto Coppi and Felice Gimondi. Even Giuseppi knew that such comments were foolish at such an early stage. Nevertheless, he believed that he could perhaps emulate later Italian 'greats such as Mario Cipollini, Paulo Bettini, Gianni Bugno, Francesco Moser, Moreno Argentin and his namesake

Giuseppi Saronni. The intense fanaticism of the Italian tifosi, (Formula 1 motor racing had copied cycling in calling its fans 'tifosi', not the other way round), had often exerted so much pressure on newly emerging talented riders that many potentially great Italians had either tried too hard or buckled under that pressure. The tragic story of Marco Pantani was one such example.

Vacchio was determined that such a fate would not be his. Now as he pedalled smoothly along the roads close to his home in Sienna, his thoughts turned to Ercole Santana. Unconsciously he crossed himself as he prayed that he would never become enmeshed in the world of drugs, blood doping and other illegal 'preparations' and aids. The careers, not to mention the health, of many sportsmen had been ruined by such practices. Santana had been looking to end the same way until in mid-season, he completely unexpectedly changed teams and was now riding for Bruce Connolly's squad Brooklin. Latterly he had been looking fitter and happier. He had gained no placings since joining Brooklin, but that didn't seem to be bothering anybody, least of all Connolly, team manager John Ryan or Santana himself. There was something very unusual about that situation to say the least. Brooklin was famed for its total anti-drugs stance and it had been widely rumoured for a long time that Santana had been very very lucky not to have tested positive. There was also the very unusual, not to say almost unheard of situation of a riding changing teams in mid-season. Very odd indeed, Giuseppi thought to himself. However, the Spaniard appeared to be benefitting from the change and that was good, Vacchio liked Santana.

Mentally shrugging his shoulders, Giuseppi decided it was time he did some real work and concentrated on picking up his pace whilst maintaining perfect balance and control. His cadence and speed increased and it wasn't long before he was travelling at over forty kilometres an hour and feeling really good. A few minutes of all-out effort and then he eased up. Like all racing cyclists Giuseppi knew that one of the secrets of maintaining interest in the decidedly arduous process of training was to ensure lots of variety in it. Unlike many of his contemporaries, however, Vacchio preferred to train alone. The solitude allowed him the luxury of uninterrupted thought during his easy pedalling breaks between the intensive intervals and in this he revelled. As he eased up after his next interval his thoughts returned to Ercole Santana. Perhaps he ought to try and be more supportive of the once highly regarded, new recruit to the Brooklin team. He resolved to try to become closer to Santana before the season ended. Giuseppi's thoughts then returned to girls. The new soigneur in the PDZ-Light team, wow she was gorgeous, built like a dream. He began devising his strategy.

Just over a thousand miles away, Santana was also in the thoughts of Bruce Connolly. Ercole had settled down much more easily with the Brooklin boys than Bruce had expected. Responding well to the welcome of Bruce's teammates and being very grateful for the easing of the tremendous pressure he had been under in the Sansor team, Santana had avoided using any illegal 'help' since joining Brooklin, of this Bruce was certain. This had been easier than Santana might have expected because of the lack of pressure put on him to produce results. He had turned himself into a loyal domestique thus far, doing his work early in a day's race then simply finishing as best he could. What Connolly had also been well aware of was that Santana needed to be kept away from other sorts of temptations in his off-duty time. To this end Connolly had contrived to ensure that Ercole had very little time to himself. Whether Santana was aware of this Connolly neither knew or cared, as far as he was concerned it was absolutely essential. There was also the very real danger to Santana posed by the bad guys. All of these things had greatly reduced Santana's depression and he was now a much happier man than for a very long time. However, it was now time for the Spaniard to pay the piper. Ercole must now be questioned much more fully in order to fill in the gaps in the jigsaw, or at least, some of them. This filling- in had been accelerated by some of the revelations of

Sarah's father when Connolly and Sarah had been to see Curzon a few days earlier. Connolly smiled as he recalled the visit.

Having won the Tour de France, still the major prize in cycling, Connolly was still desperate to win the Rainbow jersey. However, that desire did not prevent him taking a few days off, post-Tour to travel to England. He was very keen to ride there, not only because of his inability to fulfil his commitment to ride the Great Orme time trial earlier in the year, but also because it would enable him to spend a few days at Sarah's home, somewhere he had not yet visited. August was not really the best time to See England, but a relatively wet spring and early summer meant that the grass and trees were still green and fairly lush. Indeed after a very hot and dry Tour, to ride on the still damp roads and feel spray from the puddles on Connolly's feet felt delightful as he trained on the early morning on the quiet Sussex lanes. Rain during the night had left enough residual water on the roads to combine with the brilliant sunshine to produce a continuously dancing shifting mirror in which Connolly could see himself in a thousand different images whenever he chose to look. The lightest of winds was still strong enough to lift the perfume of roses in gardens in pretty villages, abundant in their second flush, and carry it to Bruce's nostrils. This was a lovely companion to the country sights and sounds which pervaded two of his other senses. He had got up at dawn, leaving Sarah fast asleep, and after a breakfast of porridge and kippers (the latter something of an indulgence), had set off for an extended training session during which he would loosen up legs left a little stiff by the thousands of kilometres of the Tour. The traffic was light and the few motorists he did encounter were considerate and Connolly enjoyed himself enormously before returning to the Curzon house a few miles from Lewes.

By this time the temperature had risen considerably and on his arrival he found Sarah in a red, black and white bikini sunbathing by the swimming pool looking stunning. Connolly smiled and blew Sarah a kiss. With no one else at home, Bruce quickly stripped off and dived in to the pool to cool off. After a couple of minutes, Sarah also dived in and swam leisurely over to Connolly. She took hold of his hand and they both swam to a part of the pool where they could stand comfortably on the pool bottom. As they kissed, she gently took hold of his balls with her left hand. His adrenalin already high after his ride, he became rock hard almost instantaneously. They continued to kiss as Bruce first took off her bikini bra and then the bottom half. She, in turn, started to gently massage Bruce's shaft. Letting the water help support her, Sarah raised herself above Bruce and agonizingly slowly yet deliciously impaled herself on him. With one hand caressing her breasts and the other one holding and squeezing her behind, they moved almost in slow motion. Connolly felt himself building and he could tell that Sarah was getting close to her climax too. Inevitably the water ensured that even though their urgency was increasing, every movement was slower than normal. Their orgasms, however, when they came in glorious unison, were no less shattering and as wonderful as ever. They slowly moved to the side of the pool still together, then, as Bruce's erection subsided, they climbed out of the water and lay together on a double-sized lounger. The warmth of the sun, their lovemaking and their sense of peace soon brought sleep to both. Neither had spoken a single word since Connolly's return from his training session.

Two hours later Bruce was shaking hands with Jason Curzon. Sarah had suggested it was time that her father was brought up-to-date with the situation and Connolly's presence in England had provided the perfect opportunity. After the usual pleasantries, Sarah left the men together making noises about meal preparation. All three knew very well that all the necessary preparation had already been done but neither man demurred. Connolly studied the man sitting opposite him over his cherry juice. It had been some time since Bruce had last met Curzon but the man had changed little. He looked almost the archetypal successful businessman but carrying rather less weight. An inch over six feet tall and just below thirteen stone, Curzon didn't look his age, although his hair was mostly white rather than grey and blue eyes still held a twinkle in them.

"Before we get to business there's something I need to ask you."

"I'm pretty sure I know what it is, Bruce, and the answer's yes of course, I'm very pleased."

"Sarah's been talking to you?"

"Not about you two."

"Ah, so that's where she gets it from?"

"You mean knowing what people are going to say?" Connolly smiled and nodded. "She's done it to you then?" Curzon now smiled.

"From the moment we met. She says that it's no big thing and that anyone can do it if they try hard enough, but I can't."

"A case of practice makes perfect I think. Anyway irrespective of all that, may I offer my congratulations?" The two men shook hands both wearing big smiles. "Does anyone else know?"

"Not yet, and that's how we want it to stay for a while please." Curzon nodded.

Sarah had obviously been waiting for the moment and now came in.

"Mr. Connolly has just asked for my permission for you to marry him, well he would have done had I given him the chance. I must say I was greatly flattered that he took the trouble. I didn't think anyone bothered about that kind of thing anymore, especially, with respect, Americans." They all laughed.

"I know I was listening." Sarah replied archly.

"Wicked girl, you're marrying an eavesdropper, Bruce." More smiles.

"Now back to business, what don't I know?"

Wasting few words Bruce quickly related the events of the past few weeks to Curzon. Some of these Sarah had partly explained to Jason but much was completely new to him as well as elaborating on what Sarah had already told him. Silence followed Connolly's explanation but he didn't attempt to break that silence getting up to fetch more drinks leaving Curzon to marshal his thoughts. When Bruce returned Sarah spoke first.

"Well, Dad, what do you think?"

"More than anything, I think that you have both got to be very careful, but of course you both know that. If what you say is right, and there seems to be no reason to doubt you, a dead Bruce Connolly is probably better for these people than a live one. However, as you have said, if that was their prime objective, one would have thought that could have been achieved by now, so presumably there are other, or at least one other, objective. Apart from that, and I presume that this is really what you are asking, I have no idea who could be behind all this," he waved his hands in the air, "whatever 'this' is." Connolly cleared his throat.

"We were rather hoping that you might be able to throw some light on things based on your 'trouble' in the past. I'm sorry if that brings up unpleasant memories." Connolly only just stopped himself adding, 'sir'. Curzon was that sort of man.

"Well my boy". The 'my boy' slipped out before he could stop it.

"Dad!" Sarah scowled after she spoke, and Connolly smiled.

"It's alright, Sarah, I almost called your father 'sir' a few seconds ago." Curzon looked rather shamefacedly at Bruce then at Sarah.

"I'm very sorry, Bruce, but most of the men of your age that I deal with regularly, lack your maturity. I shall make sure that it's Bruce from now on, that is of course, as long as you stick to Jason."

"Deal."

"Anyway, my trouble, as you delicately put it, was never really sorted out. It doesn't bring back bad memories particularly; it's just something that I prefer not to think about. It was all very involved and I was made to pay for some, let's say, bad decisions and rather foolish behaviour. At the moment I can't really see how there could be any connection between your current problems and my past ones. However, I shall look into it. Now if I understand you properly, you both think, believe even, that by some means, something valuable is being smuggled into various countries using major cycling events as a cover. You don't know by whom, or by what means but you think the valuable items are gems. The 'accidents' or whatever you want to call them are arranged to cover the smuggling, but the shooting affair at the Tour was a deliberate attempt on your life and so different to all the other 'happenings' that you think it was unconnected to the other 'accidents'. How'm I doing?"

"Pretty much spot on." Sarah spoke.

"Obviously what we really need to know is how the smuggling is being done and by whom." Curzon pursed his lips.

"I have a few totally trustworthy people who could work on this for you if you'll tell me what you would like done."

"Would it be possible for your people to find out if any large robberies of highly valuable small items, have taken place, say a week or ten days, maybe a fortnight even, before the races in which there was one of the 'arranged accidents'? We can give you the dates of the races in question before we leave."

"Consider it done. I'll put my people on it straightaway. Now I'll be getting back home."

"Aren't you staying to eat with us?" Sarah asked in a surprised voice. The garden of Jason's huge rambling house, far too large for him of course, backed onto Sarah's garden and going home was just a walk across the two gardens.

"No, I have too much to do." He kissed his daughter and Shook Bruce's hand with considerable warmth and took his leave. Earlier he had been sitting on his bedroom balcony enjoying the sunshine when he had seen his daughter and Connolly together. He had gone indoors as soon as things began to get intimate but he knew without doubt that with business over, three would definitely have been a crowd. Anyway, he was telling the truth, he did have a great deal to do and not just the research he had promised to organise for Sarah and Bruce. Curzon had decided that he would carry out his own investigation into this very disturbing business.

For their part Sarah and Bruce were arranging a visit to Sarah's London flat. Bruce and John Ryan had come to the shared conclusion that some active recovery riding after the Tour, as distinct from racing in criteriums, largely for appearance money, was the best preparation for the second half of the season. There was no reason why that riding could not be done in England provided sufficient security was in place.

Also in London, in a Knightsbridge hotel, James Dowling was interviewing Harry Matthews. Dowling smiled at Matthews.

"You did well on the last job, it went like clockwork. Everybody was so fired up by the antics at the front that no one noticed a thing as far as I could tell. Santana played his part faultlessly, so what's he doing with Connolly and the Brooklin squad? It's very puzzling to say the least. Still I'll come back to our Spanish friend in a minute. What have you managed to find out about the shooting?"

"Nothing I'm afraid. The French police have got nowhere so my source can't find out anything from that angle and our own investigations have produced nothing yet." He knew it would be a bad plan to either apologise for the lack of success or say more than was necessary.

"Hmmm. In your opinion, is it something we should be worried about or was the gunman some kind of nutcase with a grudge against Connolly?" Matthews was well aware that this was some kind of test, but for the life of him he couldn't work out Dowling's thoughts on the shooting.

"My first thought was that the guy was just a nutter, as you suggested may be the case, someone with a grudge against Connolly. But the more I thought about it, the more I came to the conclusion that it was too professional for that. So to ignore it is perhaps not the wisest course."

"My thoughts entirely." Matthews heaved an inward sigh of relief. "So do you want me to put some more people onto it or would you rather run with it yourself? There are no more jobs for a while so presumably you'll be less busy." Harry knew better than to contradict Dowling.

"I'll put more time into it myself but another legman would be a help."

"Fine, pick who you want and report back in a week in New York. Now back to Santana. What exactly is the situation with that loser and Brooklin?" Harry was on firmer ground here. Nevertheless he collected his thoughts before replying.

"He's riding for prize money only but as yet has won nothing. Connolly's guys shadow him everywhere and he's never alone, or at least, not as far as my people have seen. The word is he's not taken anything since joining Brooklin, but that was a condition laid down by Connolly. He appears to be riding totally domestique duties and that seems to suit him fine even though he's supposedly getting no pay."

"You say supposedly no pay?"

"Apparently some of the Brooklin guys are sharing some of their winnings when Santana has helped them and Connolly is turning a blind eye."

"Keep a close eye on that Spanish shit. If he talks he could seriously damage us. He's a loose end that needs tying up sooner or later. How come he was let go mid-season anyway?"

"According to the Directeur Sportif, Brooklin made him an offer for Santana he couldn't refuse. He was losing his bottle for our work anyway and wanted out. He would've been unreliable and we have enough other guys wanting to take his place."

"Okay but it seems suspicious that he's ended up with the one team we've been targeting. If he talks we have a problem. Sort it." Dowling looked down at the papers on the table in front of him and Matthews knew that the interview was at an end. He left the suite silently, breathing much more easily than when he had entered it as he closed the door behind him.

CHAPTER THIRTY

Three days later after some careful arranging of training sessions and Sarah's own business interests, Connolly and Sarah finally made it to her flat. As with most people when visiting someone's home for the first time, Connolly looked around him with interest. This first visit to Sarah's apartment, or flat as she called it, had taken some time to come about and he wished that he had been able to visit before. The flat told him a great deal about Sarah and some of this surprised him more than a little. Sarah had already told him that the flat overlooking the Thames was owned by her father, but since his partial withdrawal from some of his business interests he needed to spend little time in London.

"I'm gradually buying it off him but for a price that is much less than it's worth. I love it, it's so convenient for so many things and yet so quiet. Wander around and help yourself to whatever you want, I'm just going to change, then I'll knock up some lunch."

Left to himself, Connolly was now exploring where he could. By comparison to both his house and Sarah's Sussex home, the flat was miniscule and yet it felt good to be there. A lot of use had been made of white walls and mirrors to create illusions of space and yet it was not a case of seeing oneself at every turn. As an architect himself Connolly mentally approved of the interior designer/architect who had been so clever in making such a small property seem so relatively spacious. The first surprise however and by far the biggest, concerned the pictures. Firstly, there seemed to be no pattern or connection between them, even less than with his own. About half were very good quality prints, the other half originals. It was two of the originals which really stunned him. His knowledge of art was certainly not that of an expert but he knew that the two in question were a David Hockney and a Chagall. He couldn't help whistling quietly to himself. However valuable the flat, that value paled into insignificance when compared to the value of the two paintings, assuming of course that they were genuine.

Another original was a Rowland Hilder, also worth a fair bit. The prints included works by Sisley, Klee, Klimt and, perhaps pointing to Curzon's interest in cycling, two by De Vlaeminck. Another surprise awaited him when he looked at the bookshelves. In total contrast to his home, here there was not a non-fiction book in sight. Sarah was clearly a romantic. Russian literature was much in evidence, a copy of everything that Tolstoy had written as well as most of Turgenev, Dostoyoevsky and Solzenitsyn. Thomas Hardy, F. Scott Fitzgerald, Sir Walter Scott and the Bronte sisters rubbed shoulders with many modern authors amongst which were some who were definitely considered rather low-brow. A significant number of these were of a comedic nature. Poetry was much in evidence too, almost exclusively quite old, only Betjeman, Auden and Robert Frost representing reasonably modern poets. To confirm his view that Sarah was no prude, the E.L. James 'Fifty Shades' trilogy, Sexus, Nexus and Plexus by Henry Miller, works by Miller's lover Anais Nin and a complete collection of D.H. Lawrence were next to Victor Hugo and Marcel Proust, as well as a large miscellany of other authors' works.

The furniture was simple, elegant and very comfortable. A grey Borg-covered sofa and armchair, a coffee table, the top of which had been made from a slice of a very large log, beautifully treated and French-polished, and the wall units/bookshelves was the sum total except for the music system and its storage facilities. The carpet was of thick pile of various shades of grey all darker than the sofa and armchair. An effective contrast was achieved through the use of dark red soft furnishings with the wall units of rosewood. As Connolly was looking again at the pictures Sarah came back into the room.

"I've just put the kettle on. You like?" She waved her arm around the room.

"I do like, in fact, I like very much."

Sarah had put on a soft dark red dress with a polo neck and full skirt which matched the décor. She had put a ribbon in her hair and Connolly yet again thought that she was the most beautiful woman he had ever seen.

"Don't you want to kiss me?"

"No." Connolly replied, gently pushing her away from him. "I just want to look at you for a while." The burgeoning pout died on her lips and for an aeon they just looked at each other. It was a moment they were sure they would remember and cherish for the rest of their lives.

"I'll make the tea, or would you prefer coffee?" The spell was broken.

"No, tea will be just fine."

"Right, sit down I'll only be a moment."

Bruce sat down on the sofa which was as comfortable as it looked and decided that it would be very difficult if not impossible not to feel very much at home here.

Sarah returned carrying tray laden with tea and some sort of cake.

"Can a top cyclist's diet accommodate the occasional fattening frivolity? If it can, you'll love this."

"What is it? It certainly looks delicious."

"It's called Friendship Cake, so-called because you can only make it if one of your friends gives you a little of the basic mixture to start with."

"It tastes even better than it looks. It's delicious, it really is."

The first piece disappeared very quickly and before he could ask, Sarah pressed another piece on him. Two pieces and two cups of tea later, he sat back replete, if only temporarily. They exchanged small talk for a while and then Bruce asked about the pictures. Sarah explained that she had bought all the prints but that the originals had all been presents from her father.

"What d'you reckon they're worth?"

"I've no idea, art has never really been my thing. I quite like them but to tell the truth I prefer my prints, but don't tell Dad, he pays the insurance." She laughed then changed the subject.

"Now you've looked at me for long enough. I want you to kiss me and for a very long time. Oh and while you're kissing me, I want to feel those lovely big hands of yours on all those places you've been looking at when you weren't looking at my face."

Connolly groaned at her words and did as he was told. As they turned, Bruce's hand brushed against Sarah's breast. The red dress, whilst hardly being skin-tight hadn't hidden the fact that whilst changing she had dispensed with her bra. Now that single touch had transformed his thickening penis into a hard-on like a French stick. Their kiss did nothing to lessen the effect and Bruce had to pull away so as not to do himself a mischief.

"Anything the matter, Bruce?" Sarah asked innocently.

"No, no everything's fine, just making myself a little more comfortable." Sarah smiled and took hold of his hand.

"You haven't seen the bedroom yet. The bed isn't as big as yours but perhaps you'd like to inspect it to see if it's good enough for making love on. If you just want to look, that's fine but it certainly looks as if Willie would like to do more than that and so would Fanny, or should I say Pussy, so we can just look while they get together."

Sarah's words and how she had said them was almost more than Bruce could bear. Even during their first meetings he had never felt desire quite like this. Perhaps that was because of nervousness, or even because he didn't know how fantastic the sex was going to be. Now every time seemed to get better, resulting in the desire seemingly being heightened too. Now he was as desperate as he could ever remember and Sarah obviously felt the same. Once in the bedroom they were naked in seconds and it was only then that Bruce noticed that here too, considerable use had been made of mirrors to create a special feeling. Now of course the mirrors served an altogether more erotic purpose. Connolly had briefly seen himself having sex in a mirror during a much earlier relationship but it had never been like this. Here he was surrounded by images of himself and Sarah in every direction. Now she inflamed him even more.

"I meant what I said about us watching Willie and Pussy getting together, but that's for later. Now I need your cock and I need it desperately." Sarah pulled Bruce down on top of her and his entry was instant. He was able to thrust into her for only a few seconds before he was spurting into her with such force that the length of his orgasm and quantity of his sperm brought her to climax too. She had thought that she might have to wait for further lovemaking in order to come because of the certainty of Bruce being so quick but to her delight she felt herself coming almost as quickly as he and she threw her legs around him and clasped him as tightly as possible as she moaned and shuddered to her climax.

On reflection Sarah realised that it had been quite some time, in their terms, since they had even been in each other's company, let alone had made love. It was inevitable therefore that they would both come very quickly. Neither was it a surprise that even after coming so comprehensively, Bruce's cock was still fairly rigid. She reflected again that although some of her past lovers had been 'big boys' none had been quite in Bruce's league but much more important than that was that he had both so much more stamina and a desire that matched her own. She could only remember one boyfriend who had wanted sex as much as she had and that relationship hadn't lasted very long because although he had a high sex drive and a big dick, he also had an ego to match. This man by contrast, with so much reason to be a bit egotistical, wasn't in the least bit so. His sexual expertise was better than anyone she had been with and was by some distance the most loving, caring and selfless man she had ever met. 'And', another thrill ran through her, 'he's mine and he wants to fuck me again already. I am such a lucky girl.' She rolled off Bruce and reached for his still glistening member, now almost hard again and took him in her mouth. It was his turn to moan as she expertly fellated him to full hardness. When she stopped he feigned disappointment.

"Don't look so disappointed, stud, you'll enjoy this. I said we were going to watch Willy and Fanny. Don't look at me, look at us in the mirrors." She gestured around her. She straddled him with her vagina, just above his straining bell-end and held herself there.

"Look around you, do you like what you see?"

Now the mirrors really did get his attention. By looking sideways he could see Sarah's profile from both sides. Her superb breasts with their distended nipples now jutting forward as she knelt upright above him, now hanging heavy and pendulous as she leaned forward, her nipples brushing his chest. By looking slightly to the side of her he could see her back and hips flaring out from her waist. Sarah was looking at the mirrors too and as they looked at the same mirror their eyes locked and as they did so, she oh so slowly lowered herself onto that beautiful big cock of his. For some seconds they continued to look at each other in the mirror before Sarah leaned forward again. Bruce could now see the whole shape of her behind and decided that splendid though her breasts were, it was her ass that was her best feature. Finally by leaning back and looking in the mirror above the headboard, he could see her desire-filled face as well as soft breasts which he was now gently cupping with both hands. As she moved up and down, telling him to lie still and do nothing, he could see all of her by just looking around him. Nothing in his experience had been anything like so erotic.

Now rock-hard and aching, lying still was very difficult. As her movements were getting more and more pronounced, they were also more and more exciting. There was no doubt who was in control, Bruce both being given pleasure and being used to provide intense pleasure himself. Sarah now lifted herself off Bruce, turned around then sank back onto his penis, facing his feet. This of course afforded an even better view of her bottom. She leaned forward again and brushed his toes with her breasts before pushing back on him as hard as she could.

After a few moments of this, Bruce delighting in sitting up from time to time to fondle her breasts before lying back and feasting his eyes on her gorgeous behind, Sarah turned around again and sat on his tool again, this time sitting in the lotus position. This she did with great care as his depth of penetration was greater than she had ever experienced.

"God, but you're so beautiful, Sarah."

"God you're so big."

She was now rocking gently from side-to-side, Bruce, as he had been commanded, lying almost perfectly still. Sarah looked around her at all the mirrors. She could never have imagined anything quite so erotic.

"Now, my darling, I'm probably going to shock you terribly because I'm sure that you think of me as a more or less pure English rose but I want to say really crude things to you, I can't stop myself."

"I can't think of anything I'd want more so go right ahead. Shocked? No way. Delighted? Absolutely. Does that make you feel better, my love?"

"Oh yes, yes. Now, superstud, when you begin to think you're building, and your spunk is beginning to rise up that fucking great prick of yours, tell me because I want you to fuck me on the edge of the bed. I want that horse cock of yours all the way up my very wet, juicy cunt. I want to look at that huge pole going up me in the mirror. Then just before it's too late, take it out, turn me round suck on my titties and squeeze my arse as hard as you can. Then turn me round again and fuck my cunt again as hard as you can until I let my girlie spunk run all over that fabulous cock of yours."

Her language, the mirrors, the exquisite lustfulness and eroticism together brought on his orgasm almost too quickly for him to do as Sarah had asked but he managed to hold himself back. He loved doing her from behind and pulling out as she had asked, so he could suck her beasts and squeeze her bum staved off his ejaculation just long enough. As he pushed into her from behind for the second time he looked at himself in one of the mirrors. His tool looked bigger than he had ever seen it.

"Now! Fuck me, Bruce, oh please fuck me. Yes, that's it as hard as you can. God what a prick you have on you, Bruce, You're massive, do you know that, fucking massive? Ohhhh I'm coming all over that prick of yours, keep doing me, yeeeesss, I'm coming aaaah!"

Her last words were lost as Bruce let out a roar as he started to ejaculate and the considerable quantity of semen produced in his first climax seemed not to have affected his ability to produce copious amounts again and the satisfaction was mutually complete to an even greater extent than before. They lay for some time, happy in silence and in the warmth and closeness of each other's bodies. After lying in that delicious state of half wakefulness and half sleep for twenty minutes, Sarah nudged Bruce.

"Hungry, handsome?"

"Famished, fairest."

"Wait here, oh mighty one, I shall be but a nonce." In one graceful movement, she had risen from the bed, put on a dressing gown and was walking out of the room.

"A nonce?" Bruce asked her departing back but received no answer. He lay back and closed his eyes again. Aahh, the bliss.

"Come on then, famished. This will keep you going for a while. You can take me out later to a wickedly expensive but good restaurant and buy me dinner for allowing you to seduce me."

Connolly had dozed off again and almost a quarter had passed. A very appetizing looking omelette and salad with accompanying tea and cakes was being presented to him. Sarah's last words gradually registered.

"Whadd'ya mean seduce you? I never had a chance!"

"No, you didn't," she agreed ingenuously. "But you can still buy me dinner for not having to seduce me." Connolly sighed in pretend resignation.

"Okay I get the message, I'm buying dinner, but on one condition."

"Oh and what might that be? O forceful one?"

"You choose the place and either you drive or we take a cab."

"That's two conditions and it's taxi, not cab, we're in England now."

"My humble apologies, it won't happen again. Anyway can we eat? I'm even more famished now."

Later, as they drank their teas, Connolly became serious.

"Look, sweetheart, I have to know something."

"Hmm, ask away but it can't be as serious as you look can it? You're not going to ask about past lovers surely?"

"I sure am not. No, I guess it isn't that serious but I still need to know. Hey I've just realised, you haven't told me what I'm about to ask you. Losing your touch? Sarah smiled.

"I don't think so, but it looked as if you had something on your mind that was more serious than what I had in mind."

"Come on then hotshot, prove you've still got it, what am I going to ask you?"

"Something about the first time we met, when I was in your room and started the striptease?" Connolly shook his head wonderingly in mute enquiry.

"You were bound to ask sooner or later and the atmosphere's right, it's as simple as that. To be honest I'm surprised it's taken you so long."

"Okay, wise guy, so why did you and how come it's not very serious?"

"What I said then was more or less the truth. We needed someone who had high moral principles, single-mindedness and who was not easily distracted. The vast majority of men in the situation I put you, would have behaved differently."

"Exactly! What if you'd got me wrong and I hadn't resisted your charms. Wouldn't you have been putting yourself in a dangerous position and if not that, you could have given somebody with a shortage of morals and maybe gossip column inches, plenty of ammunition."

Sarah snuggled up to Bruce.

"Firstly, and I might shock you again now, if you hadn't turned out to be the knight in shining armour, you wouldn't have been the first one-night stand in my life and one fuck in the line of duty as it were wouldn't have killed me." She saw the look of bewilderment on Connolly's face and giggled. "I thought that might shock you. Anyway, secondly, I can look after myself and I mean really look after myself, one day I shall have to demonstrate that. Thirdly, it would have been your word against mine, and to be honest which of us has the more apparently murky, if undeserved, past? You, with your reputation for womanising, or sweet innocent me? Don't forget as well, that I'd done my homework. You might be a hard case to the fans, but anyone who is anyone in cycling knows that you're an alright guy, so I wasn't risking much."

Connolly was only half-convinced.

"Okay to most of that, but why the striptease? Couldn't you just have asked me to help?"

"Come on, you wouldn't have agreed, I thought I had to do something to make you interested. I know I succeeded because although you didn't try anything I could tell that you were tempted and it was only the gentleman in you that prevailed as it were. Actually, the tart in me rather enjoyed it. You do know I presume, that a large proportion of women have a tarty side to them but never let it show?"

"I do as of about an hour ago. Ouch!" Her punch on his arm was quite forceful.

"I'll tell you about tarty sometime if you're a very good boy." She batted her eyes.

"Okay, but you still might have got me wrong."

"I've told you already that I can really look after myself. Anyway I didn't have to because you behaved exactly as a true gentleman should have behaved." She paused. "That's because you are a true gentleman. Now, nice guy, come over here and get yourself kissed."

Later that evening, after a splendid dinner, the conversation turned to Sarah's flat. The turn was brought about by Bruce but sufficiently adroitly for Sarah not to have realised it, or so Connolly hoped. After some general conversation he raised the question of the paintings.

"Forgive me for bringing up the sordid subject of money again but don't you have any idea what the oils are worth?"

"No, as I said, both belonged to Dad and he's always insured them so I've never had reason to find out. They're both good I'm told and quite valuable but more than that I don't know. I have a vague recollection that the older one is a..." she hesitated, trying to remember, "er, Chagall?" Connolly nodded. Sarah continued.

"One of my friends said they thought it might be worth as much as fifty thousand pounds." Connolly whistled but not for the reason thought.

"Yes, that's a lot of money isn't it?"

"It sure is." Connolly agreed, adding to himself silently, about a hundredth of what it's worth. The Chagall painting of a French village was painted about 1926 as far as Bruce could remember and was from the painter's most prolific and valuable period. He changed the subject slightly.

"What about the Hockney?"

"What about It?"

"Has Jason ever given you any idea about when he bought it, what it cost, anything like that?"

"No, nothing like that. Now come on, Connolly, this is the second time you've asked me about the paintings and you brought the conversation back around to my flat. You ought to know better than to try to hide something from me, so what is it that you're not telling me?" Bruce cursed inwardly and smiled a somewhat resigned smile. He should indeed have known better. He decided to tell the true, or at least part of it, for the time being anyway.

"Well, the thing is, the fifty thousand you spoke about is a fraction of what it's worth."

"How small a fraction?" Sarah asked the question in a slightly timid voice, as if afraid of the answer.

"Brace yourself, my darling, I'm fairly certain we're talking seven figures here and that's in pounds not dollars." Sarah gasped and put her hand to her mouth.

"Oh my God."

"You could put it like that."

"What do we do now?" he was pleased to note the 'we'.

"The only real issue is whether they are the real thing or fakes. I have some friends in the art business, I could get one of them to very discreetly have a look at them, authenticate and value them, but only if you want me to."

"Oh yes please."

"Fine." He decided to change the subject. "I was fascinated by your books and in particular, what wasn't there." Sarah smiled.

"You mean the absence of non-fiction?" Connolly nodded.

It's just not on display, that's all. I'll show you when we get back."

The remainder of the meal passed uneventfully with conversation being limited to light-hearted subjects, romance being in the air but just around the corner as it were. The gentle amble home in the moonlight and the air, warm yet fresh, was sufficient to remove from both minds any thoughts of looking at books. The day was brought to its conclusion in the time honoured manner with both lady and gentleman experiencing further delight by both pleasuring and being pleasured by the other.

CHAPTER THIRTY-ONE

"Simon, I need a favour."

"Ah, Mr. Connolly. Good morning, Simon my old friend, how are you today? I'm very well, Bruce, thank you. How are you?" Connolly smiled down the phone at the rebuke.

"Yeah, yeah, yeah, etc. What about this favour?"

"Sure, Bruce, what can I do for you, although I have to say that there's not much about that would suit you at the moment?"

"No, I said I needed a favour, not that I was about to do you one, you bum."

"Bruce!" Simon de Bois Lafayette, a friend of Connolly's for ten years, sounded hurt. "Is that any way to speak to an old friend, especially one from whom you are wanting a favour?"

"It sure is when aforementioned friend owes you plenty of favours and is also what you English call an amiable rogue."

"I should have expected nothing better, you American you!" He chuckled.

"Look the favour?"

"Yes, yes but you must admit you haven't bought anything in ages and with all your splendid wins of late, congratulations by the way, you must be rolling in loot. By the way have the bad guys given up on you then?" It was Connolly's turn to chuckle. Lafayette always kept himself up-to-date with Connolly's career.

"That's too much to hope for. Anyway produce the goods on this for me and I promise I'll buy something."

"It's a deal, so what can I do for you?"

"Find out all you can about two paintings. A Chagal, 'French village' painted in the twenties I think, and 'Early Morning, Sainte Maxine' by Hockney. Who owned them, who owned them last, what they were last sold for, their current worth — you know the score. You know how much I know about art and I need an expert's help here. One more thing, can you tell me off the top of your head, if there has been much, if any business in the way of fakes of these two dudes lately?"

"Well, there's always fakes about, you know that, but I've heard nothing about either of these two."

"What about works that are missing or which have been bought by anonymous buyers?"

"C'mon, man, there's always anonymous buyers, always has been, always will be. As far as these two are concerned though, I've heard nothing."

Okay, Simon, just find out what you can and pronto would be good, like yesterday. Oh, and going back to my promise, I might be interested in something by Rowland Hilder if anything's available, or likely to be." Connolly surprised his friend only slightly more than he surprised himself as he uttered these words.

"Rowland Hilder! Fucking Hell! You, the hardcase American machine! You must be in love or involved in something equally dangerous."

"You mind your own dammed business and get to work for me. Neither of us has time to jaw anyway. You'll do what you can?"

"Of course, dear boy, when have I not? Today's Tuesday, I'll give you a call on Thursday?"

"No, you'll give me a call tomorrow. The bad guys are still out there you know and I have a feeling this might help me nail 'em." Simon sighed exaggeratedly.

"I see you haven't changed, 'Mr. Now isn't soon enough'. Tomorrow at five p.m will have to do."

"That's fine, Simon, thanks." He rang off.

For a while Bruce sat feeling slightly ashamed of himself that he hadn't been totally honest with Sarah. He consoled himself with the thought that he may have got it all wrong and alarming Sarah would have been pointless. Nevertheless, there was something not quite right about the pictures, he was sure of it. Not necessarily the pictures themselves but something about them being where they were bothered him. As far as Sarah was concerned, she was obviously completely unaware of anything untoward. With a conscious effort he put Sarah's pictures to the back of his mind and picked up the latest downloaded report from John Ryan on the team's performances in the most recent races. The distribution of these reports to all members of the team, including the support staff had been a Ryan innovation and a good one in Bruce's opinion. Occasionally brutal in places, the reports always allocated responsibility for any mistakes fairly and squarely. They also gave equally fair, accurate and generous credit when any was deserved. They had therefore always been accepted by everyone in the team quite happily. Bruce had yet to read one of John's reports that had not contained quite a number of criticisms of just about everyone, including Connolly and Ryan himself. There was never any doubt, however, that every criticism had always been valid. He began to read with a mixture of interest, pleasure (Ryan could be very witty), anticipation and mild trepidation.

Half an hour later, Connolly was beginning to generate some heat and perspiration as he trained hard on his turbo-trainer. Training in this way was not the most interesting method of getting and keeping fit but it was certainly one of, if not the, most time-efficient methods. An hour later, dripping with sweat after a very intensive session on developing his VO2max, he warmed down and then had a shower. It was his first day back in his own home since his visit to Sarah and brief though his break had been, he had felt it in his legs when he had begun his session today. A long hard ride with the boys tomorrow should do all that was necessary to bring back his edge. Without the session just completed, tomorrow would have been very hard indeed as the boys had not had the three day break. After the shower, the endorphins generated by the training made for the usual feeling of well-being and Bruce promised himself a call to Sarah after he had had something to eat.

***

"Bruce, it's Simon. Look I'm sorry I was longer than you hoped for but the job proved to be more complicated than I'd expected. I have to say though that you certainly seem to be onto something." He sounded excited. Connolly felt his pulse quicken in expectation. Would this be another important part in the puzzle, or just a pink, if not downright red, herring? He tried to sound matter-of-fact.

"No sweat, Simon. What've you got for me then?"

"Weeell... both of the pictures are supposed to be in collections."

"Supposed to be, what does that mean?"

"Would you rather put money on your friend's pictures being originals and those in the collections, fakes, or the other way around?"

"I've really no idea. Is it likely the ones in the collections are fakes?"

Simon chuckled. "It wouldn't be the first time, dear boy." Bruce pondered for a moment.

304

"With both paintings being modern or relatively so, how easy would it be to establish their authenticity? Could you do it?"

"Alas, not with absolute certainty, which is I'm guessing what you require. I know a man who can though, or rather, two guys who can. It'll cost you though. These babies don't come cheap. On top of their fee, there's the small matter of air fares, business class mind, hotel expenses and we're talking Savoy, Inn On The Park, Browns etc. my child, plus spare money doncherknow."

"Okay, I get the picture, sorry lousy pun. When could he get here and why two? Surely an expert is an expert or he's not, he doesn't need somebody to hold his hand does he?"

"Sorry, Bruce, it's the original double act, you get both or none. I'll call them, get a time and a fee and get back to you darling. Bye."

Connolly was left holding the 'phone and feeling slightly foolish as he frequently did after having spoken with Simon. He had only been home for a few minutes after an excellent training ride, just having had time for a shower, when the call had come. He now dressed, got a recovery drink and put on a CD of the second symphony of Sibelius. He sat down and allowed the music to relax him. A feeling of well-being always followed a training ride. It was as if he had been purged clean by the sweat which fairly oozed from him after a training ride such as today's. After finishing his drink, he made a snack high in proteins and after fairly wolfing it down he allowed himself to doze off. He was awakened by the buzzing of his mobile.

"Bruce, it's Simon again. My two guys could be with you the day after tomorrow, any use?"

"No I'm racing," he thought for a moment. "What about a week from today?" He heard sounds of another phone conversation at the other end. Simon spoke again.

"That's fine. I'll come with them, but I'll pay for myself. They fancy 'The Inn On The Park' and their collective fee

will only be two grand on top as a favour, you understand."
Some favour Bruce thought to himself.

"Right so that's three single rooms for Wednesday night.
Let me know what time your plane lands and I'll try to get
there to meet you. Oh, by the way, Sarah is not to know the
real reason for the visit. We shall all call at her apartment,
sorry flat, for a cup of coffee and you guys will have to make
the best of the opportunities I can make for you."

"But, Bruce, my chaps will need some time to properly
study the paintings. A quick glance is just not on."

"Bollocks, Simon. Listen you crook, for two thousand
pounds, that three thousand dollars in real money, plus all
the extras, they should be able to suss them out in ten
seconds flat, so I don't want any of that, 'they need time'
crap."

"Okay okay, Bruce. Don't get out of your pram. There's
no need to be offensive, again I might add, to an old friend."

"About four thousand dollars' worth of friend! Call me
when you know the time of your plane." He sat down on the
sofa and wondered what he had started. Why hadn't he left
well alone? If there was something shady about the
paintings, as now seemed quite likely, all that would indicate
was that Sarah's father was either a sucker or a bit of a
villain and maybe quite a big bit of a villain. When he had
first questioned Sarah she had barely acknowledged the
existence of the paintings, so why bother? He sighed. His
earlier feeling of contentment had disappeared like morning
mist over a lake warmed by springtime sunshine.

The woods around the house had been full of bluebells in
the spring but now in mid-summer many and various other
types of wild flowers were dotted about the grass in small
clumps, here, there and everywhere. He knew the names of
some of the plants but an expert on the flora of the
countryside he certainly was not. He could recognise
buttercups, daisies and dandelions of course, couldn't
everybody? He also thought he knew tormentil, or was it
tormentillo? However, most of the others were beyond him.

Although they had never talked about flowers, Bruce was certain that Sarah would know every one of them and probably their Latin names too. He decided that a walk in the woods would do him good. His minder for the day would be around but unobtrusive so there was nothing to stop him.

He picked up his tracksuit top and stepped outside. After a few minutes, the fresh air and the surroundings had done the trick and he felt better and no longer restless. Gentle birdsong, a blackbird he thought, and the chatter of some finches were the only sounds and they added to his regained feeling of peace. Further on his walk he heard the almost cat-purr sound of either wood-pigeons or stock-doves, he knew not which. The memory of his walk with Sarah in these same woods suddenly flooded back with crystal clarity. He would phone her! This minute. He began to run back towards the house, and then stopped himself. 'There is no hurry, continue to enjoy the tranquillity', he told himself, not to mention the fact that whilst completing his walk he could anticipate savouring the sound of her voice when he did ring her. This kind of self-imposed gentle torture was a kind of masochistic delight which he made last for another fifteen minutes before returning to the house.

Sarah was reading through the Annual Report of her father's company and feeling decidedly bored. Jason had asked her to read it carefully. He had not said why but he knew that she would realise that he was unhappy about something in the report. As yet she had found nothing remarkable and it was quite heavy going, as such things invariably are. There was also quite a lot of it still to read. Bruce's phone call was therefore something of a salvation.

"Oh, Bruce, my wonderful darling lover, you've saved my life! How are you my love?"

Her reaction, somewhat different to her usual laid-back, cool-as-a-cucumber, response took Connolly aback a little.

"Pretty good I guess, especially after a greeting like that, but what's up?"

"Oh nothing much, I'm just bored, I'm missing you and you're miles and miles away." He could imagine the slight pout on the beautiful mouth.

"That's what I was hoping you'd say. Come over and stay for a few days."

"Oh I would love to but I just hop on a plane I suppose? That's not the cheapest thing in the world you know boyo. Anyway I promised daddy I'd read through the company's annual report for him as quickly as I could."

"That's okay, bring it with you and I can read it through with you. Or, I could massage your feet or something while you read it." Sarah laughed.

"Oh yes that must be the greatest way of assisting concentration ever invented I'm sure. Let me think about it."

"No thinking about it, just do it. Just book the flight through Mitchell Associates. Better yet, just get yourself over to Heathrow and by the time you get there I'll have done the booking for you. Go to the Air France desk. If you can stay for three days you can see me race, which may not be a great reason for staying for you but it sure is for me. I'll see you in about four hours. Bye sweetheart, I do so love you." He rang off before Sarah could make any protest. He suddenly felt marvellous. To celebrate, he made himself some tea, booked Sarah onto the most convenient flight, put on a Sinatra album and settled down to read a new biography of Napoleon Bonaparte. Two hours later he was on his way to pick up Sarah from the airport, feeling extremely sunny in spite of the now dull and overcast day.

Meanwhile in London, Sarah was feeling a little like she had been hit by a train. He really does need me doesn't he? she thought delightedly to herself. A quick call to Curzon to explain what she was doing and promising him to have the report ready in four or five days' time, and then she was packing feeling just as sunny as Connolly. The day had improved immeasurably.

CHAPTER THIRTY-TWO

The visit by De Bois Lafayette and his associates to authenticate the paintings turned out to be easier than Connolly had anticipated. He decided that Sarah's visit to France would give the trio the time they supposedly needed. Bruce asked Sarah if there was someone who could let Simon into to the flat to value the paintings whilst she was away. She was of course aware of Bruce's view as to their value and if he was right, they would almost certainly be under-insured so was satisfied that the visit was necessary. Bruce still felt a little uneasy about his economy with the truth but it was too late to do anything about it now. Sarah arranged for a friend to be present at the appointed time. Thus it was that the three men now stood in the flat. They then independently checked the two paintings whilst Simon talked to the other one each time. All three then sat down, drank some tea then made their way back to the hotel.

Bruce and Sarah had only just returned from an exploratory visit around the villages reasonably close to Bruce's home after which they had enjoyed a splendid al fresco lunch of local crab salad at the local restaurant favoured by Bruce when he ate out. Fortunately for Bruce Sarah was showering when the call came from Simon.

"Afternoon, Bruce." De Bois Lafayette sounded excited. "The paintings are definitely genuine." Connolly held his breath and then expelled it slowly.

"And that means?" There was a slight pause.

"That means they are stolen, dear boy."

"Sure?"

"Absolutely. Even so I've asked my guys to go and have a look at the supposed genuine ones in the galleries just to make doubly sure but neither they nor I have any doubt."

"What'll this mean?"

"You mean as far as my guys are concerned?"

"Yes."

"You not only paid for their expertise, you paid for their silence. The only person who is ever told anything is the person who pays them, oh, and me of course. That's why they cost."

"Hmmn. So what do we do now?"

"Well, I'll let you know about the galleries ASAP, but really the 'we' is just you, dear boy. We've done our bit. As far as all three of us are concerned, our visit to your friend's flat, I'm assuming it's a friend, never happened. The rest is up to you old fruit."

"Yeah I guess it is at that. Just one more thing, leaving aside the dubious nature of their ownership for a minute, when you get back about the galleries would you be able to give me some idea about their approximate value?"

"Sure no problem."

"Okay, thanks, Simon, I owe you one."

"Music to my ears, old chap, music to my ears. On that subject, are you still interested in a Hilder because I've had wind of a couple possibly coming up?"

"What? Oh yeah sure. I'll get back to you."

Stolen! What the fuck did he do now? Did he tell Sarah? Did he tell Jason? Did he tell anybody? Damn! He should have asked Simon to find out, if he could of course, when the paintings had been stolen. As soon as he thought the thought, he realised what a stupid thought it had been. It would seem that no one knew they were stolen, or if they did they weren't going to make it common knowledge. His thoughts went round and round getting nowhere and it was with a start that he saw that Sarah was standing smiling at him, looking even more beautiful than ever, if that was possible.

"You're looking very serious again, in fact more worried than serious. What is even more worrying to me is that you didn't once take a peek in the shower. What's wrong?" He knew from past experience that he had to come straight out with it.

"I didn't take a peek in the shower as you put it, though I certainly intended to, because I was on the phone. That was Simon."

"Aahh, bad news presumably. They're not worth very much after all?"

"No, the absolute opposite, they are both genuine and worth millions." He paused.

"How, my darling, is the fact that I'm now a multi-millionaire, bad news?"

"They are stolen."

"Stolen! They can't be. Dad is not a thief, your friend Simon must have made a mistake! Bruce held up his hands in a placating gesture.

"Hold on, sweetheart. If Simon did make a mistake, so did his mates and they're the best in the business. Their little one day visit cost me four grand." Sarah made a 'wow' shape with her mouth but said nothing. "They are checking the paintings in the galleries but they are certain that they are fakes. Now don't go jumping to conclusions or throwing things at me. First off there is no reason at all for Jason to know the paintings are stolen. Loads of owners are in exactly the same situation. Secondly, Simon's guys are the business when it comes to discretion. Nobody will have any idea that the paintings have been checked, so nobody will be any the wiser. Thirdly therefore, there is no need for us to do anything at all until we decide we want to. The only thing we need to decide fairly quickly I suppose is whether you want to tell Jason."

"What do you think?"

"About telling your dad, or the whole situation?"

"Both."

"Telling your dad has got to be your decision. As for the rest, like you I can't see Jason as an art thief, or any kind of thief for that matter. I'm for letting sleeping dogs lie for the moment apart from telling Jason maybe, but as I said, that's your call. In some ways I regret having to tell you, but not telling you would sooner or later resulted in me having to tell lies or something akin to that and I've promised myself never to lie to you about anything. I'll even tell you when you get a fat ass."

"Cheek! What do you mean, when, don't you mean if? Anyway, I won't get a fat a... bottom! So there!" The joke was enough to bring a little smile and Sarah visibly relaxed. They smiled, moved towards each other and kissed for a considerable length of time. Sarah gently moved out of Connolly's arms and put up a forbidding finger.

"Where were we? Oh yes. Okay so the decision about telling dad is mine but in my shoes what would you do?"

"To tell him may take the decision as to what to do next, if anything out of our hands, which may or not be a good thing. If he doesn't know they are stolen, his reaction is going to be pretty much the same as yours. If he does know, he then has to make the decision about telling you how he came by them, even though we both agree it's highly unlikely he stole them. There is another factor though which is a bigger worry. What if there is someone else out there who knows they're stolen?"

"Oh my God, yes, I never thought of that." Sarah thought for a while. "We, need to tell him don't we?"

"I think so yes, but how about this for an idea? Why don't I tell him? For the moment Jason need not know that you know, after all I was the one who started all this off. The other advantage of that is that your dad is likely to feel less embarrassed if there is something not quite right, with me than with his favourite daughter."

"Isn't that being dishonest?"

"If he asks if you know, I'll tell him the truth but if he doesn't ask, I won't mention you. How's that?"

"Yes I can live with that. Connolly, for a bike rider you are remarkably smart."

"Oh thank you kind lady, you sure say the sweetest things. Now, you observed earlier that I had failed to snatch a peek of you in the shower. What about a rewind?"

"Only if you come in with me after your peek."

"Oh now I can live with that very easily."

CHAPTER THIRTY-THREE

Much as Mary Opperman was interested in cycling, especially cycle racing at the highest level, the continual watching of DVDs and videos of events, many of which she had already seen, was beginning to pall, to say the least. Worse still was the fact that she had failed to spot anything of help concerning the 'accidents' which had befallen Bruce.

"It's no good, Bruce," Mary told Connolly over the phone, "I've looked at almost all of the races in question and I haven't seen anything at all remotely suspicious or even slightly helpful. I'm sorry."

"Don't be, we've had one piece of luck. One of the enemy, so to speak, has come over to our side, a relatively small fish admittedly but better than nothing I'm sure. I can't tell you who it is because I gave them my word, but I'm sure you'll work it out for yourself."

"Is it going to make much difference?"

"Hopefully it will but it's too early to tell yet."

"Do you still want me to look through the rest of the tapes though?"

Connolly couldn't help laughing at the lack of enthusiasm in Mary's voice.

"I guess so, but maybe look more at the people than at the action, not just the riders but the people around the action. Okay?"

"Yes sure, Bruce, I'll get back to you if I get anything."

"Thanks, Mary, bye."

For several minutes Mary sat by the phone wondering whether Bruce was clutching at straws or really had some reason for asking her to concentrate on the people involved rather than on the action itself. She sighed, Bruce wouldn't ask her to waste her time, she was sure of that. She picked up the next DVD, put it in the player and sat back to watch. There was nothing worth watching on the telly anyway and Henry was away.

Meanwhile in France Connolly sat thinking about his fellow professionals, many of whom he had known for a long time. Santana's personal revelations had certainly surprised him to some extent although he had been aware of the whispers and gossip surrounding the Spanish rider in the past few months. He was well aware, as was anyone associated with cycle racing, that doping in some form or other had been a part of life in the professional peloton since the nineteen thirties and quite possibly before that. Since the Festina scandal of 1998, the use of blood-boosting EPO and other highly advanced products had brought the sport to its knees. However, the signs were that the authorities were, if not ahead of the cheats, were at least, keeping up with them. The consensus was that many fewer riders were cheating than previously and those who were cheating were mostly getting caught. In addition penalties were getting harsher (not before time in the opinion of most people), bans becoming longer and in some cases, for life. Nevertheless there were still many people making money out the various cheating measures that were being used. Bruce was too experienced and had been knocked around the edges too much to be either shocked or hurt that fellow professionals had deliberately caused him loss and injury. He was much more frustrated by his inability to identify who these people were.

After a while he went to his PC and began entering the names of all the current professional riders in the peloton and alongside that, made notes about their current standing in the sport, their age and anything else which might indicate whether there was anything about them which might make them either a target for blackmail or be tempted by money to turn on their fellow riders. With over four hundred riders he realised that this was no five minute task and he decided that it might be opportune to bring in Sarah's group's resources at this point. It was also an opportunity to talk to Sarah. Her visit had been delightful but all too brief and he was sure that she would appreciate a chat as much as he would. The romantic part of the conversation was as pleasurable as both could make it but eventually business took over.

"I think it's time I met the guys in your group, or at least the important ones. I also reckon we need some help on the research front. It's too much for Mary on her own. I talked to her earlier and she's working her butt off to come up with something but so far, zilch. Now that we've got you-know-who on our side, we can show your guys something."

"As it happens, my guys, as you call them, have also, very politely, requested a meeting with superstar Connolly, so that works out very well. They have expressed both great concern for your safety and equally considerable gratitude for your efforts."

"Great. Anyway, make this meeting as soon as possible, it's ages since I saw you." Sarah laughed whilst thinking to herself, oh my, has he got it bad.

"It's only been three days, you big softy."

"That's ages as far as I'm concerned. You've got my racing and training schedule so you know when I'm available."

"Not seeing me will be doing you good, saving all that energy for racing."

"You have a one-track dirty mind, Miss Curzon, I was talking about seeing you, nothing more." She laughed again.

"Oh yes, I'm sure you were. In that case I'll arrange the meeting so that there's no time for anything else. Bye, lover, love you." She rang off still laughing before Connolly could say anything else.

Although the day was not a good one as far as the weather was concerned, the day's training still had to be completed and half-an-hour later Connolly, Pedro-Luis, Sean, Joe and ten other members of the Brooklin squad were pedalling very rapidly along the lanes of Brittany preparing for the only Pro-Tour race to be staged in England this year, the 'Surrey Classic'. A classic in name only, it had nevertheless attracted a high quality field and was using most of the course used for the Olympic Games road race. The race was due to be held the following weekend so for Connolly his meeting with Sarah's group would be easily fitted in. The misty damp day with a stiff breeze made riding hard and not especially pleasant work. As all the riders had ridden quite a few post-Tour criteriums as well as other races, a four hour ride was judged by Connolly and John Ryan to be long enough. Ryan in the accompanying car was more than happy with the riders' efforts. Later after showers and a meal, Pedro, Sean, Joe and John were relaxing in Bruce's lounge.

"So what's the plan for the English race, John?" Colmos asked.

"Bruce will be riding for points but it would be great if one of you three could win. All the other big guns will be watching Bruce, so one of you could possibly slip away. Anybody fancy their chances?" He looked at the three, two of whom instantly turned to Joe. Always noted for his taciturnity, Romain was slow to respond.

"They're looking at you, Joe." Connolly prompted Romain. Joe slowly smiled.

"I guess I could mebbe do a bit I suppose, but only with some help you understand."

"All the help you need, pal," "Naturally," and "Just say the word," were the three instant responses.

"Good, that's settled then. Bruce goes out for some points and the other teams waste energy chasing him. You three keep your powder dry on the Box Hill circuits and try and keep fresh for the run-in to London. Powell will be the main threat I think. He's still in good form and on home turf he'll really be up for it. Only a couple of hours on the bike tomorrow but make it high intensity intervals, a day off after that, then we travel. Right you guys I've things to do, places to go, people to see." Ryan was clearly well satisfied. Pedro, Sean and Joe made their goodbyes and followed Ryan out.

Once alone Connolly settled down to listen to Vaughan Williams Symphonia Antarctica whilst reading an interesting, if somewhat favourably biased biography of one of his current rivals in the peloton. While looking at one of the photographs in the book, he suddenly felt a surge of excitement. The photograph showed the finish of the previous year's Milan-San Remo classic. In the sprint for the line, Bruce had been brought down when in a super position to take victory. The win instead had gone to Frederick Vachot. What interested Connolly was neither Vachot winning or seeing himself sprawled on the tarmac. In the background in about twentieth position was the cause of Bruce's excitement. He had been a professional cyclist for over ten years. He had always taken great interest in all his fellow professionals, even the ones who only lasted a season or two. This rider interested Bruce enormously as he was completely unknown to him. What was also of great interest was that riding next to 'Mr. Unknown' was Ercole Santana. No way could that be a coincidence. It was definitely time for an in-depth interview with the team's newest recruit. Bruce jumped to his feet and rang Ryan.

"John, sorry to be a pain in the ass but get hold of Santana as soon as you can and bring him over here. I've just seen something that is very interesting. Whatever it takes, bring him. If I've ruined a hot date for you I'll make it up to you. Believe me, you'll think it's worth it." He sat down again to plan the interview with Santana. He couldn't afford to louse it up.

Half an hour later the sound of a car scrunching up the gravel announced the arrival of Ryan and Santana. Connolly went to the door and was surprised to also see Pete Weiss standing there. Connolly raised his eyebrows at Ryan.

"As you had asked Pete to keep an eye on Ercole during the past few weeks and having had a chat with him earlier, Pete telling me that Ercole continues to improve in both health and temper, I thought having him with us might help Santana relax a little." Ryan's words were whispered as he strode in leaving the other two a little way behind.

"Good thinking."

Whilst it was certainly the case that Santana had been healthier and happier since joining Brooklin than before, Connolly had seen that for himself in racing and training, he was pretty much in the dark concerning his state of mind during off-duty hours. According to Weiss, who had roomed with Santana more or less constantly, the Spaniard was no different to any other member of the team. Gone was his twitchiness, hesitancy and surliness. By no means, the centre of attention, Santana nevertheless didn't stand out as the lonely figure he had been, towards the end of his time with Sansor-JD. Now as the four of them sat down, Ercole looked fit and at his ease.

Connolly went straight in.

"Ercole, I'm not known for messing about. I've asked you here because it's time for you to pay the piper." A look of bewilderment crossed the Spanish rider's tanned handsome face.

"Er, pay the piper?" Connolly chuckled a little, dispelling the tension which had surfaced when Bruce had mentioned payment.

"Sorry, Ercole, I forgot that you don't understand some of the idioms in English. What I mean is, we got you out of a mess and now it's time for you to pay us back by helping us."

"Ah, I understand." The Spaniard's answer was a little guarded.

"Let me tell you what we know or at least think we know. We are more or less certain that some kind of smuggling racket is going on during many of the big cycling events and we have pretty much worked out what is being done and to some extent how. What we don't know are names, Ercole. Names of the guys involved in the racing itself and names of the masterminds behind this business. We've left you as long as we could but we can't leave it any longer. Several people have been killed, others, including me, almost killed and others badly injured. I'm still here more by luck than judgement and unless we get to the bottom of this rotten business quickly, others will surely be killed. So, Ercole, who is involved, who runs the show?"

The air of ease had now completely left Santana and fear was now etched all over his face.

"You know that I cannot tell you that."

"Why not?"

"Because I do not know." The answer was clearly a lie.

"Bullshit, Ercole! You're a poor liar. Just in case you think that your ex-buddies have lost interest in you and you're safe now, think again. Since you joined Brooklin, at least two of my guys have kept a close watch over you all the time. We've lost count of the number of times they've seen suspicious bozos eyeballing you. Without Brooklin you'd be history. Don't forget, pal, YOU came to ME for help, not the other way around. Now try as we might, there's no way we can protect you for the rest of your life. The only way to keep you, and the rest of us for that matter, alive indefinitely is for you to point the finger at these bastards so that we can get 'em. In case you're wondering, you don't have to worry that after a few years in some cosy pen, these guys will be out on the streets and able to have another pop at you. We've managed to keep all this away from the cops so far and that's how it's going to stay. 'Accidents' can happen to black hats as well as to white ones. You give us some names and we'll make sure that a few very nasty accidents happen to these fuckin' shits for a change. So don't piss me about sunshine or you'll be back out there on your ass and you'll just have to look out for yourself."

Weiss couldn't ever remember Connolly speaking like this before and he had never heard him use any derivation of the word 'fuck'. There was no doubting the sincerity in his voice or the inherent menace either. It certainly scared Weiss and Ryan looked a little taken aback too. Obviously Santana didn't like it much either. He took a deep breath.

"Apart from the 'extra guy', I know that there is only one rider in the peloton who is involved. That has been me quite often in the past. It wasn't always me though, and I could only make educated guesses as to who the other rider or riders might be when it wasn't me. When it was not my turn I tried not to look too closely. I have seen two other people who are as you say, 'bosses' but I'm sure that there is at least one other person who is their boss. One of the two I've seen is called 'Sad Sam, I think and he's been around the circuit for a few years. I don't think he is very important but he's a killer I'm sure. The other one is his boss but I don't know his name." Connolly wasn't impressed.

"As I said earlier, you make a crap liar. One lousy name! That's all you can come up with? We can do fuck-all without some names, Ercole, so come up with something more than 'Sad Sam' or I'll start to get a mite angry. The other rider or riders, you must know a name or names. What's the name of the 'extra' guy? Come up with something, Ercole, or I swear you're outa here pronto." There was not the faintest trace of anything but threat in Connolly's voice now and Ryan and Weiss were profoundly glad that they were on his side. Santana looked stricken and was sweating profusely.

"I swear to you, I know only that at every targeted race, one of the peloton is in the pay of the gang. He keeps his eye on the goods. I have never known any names. I swear this by the blood of my mother!"

Although he hated to admit it, Connolly thought that the Spaniard was telling the truth. He looked at Ryan and Weiss and both nodded almost imperceptibly.

"Okay, but do you know the names of the 'Sad Sam's bosses?" Santana clearly fearful for his life, nodded in answer to the question.

"A nod is no fuckin' good, what are their names?" Connolly face was inches away from Santana's as he hissed these words. Now Ryan spoke for the first time.

"Look, Ercole, sure as hell is hot, without Bruce, you'd be all washed up by now and almost certainly dead. Okay so you've worked hard at getting straight but you still owe the man big-time. On top of that, how long do you think the bad boys will give you before they decide your time is up?" To make sure that Santana knew they were all singing from the same song sheet, Weiss now chimed in.

"Staying with us, Ercole, you've got a good few years left as a rider with some more wins, as well as staying alive. You split from Bruce..." and here he paused so that Santana could realise the full implication of his words, "and they'll waste you as fast as you can say sprint. You're history, man, history. You've got a big nothin' in front of you, nothin' but the big sleep."

Large beads of sweat were now visible on Santana's forehead and beneath the suntan he had turned pale.

"If I tell you his name, I'm a dead man." His voice was pleading but Weiss ploughed on.

"If you don't tell us, you're on your own so you'll still be a dead man and maybe a few more of us too. Now wise up, asshole, and give us a names or I swear I'll throw you out that door myself and then we'll listen for the gunshots."

Weiss having taken over the questioning now allowed the silence to lengthen and the tension to heighten even more. Connolly, Ryan and Weiss all seemed prepared to wait for ever. With a kind of half-sob, the Spaniard rose to his feet and made for the door.

"I must go." He tried to open the door without success.

"It'd be a lot better if you sat down, Ercole." Connolly spoke very quietly now. "None of us is going anywhere 'till you tell us what we need to know. Sorry 'bout that." He didn't sound in the least bit sorry. Santana slumped back in his chair and seemed to crumple up inside. He sat for what seemed a long time and when the admission came it was almost a whisper.

"Sam's boss is called Harry," he paused, "Harry Matthews I think. I don't know his boss's name, I swear to you. The only other thing I know is that I've heard Sam and Harry mention a 'D' who I'm pretty sure is their boss."

"Sorry, Ercole, I got the Harry but didn't quite catch the other name."

"I said his name is Matthews." He paused. "I have only heard his boss called 'D' and this was mentioned by accident, and I don't know whether that's the initial of his first name, or his second name and I've never seen him, so I know nothing about his looks, how tall, anything like that." The faces of the other three broke into smiles.

"Attaboy, Ercole." Weiss stood up and patted Santana on the shoulder. Connolly also went over.

"You won't regret this, I give you my word. We can really get moving now." Santana still sat in his chair. A frighteningly loud crash split the silence and Connolly, Ryan and Weiss swivelled to see what had caused it. Santana didn't move, he'd been shot by the bullet that had smashed the window.

CHAPTER THIRTY-FOUR

For several hours Bruce Connolly had been trying to put a name to the face of the rider he had never seen before. The biggest problem was that although the rider's face had been clear in the photograph, his body had been obscured by other riders, notably Santana and it was impossible to see his jersey. Team identification was therefore also impossible. Checking through each team's riders at the time of the event in question by talking to the various team managers had so far yielded nothing and the American was beginning to feel frustrated. His task wasn't made any easier by the fact that he couldn't fully explain to the team managers why he needed the information. Nevertheless, the breakthroughs were beginning to come. Somebody somewhere must know both a 'Sad Sam' and a Harry Matthews. He now felt that he was close to another piece of the puzzle. Only four more team managers left to ask. Half an hour later he was finished. Every name provided by the managers was known to Bruce and none of them was the man in the photograph. That meant one of two things. Either one of the managers had kept one name from Bruce, or the rider in question didn't belong to any team. If the latter was the case how come no other rider had noticed him and said something? If on the other hand, one of the managers was lying, which one? Irrespective of which was correct, it certainly seemed a good bet that the rider was the smuggler, or one of several perhaps.

Given that Bruce knew all the managers fairly well and trusted them, he turned to the practical difficulties of the other alternative. As it was impossible for any rider to start a race without signing on at the start, a 'rogue' rider would have to join the race en route. With television coverage now virtually continuous, especially in the major races, this rider must have been shielded from the moment he joined the race until its end, or the point of his disappearance from the race. It seemed unlikely to Connolly that such shielding could be accomplished by one rider, so several riders from one team would be required or individual riders from several teams. The former seemed much more likely. But why, wondered Connolly, had nobody said anything? As he thought about it, the answer presented itself. Connolly himself had never noticed anything untoward. If he hadn't why should anyone else? With frequently over two hundred riders in a race no one is going to be bothered about who is or isn't there. In addition new riders quite frequently join a team mid-season, especially young riders, so an unfamiliar face isn't going to be noticed. With growing excitement Bruce called Sarah, Ryan and Henry Mitchell. Explaining only that he was fairly sure he knew 'what was being done', but not yet by whom, nor exactly how it was being managed, he made arrangements to meet the other three the following day in England. Sarah was delighted to hear that he was leaving immediately and stay overnight before going on to their meeting.

It was some time since Bruce had been alone. The 'minder' arrangements set up by John Ryan had worked very well and Connolly decided that as he was still likely to be in danger, he needed to keep those arrangements going. He called Sean Brean to tell him that he would be needed for a couple of days and to pack his training bike as the two of them would be leaving for England ahead of the others. Sean was pleased with the news. Bruce told Brean he would pick him up in an hour's time, quickly dismantled his own bike and put it in his bike box, then putting the box in the car. Some quick general packing and a phone call to the team's administrator to make the necessary arrangements regarding his 'whereabouts' as required by the UCI and twenty minutes later he was on his way. Comfortable timing, he told himself, when only ten minutes away from his teammate's apartment. Then a muffled 'bang!' told him he had punctured. The ABS avoided any handling problem but Connolly knew he couldn't afford to waste much time changing the wheel. He quickly pulled up, jumped out of the car and opened the boot. As he bent over to get the jack out, he felt the hairs on the back of his neck rise. He whirled around quickly but not quickly enough and the swinging cosh caught him on the side of the head. A second blow hit him on the back of the neck and blackness engulfed him. Just before the second blow fell, he recognised only one thing about his assailant, the smell.

For about the tenth time, the tall slim Irishman looked at his watch. Connolly's half an hour had almost doubled. This was completely out of character for his team leader. Enough was enough, he would call John Ryan.

When the call had come for him to accompany Bruce, Sean had been very keen to go with him to England. In the young Irishman's eyes, the American could do no wrong. Hero worship? Undoubtedly. Gratitude? Certainly. Friendship? To Sean's delight, this was developing day by day as his awe of the American was gradually being replaced by genuine liking. To some extent, Sean was still unconvinced of his own ability and treated his steadily increasing roll of victories with slightly perplexed wonderment whenever they occurred. As a boy in Dublin, Sean had been captivated by the exploits of his fellow countryman and namesake Sean Kelly, probably the greatest ever after Eddy Merckx and certainly the best one-day rider never to have won the Rainbow Jersey. Kelly had been the one hero of the young Brean and his background was very similar to that of the colossus from Carrick-on-Sur. Kelly, for his part, *had* encouraged the younger Sean and this had obviously added fuel to the ever-growing inferno of hope, aspiration and determination. However, Kelly had long been retired when Brean began to make a name for himself as an amateur. It was from the somewhat unlikely location of America that Sean's most influential mentor came. Unknown to Brean, it was the great Irishman who had pointed out his namesake to Connolly. The American's initial response while watching Brean race for the first time was, "The kid's all arms, knees and elbows." That the Young Irishman was awkward on a bike was beyond question. However, by the end of the race Bruce had made up his mind about Sean. By this time Connolly had become Sean's new idol and Connolly's offer of contract and a generous one at that considering his inexperience, had bound him to Connolly for ever. As Sean's successes multiplied, subsequent improvements to Sean's contract, did nothing to diminish his loyalty, and affection, as strong as any in the annals of sport, had developed and was still growing.

With perspicacity surprising in one so relatively young, Sean had rapidly seen through the veneer of aggressiveness to the sensitive and cultured man beneath. He was also the first in the team to realise that Bruce's attachment to Sarah was meaningful and highly significant for the whole team. All these emotions made the American's non-appearance more alarming and he was certain that something was wrong. Bruce was as meticulous about punctuality as he was about everything else. Over the phone he explained the situation to Ryan. John told Sean to go to Bruce's house and wait. He then phoned Raymond Dragonard. His response was that the police should be informed immediately.

"We have played the detectives for far too long, John. It's time to leave this to the professionals. We shall have to pray it is not too late. I'll get back to you as soon as I've talked to the police." He was as good as his word and phoned back a few minutes later.

"We are to do nothing for the moment. If and when the kidnappers contact us we must tell them immediately. Now who is going to tell Miss Curzon?" At that moment Ryan's mobile rang. "Just a moment, Raymond, my mobile's ringing."

"John, it's Sarah. I've just had a call from an awful sounding man about Bruce. He said that they had kidnapped him, that they would contact us tomorrow and not on any account, to contact the police. Is it true?" Whilst she was clearly upset, there were no hysterics. Ryan was impressed with her self-control.

"It certainly seems like it. Just hang on while I relay that message to Dragonard." He quickly talked to Dragonard and promised to ring him back as soon as he had sorted Sarah out. He then went back to his mobile.

"Now, Sarah, firstly are you okay?"

"Yes, I think so, but what should I do?" Again, no histrionics, just an amazingly composed acceptance of the situation. Ryan's estimation of Sarah increased yet again. He thought quickly. Self-composed or not, she would be better off with something to do.

"Right, alert a few of your people to the situation with Bruce, but only the ones you can trust with your life. Then ring Henry and tell him. Then get yourself over to New York and stay with him. Don't worry about the cost, Brooklin can afford it, oh, and go first or business class, whichever you prefer. Also, don't worry overmuch about Bruce. As you well know, this business has been going on for a while now and if the bad guys had wanted him dead they would have seen to that by now, added to which he's old enough and ugly enough to take care of himself." He managed to instil confidence into Sarah even down the phone and when he rang off she sorted out the tasks Ryan had given her. The next flight from Heathrow to New York was on American Airlines and whilst her preference was always for British Airways, the American-ness of the airline was somehow a small comfort. One of the stewardesses aware that Sarah's booking had come through Brooklin and who was interested in cycling, took a little time to talk to her about the Brooklin team, obviously unaware of Sarah's relationship with Connolly.

"They're nice guys, all of them, well the ones I've met anyway, different to each other but always polite, cheerful, a little cheeky sometimes but nice with it, never offensive y'know, even the boss man."

"You mean the Manager, John Ryan?"

"No, the well-known one, Mr. Connolly." Sarah smiled in spite of her worries. "He's a real dish as well as being really nice. I guess you must know them all pretty well if you work for the team?" It was far too complicated to explain, so Sarah just smiled again and said, "Yes, pretty well."

"That Bruce Connolly he's really something isn't he? Quieter than the others but sooo gorgeous and what a fantastic win in the Tour de France. Do you know him well?"

Sarah smiled again as she thought of what she would like to say, 'Well he's shagged me stupid quite a lot of times, does that count?' thought better of it and simply answered, "Yes, I suppose I do really." The stewardess was charming but things were becoming a little difficult for Sarah and she was relieved when a call from another stewardess saved her from further questioning. To prevent further interrogation, well-meaning though it was, Sarah tried to immerse herself in a book and after a while dozed off into a troubled sleep.

Meanwhile, having been very superficially apprised of the situation by Sarah, Mitchell had asked Mary to stay at the office for as long as was necessary. Since the night of the dinner their relationship had progressed very satisfactorily for both of them. Lack of opportunities had meant that sex had been all too infrequent but this had also meant that when it had been possible it had been mind-blowing. Whenever other members of staff had not been in the offing Henry would steal a kiss and Mary would respond very warmly, although she was careful never to make the first move. However, on the few occasions that they had been able to get together away from the office, Mary had let Mitchell know how much she wanted him in no uncertain terms. Although Mitchell had said little to Mary about the reason for both Sarah's visit and his wanting her to stay at the office, it was obvious that he was worried. Since it involved Sarah, Mary reasoned that the worries were to do with Bruce. Mary had been aware for some time that Connolly was leading a rather more dangerous life than the average cyclist but she had always thought that he seemed so capable and well able to take care of himself. Hopefully Henry was worrying unnecessarily, then again, perhaps not.

Two hours later, Sarah's expression when they first saw her at the airport and then her first words confirmed their worst fears. On the way to Henry's house, the full story of what had apparently happened to Bruce as far as Sarah knew it was related and by the time they arrived at Mitchell self-designed villa, the mood was sombre. Mary went to make some tea and Sarah slumped onto the very comfortable sofa. The phone shattered the silence as Mary brought the tea tray in. Henry snatched up the phone.

"Henry, it's John. We've heard from the bad guys again. They've got Bruce, he's okay and I've talked to him. He sounded a bit fuzzy but he was knocked out so that's hardly surprising. Apparently he's unharmed apart from a few bruises. That's the good news. The bad news is they're not going to release him until after the end of the season. Any attempt to discover his whereabouts or to continue our general search and investigations, their words, will result in gradually increasing amounts of injury to Bruce and eventually his death. Pictures of the injuries inflicted will be forwarded to us should we disobey them. We are to tell the police that Bruce has been found suffering from a complete loss of memory after a fall from his bike and will be unable to race until he fully recovers. I'll let you pass all this on to Sarah and Mary and I'll contact Raymond. Perhaps you can ring me back in say, half an hour?"

"Sure, John, bye." Henry passed on the news to the two women. For a few minutes there was silence which enveloped the three in a blanket of frustration and helplessness. Eventually, however, anger began to surface.

"Surely they must know that as it was, relatively speaking, a long time after Bruce disappeared, before they rang me, someone would have been bound to contact the police. Are they so stupid they haven't worked that out?" Henry and Mary smiled briefly at Sarah's outburst. Mitchell moved over and put his arm around Sarah's shoulders.

"Sarah, we can't overlook the fact that we believe, do we not, that the bad hats have inside information? They often seem to know one heck of a lot about Bruce's movements." Mary now spoke.

"Why don't we suggest to John that he ring the police in France with the lost memory story and supposedly calling them off? When he does so he makes sure that enough people in the team know that he's doing it so that the 'mole' hears about it. Then privately he contacts the Chief of Police and gives him the real picture?"

"That's a cracking idea, Mary," this from Sarah.

"It certainly is," confirmed Henry.

"Hang on though," this was Mary again, "there is still the possibility that the inside man may somehow find out about John's second call. We don't want to put Bruce in any further danger." Sarah now spoke again.

"What if one of us calls the Chief of Police with the real situation, no one else will know anything about that call will they?"

"Spot on, Sarah," said Henry, "I'll call John now."

CHAPTER THIRTY-FIVE

Bruce Connolly had read numerous books in which one or more of the characters had experienced the kind of treatment to which he had been recently subjected. As he gradually regained consciousness Bruce felt far worse than the descriptions in those books had suggested. Apart from the pain, itself absolutely awful, there was the worry about his actual bodily health, something never mentioned in the stories. This he reasoned was because it would indicate something less than heroic on the part of the heroes in the books. Every time Bruce woke he firstly worried for a few seconds whether he had been left to die and that was frightening in itself. As that fear diminished he then began to worry about whether his career as a cyclist was finished. Other worries jostled for space in his head as each time of consciousness came and went. Several times after he first came to, he had merely tried to move into a more comfortable position only to have to give up as the pains were too intense. They only subsided if he lay completely still. Each time he slipped back into a semi-conscious state and several hours passed this way.

After what Connolly guessed to be half a day but was in fact half of that, he found he could sit up if he moved very slowly and carefully. Although it was very dark in wherever he was, he could make out a few details of his prison, as a little light was entering through cracks around, what he could now see, was a door. He could also make out what appeared to be a crack across the door. Stables! Of course, that was the smell he had half-recognised as his unknown assailant had hit him. The same smell was all around him now.

Although now able to sit up, any further movement was going to be extremely difficult if not impossible. He was bound very tightly. Thankfully he had not been gagged and he wondered about crying out for help. He quickly discarded the idea. He would not have been left ungagged if his cries for help could have been heard by innocent ears. He decided to lie back in his original position and await events. At least his worries about his life and his cycling career had gone. His injuries were painful but neither life nor career threatening, of that he was fairly certain. After what he judged to be about half an hour since waking, he heard footsteps approaching and then bolts being drawn across. What sounded like two men (there were in fact three), entered the stable. An uncultured English voice said, "E's still out, you must've 'it 'im pretty 'ard." An American voice answered:

"He's reckoned to be a tough guy − I had to make sure he was out cold."

"I s'pose so. Let's 'ope 'e's not dead." Connolly felt fingers on his carotid artery and managed not to flinch at the contact.

"E's still breathing okay, now what?" A third voice, this one with a French accent and with more authority in it said:

"We leave 'im 'ere and check on 'im in an hour. Check 'is ropes and the bolts when we leave."

Bruce felt the ropes around his ankles and wrists being pulled, and then the sounds of movement were followed by the opening, closing and bolting of the door. Silence ensued. If Bruce was going to do anything he had an hour in which to do it. For a few minutes the sheer hopelessness of his situation, together with the distinct possibility of him missing the World Championship brought him close to despair. Breathing slowly and deliberately calming himself, however, he began to banish the negative thoughts and concentrate on how to improve his situation. There were three of the bad guys at least and clearly they would have no compunction in knocking him about as much as was necessary to keep him prisoner. On the other hand, they had to keep him alive, the English voice had been distinctly worried when it had hoped he wasn't dead. That was one thing in his favour. He slowly sat up again and waited for his head to clear. He wished that he could see a little more clearly. Although his hands and feet were tied tightly, at least they were not tied together. With considerable difficulty therefore, he was able to stand up. Equally slowly he shuffled up to the wall in which the door was placed. He guessed that this was either an empty stable or a tack room. In either case it hadn't been used to keep horses in for some time. Not really knowing why, he felt along the walls one by one. He had been vaguely hoping that there might be something he could use to try and cut the ropes with. Unfortunately, the walls appeared to be completely smooth. He circled the room again this time moving his hands up and down as much as the ropes would allow him but still without success. He calculated that most of the hour before the next inspection had now passed so he made his way back to his original position. When the kidnappers came in, the brief influx of light might help him to spot something that might help him. He had judged the time fairly accurately as it wasn't long after he had managed to sit down that he heard the sound of approaching footsteps.

The door opened and simulating awakening, Connolly slowly opened his eyes and groaned. Blinking, he rapidly looked around him, taking in as much detail as possible.

"'E's come to worse luck." The Englishman was the first to speak. All three wore Halloween masks so they were obviously intending that Connolly would ultimately be freed. This thought cheered him up considerably.

"Where am I?" He mumbled much more feebly than he felt.

"Never you mind, yank, 'spect you're 'ungry?" The Englishman was still the spokesman.

"Thirsty." Bruce mumbled again.

"Well, we'll get you something to eat directly an' 'Enri 'ere'll keep you company while you eat it. I'll see ya later me ole china." With that two of the three disappeared, leaving, presumably Henri, by the door which had been left slightly ajar, presumably to provide some light. Henri had been pointing a gun at Connolly throughout the conversation. He appeared to be totally comfortable with the weapon and was clearly used to handling a gun. After a couple of fruitless attempts at conversation, Connolly awaited the arrival of food and drink with some anticipation as he realised that he was very hungry. Unfortunately the light had revealed absolutely nothing that might have helped Connolly escape. He desperately tried to think of other means by which he could get free.

Sometime later, the food and drink arrived. The Englishman very carefully untied Bruce's hands and, after a few whispered words to Henri, left. A light was now switched on and Connolly's more leisurely inspection of what was now clearly recognisable as a stable, confirmed his fears. All the walls and floor were devoid of anything. Nevertheless, he ate the more than fair meal quickly, quite enjoying it in spite of the circumstances, deciding that it was better to do his thinking on a full stomach. As he put the empty plate down there was a loud knock on the door.

"Henri, open up." It was the voice of the third man. Clearly well aware of Connolly's reputation as a hard man, Henri kept Bruce covered by the gun as he unbolted the door which he had bolted when the others had left previously. The others now came in and handed Connolly a mobile phone. He was given very clear instructions as to what to say to John Ryan after the chief bad-hat had spoken to Ryan. The phone call concluded, Bruce was tied up again and left alone. Try as he might to be positive in his thinking, the increasing likelihood of him being prevented from competing at the

World's and winning the Rainbow Jersey, dampened his earlier hopefulness. Instead of thinking about himself therefore, he tried to think of possible motives for his kidnap. There didn't appear to be too much logic but that was presumably because he wasn't looking at things from the villains' viewpoint. He progressed no further than concluding that it appeared to be the case that an absent Bruce Connolly was required but not necessarily a dead one. It wasn't long before the combination of food, his tired and slightly fragile state and the pointlessness of doing anything else, sent the American to sleep.

The door of the stable being opened woke Bruce. The same guards brought in another meal without saying a word. He looked at his watch to see that almost a complete day had passed since his capture. Anger and frustration threatened to engulf him again as the hopelessness of his situation filtered again into his still sluggish mind. How long had Sean waited before calling Ryan or the police? Did anyone else even know what had happened? Did Sarah know? Had Sean been kidnapped too? These and many other questions together with their implications chased each other through his mind as he began to think with increasing clarity. He ate his meal. His legs were still tied but his hands were free. He thought of various schemes to try and escape and came to the conclusion that his only chance was to make a break, the next time he went to the john.

It would doubtless have been of some consolation to Connolly if he had known that the enemy camp was in something of a quandary. James Dowling was not used to indecisiveness and he didn't like it. The abduction had been a success but what did they do now? He had had the kidnap forced upon him. Sergio Indurrana had made it clear that the boss wanted Connolly out of the way until the end of the season so that the remaining operations would be less risky. Dowling's own experiences had taught him that kidnapping was never as easy as it might seem. The 'what happens afterwards' bit is always a problem, as indeed it was now. Connolly couldn't be kept where he was indefinitely so a move to safer more secure premises was essential and soon. In addition, he wasn't overconfident in the ability of the abductors. They weren't not of his choosing, but were from Indurrana. Dowling had not stopped short of murder in the past but Connolly was now very well-known outside cycling as well as within it. To murder him would result in a very heavy investigation just when their activities required the minimum of spotlight for just a few more weeks. Yes, Connolly had to be kept alive and he would have to be moved. Not for the first time, Dowling cursed himself for not arranging the whole kidnap himself. His underlings had let him down again and now he had to make some quick decisions. After a few minutes more thought he phoned Harry Matthews and gave him very clear instructions. Having now satisfied himself as to Connolly's future security, Dowling turned his attention to the next smuggling operation. It was with no small satisfaction that he completed the task two hours later. Now all he needed was sex. He picked up the phone again.

At about the same time, Connolly completed his escape plan in his mind, if it could be called a plan. The bad guys would be ever vigilant, that much was obvious and he didn't hold out a great deal of hope for the success of his 'plan'. However, doing something, however futile it might appear, had to be better than lying in the stable getting increasingly uncomfortable and even more frustrated. If he failed to get away soon he could kiss his 'Rainbow' aspirations goodbye.

"Hey!" Bruce shouted at the top of his voice. Nothing ventured, nothing gained, but it felt rather like attacking in a race into a force nine gale. He shouted half a dozen more times without any result and then gave up. Time passed and then he heard footsteps approaching. At last, he thought and tensed. He heard the door being unlocked, then opened and then saw an arm appear. A knife was thrown onto the floor.

The door closed and Bruce heard the footsteps fade away.

Although momentarily confused by both the suddenness and strangeness of the events, Connolly rapidly shuffled over to the knife. With some difficulty he cut himself free and got to his feet. Intense pins and needles shot through him when he first stood up but he quickly rubbed some life back into them. Very carefully he opened the stable door and looked outside. Around the corner of the nearest building, an arm, it looked like the knife throwing one, was beckoning. Without hesitation Connolly ran towards it.

Co

CHAPTER THIRTY-SIX

For the umpteenth time Henry Mitchell looked at his watch, then at Sarah and then at Mary, both of whom were looking anxious. Conversation had long since died. They were waiting for a call from Ryan who had promised to ring at four o'clock, or before, if he had any news. It was now almost a quarter to four and as the afternoon wore on so the three of them became increasingly depressed. With an explosion of sound which jangled their already stretched nerves, the object of their collective concentration burst into life. All three sprang to answer it but Mitchell was way ahead of the other two.

"Yes!"

"Henry, I'm okay so there's no need to worry. Is Sarah there? I need to talk to her right now and then I'll talk to you again when I've spoken to her."

Mitchell had never felt such relief flow through him and he was unable to say anything as he handed the mobile to Sarah. Still looking apprehensive, Sarah took the phone and said hello very tentatively.

"Bruce!" The relief in her voice was as obvious as Mitchell's emotions had been repressed. "Are you alright? Where are you? What on earth happened? Are you safe? How did you..." Connolly interrupted her with a laugh.

"Hey steady. I'm fine but we've got to move fast. Get hold of John and Pedro, oh and Sean as well. Get them to meet me at Terminal Five at Heathrow say midday London time tomorrow. Then get Henry and Mary to get Val Cornell, Rosalind Lewis and Raymond Dragonard over to the race headquarters at the Leeds classic the following day, say an hour before the start of the race. Got all that?"

"Yes, sure. But why?"

"I'll explain it all when I see you. Make sure that you're always with John and be careful. The bad guys aren't going to be too pleased I got away and they might go for you next. I love you very, very much. Now I need to talk to Henry again. See you tomorrow."

"Bye, Bruce. Oh, Bruce, I love you so much too. I didn't really know until this awful business. Are you sure you're not hurt?"

"Sure I'm sure. Now quit worrying and let me talk to Henry again. Sorry to be in such a hurry but I gotta get a move on."

"Sorry, Bruce, bye." She handed the mobile back to Mitchell and then sat down and began to weep silently. Mary went over to her and put an arm around her.

"The big lug's okay I presume?"

"Oh, Mary, I'm so sorry. I'm being selfish indulging myself in tears. You and Henry must be just as relieved as I am." Mary put her other arm around the younger woman.

"I guess I'm pretty fond of Bruce, yes, but I reckon old Henry was having a bit of trouble a few minutes ago, so don't bother yourself. I guess I'd be a bit weepy in your shoes right now."

By this time Mitchell had finished talking to Connolly.

"Right, from what Bruce tells me, we've all got things to do so let's get to it."

"Hold on a minute you two." Mary now chimed in very strongly at this point. Would one of you please tell me what's happened and what it is that we've all got to do.

Don't forget that I didn't get to speak with he of the blue eyes, wonder-willy and golden balls."

Sarah and Henry both looked astonished at Mary, said "Mary!" in unison and then collapsed in fits of laughter.

"What's so funny?" Mary looked slightly embarrassed and slightly miffed at the same time.

"You are." The two replied together. Mitchell went behind Mary and wrapped his arms around her.

"That was absolutely priceless but as you never say anything even slightly risqué, we were both a bit surprised." He turned her around and kissed her for a very long time, seemingly oblivious of Sarah. For her part Sarah was thrilled that at last Henry had demonstrated in the most dramatic way possible that his affection for Mary equalled that of hers for him. From being in the depths of despair, all three were now on cloud nine. In a few sentences the situation was explained to Mary and all three then set about carrying out their instructions.

"Before we get too much into this and before I forget, I must ask you something, Mary." Sarah had a twinkle of mischief in her eye as she spoke.

"Ask away." Sarah winked at Mitchell as Mary replied.

"Well, the blue eyes are obvious, but how do you know Bruce has a wonder-willy and golden balls?" Henry collapsed laughing again. Mary grinned hugely too, took Sarah's hands in hers and looked very seriously in her eyes.

"Well, you know how it's said that every virginal young man should be introduced into the delights of sex by an experienced older woman?"

"Yes," Sarah replied, not knowing what was coming next. Mary hesitated; Henry had started to blush but clearly couldn't move. Mary spun out the silence increasing the tension.

"Well, that wasn't me." They all laughed uproariously.

"Mary, you are terrible and you still haven't answered my question." Sarah was still giggling.

"I can't stand this anymore, I'll make my calls from the den." Still chuckling himself, Henry made his exit.

"Sometime when we can gossip a bit, I'll tell I promise. It's nothing for you to be worried about, sweetheart." Although Sarah knew that Mary had liked her from the beginning, this was the first time she had used such a term of endearment and she was deeply touched by it as it was obviously sincerely meant.

"Oh I never thought it was, but it sounds intriguing. Promise you'll tell me as soon as you can."

"Let's get these jobs done and then I'll tell you. It'd be better if it was our little secret though, so we'll have to get rid of Henry. That shouldn't be too difficult though."

The two women shared a conspiratorial grin.

An hour later the three had completed all that Connolly had asked and Sarah had packed ready to fly to Heathrow the following day. Mary winked at Sarah.

"I feel like a breath of fresh air after that, do you fancy a walk, Sarah?"

"That would be lovely, yes."

"What about you, Henry?"

"Why do I get the distinct impression that I would be about as welcome as a headache?"

"That's probably because you would be but... we would put up with you wouldn't we, Sarah?"

"Oh, absolutely."

"Off you go but don't forget what Bruce said about taking care."

"Yes, boss." The two women grinned at each other again.

As soon as they were outside Sarah put her arm through Mary's.

"Now come on spill the beans, I'm intrigued because you didn't just say those things as random comments did you?"

"No, but I surprised myself as much as I surprised you two, I suppose I should be ashamed of myself really because I'll almost certainly come across as some kind of dirty old female pervert, but somehow I'm not. I do hope that what I'm going to tell you won't either shock or offend you though."

"Well, as to shocking me, as I keep saying to Bruce, I've been around the block a few times and how can I be offended when I've practically begged you to tell me."

"Okay, you asked for it. When Bruce was little I used to baby-sit from time to time, not regularly, special occasions kind of thing. Later, from when Bruce was about nine, I was asked to child-mind, quite often staying over. This went on for several years, more so that Bruce's parents could be sure that he would eat properly and go to bed at a reasonable time, than because of any safety issues. In truth I enjoyed it and although I wasn't paid, there was always a nice present. Bruce was also much more enjoyable company than any other adolescent I'd ever come across. Now I was sufficiently acquainted with the ways of young hormonal males to make sure that I never went into his bedroom unless asked. I had two brothers and jokes about the amount of time they spent in the bathroom, not to mention the occasional careless leaving around of 'Playboy' and other more explicit male magazines, were frequently made by both Mum and Dad. Here's a quick question for you. Are you a penis kind of girl or a cock kind of girl?"

"Oh definitely cock, penis is too clinical, although sometimes it's the right word, if you get my meaning. I must say you are full of surprises today, Mary, but I love it."

"Good. Anyway it seemed to be that wanking was my brothers' favourite occupation, if their time in the bathroom was any guide. Now I was no goody-goody when younger and had pleasured myself too. However, I had never seen my brothers doing it and had not experienced it with any of my boyfriends at that time. As I said earlier, I will now certainly come across as some kind of pervert, but this particular evening I heard Bruce go into the bathroom and he didn't close the door. I heard water running into the sink and thought, that's strange, it's not anywhere near bedtime, a boy washing unnecessarily, whatever next? Bruce must have been about thirteen or so at the time. Then I heard some slight moans, and stifled grunts and I knew what that meant. I just couldn't help myself. I crept up to the door. You could see the mirror and there was Bruce washing his cock. The thing was, by this time I'd seen a few guy's cocks before as well as some porn, and even at his age Bruce's dick was bigger than any of them. It was so big! The thing was, I discovered later, that this was his first ever time. As he started to shake and lose control, he suddenly looked in the mirror and saw my reflection. I didn't know what to do and neither did he. He looked absolutely stricken but of course being the first time he couldn't stop himself. I decided to go in as if it was nothing. He clearly didn't know what was happening, his naiveté was endearing. I remember as if it was yesterday. He said in a kind of strangled voice, 'I feel funny, nice but funny, my thingy feels very strange. Mary!' It was a kind of cry for help. Then he just looked at his dick and after what seemed an age it started to jerk and began to ejaculate. He was almost crying. By this time of course I had heard that masturbation frequently brought with it a sense of guilt immediately afterwards and it suddenly seemed that Bruce realised the apparent enormity of what he'd done. He started to apologise again and again as he frantically got dressed.

"I'm so sorry, Mary, I feel so ashamed. What must you think of me? I feel terrible."

"It obviously hadn't occurred to him that I'd behaved pretty badly too. The whole thing had made me as horny as hell and I desperately wanted to make him feel better but wasn't sure what to do. I decided to be honest. Hey, first off don't you know what you've just done? He shook his head.

Hmm, well it's called masturbating, but there are lots of slang terms for it, the most common one being wanking. He had been looking shame-faced at the floor but now he looked up. Ah you've heard that word, I can see. You didn't know what it meant? Another shake of the head. Well now you know and I can tell you that every boy does it. You mustn't feel ashamed about it; it's something that people with no intelligence frown on and call sinful, even though they almost certainly do it as well. Anyone with common sense knows that basically for someone like you, who can't have intercourse, it's an outlet for your sexual urges. Don't sweat it, it'll be our secret unless *you* want to tell people about it. Just so as you are clear, you'll want to repeat it again fairly quickly and it isn't wrong. In future though, it might be a good idea to make sure the door is locked. Now how about I make us a hot chocolate each? For the next few days and weeks he was so sweet to me. A couple of times he came out of the loo with a towel wrapped around something that looked suspiciously like a magazine when I was opposite the door. Both times I smiled and winked and he smiled back but blushed furiously too. So, you lucky girl, I know what you've got for yourself and I have to say it couldn't have happened to a nicer girl. Now do you think I'm a shameful hussy?"

"Of course not, I thought it was quite a thrill when I first saw a boy shoot off, so I know where you're coming from. Tell me though, has Bruce ever mentioned it again?"

"No never. Anyway now you know why I think of him as wonder-willy." They both giggled again. "Time to get back I think." Sarah nodded, linked arms and they walked back in a companionable silence.

In the meantime, Connolly had discovered that he was in Brittany which was good news as far as him getting to England was concerned. He was now in the flat of Jerome, a friend in Rouen to where he had driven the car he had found parked in the lane which had led to the stables. As the car had been unlocked with the keys in the ignition, Connolly

345

had assumed it had been provided by his angel of mercy. If not it was too bad. It was now parked in his friend's garage out of harm's way. He still had no idea who had engineered his escape but to be on the safe side he had used his knowledge of Rouen and his not inconsiderable driving skill to lose anyone who might have been tailing him. The only thing that he could be certain of was that the arm that had beckoned him was very slim, either that of a female or a very young man. He would worry about who had freed him and why, all in good time. Sitting in an extremely comfortable leather armchair in Jerome's flat Bruce relaxed for the first time in several days. He was safe, of that he was certain. Jerome was an ex-teammate of Bruce who had been forced to quit racing after a particularly nasty racing accident during a team time trial had left him permanently disabled. He was by no means immobile however and Bruce had made sure that Jerome had received a very generous amount of financial compensation.

Remaining in cycling had always been Jerome's long-term career plan and the accident had brought forward retirement by a few years. With the help of a few introductions from Connolly, Jerome had quickly carved out a successful post-racing career as a writer of highly regarded cycling books and as a TV commentator. Recently he had moved into race organisation and was now a key member of the organising teams of a number of prestigious races. His gratitude to Bruce had always been unbounded and he saw far less of Connolly than he would have liked. He was now in grave danger of killing the Brooklin leader with kindness in his desire to please him. Eventually Connolly had been able to dispatch Jerome off into town to buy him a few necessities, leaving Bruce to organise both his thoughts and actions.

Considering all that had happened, he didn't feel too bad. His head still ached slightly and the bump on his head was still tender. He felt stiff in places and his body was telling him he hadn't been on a bike for a few days. He decided that he would start the Leeds Classic but not

346

necessarily finish it, helping his teammates where he could. That way the bad hats might feel that they had achieved some measure of success and his rivals might begin to think that he was losing some of his form. This of course was working on the assumption that the events of the past few days hadn't debilitated him more than he thought.

He next decided to check on his house. As the remainder of the Brooklin team had by now left for England, he rang Pedro's girlfriend Natalie and asked her to carefully check on his home, making sure that she took someone with her. He also asked her to ring him from the house, as and when she was sure everything was okay. Connolly was now feeling very tired. He set his alarm clock for four hours' time and crashed out on Jerome's very comfortable bed. His very heavy sleep was broken three hours later by Jerome's phone. He reached for the bedside extension and mumbled into it.

"Bruce, is that you? Are you alright?" Natalie sounded very worried.

"Yeah I'm fine, just woke up, that's all. What's the problem you sounded worried?"

"No nothing, it was you, you sounded terrible. No the house is fine, but someone left a note." Connolly's stomach tightened. "I opened it, I hope you don't mind, actually it's too bad if you do isn't it?" She giggled. "It says, 'Bruce you must meet me at the Crown Hotel in Harrogate, on Saturday at 5:00p.m. in the residents' bar.' It's signed V.C. and the must is underlined. Is that okay, Bruce?"

"Yeah that's fine, Nats, you're a star, I owe you one. See you at the World's. Bye."

"Bye, Bruce, good luck." They rang off together Connolly reflecting that he wasn't the only guy who'd got himself a very competent, pretty much unflappable girl who was gorgeous as well. I'll have to tell Colmos to get his ass into gear with that girl he thought.

V.C., presumably the journalist again? She had wanted to meet him before. Could her's have been the rescuing arm?

It was looking likely. If so, why had she remained out of sight when he had escaped? No doubt she would explain everything when they met.

Bruce now busied himself with preparations for his visit to England and he began to think in cycling terms again. After the return of Jerome with his goodies and a brief but meaningful thanks and goodbye, Bruce in a state of quiet elation, if such a thing is possible, took a taxi to Paris and the airport. He travelled Business class, expensive and a tad self-indulgent perhaps but what the hell; it was time the team's sponsors looked after its leader a bit better he decided. During a surprisingly enjoyable flight, Connolly briefly dozed off and arrived at Heathrow feeling remarkably fresh. He decided that in the time left before he was due to meet the others, he would do a little sightseeing. It seemed years since he had played the tourist. He checked into his hotel (one suggested by Mitchell), and went first to Madame Tussaud's. The queue was enormous, quite normal of course but a surprise to the American. Connolly didn't do queuing so he went instead the Planetarium, which he thoroughly enjoyed. The queue to the waxworks was even longer now so Connolly decided to indulge his interest in painting and visit the National Gallery. He went on the Underground to see how it compared with the Metro. It was whilst he was on the tube that he first sensed he was being followed. An unnecessarily long examination of the Underground map, which allowed a train to come in and leave without Connolly, and then a little weaving about on Trafalgar Square, turned his suspicions into fact.

The man was of medium height and a slim build and was unremarkable apart from a slight limp. How dangerous was he? Was it worth the risk of confronting him? He decided to let things lie for a while and went to the Gallery restaurant for something to eat and drink, having suddenly realised that he was famished. Pausing for a while would also reassure Mr. Brown, as Bruce had christened him because of the suit he was wearing, that Connolly was still unsuspecting. An excellent, if somewhat expensive ham salad and equally fine pot of tea took forty-five minutes after which Bruce took two hours looking at Paintings from the Italian and Flemish schools. Titian. Canaletto and Tintoretto were probably Connolly's favourite painters but he also had a high regard for Maurice de Vlaeminck. De Vlaeminck was a forbear of Roger de Vlaeminck, four times winner of Paris – Roubaix, and numerous other classics and World cyclo-cross champion and his brother Eric, seven times World cyclo-cross champion. After this very pleasant interlude Connolly decided to continue with his cultural expedition and hit the record shops around Piccadilly and buy some CDs.

Occasional checks during the CD buying confirmed the presence of 'Mr. Brown'. By now he had ceased to worry and was merely intrigued. He didn't feel in the least bit threatened and decided to let sleeping dogs lie a bit longer. Really indulging himself Bruce bought the complete Wagner Ring cycle, a new recording of all the Vaughan Williams symphonies (Bruce had always been a sucker for English music), and a new set of Aaron Copland orchestral works. He then got a cab and went to his hotel. To Bruce's considerable surprise, as he was getting out of the taxi, 'Mr. Brown' came out of the hotel, paid the taxi driver, then gave him what sounded very like instructions, then turned to Bruce and smiled.

"Excuse me, Mr. Connolly," seeing Bruce's all-encompassing look around him for a way of escape he quickly continued. "It's okay, I'm with the good guys. Please hear me out."

"Okay but make it quick. I know you've been following me all day and I haven't much liked it."

"Fair enough. You've known I've been following you because I wanted you to know. Believe me, if I hadn't wanted you to see me you wouldn't have. I've been following you since you picked up the car outside the stables in France. I work for the same outfit as Val Cornell. We have, shall we say, been looking after your interests. Look before we go any further, how about a coffee and a bite to eat. You obviously enjoyed your tea and salad but I had to keep my eyes open. I'm thirsty as hell and so hungry I could eat a horse with its hair on." Bruce laughed.

"Sure, both the coffee lounge and the restaurant are very good here."

Five minutes later both men were nursing cappuccinos in the coffee lounge. Connolly had ordered prawn jacket potato and his guest a mixed grill to be served in the restaurant when they had downed their coffees. The coffee lounge had a relaxed feel to it, the colour scheme being mostly cream, brown and white, the comfort of the sofas rivalling that of Bruce's own furniture. He discovered that he was beginning to like 'Mr. Brown' but quickly put his business face back on.

"Okay back to the earlier events of the day. So it was Val who helped me escape?"

"Good Lord no, it was one of the stable girls. It isn't only the villains that can use bribes you know. I was in the boot of the car, and then I stayed in a small hotel opposite your friend Jerome's place until you left for the airport. I was four rows behind you on the plane." Connolly was astonished truly lost for words. When he found his voice he it was somewhat accusatory.

"It's obvious Sarah didn't know anything about this 'protection service', wasn't that bloody insensitive to say the least?"

"It must seem so yes, but we couldn't take the risk that she would let slip some kind of comment that might let your 'mole' know about us." Connolly thought about this and then nodded.

"Actually, another colleague of mine has been helping me today but we made sure neither you nor anyone else knew about him."

"Anyone else, what's that supposed to mean?"

"We weren't the only guys following you today. One of the reasons I didn't try too hard to be inconspicuous was that we wanted the black hats to know you were being "looked after". Connolly was surprised again.

"How many bad guys?"

"Two and they weren't trying to be seen, they just weren't very good."

"What's your name?"

"Let's just leave it at Sam shall we?" Connolly's face split into a grin.

"What's the joke?"

"Well, I had mentally christened you Mr. Brown."

"The clothes you mean?" Bruce nodded assent. Sam still looked perplexed.

"So what? That doesn't seem so funny to me. Have I overdone the sauce without noticing or something because I have no idea what you're talking about." Connolly smiled again.

"You're not English are you?" Sam shook his head. "Canadian."

"If you were, you'd understand the joke about Sam Brown. It's not important, don't sweat it. Look, I'm obviously very grateful but who was following me?"

"Our guess is that the two we saw were just keeping an eye on you. There may have been more who were better at keeping out of sight. Had they wanted to snatch you again they would have had to get rid of my pal and I first." Connolly began to feel more optimistic and a little elated about the events of the day.

"We must be getting close to them for them to take risks like this."

"Yeah, probably worried enough to kill again." Some of Connolly's elation went out of the door at this point.

"Again?"

"Sure, the foot soldiers of this bunch have killed at least six people this year."

"Six! But if you know who they are and what they've done why haven't you gone to the police?" Sam raised an eyebrow.

"You've been to the police about your problems I presume Mr. Connolly?"

"Ouch!"

"Exactly. These people don't leave notes telling people what they've done. Evidence doesn't exist." Somewhat chastened Connolly could only nod again.

"Humble pie time I guess. Okay, what do we do now?"

"Eat and then sleep, Mr. Connolly. I'm staying here too, so is my colleague, who incidentally has been watching us the whole time since we sat down and who will also be in the restaurant while we eat. You've probably guessed it, we are in the rooms each side of yours."

"I'm getting more and more nervous by the minute. Oh, by the way, lose the, 'Mr. Connolly', it's Bruce." Sam smiled and shook Connolly's outstretched hand. Bruce had not been entirely joking when he said he was getting nervous. For the first time he realised that a lot of people were involved in this business. At the outset it had seemed that it was Sarah's group who were depending on him, it was clearly the case now that he was dependent on them for his continued existence. A thought struck him.

"How do I know you are who and what you say you are? You could just as easily be a villain as a hero. Maybe these others are the ones who are trying to look after me and this is a much more subtle way of kidnapping me, not the other way around."

"That's better, I was beginning to think that the bang on the head had done some real damage. For a start, here's my press card. Secondly ring this number."

"Whose is it?"

"Just ring it. I swear after the call you'll have no doubts about me." Connolly took out his mobile but Sam laid a hand on his arm, shook his head and pointed to the public payphone in the hotel lobby. Bruce went out of the lounge and dialled the number. A vaguely familiar female voice answered by just quoting the number.

"Who is this? Bruce asked.

"Why hello, handsome, long time no see, or hear. Glad that you're in the land of the living again. I presume that Sam is looking after you properly?" Connolly grinned.

"Val! Yeah, I'm fine now and your boy here is really doing the business. I guess I owe you guys my life."

"No, I very much doubt that, you're much too valuable alive than dead, of that we're certain. As far as thanks go, it's we who owe you. We also owe you an apology for letting you get snatched, that was sloppy and shouldn't have happened."

"If you say so. Anyway, how are you?"

"I'm fine too but we can have a chat tomorrow. Now if I know Sam he'll be champing at the bit for food, so go and get yourselves a meal and a good night's sleep. I'm looking forward to seeing you tomorrow. Bye, Bruce."

"Bye, Val." Connolly put the phone down and then went back to Sam just as the waiter came to tell them their meals were ready.

"That's some lady you got there, Sam."

"Yeah, I guess it is. C'mon let's eat, I'm starving."

CHAPTER THIRTY-SEVEN

Rumours about the disappearance of Bruce Connolly had been circulating within the cycling community for some hours. It seemed that he had disappeared somewhere in France, on his way to the airport to fly to the U.K. for the Surrey Classic. That there had been involvement of some criminal element or other had not been denied by those closest to the American. As it was well known that Connolly's stated intentions for the season were to win the Tour de France, the Rainbow jersey and end the season as world number one, his presence at all the World Tour counting events, the Surrey Classic being one of those events, was virtually automatic.

Connolly's closest rivals for the number one spot, Roger Powell and Giuseppi Vacchio, out with their respective teams on the Surrey Classic course, met after completing their pre-race reconnaissance.

"Ello, Roger, not a bad course eh?" The Italian smiled at the Englishman as he spoke. Powell, having lived for most of his life in Yorkshire, was more familiar with the roads all around Leeds and the Pennines but had raced around the roads of the current course fairly frequently before getting his contract with his current team and had always done well here.

"Yes, I love it around here anyway, although I would've preferred a longer race to be honest. Of much more importance, Giuseppi, it's a bad business about Connolly."

"Never fear, my fren', that American, 'e is indestructible. 'E will be back." Roger was not convinced.

"I'm not so sure. There are obviously some pretty nasty characters involved in all this and the more we hear about that shooting during the Tour, the more the whole thing takes on the look of a gangster movie."

A frown appeared on the handsome face of the young Italian.

"You believe that Bruce is in some danger then?"

"I'm no detective, Beppi, but asking around I've found out that quite a few people are now convinced that the 'accidents' which happened mainly to Bruce and his team during the last two seasons, were not accidents at all. When you count how many of the 'accidents' happened to Brooklin it begins to look as if they were deliberate attempts to harm Bruce or the team as a whole."

"If you are right, the rest of us are not in any danger then?"

"There have been other 'accidents' which didn't involve Bruce or Brooklin but my guess is that they were just camouflage as it were to confuse things. So that might mean that we all have to be careful, but yes, it seems that the shooting on the Tour, and now this would suggest that whoever is behind it has decided that there is no point in pretending anymore."

"One thing I am certain of, my fren', is that rumours are always best ignored. The wise thing is to wait for facts. Bruce, is as the Americans say, a tough cookie. 'E will not be easy to kill." The Englishman remained unconvinced and downcast.

"Oho, what is this? 'Ero worship of an American by an Englishman?" The Italian teased Powell.

"The guy's the best there is and we both know it. Perhaps more importantly, not only is he absolutely straight, but underneath the hard-case cover, he's a really nice bloke." Powell's passion surprised Giuseppi.

"Okay, okay, mama mia, I'm sorry. I do agree with you, I just did not realise that you felt so strongly." Powell's smile acknowledged Vacchio's apology.

"I just wish there was something we could do." Roger added.

"Perhaps when 'e gets back, we could keep the eyes on 'im, as you English say, whenever we race again."

"That's not a bad idea at all. Yes, let's do that."

CHAPTER THIRTY-EIGHT

Although John Ryan was not exactly ecstatic about what he was now about to put into operation, he knew that a great many things may well depend upon the outcome. Convincing himself of the necessity of checking on Judith's past had in itself, been fairly easy − amongst other things Bruce's life may well depend upon it. In addition, the whole sport of cycling was also in danger of being seriously damaged, not to mention the very important matter, as far as he was concerned of his future with Judith. Whilst he had been completely sincere when he told her he didn't care about her past, he was wise enough to realise that she would need to know that he was au fait with all that had gone before in her life.

Now facing him was a very innocuous-looking, surprisingly young, private investigator. About five feet eight inches tall and weighing no more than one hundred and fifty pounds, Ryan put the man's age at about twenty-five. Sandy- haired with pale blue eyes, he looked about as far away from the conventional perception of a private detective as could be imagined. It was only when one looked into the pale blue eyes that a hint was given of some considerable inner strength. Ryan now explained the situation to the investigator, whose name was Matthew. He didn't enlighten him on the exact nature of his relationship with Judith but stressed the importance of needing to know everything that Matthew found out, however seemingly trivial, especially regarding the people with whom Judith and her sister had had any kind of relationship, however brief or apparently inconsequential.

The detective's manner certainly helped and as Ryan shook his hand, he had a feeling that he had taken a positive step to help Connolly. It was now time to see Raymond Dragonard. It had been a few days since the team's manager had seen either John or Bruce and it promised to be a fairly interesting meeting as Dragonard had made it clear he had not been best pleased to have been kept in the dark recently. Ryan's reception, however, was considerably more cool than he had expected. For well over two minutes with no pleasantries exchanged beforehand, Ryan had to endure accusations of gross negligence, mismanagement, deliberately withholding information and generally performing incompetently. Worse was to come. Before Ryan had any opportunity to explain what had happened and why Dragonard ended his tirade thus:

"You could have caused Mr. Connolly's death. Had he not been assisted in escaping there is no saying what may have happened. In short the company has lost all confidence in you and it has been decided to dispense with your services. This envelope contains a very generous settlement and you will find that everything is legal. Good-day to you, Mr. Ryan. You know the way out."

Ryan was absolutely stunned.

"What about Bruce? What has he had to say about this?"

"Mr. Connolly has not been consulted but he will not be able to help you in any way on this occasion. This interview is at an end."

John left very quickly. Feeling both very angry and equally perplexed he decided to phone Bruce in England. He caught the American just before he and Sarah were about to go out for the evening with Henry and Mary.

"Sacked! He can't do that and he knows that. What in hell's name is going on? Sorry, John, that's a fool question, you wouldn't be ringing me if you knew the answer. Look can it wait till the morning? We're just off out but I'll get to Dragonard first thing after breakfast. Do me a favour, John. Write down everything he said as accurately as you can and fax it to the hotel here as fast as you can."

"Yes sure, Bruce, but why?"

"Just do it, John, I'll get back to you tomorrow and don't worry." He rang off. Ryan would not have felt quite so helpless if he had seen the light in the American's eyes.

For a few minutes, Connolly sat and did nothing, and then he picked up the phone and rang two numbers, one in America and one in England. The instructions to both recipients were identical, brief and succinct. When he had finished he turned his attention to the evening ahead. Meanwhile in France Ryan decided that he could do nothing to help the situation so after having faxed the information asked for by Bruce he decided to go to a concert. He knew that Judith was tied up with her own team matters so he chose a performance of Shostakovich's seventh symphony, 'The Leningrad' being performed by the Berlin Philharmonic under Simon Rattle at the Paris Conservatoire. It was a good decision. He thoroughly enjoyed the performance, not surprisingly, out of the top drawer and slept very well.

Back in England, Connolly had put the peculiar behaviour of his sponsor's chief representative out of his mind and was preparing to enjoy himself. Neither of the women had been exaggerating when indicating to each other that they were going to pull out all the stops as far as dressing was concerned. Sarah was at the beginning of that age when women look at their very best, whilst Mary, although closer to the end of that period than the beginning, still possessed an excellent figure and extremely attractive features. The men had been sent down to the bar to order drinks. All four were aware that a grand entrance was being set up and all four wanted to enjoy it. Nobody was disappointed. The response of the other occupants of the hotel foyer and bar through which Mary and Sarah walked was identical to that of the other diners at Sam's restaurant a few months earlier. The men all wished they were Bruce or Henry, the women all wished they were Sarah or Mary.

Mary's floor length dress was of black velvet with only a sequinned belt for decoration. The briefest of shoulders went into puff sleeves of elbow length. Plunging neck and backlines revealed a little but promised much more, creating a very sensual image, heightened by the fact that Mary looked as if she had been poured into the dress. A pearl studded black velvet choker and matching bangle, together with black patent leather high-heeled open toed shoes completed a stunning ensemble. Both Bruce and Henry looked open mouthed as she came into view.

"Bruce my boy, I have really wasted far too much time already, I don't intend to waste any more."

"Attaboy, Dad." Ben felt very pleased to see his father so happy.

At that moment Sarah came into their view having been behind Mary up to that point. Like Mary, Sarah looked as if she too had been poured into her dress which was of dark red silk. Even though the dress showed off her figure to perfection, it managed to avoid looking in the least bit suggestive. Also of full length the dress was open down the front revealing tantalising glimpses of Sarah's splendid legs. A heart-shaped neckline revealed a little décolletage but this added to the elegance of her outfit. Very narrow shoulder straps showed off her blemish-free skin perfectly and pearl earrings, necklace and bangle together with pearl coloured pumps completed her outfit.

"Yours is absolutely gorgeous, Dad, but I still prefer mine," joked Connolly after absorbing Sarah's beauty. The men stood as the women reached the table and together as one said, "You look beautiful," at which all four laughed. The evening seemed to fly by, another excellent meal if not quite up to Sam's standard, a first class floor show and some dancing enabled all four to relax after the tensions of the past weeks. Later in their respective rooms, Henry having given up the pretence sleeping in a separate room to Mary, each couple remarked how well matched the other two were and then, after blissful lovemaking fell into equally blissful sleep.

When Connolly woke up he instantly knew that there was something at the back of his mind which was of vital importance to the solution of their problem. He made some tea without waking Sarah and sat down to think. For a while he let his thoughts ramble around. Something had prompted the feeling that he knew something which he couldn't put his finger on and he knew that eventually the thought would return. It had something to do with Sarah, of that he was certain so he now tried to concentrate his thoughts in her direction. Sarah, Sarah's group, Sarah's involvement, the things she had said, her past, her family. Something was coming there. Yes! Idiot! Of course Jason Curzon. There had to be some value in talking in depth with Sarah's father about his problems in the past. That he had had problems in the past was fairly common knowledge. That he had dropped out of cycling sponsorship rather than let the sport be possibly dragged into the gutter was less well known. Exactly what the problem or problems were and how much those difficulties had affected Curzon both financially and in other directions Bruce didn't know at all. He decided it was high time he found out. Instinct told him not to mention his intentions to Sarah. Checking that she was still asleep, he dressed quickly and silently and went down to the hotel lobby where he used the payphone. Only the night porter was there and after exchanging pleasantries, Bruce called Curzon's number. A sleepy voice answered "Hello".

"Sorry to disturb you so early, Jason, it's Bruce Connolly. I need to talk to you as soon as possible."

"Okay, Bruce, things are fairly quiet for the next few days, you pick a time and a place."

"How about now? That is as soon as I can get over, say in about an hour?"

"Fine by me. You can join me for breakfast. See you then. Bye."

Bruce put the phone down. Another quick call to Henry to put him in the picture and a note left with the hotel porter for Sarah and he was away. The roads were clear of traffic as it was so early and he was alone on the roads. Even the M3 was virtually deserted. Dawn had just broken and the sun's early rays were just beginning to edge over the skyline. There was the possibility that Jason may give him information about the past which was less than pleasant. Nevertheless Connolly felt good. The relative smallness of England compared to the States had always delighted him as had the frequent variations in the climate. Okay, the rain could be a drag but nowhere over here was there the dreadful humidity of many places in America. As Bruce drove along, the red and gold in the sky was gradually turning to that indescribable hue which is suddenly blue. Now in late summer many of the trees were not as green as they had been and the rich coppery maroon of an occasional copper beech stood proudly as if reminding everyone that a tree did not have to be green to be beautiful. Here and there kestrels hovered alongside the M3 waiting with infinite patience for their prey to break from cover and once to his great joy a pair of red kites flew over his car. Later, alongside a river a grey Heron took off, the slow beat of its wings deceiving Connolly as to the speed at which it was travelling. So transfixed by this, for him, unusual sight, Connolly slowed the car so as to be able to watch clumsy looking yet somehow elegant natural aviator as it paralleled the motorway for a few hundred yards. Too soon his idyll was broken as gradually traffic joined the motorway and his thoughts turned to his meeting with Curzon. Connolly reached Jason's house in five minutes under the hour and he was waiting for Bruce on the gracefully sweeping gravel drive and took him straight to the breakfast room. His greeting was warm and effusive and Connolly's immediate thought was that either Curzon had nothing to hide or he was an extremely good actor. Breakfast over, which included a new introduction to Bruce, black pudding, unusual but certainly to his liking, Curzon turned the conversation to business.

"Whatever it is you wanted to talk to me about it must be important to get you out this early."

"Yes, it is and I was kinda hoping you might have some idea what it was." The American didn't smile. Curzon got up, still holding his cup of tea and walked across to the window. Looking across the lawn he seemed to gather himself and then began to speak.

"How much do you know about my business, Bruce?" Connolly decided not to bluff.

"Not very much. I've heard rumours of course, I guess everybody has but no facts and I don't deal in rumours."

"So I've heard." Connolly raised his eyebrows questioningly.

"Oh I've done quite a bit of research of my own, Bruce, after all, you've been spending quite a bit of time with Sarah — serious time I gather." Connolly nodded and the two men smiled.

"Fair enough." Bruce waited for Jason to take up the conversation but Curzon was also waiting. Bruce took the plunge.

"All I need to know is whether your past problems could have anything to do with my troubles of the past couple of seasons. You heard about the attempted murder I presume?"

"Yes!" Curzon almost spat the word out. For a moment Connolly could see that an inner rage was being tightly controlled. It was only momentary however and Jason's habitually calm exterior was virtually instantly back in place.

"Frankly I don't know whether the events of ten years ago are connected with this appalling business with you or not, but if you think it worthwhile for me to tell you all about it, I'll gladly do so, well perhaps not gladly, but at least, willingly. You must promise me one thing though."

"Sarah?" Bruce asked. Curzon nodded.

"I can promise to tell her nothing of what you are about to tell me and keep that promise but if there is something that is connected with the current situation and I use that information to help me she might find out anyway." Jason shrugged.

"I'll have to risk that. Just don't you tell her."

"Okay, you got a deal. Now fill me in on whatever happened. For what it's worth, even with the little I did know I figured that you were probably protecting somebody and that was why you pulled out. I'd also guess that there was some blackmail somewhere. Am I close?"

"Close enough."

When the American left Curzon's house almost two hours later, he had quite a few more answers. He also had some more questions to ask a few people. As he drove away, a smile played around the corners of his mouth. There wasn't a ghost of a smile in his eyes.

CHAPTER THIRTY-NINE

Jessica Taylor, alias Joanne Turner felt absolutely wretched. Judith and she had seen little of each other for several years, but they had once been very close, particularly while they had been working together. However, whilst not being an angel, Judith had stopped quite a way short of getting involved in some of the activities which Jessica had been quite prepared, even keen to get into. Jessica had made quite a lot of money, most of it from questionable sources, by equally questionable means. After her early relative recklessness and the breakup of their act, Judith had taken the safe route, steady relationships and respectable jobs, which to Jessica had seemed to get Judith nowhere. Of a fairly amoral nature, Tina's own life was not something she was ashamed of even though she supposed she ought to be. The money men had paid her for her services they would have spent on other things and if she hadn't taken part in the porno films there were plenty of others who would have gladly taken her place. When to that was added the fact that she had never indulged in any sexual activities under any duress, she felt that she had nothing to regret. She had sometimes felt sorry for Judith, but she knew that sympathy was not what Judith would have wanted; neither did she want anything to do with Jessica's world. Their separate paths had been taken with philosophical acceptance if not ecstasy by both and each had been happy enough to leave things as they were.

Until now.

Jessica liked sex and she particularly liked it when it paid as well as it did with John Donne (the poetic pseudonym amused her), and even more so when the big pay day had as a bonus, a big dick with it. Never before, however, had he asked her to do to or for that matter, with what she thought of as innocent people. That J.D. was a crook she had no doubt. Of the scope of his crimes, of the harm, pain and terror inflicted on his victims, either by his own hands or as directed by him, she had no knowledge. For the first time in a very long time Jessica was frightened. Until this situation had arisen, she hadn't realised quite how alone she was. She didn't know what to do or who to turn to. As yet she didn't know exactly what she was going to have to do but she knew it would be bad. She would no longer be a prostitute used by a criminal, she would be a criminal herself. Worse than that she knew that her sister was in considerable danger.

A couple of hours later on the other side of the city, James Dowling, unaware of his occasional 'employee's' feelings, was receiving the latest report from Harry.

"Two point four million from the Tour, nearly six hundred thousand from the autumn classics so far, with just the 'Cools' to come. The total for the season stands at just under six and a half million." (Surely the boss would be pleased with that? − God it was hot in this bloody office.) Harry waited, not daring to move a muscle, hardly daring to breathe, lest his face should twitch which might be interpreted as being a smile. Eventually Dowling looked up and smiled, if thinly, himself.

"You've done well, very well in fact. You'll get your pay as usual and then a bonus as soon as the Cools is finished and we get the total there." He passed over an envelope, a satisfyingly thick envelope. Harry wondered about a smile himself, or a word of thanks perhaps, thought better of both and remained silent. It was the right decision.

"One thing I like about you, Harry. Most of the time you say the right thing, which is nothing. Finish the season with the Cools, the stuff will be brought to you at the usual time, here." He passed over a slip of paper with an address on it. Harry read it twice very carefully then tore the paper up and swallowed the pieces.

"Then it will be collected here." The same procedure was followed.

"I assume that the rest is all under control?" Harry nodded.

"Good, in that case, I'll be in touch when I need to see you again, probably Milan-San Remo." He looked down again. Harry knew what to do next. He left. On his way out he passed the reception desk and seeing that Jessie was on duty and feeling more relaxed than he had for many months, he decided to chance his arm.

"What are my chances of a date?" Jessie looked at him for a long time. Eventually she spoke.

"Now give me one good reason why I should. After the last time you could have died for all I knew. It was a one-night stand without the night." He could see that there was a smile lurking there somewhere. He tried a joke himself.

"I didn't get the chance of a stand either though did I?"

"Don't push your luck and I'll consider it. Ring me tomorrow."

"Now or never girl." He was now smiling broadly.

"In that case, never, see you hotshot."

"Okay, okay, you win. I'll settle for tomorrow night at say Enrico's?"

"Listen dumbo, what you'll settle for is a 'phone call tomorrow or nothing. Now shoot the breeze someplace else, I've got work to do."

She went back to her computer without looking at him but the smile was broader now.

Dowling meanwhile was presiding over a small meeting in his office. He had been joined by Sad Sam and Joanne Turner who were listening to Dowling in varying degrees of fear as well as attention and trying very hard not to betray any evidence of either emotion. Having outlined the arrangements for the Cools as discussed with his previous visitor Dowling turned to Sam.

"So?"

"He's dead, no fuss, one bullet, the others didn't see a thing."

"Others? Who else was there?"

"One of Connolly's teammates, Weiss I think his name is."

"Did Santana tell them anything?"

"I couldn't tell." No apology, just a statement of fact.

Dowling looked annoyed.

"I told you to make sure that you shut him up before he could talk."

"You told me to make sure, but I didn't say I would. You wanted him dead without Connolly knowing who did it. That's what you've got."

Dowling was about to say more but decided against it. Sam was too good to alienate.

"When are you going to take care of Harry?"

"After the drop at the end of the Cools."

"D'you know where he spends his time?" Sam gave him the benefit of a withering stare before answering.

"When I do my job, you pay me, when I don't, don't pay me. Okay." No emotion in the voice, laconic almost to the point of boredom. The other two audibly gasped at Sam's apparent foolhardiness, but Dowling said nothing, merely looking a little more sour than usual.

"Okay, just checking." He bent down and passed another envelope to his hit man who nodded in acknowledgement.

Dowling now became more businesslike again.

"Let's turn to the matter of Bruce Connolly, John Ryan and Judith Taylor." He turned to Joanne. She smiled but her heart was pounding.

"What's the matter, my dear, you look a little flustered?"

"I'm fine, thank you."

"I just wondered, you're not your chirpy self today."

Could he know? If he had looked at Judith carefully, surely he would have seen the resemblance, even with her different colouring and hair styling now. Her heart was pounding but Dowling appeared satisfied. He looked round at the three impassively.

"It is becoming imperative that Connolly be silenced. I wasn't certain that this would become necessary, but now I'm sure that it is. It would appear that he and his little band have some idea of what is happening, but not who is operating our scheme or who is behind it. It is only a matter of time before someone opens their mouth to the wrong person. In our favour is the fact that as far as we can tell, Connolly has made sure that the police have been completely kept out of everything. The Cools is our last 'dealing' race this year and Connolly will almost certainly have worked that out for himself. He will be trying as hard as he can to catch us out. We shall therefore have to fix him before he can fix us as it were. You," he pointed at the man unknown to Joanne, "will have to organise that. Study the route and find a place where the coming off will prove fatal."

"It isn't that easy, boss." The protest was somewhat nervously uttered.

"So far you have been paid very well for doing very little. Now is the time to do something to justify the money I pay you. Do I make myself clear?"

Frightened into silence and not trusting himself to speak, the man nodded in acquiescence.

"Good." Dowling looked slowly around the group.

"A lot of money rests on this race, not to mention the elimination of Connolly and the tying up of a few loose ends."

He turned to Joanne and she dreaded what was coming.

"You know what to do as far as the Taylor woman is concerned?"

Joanne knew that she had to show both enthusiasm and certainty in her answer and she said "Yes" very firmly. Dowling appeared pleased.

"Good. Everybody knows what to do, so get on with it."

Since dismissal was normally Dowling simply going back to whatever he had been doing, this was real eloquence. However, the three knew better than to allow such a matter to evoke any response and all left the office quickly.

Joanne had been alternately dreading then hoping that she would be asked to stay. Although frightened of him, she nevertheless could not stop thinking about how satisfying and exciting sex was with him. It seemed that this additional power he, seemingly unknowingly, had over her, had heightened his attractiveness for her. So as the three entered the lift she felt the peculiar feeling of relief and disappointment. This was then succeeded by a feeling of self-loathing. How could she feel any attraction, even a physical one at its basest level for a man who was making her harm her own sister?

Stopping the lift at different floors and then leaving the building at slightly different times by different exits minimised the possibility of anyone casual observing making any connection between the Dowling's three associates so Joanne was at least spared the necessity of making small talk with the others. With a heavy heart she made her way to her apartment. Why did Dowling want Judith? If he was going to eliminate Connolly during the race why did he need to get Ryan as well? Both men had shown themselves well able to look after themselves in the past. Why did Dowling need to get involved in something which could well turn sour on him? Take the money and run was surely the sensible option? It had worked perfectly for a long while and had brought in a lot of money. Still she knew what the result of her betraying Dowling would be. She shivered at the thought and did her best to think of other things. As she reached her block she received a particularly bright smile from the commissar, a not-unattractive man of about thirty known to Joanne only as Bernard.

"Good afternoon, Miss Turner."

"Good afternoon, Bernard, you are looking very pleased with yourself."

"Not as pleased as you will be in a few minutes, Miss."

"Hmm?" In her somewhat preoccupied frame of mind she didn't feel like sorting out any riddles so carried on with as bright a smile as she could manage. When she reached her flat there was a note on the bed.

It read, *'Go down to the garage. There are two items there with your name on them. Choose one and tell Bernard your decision, he will do the rest. Consider it a bonus.'* There was no signature but she knew who it was from. Two minutes later she was walking into the underground garage.

A dark blue 5 series BMW convertible and a white Porsche 911 with a black soft-top, both brand new, were parked side by side with notices saying Miss J. Turner on their windscreens. Behind them sporting a smile which was trying to become a grin all the time was Bernard. Caution told her that Bernard may well be questioned regarding her reaction so she widened her eyes, squeaked with delight and ran to the cars. In truth she didn't have to work too hard to appear enthusiastic.

"You're to test drive them both before deciding, Miss."

"Ooh, lovely." She hesitated for a minute.

"I'll try the BMW first."

"Certainly, Miss. I shall remain here until your return."

"Thank you, Bernard." Joanne loved driving and was soon thoroughly enjoying herself. After half an hour's fun in each car, she handed the keys back to Bernard.

"It's the Porsche, but only just."

She left Bernard looking wistfully at the cars and went back to her apartment. In spite of her conscience she couldn't help feeling excited about her gift. Obviously it was a case of the man who pays the piper calling the tune, paying a bit extra for more difficult pieces of musicianship but for the moment she dismissed the thought. Until she had to play her part in the Cools, whatever part that turned out to be, she could indulge herself in some fun driving somewhere. She sat back in her sofa and began to plan where she might go for a few days. She would have to clear it with her benefactor of course but he could hardly make the gift then refuse to let her use it could he?

At the same time in his office, Dowling was being apprised of Joanne's reaction to his gift to her. He was obviously satisfied with the report.

"Thank you, Bernard. Keep me posted on her movements."

He put the phone down with a smile on his face, but again one that didn't reach as far as his eyes.

CHAPTER FORTY

Very few of the greatest cyclists throughout the history of cycle racing had failed to win the world professional road race championship and thus be entitled to wear the coveted Rainbow Jersey throughout the following twelve months. There are a few glaring omissions from the roll of honour: Irishman Sean Kelly, Jacques Anquetil and Roger de Vlaeminck are probably the most obvious candidates, although De Vlaeminck was world professional cyclo-cross champion. Bruce Connolly was determined that he would not be another who would fail to ride the rainbow.

For this year's championship, most factors were in Connolly's favour. Firstly he was winning again, and winning well. He was at his fittest and on form and the other main contenders feared him, always a big plus. He was also close to home – the course was centred around Rouen and he had an excellent team around him. Ordinarily professional cycling races are contested by sponsored teams often containing riders of several different nationalities. The world championship, however, is contested by national teams. In theory in the world championship, trade team loyalty took a back seat to national prestige but in practice many riders still rode for fellow sponsored teammates, rather than for their compatriots as it was the trade team that paid their wages and would be hopefully giving them new contracts. In simple terms you didn't bite the hand that fed you. In Connolly's case he was doubly fortunate in having some very strong

Americans in his own team – Pete Weiss and Joe Romain. As the sole Irish representative, Sean Brean, had no fellow countryman to ride for anyway and good though he was, he wasn't really a contender so had privately told Bruce that he would ride for him unless he was on a super day and thought that he had a chance to win himself. The same sentiment had been expressed by the other American big hitter Mark Andrews of the Ruff-Stuff Jeans team. Also in his favour was the weather, the day being unusually cold for a French September day and Bruce was one of a relatively small number of riders who excelled in bad conditions.

As Bruce viewed the day, he hoped that the heavy looking clouds scudding across the leaden sky would bring rain, lots of it. Against all these considerable advantages stood one major disadvantage. Even in a race which was as much of a lottery as the world championship normally was, Bruce was most people's favourite to win. The riders, journalists, bookmakers and fans all saw Connolly as 'the man most likely to'. With that kind of pressure, the marking of Connolly would be intense. If he was to win, it would be necessary for him (and/or his team-mates) to make attack after attack in order for him to thin out the opposition. In spite of his Tour victory, Bruce had made no secret of his priorities at the beginning of the season and winning the Rainbow Jersey had always been his major target.

The bookmakers saw his main rivals as being Frederick Vachot and Miguel Velasquez, [7-1], Roger Powell and Giuseppi Vacchio, [9-1], Mark Andrews, [10-1], Amaroso Sarro, [12-1] and Bruce's own teammate Joe Romain at 15 - 1. Connolly's own odds were 3 to 1. Bearing mind the nature of the race, and his relatively recent string of bad luck, notwithstanding the successes so far this season, such odds were ridiculous. It only took a puncture at an inopportune moment and the race was lost. Bruce, although as nervous as he could ever remember before a race, was also feeling confident.

The race was to be waved away by the legendary Frenchman Bernhard Hinault from the city centre after which it was neutralised for five kilometres out of the city. Ten laps of a twenty-four kilometre circuit around Rouen would then be followed by six laps of a four-and-a-half kilometre finishing circuit. A much more hilly course than had been used for recent world championships, it was thought highly likely that there would be many retirements today, especially if it rained.

As befitted the most important single day race in the cycling calendar, the crowds were enormous all around the circuit. The retirements of Hinault and Fignon in the eighties and nineties had left French cycling largely bereft of real talent. There had been many good French riders since then but no Frenchman had won the Tour in almost thirty years and no one but Fignon had ever looked even close and that had been twenty years ago. Nevertheless, the French cycling fans were still as enthusiastic as ever and endlessly optimistic, especially for one day races. The only French riders in the current peloton with real class were Frederick Vachot (well-fancied today), Jean-Luis Bobert of the Santiamo squad, young enough to develop into a really good rider, Gilles Duclat of the Selma-Consor team and the leader of the Citrive-Minerva team, Antoine Delacroix. Only Vachot and Delacroix could be seriously considered as having a chance of winning today. In years to come Connolly's young new recruit Jean-Luc Bernardt could turn out to be the next Hinault but not yet.

Knowing how important victory was to Bruce, Sarah, Henry, Mary, were amongst the huge crowd, but in a somewhat privileged position, as Raymond Dragonard had reserved some grandstand seats for them overlooking the finish some weeks earlier. John and Judith were to join them after the race had begun and they had finished their pre-start duties.

Roger Powell had plenty of support too. Sally, his parents and a significant number of members of the English cycling club of which he was still a member in spite of his successes, were all wearing "Powell Has the power" T-shirts. A very large contingent of Italian fans, always the most enthusiastic supporters would ensure that Sarro, Vacchio and all the other blue jerseyed Italian riders would not be lacking support.

After handshakes, pats on the back and a few kisses from nearest and dearest the riders, numbering over two hundred assembled at the start and after a mercifully short preamble, they were off.

It had now been some while since any 'accidents' had befallen the Brooklin team and in particular its leader and since the race was contained within a fairly small area in just one country, Bruce et al were firmly of the belief that nothing untoward would happen today. Normally the opening laps of the World Road Race championship are something of a procession. All the riders are usually unwilling to expend too much energy with such a long and hard race in prospect and early breaks are usually allowed to go off the front. The riders in such breaks are usually little fancied and can enjoy a few moments of glory, especially television glory. Connolly was well aware that today he would have to wage a war of attrition, gradually eliminating rivals by frequent attacks. He could not let too many laps go by therefore before beginning the elimination process. By the end of the first two laps there had been two attacks by virtually unknown riders which had come to nothing. The expected rain now began to fall and Bruce nodded very discreetly to Joe Romain that any time soon would be a good time for him to make a break.

Joe waited until the hardest part of the lap was approaching, a combination of a number of sharp climbs and a headwind, and then smoothly accelerated away. Romain was considered a fairly dangerous rider so it was no surprise that several other riders quickly jumped after him. Connolly waited until he judged it wouldn't be too obviously a two-man band then followed and rapidly caught up the fairly fast moving break. He sensed other riders following and he hoped it was some at least of the big hitters but he didn't look round. It wouldn't do to show his concern at this stage. He need not have worried. Early in the race though this was, such was Connolly's form and reputation that he was not going to be allowed any rope at all. With Joe with him, the other favourites couldn't afford to take any chances and Vachot, Powell and Delacroix had jumped as soon as they saw Connolly follow Romain. All three were accompanied by a teammate and they were then followed by Sean Brean and two Swiss riders of no mean ability.

For the next two laps the break continued to gain ground on the peloton, all the riders contributing to the effort even though some did more than others. During the third lap of their breakaway however, Powell sensed that the tempo was dropping slightly and broke away from his companions. Immediately Romain looked at Connolly who shook his head. With so much of the race still remaining such a move was suicidal. If any of the other breakaways decided to follow the Englishman that would be a different matter, especially if several did. The rest were thinking like Connolly however and decided to let Powell stay out on his own and use up some energy. After a few minutes, Roger, having gained thirty seconds but seeing that no one had followed to help him stay away, decide that enough was enough and allowed himself to be caught by Connolly's group. When this happened, by unspoken mutual consent, the group, deciding that it was unlikely that the peloton would allow them to stay away for the remainder of the race decided that they may as well save some energy themselves and allowed themselves to be caught. The chase would have already tired many in the bunch anyway. A few minutes of easier pedalling resulted in the break and the peloton coming together again and the survivors settled down.

The race now stayed together for the next fifty kilometres. Just over one hundred and fifty kilometres had now been covered and Miguel Velasquez now attacked, assisted by one of his teammates. Following the Brooklin pattern, Jean-Luc immediately took off after the escapees to police the move and he was joined by Giuseppi Vacchio. This break worked well for another ten kilometres and their lead reached one minute. A puncture to Vacchio proved their undoing and by the two hundred kilometre mark, the field, now down to one hundred and thirty riders, was all together again.

With just one lap of the big circuit left, Connolly decided that he would launch a major attack. He didn't expect to drop all of the major opposition in one hit, it would be necessary to attack again later he felt sure but to eliminate three or four of the big threats would be good. The original plan had Pete and Sean going with Bruce, the remaining Americans helping to control the chase by keeping at the front and hopefully slowing the bunch down. The unknown quantity was Mark Andrews. As surreptitiously as possible, Bruce moved to Andrews' side.

"How d'you feel, Mark?"

"So-so", was the noncommittal reply.

"So you still rate yourself for this then?" This time Andrews merely smiled. Connolly smiled back and after a couple of minutes rode back to Joe, Pete and Sean.

"We can't count on Andrews, so watch him. You guys ready?"

Nods from the others.

Connolly without really seeming to do so, gradually moved through the bunch and after five minutes was near the head of the race. He tensed to make his move but before he could sprint away, another rider did so first. A blue Italian jersey streaked away followed by another. Connolly immediately took off after them with Sean and Pete on his wheel. Italians had had conspicuous success in the eighties, nineties and 'noughties', in the world road championships. Mareno Argentin, Maurtizio Fondriest, Gianni Bugno, Mario Cipollini and had all won the rainbow jersey some of them winning it twice. A considerable number of silver and bronze

378

medals had also been won. Today they were clearly hoping to continue the tradition.

Amoroso Sarro and Giuseppi Vacchio were now in effect riding a team time trial and Connolly, Weiss and Brean followed suit. With strength in depth in the peloton, the Italians could carry out effective blocking tactics for a while at least and with Connolly's teammates in the bunch also able to help with the blocking most of the crowd were of the opinion that now the final selection had been made. Three other riders thought differently, however, and just before it would have been too late to try and bridge across to the break, a tremendous effort by Mark Andrews, Felice Brambani, the new leader at Sansor-J.D. since Santana's departure, and Roger Powell, swelled the break to eight.

It had taken the remainder of the last big circuit to achieve this, for Connolly at least, desired objective. As they came onto the finishing circuit for the first time only twenty-seven kilometres remained. The crowds around the course speculated as to who would do what as far working was concerned. Connolly had no real weaknesses and was one of the two or three best sprinters in the group. However Sarro was probably the best climber and Andrews was well-known for being able to maintain long lone breaks. Powell and Vacchio, although having achieved excellent wins had yet to show their full potential. Neither Weiss nor Brean were likely to figure on the podium but would be able to help Connolly. It was equally possible that two of the three Italians had agreed to sacrifice their chances for the other one.

The first circuit was completed with all eight still together, all sharing the work. The bunch were now at two minutes. In the second lap Connolly had his first slice of bad luck – Weiss punctured. Even a rapid wheel change wasn't rapid enough for him to get back to the seven, so Connolly only had Brean to help him now. Immediately Weiss flatted Brambani and Andrews attacked. Were they trying to break away for themselves or trying to weaken the Irish-American duo? Powell and Andrews might well have struck up an alliance. There is no time to mess about in such circumstances and a lack of response from the other two Italians and Powell, suggested teamwork. Sean therefore took off in pursuit and caught the escapees fairly quickly. Confirming Connolly's analysis as soon as Brean caught Brambani and Andrews, they eased off.

At the start of the third circuit the seven were still together and things were somewhat clearer. Andrews had apparently decided that if couldn't win he would prefer an English winner rather than another American. Connolly was also sure that Brambani was there to help Sarro and Vacchio. For two more laps the seven took turns at the front, ensuring that the pace was too high for the bunch to catch them. At the beginning of lap five the lead was up to five minutes and Connolly decided that it was now or never. He nodded to Brean, dropped to the rear of the group and a hundred metres before they hit the bottom of the toughest climb on the circuit, he stood on his pedals and was off catching all but the Irishman slightly unawares. With legs pumping like pistons, heart thumping, every muscle straining, he pounded the pedals round like a man possessed. Brean taking protection from his leader, there was a significant headwind at this part of the circuit, struggled manfully to keep with Connolly and just after they breasted the summit, managed to get in front of Bruce so that Connolly could get a tiny bit of respite. For two hundred metres the Irishman led then heard the bang and felt the thump of the puncture at the same time. Realising the effect this would have on his pursuers Connolly again dug into whatever reserves he had left. This second piece of bad luck should have been his undoing but the Rainbow Jersey was going to be his, dammit!

His last attack had done considerable damage. Risking a quick look back, he was pleased to see that only Powell and two of the Italians were still close enough to have a chance. Bruce now used all his experience. He continued to keep up a high cadence but did not keep going at full gas. The other three were clearly having considerable difficulty in bridging across but with just over one lap to go the four came together. As the three chasers relaxed slightly having caught Connolly, he jumped again!

Not quite knowing where his power came from, in the space of a minute he made the Rainbow jersey his own. As Connolly jumped again, the other three had nothing left after their desperate chase and could only watch him ride away from them. At the bell he had made a minute on them and Powell, Brambani and Vacchio had decided to wait and sprint it out for silver and bronze. Bruce was taking no chances however, too many punctures at crucial moments, too many 'accidents' and too many disappointments made him ride as hard for the last lap as he had at any time in the race. Adrenaline was clearly helping a good deal too but the last three-and-half kilometres through Rouen were as good as any he had ever ridden. The absence of a Frenchman in the break meant that Connolly was the crowd's favourite and to him steaming round the circuit at such speed that he almost caught the remains of the peloton, thrilled the huge crowd. With the memory of the puncture during the last big stage of the Tour still vivid in his memory, he flashed down the finishing straight, praying not to hear the bang, which of course, never came. He crossed the line with his hands aloft in the traditional two-handed victory salute, with a smile as wide as the Grand Canyon. He had been delighted to win the Tour but the euphoria he was feeling as he free-wheeled towards his helpers and supporters was greater than even that. As he came to a halt, he was enveloped by a crush of well-meaning bodies but saw the two faces he was most looking for, John Ryan and Sarah. Without too much ceremony Ryan and a couple of mechanics bundled well-wishers and reporters out of the way to allow Sarah and Bruce to embrace, or more accurately, smother each other. As moments go, it was the sweetest either could remember.

In the sprint for second, if sprint was the right word, a tired but still delighted Roger Powell edged out both of the Italians who couldn't be separated either by the judges or the cameras.

A few rainbow jerseys had been won in the past by luck, some by sheer brilliance and some by sheer hard work. Occasionally the best man on the day had not won; sometimes one of a number of equally worthy riders had had a little bit of extra luck; and sometimes one man had been head and shoulders above the rest when winning the world crown. This was one such time!

CHAPTER FORTY-ONE

The Cools Classic was one of a relatively small number of American bike races which attracted an international field of real class, in fact the only other one was the Tour of California, but that was a stage race and held in May. In the seventies the similarly named Coors Light Classic had been the first American race to attract foreign riders of note and this had been followed by the Tour de Trump and the Tour Dupont. Bernhard Hinault in his La Vie Claire years, and Greg Lemond and Mexican Raoul Alcala had scored notable victories in these races. This year for the first time the Cools had been added to the World Cup and this had added a huge amount of both prestige and interest. The prize list was very attractive and no expense had been spared in accommodating the teams. It said a great deal for the enthusiasm and influence of the organisers that they had managed to get part of New York closed to traffic. Prior to this event only the New York marathon had been granted such a privilege. Previously, it had been considered impossible for such a happening ever to be arranged but such was the power of advertising, the recent huge increase in the popularity of cycling in the U.S. and the persuasive skill of the organisers, that for approximately six hours on a Sunday in late September, cycling would be king!

To minimise the disruption to the city the race was due to start at 7 a.m. and to end depending on the race speed of course at around 1 p.m., the racing being broadly based around Central Park. Starting in Queens, and then crossing the Queensborough Bridge, the riders would go down East Fifty-Ninth Street, then West Fifty-Seventh Street, before turning right along Henry Hudson Parkway with the Hudson River on the riders' left. Turning right on at West Ninety-Sixth Street, they would then go through Central Park itself, along East Ninety-Sixth Street, then right down Lexington Avenue, joining the circuit at East Fifty-Seventh Street. The lap distance was almost ten miles and there were twelve laps in all, before the race turned left at the end of the last lap for the final sprint across Queensborough Bridge, the race finishing on the Queens' side of the bridge. In truth, the course, although not unattractive and certainly interesting had no climbs to speak of but there was a very strong wind blowing which would make the stretch down Lexington very hard. Even as the day dawned, bright but cold, the hardiest fans had begun to gather at the best points on the course. As a spectacle, the event was beginning to look distinctly Continental with French, Italian, Belgian, Dutch and Spanish teams being well represented as well as British, Australian and American teams in abundance reflecting the increased globalisation of cycle racing. Many continental sponsoring companies were using the opportunity to advertise their wares to the Americans – ice cream, chewing gum, banking, cycling accessories, computers, a world-wide delivery company and a health drink firm were all vividly displayed and already there were plenty of free gifts a la Tour De France style being given to the early arriving fans.

The stiff breeze was blowing the trees in Central Park and leaves were blowing about in crazy patterns. The early sunshine, though without much warmth, nevertheless gave the whole scene a warm glow and the paucity of both people and vehicles helped to create a much more peaceful scene than is usually associated with the Big Apple.

Ten minutes later the air of calm had evaporated from the vicinity of the start area as, one by one, the teams arrived. Ruff-Stuff Jeans, Corvette - U.S. and Williams N.Y., the three most local American teams arrived first. PDZ-Light, Bianchi-Jerez, Santiamo and Mercia-McConnell soon followed. The British teams ABC-Mercian, A. & J. - Brachman and United Foodstuffs were next and Brooklin, Sansor -J.D. and Selma-Consor were the last to arrive. Three American espoirs teams had also been invited with the newly formed Australian squad Unica-Green Bay bringing the total to seventeen teams of tem men each, a total of one hundred and seventy riders.

Brooklin had two strategies for the race. Connolly needed a top five placing to keep him in contention for the World Cup, unless of course all the other main contenders failed to score. To achieve this Ryan instructed the team to work for Bruce. If however, either Bruce was not feeling too good or all the other top World Cup riders were by the later stages of the race clearly out of it, they were to switch allegiance to the team's best sprinter, Ron Morrow to help him win if the race ended in a bunch sprint. Ron himself was excused supporting duties until the later stages of the race.

In addition to this the trusted few had been told by Ryan to leave the rest of the team to look after Bruce and keep their eyes out for the bad guys in exactly the same way as they had at Paris-Brussells. It was now just after six-thirty and the riders were signing on, receiving last minute pep talks from their managers, kisses from wives and girlfriends, and food and drinks from their helpers. Sarah kissed Bruce as Judith kissed Ryan. Connolly rode and Ryan drove off in the direction of the start. As they left neither saw a woman, who would have been slightly familiar to them, go up and speak to Judith, smiling as she did so. After a few words the two women walked off together.

The plans formulated by Dowling and his associates had been carefully laid, even more so than those aborted in Paris-Brussells. Connolly was to be taken out just over halfway through the race. Before that, however, a message was to be relayed to Ryan that Judith had been kidnapped and Ryan was to pass that message on to Connolly. He would also be told that any plans Connolly et al had for interfering in the bad guys' plans must be dropped or they would never see Judith again.

As the riders wound their way across Queensborough Bridge from the start, such possible eventualities were not even being contemplated by Connolly. Still in the neutralised part of the race, the riders had time to look down onto the East River and Roosevelt Island. The early morning sun shimmering on the water was so beautiful that the riders' minds were, if only very briefly, taken away from the job in hand. The water traffic, if not as romantic or attractive as in decades past nevertheless looked almost jolly despite the fairly drab colours and uninteresting cargoes. The breeze was whipping up the tops of the waves and as Roger Powell looked at the lighters moving up and down the river, some of the lines from John Masefield's poem 'Cargoes' came into his mind, *Dirty British coaster with its salt-caked smokestack butting up the Channel in the mad March days.* The boats weren't coasters, it wasn't March, and it wasn't the Channel but the thoughts made Powell feel a little homesick. Suddenly he had no time to think anything as the flag dropped to signify the end of the neutralised zone and the race started in earnest.

With so many domestic riders taking part all keen to make their mark in front of the already large home crowd, the racing was certain to be fast and furious. So it proved and for the first four laps, numerous attacks from either home based riders or American riders in foreign teams ensured lots of action for the crowd to appreciate. Monitoring and chasing down the more serious attacks meant lots of work for the top teams. The race then began to settle down somewhat but even so as with all city centre races it remained exciting with slower riders being eliminated as they were lapped. With three tight corners and the roads through Central Park being greasy, there were several accidents. None were serious but they resulted in a few injuries forcing the riders in question to abandon.

Connolly had to ride fairly hard and carefully to keep in contention and he hadn't had much time to think about the bad guys or how his teammates were doing in tracing them. Twice he had to swerve violently to avoid other riders who suddenly careered across in front of him but by lap six the field was down to just over a hundred riders and the attacks had subsided for the moment. A Brooklin jersey came alongside. It was Joe Romain.

"You've been deliberately switched at least three times, Bruce."

"Are you sure?"

"Pete and I have been behind you all the way. It's not been the same guy and the guys who have gone across you haven't done it deliberately but they been leaned on by one guy who neither of us recognise. I've told Sean to come up and ride shotgun while Pete and I try to sort this guy out. The others are looking for the switch, if there is one." Bruce nodded his agreement. Then thinking quickly he waved for Joe to come back up to him.

"I've just had an idea. If I attack hard but not so hard that somebody really determined to keep with me can't, you two tagging along as well, the chances are, our boy will have to join me if he's going to get me. A few others are bound to follow. He wouldn't be able to afford to let me go. Worth a try?"

"Sure. You feel strong enough to go for a long one?"

"Is the Pope a catholic?"

"Sorry, stupid question. Okay, just let me warn Pete and Sean and then we'll go for it."

The conversation had been noticed by quite a few riders and Connolly knew they would assume that he was planning something and it wouldn't be the menu for the evening meal. There was no point in going for the break straightaway as the other teams' riders would be ready. He waited for a while then halfway down Lexington and therefore still into the wind, he mentally gathered himself then jumped on the pedals as hard as he could. He shot past the riders at the front of the bunch, Romain, Weiss and Brean following immediately. The reaction from the bunch was a bit slow in coming. For four riders all from the same team to be away in a break was virtually unheard of even with the distance that was still left in this race. It also spelled 'finis' for the other riders if it was not pulled back pretty quickly. Fortunately for the peloton it was not the Brooklin intention to break away on their own they had to try and take the bad guy with them. When the four saw the damage that Bruce's attack had wrought they eased off slightly and were rewarded a few seconds later by the sight of another half-dozen or so riders trying to get across.

By now the four had reached the corner of Lexington and East Fifty-Ninth Street. As they swept around it, they slowed but not too obviously to allow their pursuers to catch up. As Connolly wanted to win the race, he still needed to keep the pace up to keep away from the peloton and to build up their lead. Gradually the six pursuers caught the four and then two more joined the breakaway. One from Santiamo, two from the Selma-Consor team, three from Sansor-JD two from Roger Powell's team and one from the Ruff-Stuff Jeans team made up the pursuers. Connolly tried to analyse the opposition both from the race point of view and from the personal danger aspect. Which team posed the biggest threat? Ruff-Stuff, Santiamo, Selma-Consor, Sansor-JD... Suddenly, as if seeing it for the first time which in a sense he was, Bruce saw the JD rather than the Sansor. Surely it couldn't be that obvious could it? He rode up to Weiss.

"What do you know about Sansor-JD?"

"They're always there or thereabouts."

"No, not the racing team. What do you know about the team sponsors?"

"Not much. Sansor make sports clothes I think. No idea about JD." He paused thinking, and then realisation as the penny dropped for him too.

"Oh my God! J.D... James Dowling. It can't be that simple surely. We can't have been that fucking stupid can we?"

"It's Ercole's old team. It must be that." Connolly replied. He stopped talking as Van der Eyysen, one of the riders from Sansor-JD tried to attack and the others reacted to bring him back. Weiss and Connolly were caught napping slightly and as if to confirm their suspicions Brambani didn't react immediately either and waited a little behind the Americans until they set off chasing down the rest of the breakaway. A few minutes' chase brought them all together again and everyone settled down.

"Whatever you do don't get caught at the back with Brambani, Harnot or Van der Eyysen. I'll tell Joe." Weiss rode up to Romain, whispered a few words then rejoined his leader. He nodded as he came alongside Bruce. Then as the ten riders gradually increased their lead over the bunch, the Brooklin team car came alongside the riders. Ryan signalled to Bruce who manoeuvred himself alongside the car. Alarm was etched on the Directeur Sportif's face.

"Judith's been kidnapped, Bruce. If you or any of the team try to do anything to get in the way of whatever these bastards are planning, whatever that might be, we'll never see her again."

Connolly said nothing for a few seconds. Ryan was clearly very upset.

"Okay, John, we shoulda seen it coming. We realised a few minutes ago that the JD in Sansor-JD is obviously James Dowling. How we could have missed something as fucking obvious as that is beyond me. That was the one name Ercole gave us before he was shot. Anyway we reckon that one or more, likely both Brambani and Van der Eyysen are up to no good. There's only one thing we can do. I'll go for broke, try to get the bastards to chase me or hopefully leave me alone. Lay off trying to catch anyone up to any nonsense as far as smuggling is concerned and we'll try to get them another time."

"What about Judith?"

"She's not likely to get hurt. This is just another frightener. They're just using her as protection. We'll get her back all in one piece don't worry."

Quickly Connolly relayed the information to his teammates and they quickly agreed what to do. There were now three laps left. They decided to wait until they reached Lexington again before unleashing their attack. This would be into the wind and therefore more difficult to counter. Before that, first Romain, then Connolly himself would try a couple of softeners through the Park. Weiss would then lead out Connolly for real as soon as they turned onto Lexington from East Ninety-Sixth Street.

The two semi-attacks in Central Park succeeded in dropping Luca Frenchini, Adam Padston and Adrie Van der Eyssen, the Dutchman obviously suffering from his earlier attack. As the remainder came out of the Park, past the Cooper Hewitt Museum, Weiss moved smoothly up to the front. Slightly puffed after their chase through the Park, the seven others were left as Weiss sprinted away with Connolly looking as if he was glued to his wheel. For a few seconds Weiss led Connolly at a phenomenal rate then, as he faded, Connolly moved smoothly past. Only two riders made any attempt to follow the Brooklins and it was no surprise to Bruce as he looked back to see that it was the red and yellow jerseys of the Sansor riders who were working furiously to get up to him. They passed a by now jaded Pete as if he was standing still. Connolly had to make an instant decision. He was far enough away from them still, and he felt strong enough to keep away. Neither Brambani nor Harnot were in Bruce's class, but would that help him and Judith? The decision was surprisingly easy. He eased very slightly over the next lap and allowed the Sansor riders to come up to him. Now was the moment of truth. If they tried to leave him, as would be the norm expecting a lone breakaway to be tired, that would indicate genuine racing intentions. Catching the American the Sansor riders both slowed slightly to his pace.

Connolly tried to look surprised and did what they would expect an innocent rider to do in the circumstances, he tried to break away again. He didn't try too hard however and they had no trouble catching him. He glimpsed the two signalling to each other. It wasn't clear what was intended, but obviously, something was. Where would they make their move? More importantly how? The least populated part of the course was along the Henry Hudson Parkway, the wind and the river together made that section somewhat inhospitable.

As if to give Bruce a clue as to the 'how', he felt rather than saw, the two station themselves on each side of him and a metre or so to the rear. They were now turning off West Fifty Seventh onto the Parkway and Connolly thought he knew what they would try to do. Somewhere along the Parkway, when with the tailwind they would be travelling at their fastest, they would sandwich him. It would be difficult and dangerous for them as well as for him but these guys weren't playing for nickels and dimes and it was obviously necessary to down Connolly. No doubt there would be other hoodlums lurking in the crowd if any other touches were necessary to complete his demise.

They were about a hundred metres along the Parkway, their speed building after the corner, when Bruce decided to make his move first. He jumped on the pedals and pushed for all he was worth, his thigh, calf, shoulder and forearm muscles strained to their limit. For a few metres he pulled away from the other two but they were stronger than he had thought possible. He should be leaving them with the effort he was making. They must be on something, something bloody good! He tried again but only succeeded in opening a gap of a few metres. With a sickening feeling he realised that he just wouldn't be able to ride away from them. Dear God, what could he do? He heard and felt them coming closer on each side of him, there was absolutely nothing more he could do!

CHAPTER FORTY-TWO

At the race headquarters, James Dowling, present at an event for the first time in two seasons, was conscious that although things seemed to be going well, there was still much to be kept under control. He was never happy to be seen at events, even though his company was the secondary sponsor of a team and a successful one at that. He had no real interest in cycling as such; he had seen the sport merely as an effective way of advertising and latterly of course a brilliant way of making a lot of money on the side. The amounts produced had exceeded his most ambitious expectations, the only drawback having been the necessity to involve Indurrana and his cronies in order to obtain the smuggled goods in the first place.

The abduction of Ryan's tart had been amazingly easy. The similarity in appearance of Judith and Joanne was extraordinary.

Now looking at the race on the huge TV screen, he had to admit that he was relieved that the Sansor boys had managed to get Connolly to themselves. It shouldn't be difficult to bring about the 'accident' along the Parkway and the insurance of having some of Harry's men in the crowd over there should tie up any loose ends. If the accident didn't waste Connolly, they certainly would. It would be the end of the careers of Harnot and Brambani, of course, they would be tested and found positive of course and get banned. But that was part of the plan the drugs would explain their erratic and dangerous riding. They of course would receive ample compensation.

He looked at his watch. It was almost time for his 'minders' to join the race. This was going to be more difficult here as there was very little open space and was made even more difficult by having had to doctor several bikes thereby requiring several attendant riders. On the plus side, the elimination of riders for all sorts of reasons made it more difficult for officials to know exactly what was going on, especially at the end of a race away from the front where the interest was. The only cloud on the horizon was whether or not Santana had told Connolly anything of value before he had been shot. If he had been able to point the finger at Dowling, presumably Connolly would have done something by now. Comforted by this thought, he decided to make his way to where Ryan's tart had been incarcerated. He wanted to be away from the race area by the time the 'accident' happened and be back in his office by the end of the race presentations. As far as he could tell, Connolly's teammates were making no attempt to do anything other than race normally. Connolly himself was clearly simply riding to win. Dowling quietly slipped away. A few minutes later he was followed by one of his faithful minders and Harry Matthews' secretary Jessie.

Halfway along the Parkway Harry Matthews was sweating again. God how he hated Dowling. He cursed himself. There was nothing he could do to escape the man's clutches and he knew that as soon as he made a mistake he would end up with a pair of concrete boots. He wrenched his mind away from his fears and tried to concentrate on the race. Connolly and the two Sansor riders were now well out in front and on the next circuit, the last, they would bring Connolly down as damagingly as possible. Harry looked along the Parkway to where a group of spectators stood. A cursory glance would have passed over them as just fans. A closer examination would have revealed that there was no emotion being shown by any of them, that all were men, and that they appeared to be screening something behind them.

The items in question were bikes, none in Sansor colours, and three riders, in the same colours as the bikes. Matthews looked at his watch. Right on cue, two Sansor riders came past him, raised their hands in the universal cyclists' signal indicating that they had a problem, and came to a halt by the group of men. The bunch sped by a few minutes later and as they passed the men, the two cyclists jumped back on their bikes and chased after the bunch. A keen observer would have noted, however, that only one rider was in Sansor colours. Seconds later, another two Sansor riders also stopped and the process was repeated. A few stragglers then passed and then the process was repeated a third time. Shortly after all this the Sansor riders replaced by the 'plants', rejoined the race. In all the hustle and bustle and excitement no one noticed what had happened.

Matthews heaved a sigh of relief. That was one hurdle safely overcome. At the end of the race, the two plants having by now located the doctored bikes, would ride to the finish as close to them, then when the excitement brought about by Connolly's accident, diverted everyone's attention, the plants would indicate to the equally fake mechanics, which were the bikes to take. Mechanics, riders and bikes would then disappear, the mechanics leaving two replacement bikes so as not to arouse suspicion. The few thousand pounds in value of the spare bikes would be carried by the bike manufacturers anyway. Matthews looked at his watch again. It wouldn't be long before the three leaders would be passing him on their final lap. He heard the roar of the crowd and saw the three leaders swing onto the Parkway. Connolly was still leading with a Sansor rider on each side of and slightly behind him. Any moment now they would take him.

Dowling unaware of exactly how the race was progressing had almost reached the warehouse where Judith was incarcerated. The kidnapping had been very easy indeed. Joanne had merely identified herself and suggested a cup of coffee. It being early morning, it would be easy to call a cab Joanne had said and the one that had picked them up had, of course, been laid on by Joanne. As Judith had climbed in two men had run out of the crowd of spectators, pushed Joanne very convincingly out of the way and on to the sidewalk and followed Judith into the cab. As she started to scream one of the men had put a hand over her mouth and at the same time she felt the prick of a needle in her right hand. After a very short while she ceased to struggle and lost consciousness. When Dowling arrived she was still unconscious and her two guards had had to do nothing. For convenience' sake the substitute bikes had also been brought here, but as always, having an eye on security, Dowling would be able to view the whole proceedings from an office overlooking the warehouse floor without anyone seeing him. The guards employed by Matthews and unaware of Dowling's presence simply had to keep the girl until Sad Sam or Matthews himself came to collect her. Dowling looked at his watch; the race should be finishing in a few minutes. It would take about half an hour for the bikes to be picked up and brought over, but better to add say ten minutes for possible traffic problems so he settled down to wait.

Connolly could now see the Sansor rider on his right, he looked to his left and as he had expected, there was the other one coming up. Then they moved slightly outward of him and he knew It was only seconds before they made their move. The three riders were travelling at well over sixty kilometres an hour, the adrenalin was pumping and Connolly no longer felt concerned about his safety. He felt rather than saw the two riders beginning to close. The hairs on the back of his neck stood up. His timing had to be perfect. At the last millisecond he slammed on his brake levers as hard as he could and thankfully with a dry road he didn't skid but almost stopped. The other two were caught completely unawares. They had expected Connolly's body to be there and suddenly there was nothing. The gap left made them overbalance and they fell into each other with a terrible crash.

Harnot flew into the air, the force of the impact forcing him out of his clipless pedals, he cart wheeled crazily, hit the

395

road with sickening force, landed on his head, broke his neck and was killed instantly. Brambani fell into the road and immediately became entangled in the chain sets, pedals and gears of both bikes. The teeth of one of the chain sets ripped into his left leg, the right one being broken by the impact with the road. He screamed as he slid along the road, blood streaming from his multiple cuts. After what seemed an eternity to the stunned watching crowd who had begun to boo as they saw what the Sansor riders were going to try and do to Connolly, Brambani came to a halt, lying in the road still attached to his bike and screaming for help. Miraculously Connolly swerved around the wreckage of men and machines, built up his momentum again, in spite of the shock and continued on his way unaware of the seriousness of the injuries. Inevitably the bunch slowed when it came to the scene of the accident and Connolly had no trouble crossing the finishing line on Queensborough Bridge first, in spite of now trembling. The crowd, mostly American, of course, were ecstatic about Connolly's win and as usual at the finish of a race, he was instantly mobbed by reporters, but fought his way to the team car which had just pulled up and climbed in. Frank Costello was at the wheel.

"Where's John, Frank?"

"He's in the other car, he stopped by the accident. It looked pretty bad, Bruce. Harnot hadn't moved at all and Brambani was screaming blue murder. There was a lot of blood about."

"It should've been mine as far as those two were concerned. Get a message to the dope control, Frank. Do what you can to make sure they're tested. The way I was riding, those two must've been on something to keep with me. Do you know about Judith's kidnapping?"

"Yeah, John's worried sick."

"Get me in to the control as quick as you can, and then check on Pete, Sean and Joe, they might have some interesting news. Then get back to John. Let's move it, Frank."

Harry Matthews had watched fascinated as he saw Harnot and Brambani preparing to sandwich Connolly. Then, suddenly unaccountably, feeling ashamed that such a fine athlete was about to be seriously hurt even possibly killed, he had been delighted when Connolly had outfoxed the other two. In the microseconds that followed, his emotions ran riot. Horror at the sight of the crash and its obvious seriousness was immediately followed by fear for himself because of the repercussions of what would certainly be seen as his failure. This, in turn, was succeeded by shame that he should be thinking about himself as two men lay seriously injured, relief that Connolly was alright and finally, the realisation that here was the opportunity to get out of the hellish mess he had been in for so, so long. These thoughts galvanised him into action. By now it was obvious that although the two riders were badly hurt, one lying ominously still, there were more than enough people about to provide whatever assistance was required. Matthews newly discovered conscience didn't trouble him therefore as he moved away, quite sure that he had to find Dowling.

It was obviously a day for sudden reappraisals of one's position. As soon as Jessica picked herself up off the pavement, she too felt a kaleidoscope of feelings rush through her as had her criminal colleague Harry: fear for herself, relief that she had played her part in Dowling's scheme successfully, fear for her sister, then utter revulsion of herself. Many solicitous hands had helped her to her feet and equally concerned souls had offered her drinks of tea and had tried to persuade her to sit down. Her mind in turmoil and her heart worse, she got away from her would-be Samaritans as quickly as she could and tried to think. Her fear of Dowling had completely evaporated at least temporarily and she knew she had to find her sister. Hopelessness gripped her as she realised she had no idea where Dowling's goons had taken Judith.

"You bitch!" A female voice hissed at her with considerable venom. She turned around in surprise and alarm. The woman seemed slightly familiar but she couldn't place her for the moment.

"You absolute bitch! You might have fooled the crowd and that poor girl, but you didn't fool me. I know something of your game. I've been watching you for months."

Recognition flooded through Jessica, the woman was one of the secretaries in Dowling's company. She couldn't remember her name; she seized upon her as a lifeline and grabbed hold of her arm.

"You must help me, they've kidnapped my sister!"

"Your sister!" This time it was Jessie's turn to be surprised.

"Yes, I know what it looks like, and yes I've done some bad things but you've got to help me. I don't know what to do."

"Help you do what?"

"Rescue my sister. It's all to do with the Bruce Connolly business, but I'll explain later." Suddenly a thought struck Jessica.

"Anyway, what are you doing here?"

Jessie smiled slightly.

"Before I say anymore, how do I know I can trust you? What you've just said could be all eyewash."

"I swear to you I realise what a mess I've got myself into and I'll do anything to firstly get my sister out of danger, and me out of the mess I'm in. Please believe me." Jessie looked appraisingly at Jessica for a while then shrugged.

"Okay, well I work for Harry Matthews and just lately we've been, shall we say, getting on pretty well together. I've had my suspicions for a long time that something wasn't quite right about the firm. Too many nameless people coming to see the boss and us never seeing him. The letters we typed never having any pattern to them as you would see in a normal company, and most of all, too much money for too little work." She stopped, thinking for a moment.

"What's the matter?" Jessica asked looking even more worried.

"We're not getting anywhere here, let's drive while we talk."

She called a cab. Having given the driver an address that meant nothing to Jessica, Jessie carried on with her explanation.

"Anyway, two days ago Harry came down from 'above' looking very worried, well frightened really but he wouldn't tell me what the problem was." Jessica interjected at this point.

"Was that the last time I came in?" Jessie thought then nodded.

"Yes, I think it was, in fact I'm sure of it."

"Well, in that case I'm not surprised he was frightened."

"You and Harry involved in the same thing?" Jessica nodded.

"Hmm. Anyway I decided that it was about time I tried to find out a bit more about the business of the company in my own way. Bosses never ever give credit to people like me. Because they hardly notice us, they think we don't notice things either. Anyway to cut a very long story short, I found out that after today's job, whatever that job is or was, the thin miserable man, has to eliminate Harry."

"You didn't find out how, where or when?"

"No, I just came along here, hoping for the best. It was a complete fluke that I happened to spot you this morning. I'd seen you in the building several times. That coming down and leaving separately lark isn't half as clever as his nibs thinks you know. I worked out some time ago that you, that odious thin guy and Harry frequently came in on the same days and that you were involved in something together so it seemed a good idea to follow you when you left this morning. I'm trying to help Harry. Now it's your turn to convince me that we're on the same side. From where I'm standing it isn't all that clear."

In as few sentences as she could, Jessica told Jessie as much of her background and involvement in the Connolly affair as was necessary to convince her of her change of heart. The 'Connolly affair' as Jessica called it was of course new to Jessie anyway, so Jessica briefly explained what it was about.

"I wouldn't blame you if you thought me a wicked person."

"Why? Because you opened your legs when it might've been more sensible to have kept them closed? Anyway, lots of wives behave like tarts with their husbands. The guys pay their wives for fucks by buying new clothes, expensive holidays, and new washing machines, whatever. At least you're honest. As for being sensible, I've opened my legs more than once for the wrong guy. Hung like donkeys mind you, but wrong. Anyway as we're all girls together, I guess the boss is pretty good in the sack huh?" she laughed.

The openness of this woman helped Tina and she couldn't help laughing with her.

"I guess so, and yes before you ask, he's hung like a horse too, but he's still very bad news, I've known it all along, I was so stupid. He's a real bastard."

"They always are, honey." By this time Jessie was clearly convinced of Jessica's true feelings and was anxious to be doing something both for Harry and for Judith.

"Find someone in the Brooklin team to take you to either Connolly or Ryan, probably Ryan, and tell them what you know and what you've done. I have a couple of things to do myself. Off you go and try not to worry. Bye."

By this time the cab had reached the edge of the race route near the race H.Q. Without giving Jessica a chance to say anything, Jessie asked the driver to stop and she got out. Jessica still felt frightened, but for the first time for a long while, in her heart she didn't feel totally ashamed of herself.

CHAPTER FORTY-THREE

Harry hadn't been told exactly where Dowling was going to take the Taylor girl but he knew it was an unoccupied office block cum warehouse somewhere in Queens. That still left a great deal of ground to be covered and he knew that he would need some luck if he was going to find Dowling today. One didn't need to be a medium to foresee that after the 'accident' Dowling wouldn't hang around. What Harry didn't know of course was whether the operation with the doctored bikes had been completed satisfactorily. His part had gone well enough and the hoo-hah with the 'accident' itself would certainly divert attention. Having thought about that, Harry realised that it didn't matter much to him anyway. Having made up his mind to break away, he knew it would eventually have to be Dowling or himself, if Harry got that far of course. He had by now crossed the Queensborough Bridge and was almost at Thirty-First Street when the necessary stroke of luck presented itself.

As he had been driving he'd been trying to remember any little snippets of conversation he'd heard in Dowling's office which would help him. As he pictured the desk, he saw in his mind's eye the doodling on Dowling's pad. He could picture various numbers, the word 'Queens', some meaningless, well meaningless to him anyway, squiggles and another name which hadn't really registered at the time. He tried to concentrate on the name. At the junction of Thirty-First Street and Jackson Avenue, he decided to try down

Jackson. Halfway down he saw the name that brought everything together. 'Clarkson House'. In a revelatory flash, he was sure that that was the name on the pad. As the traffic was fairly thin he was able to slow down a little as he drove past. As far as he could tell, it sure looked unoccupied. He felt a tingling in his scalp and up and down his spine. He drove past until he found somewhere to park. Deciding that there was nothing to be gained by secrecy as Dowling wouldn't have any inkling of his change of heart, he made no attempt to find anywhere particularly unobtrusive. He walked back up Jackson and tried the double doors of the Clarkson building. They were firmly locked but this was to be expected. A walk around the building was obviously the order of the day. As he began his reconnaissance he failed to notice the figure on his tail. That same figure had been following him since he had left his hotel first thing in the morning.

There were several entrances but they were all locked. Did he try to break in or wait outside and hope for some unexpected development? More perhaps because he felt that doing nothing might chip away at his resolve, rather than for any other reason, he decided that he would try and break in. Halfway along the back of the building, there was an alley. Without hesitation he entered it and walked quickly along it. It wasn't long before he saw a window, open sufficiently for him to put his arm through. He was then able to open the larger window next to it. Less than a minute later he was inside. He stood perfectly still and listened very hard. For some seconds he heard nothing. Then, satisfied that his entry had not been detected, he began to move as silently as possible about the building. After about twenty minutes, by this time at the very back of the building, he heard a very faint murmur.

Isolating the noise, it became clear that desultory conversation was being carried on in an office now directly in front of him. Heart hammering, he moved up to the door and listened again. He thought he could hear at least two voices but there could be three. None of them were female though. He wondered what the hell to do now. The question was answered for him.

"Go in, Harry, the boys will be pleased to see you." The voice frighteningly familiar, was Dowling's. At the same moment, Harry felt something hard pressed into his back. He recognised a gun when he felt one.

In the meantime, at the race, after Connolly had won and as quickly as he could, he looked for Sarah, Ryan and his team members. Sarah found him and accompanied him to the podium but neither of them could find Ryan. The presentations were mercifully short in view of the death of Harnot but rumours were beginning to circulate concerning what Brambani had told the police before he was taken to hospital.

"Where's John? Do you know anything about Judith? Did the guys spot anything in the race?" Bruce's questions were halted by a raised hand from Sarah.

"Whoosh! Hold on! Where are we rushing off to for a start?"

Bruce stopped, looked at Sarah as if she was stupid for a second, and then began to look a little foolish.

"I see what you mean. Okay tell me what you know. I'll change in the bus as we talk." They reached the bus, fortunately before anyone else and got in.

"Now, we don't know where John is, or anything about Judith. That's the bad news. There is some good news though. The switchings of riders were picked up by some of our lads and the extras are being followed as we speak. That's all taken care of. Pete and Joe don't think that the villains know that they were spotted. What we have to hope for is that wherever the doctored bikes are being taken is also where Judith is being held captive."

"So what do we do now?"

"Nothing 'till we hear from Pete, Joe or Sean who are following the bad guys, or from John, who as I say, we don't know anything about." She hesitated for a moment and then took his hand.

"I was so scared for you out there. You could easily have been killed."

"I guess that was the general idea. I can tell you I was none too happy myself, in fact pretty terrified to be honest."

"You didn't look it. Mr. Ice-cool in fact." In that instant all her cool went and she threw herself into his arms.

"Oh, Bruce, I do love you so very, very much. I don't think I realised quite how much until today."

"Hey, kid, relax, Mr. Indestructible me. Everybody knows that. Still I'm not complaining if my popularity has risen a few points."

"Be serious!"

"I am being serious. The more you love me, the better I like it. That's pretty serious for me." He gave her a bear hug and they were silent for a few seconds.

"Bruce, do you know what happened to the two who tried to sandwich you?"

"Not exactly. One thing I do know is that I really thought they had me. How are they anyway?"

"One's dead, Harnot I think, the other one looks fairly smashed up but he was singing like a bird apparently when he was carted off to the hospital. Dowling's name was apparently mentioned several times. The police want to talk to you but there is absolutely no doubt about their guilt. Before you ask, no one seems to know where Dowling is.

He was apparently seen around the start area very early this morning but no one's seen him since."

"Isn't there anything we can do?" She gave him an old-fashioned look.

"Okay, okay, so there's nothing we can do." By this time Bruce had changed into a tracksuit.

Sarah smiled for the first time since the race began.

"While we sit on our thumbs, we could try and see exactly where we are, what still needs to be sorted out and whether we can tie up some loose ends." Bruce nodded in assent.

"Okay. We know what has been going on, how it's been done, and largely by whom. James Dowling has clearly been running things but it's my guess there's somebody above him. We also know that Judith's sister has been involved in some way." Sarah jumped in here.

"Oh yes. It's pretty certain that that it was her who has used a number of names in the past, who arranged the kidnapping."

"Figures." Bruce nodded. "Judith wouldn't fall for any old scam and even though she's seen the photos, just seeing her sister might well put her off her guard long enough. Anyway, what we need to do, apart from getting Judith back in one piece, is to get Dowling with some of the goods, get him to spill the beans on the other guys and find out who pulled the triggers on the murders."

"That seems like a pretty long shopping list to me," Sarah was frowning, "and there are a couple of things you've missed."

"Such as?"

"Such as, who is the spy in the Brooklin camp? Secondly, Why?"

"The second one's easy. Money."

"Probably, but I have a feeling there's more to it than that."

"Ah, yes. Your 'feelings'."

"You may mock maestro, but mark my words." They both jumped as the phone in the bus buzzed.

"Yes, she's here." The driver passed the 'phone to Sarah.

"Sarah, it's Joe. We followed the crooks, after two car changes mind you, to an office block on Jackson Avenue. It looks as if it's not being used at present. Get here as soon as you can. We'll be waiting a little way along from the office block which is called the Clarkson Building. We're in the dark blue Lincoln and we're pretty sure we haven't been spotted. Don't hang about."

"Okay, Joe. You all be careful." She handed the phone back to the driver.

"Right, Leon. Jackson Avenue and step on it."

CHAPTER FORTY-FOUR

Whilst none of the main actors in the drama were aware that the climax was fast approaching, each sensed that something of significance was about to happen. From different points, Dowling, Connolly and Sarah, Ryan, Harry Matthews (without him realising it, suddenly promoted from bit-part player to main support), Jessica and Jessie (like Harry now of much greater importance than hitherto), were all converging on an office block in New York where the other major player, Judith Taylor, was already on stage.

A short while after Harry's arrival and his very unwelcome welcome from his employer, Bruce and Sarah met up with Romain and Weiss, both to Connolly's astonishment, armed. Shortly to arrive were the two other women and one last ace-in-the-hole of whom only one of the eight was aware, who was still some miles away.

As far as Dowling was concerned, he had two urgent problems to resolve – the anticipated one of Ryan's tart, and the unexpected one of Harry Matthews, who by now should have been taken care of by Sad Sam or one of his acolytes. The unsatisfactory nature of that aspect irked him considerably but he drove it out of his mind as he sought to conclude the current business. He had Harry tied up for the moment and was now concentrating on his merchandise. The bikes were now being stripped of their exceedingly valuable cargo. From within the handlebars, the seat pillars and from under the saddles, in the last case, in slim black plastic cases that looked for all the world as if they were part of the saddles, Dowling's hoods retrieved chamois leather pouches and passed them to their boss. His eyes alight in expectation., Dowling very carefully emptied the contents onto a small baize covered table. Diamonds. Perfect River diamonds, the highest value diamonds in existence. Almost priceless because of their purity and, of course, their rarity. Dowling's worries were banished as he feasted his eyes on the fortune in front of him.

A door creaked. He froze. All the others in the office looked at him. He motioned to his thugs to get behind the door. Silence reined again. Dowling very carefully gathered the diamonds into their bags and then he moved to the door. The sequence of events that followed was extremely rapid and a great deal happened in a very few seconds.

Dowling pulled the door open, Weiss and Connolly almost fell into the room. One of the thugs hit Connolly with his gun and the other shot Weiss.

"You fucking moron!" hissed Dowling as he ran from the door not realising that a little way behind Weiss and Connolly had been Romain with Sarah behind him. Joe shot the man who had shot Weiss, as he entered the room, turning as he fired. The two thugs fell into each other and Matthews stuck out his legs causing Dowling to trip. He stumbled but didn't fall and was able to get to Judith and put a gun to her head before Joe could do anything about it.

"Back off and put the gun down now!" Dowling barked.

Joe hesitated clearly not relishing being unarmed.

"Do it moron or she dies!" He clearly meant what he said. Joe did as he was told.

"Miss Curzon isn't it? Do come in. The party just wouldn't be the same without you." Dowling didn't smile. "You," he pointed to the uninjured hood.

"Pick up the diamonds, we'll take this one with us. Miss Curzon, over here." He pushed Judith away grabbed Sarah and moved towards the door.

"All the lines you've heard in films about not doing anything rash, they're the ones to take note of now. However, before we go, you, Harry, were going to end your miserable life anyway. You were just lucky for a few hours — Sam must be having an off day. It was only for a few hours though. Bye, Harry." He raised his gun and pointed it at Harry's head. The silence was palpable. It was broken by a groan from Connolly. As if a signal, the groan was followed by the deafening sound of a gunshot!

Sarah and Judith screamed together. Harry's face had a stunned expression on it as he slumped to the floor. Dowling's henchmen looked equally shocked. Milliseconds later Dowling crashed to the floor, his gun still in his fingers, now lifeless fingers, shot through the heart by a bullet from Jessica's gun. She and Jessie had met up on the way to the office block and the sound of the fighting and the earlier shots had masked their approach. Jessica was now trembling and began to cry quietly. Joe was the quickest to regain his wits and he was able to grab the gun from Dowling's thug, hit him with it, and then satisfied he was out cold and there was nothing to fear from the other hood, he went to check on Weiss and Connolly. Bruce was slowly coming to and Pete was breathing. The shot had struck a glancing blow to his head and there was plenty of blood about but he was in no danger. Sarah meanwhile had called an ambulance.

Joe cut Harry and Judith free and then helped Bruce to his feet. Reaction was now setting in in different ways. Judith rushed over to Jessica put her arms around her. Jessie was employing much the same manoeuvre with Harry. Sarah and Joe now tied the two villains together, patching up the wounded one as well as they could.

For three men who had spent most of the day competing in an extremely hard event in one of the hardest of sports, Connolly, Romain and Weiss had performed miraculously, especially Joe. Now all three were ready to drop. Before that luxury, however, there was some tidying up required, Connolly roused himself and rang Henry. He quickly explained what had happened and Henry assured his son that he would do all he could to sort out the small matter of the police as discreetly as possible. True to his word, he arrived a few minutes later just preceded by the paramedics and accompanied by three men who were not introduced but who were obviously plainclothes policemen.

Assurances having been given about statements the following day. Everyone was allowed to leave, some with Henry, some in Bruce's car, driven by Sarah. Henry's offer of accommodation for the night was gratefully accepted, and all but Pete who was being kept in hospital for observation were keen to take to the numerous beds in Henry's house as soon as they arrived. Before that, however, Henry explained the non-appearance of Ryan.

"He called me just after the race finished. He hadn't been able to find out anything nor find any of you and was frantic with worry. He left me a number to call as soon as I knew anything and as soon as Bruce rang me I rang John. He was obviously very relieved especially about Judith, then said to give everyone his best. He said he was onto something and would call back in the morning."

"Is there anything else to be done now though?" This from Mary, who had been at Henry's house all the time.

"Yes, I'm afraid there is. Two things really. Raymond Dragonard is the first and a certain highly regarded cycling authority being the other. However, both of those can wait until the morning when we're not all out on our feet." Connolly's tone made it clear that that was that for the night but everyone was too tired to argue anyway.

The following morning after a good night's sleep and a superb breakfast courtesy of Mary, all except Harry, Jessica and Jessie gathered in Henry's lounge.

"You mentioned last night that Dragonard was somehow involved, Bruce?" The questioner was Joe.

"I'd had my suspicions for a while. As a few people know, the Brooklin team is a little different to all the others.

410

Although the firm Brooklin do provide some of the sponsorship, and Dragonard was their man, most of the financial backing has always come from a source which has been kept secret, even from me. I didn't find out who the source was until very recently. The really weird thing about the backing was that from the outset, I was invited to be team leader with absolute choice as to who would ride for us, how much they would be paid and when and if anyone had to be fired. Dragonard was introduced to me as the Brooklin representative, he being quite agreeable to all of this. Brooklin were putting up twenty-five per cent of the finance and would therefore receive the same percentage of the income. Both Brooklin and the unknown benefactor provided accountants to jointly check the books. Things were swell for the first couple of years, but as the accidents happened Dragonard began to argue with me; and with John for that matter, more and more. Finally, as you all know, he tried to sack John, something which he knew well enough was not in his power. Since then he's disappeared. It's my guess that latterly he's been on Dowling's payroll and he's been organising, through one of the mechanics I'd guess, the leaking of information to Dowling. "

"Presumably this was the same mechanic who tampered with your bike in England?" Henry interjected.

"Can't we find out who it was?" Mary sounded affronted.

"I figure it's too late and he'll be long gone by now. It will be difficult, if not impossible to prove anything and he's only a very small fish anyway. For what it's worth, I don't think we shall ever find out who killed Santana either. Ercole had told me about this 'Sad Sam' character but neither of the guys yesterday fits his description."

"And I thought it was all over." Sarah sighed wistfully. Bruce smiled and squeezed her hand.

"It almost is, hopefully John may have some more information when he gets back. Anyway, I'm certain the smuggling business is over. The publicity will be enough to keep everybody very watchful for a long time to come."

"How's the Sansor rider?" Judith spoke for the first time.

"He'll live." Henry grunted rather disgustedly.

"What..." Sarah was interrupted by the doorbell ringing. Mary returned with John in tow and an unexpected visitor.

"I think you know Bruce and Sarah", Ryan began and then he introduced the other members of the group.

"Ladies and gentlemen, for those of you who don't know him, this is Sir James Stirlingson, the British Minister for Sport." Everyone nodded. Judith however was not interested in Stirlingson. She ran over to Ryan and flung herself around him. To his credit John did the same to her. Only Stirlingson seemed embarrassed by this show of emotion.

"I guess John has filled you in on what's been happening, Sir James? Bruce asked.

"Yes a little. I, er, expect that you are wondering why Mr. Ryan has brought me over here?

"Just a little," Henry replied looking puzzled.

"Perhaps I can explain," Ryan began, gently disengaging himself from Judith but still holding her hand.

"After the race, whilst wondering what the hell to do, I saw Raymond Dragonard leaving the circuit. So, since there seemed to be nothing else I could do to help, bearing in mind that he'd disappeared after trying to sack me, I decided to follow him. To cut a long story short..." Bruce interjected at this point.

"We've pretty much reckoned out friend Raymond's part in all this."

"Good, that simplifies things. Well, eventually I caught up with him but kept out of his sight. He was making his way back to Queens by the look of things when he heard or something which caused him to change his mind. I thought he'd spotted me, but that wasn't it. He suddenly turned his car around, bloody dangerous actually and hared back the way he had come. As he raced off another car accelerated after him and I turned too, more safely I assure you and tried to follow them. Dragonard was driving like a lunatic, so was the other guy for that matter. How they didn't hit anything I'll never know. Dragonard had almost reached the bridge when a cab came out of a side street. Dragonard had to really slam on his anchors. The other car caught up, went alongside and the passenger in the other car shot Dragonard in the head."

Ryan sounded appalled.

At that moment, Jessica, Harry and Jessie, who hadn't been awakened for the meeting, walked in. The effect of their entrance was exactly what Connolly would have wished for. Jessica stood stock still, alarm, fear then panic succeeding each other in her eyes and on her face like pictures from an old cartoon film. Even Stirlingson for all his political and diplomatic training and experience couldn't hide his astonishment. He recovered much more quickly than Jessica however. Instantly realising from her body language that Jessica had been accepted into Connolly's circle, he decided to attack first.

"Don't you know who this girl is?" he almost shouted pointing at Jessica.

"Well, first and foremost, she's my sister." Judith's extremely polite but ice-cold reply was ignored by the Englishman.

"She's nothing but a prostitute, a very expensive one I might add. She's also a close associate of James Dowling of J.D.Textiles, who sponsors one of the pro cycling teams."

"Was Stirlingson, was." Connolly's omission of Stirlingson's polite title was deliberate and did not go unnoticed by the politician.

"What do you mean, was?"

"Well firstly," Connolly motioned to Joe who moved to the door.

413

"Jessica disassociated herself from Dowling some time ago, and secondly," he paused to tease Stirlingson along, "Dowling is dead."

Connolly looked at Jessica, almost imperceptibly shook his head, and then spoke.

"He was shot yesterday by an unknown assailant in an unoccupied office block where this lady was being held against her will. I didn't see the man, but a witness described him as being very thin with a mournful look about him. Does that description ring any bells?"

"Why on earth should it? I'm not in the habit of consorting with hoodlums." Stirlingson was now clearly feeling easier.

"No, of course not and yet you seem to know all about Jessica here." Connolly left the comment hanging in the air."

"Anyway, do you know why Dowling was killed?"

"It may have had something to do with the fact that he was about to kill this gentleman," Bruce pointed to Harry. "Of whom, I believe, you have some knowledge?"

"I've never seen him before in my life; I don't know him at all." The minister was all bluster now.

"I didn't say you did know him, I said that you knew of him. Would you care to explain this, Sir James?" Connolly thrust the photograph of Jessica and Stirlingson taken at the previous year's Tour of Lombardy.

"If you can't, I'm sure that Jessica here can, or as you probably know her, Joanne Turner." The bluster was beginning to waver but Stirlingson was not yet down.

"I came here to try and help and to see how much progress you had made. All I get is this harassment. I've got better things to do than waste my time with you people." He turned to go but found his way barred by Romain.

"Move out of my way you silly little man or I'll move you." Joe didn't look in the least bit interested in moving. Now it was quite true that Joe was neither particularly tall nor particularly broad. So Stirlingson, older but apparently stronger could have been forgiven for thinking that he was easily a match for the cyclist. He tried to push past Joe and found himself lying on the floor in a matter of milliseconds.

"Now, Mr. Stirlingson, we are not the police so are not bound by whatever codes of procedure that may have to abide by. You were the passenger in the car, you were the person who killed Raymond Dragonard. Several friends of ours have died because of Dowling and his gang and we know that you are involved in this smuggling ring right up to your dirty neck. Unless you start to tell us all you know from the beginning, you will follow those friends, except in your case it will be to Hell. Now talk."

"I have nothing to say. I don't know what you're talking about. If you think one photograph and the word of a whore is proof. Pah!" The bluster was still there in force. Connolly turned to the others in the room.

"Joe, John, Harry stay, the rest leave. The next few minutes may not be pleasant."

Henry led the ladies out of the room. As they did so Stirlingson tried to get to his feet. Romain thumped him very hard in the solar plexus and he collapsed writhing on the floor.

"Now you'll have noticed that ole Joe here is pretty handy and I'm going to remind him, one by one, of the things that Dowling and his gang, and therefore you by association, have done to hurt him, me or one of our friends or colleagues and at each reminder he's going to hit you very hard and hurt you a lot. It won't be long before he starts to break things until you tell us what we want to know. I'd guess he'll start with your arms then fingers probably then legs or perhaps ribs. What d'you reckon, Joseph?"

"Arms first definitely, then legs I think." Stirlingson's bluster had almost but not quite disappeared.

"You wouldn't dare!"

Connolly nodded to Joe and said, "Let's start with the killing of Ercole Santana."

"I liked Ercole you bastard, I liked him a lot." Romain grabbed hold of Stirlingson's left arm, pulled it up behind his back and jerked very hard. Stirlingson's scream almost drowned the sound of the breaking bone.

"Now, I'll ask you each question only once. Was Dowling the top man?"

"For God's sake please do something about my arm."

"All in good time, answers first, there's a good chap." His exaggerated upper class English accent didn't amuse the English minister one bit.

"No, he wasn't."

"That's better. Were you the main man then?"

"No, No. I was just their man on that precious committee."

"So you know what the next question is, who is the boss man?"

"I can't tell you, I'll be a dead man."

"If I let Joe start you'll leave here a dead man, sunshine. Joe, you remember last year's Tour of Flanders, you and me walking away with it and this shit's cronies pulling that banner down on us?"

"I sure do, boss." Romain took hold of the Englishman's other arm.

"No, no more, I'll tell you." He looked and his eyes widened in absolute terror. Seeing his look Connolly and Romain turned in the direction of Stirlingson's horrified stare and saw at the open French windows, a tall thin man dressed entirely in black and masked. As they gazed transfixed like a snake by a mongoose, the silenced gun in the intruder's hand spoke once and the 'phut' sounded more frightening than the usual roar of an unsilenced gun.

Connolly and Romain dived for cover but need not have feared. After the one shot, the assassin had disappeared.

Stirlingson was dead of course and with him all hope of further progress. As Connolly picked himself up, he cursed long and loudly but he knew it was to no avail. There was still someone free out there, someone who had made a great deal of money and had caused the death of a significant number of people, as well as injuries to many more. Perhaps there was still something that could be done, but exactly what he had no idea.

A few hours later and many miles away, the small blonde-haired man steepled his fingers again as Sergio Indurrana related the story Dowling's demise, the death of James Stirlingson and the end of the diamond smuggling chain. He just managed to keep his elation at Dowling's failure out of his voice. The reaction from Indurrana's boss was phlegmatic.

"The loss of the diamonds and the future income from them is unfortunate, the deaths of Dowling and Stirlingson are not. Is there anything, however minor which could be traced back to us?"

"Nothing at all. There are still three of Dowling's goons alive but they never knew that there was somebody for whom Dowling was working. I can arrange for their elimination if you wish it?" The blonde-haired man shook his head.

"If they know nothing there is no point in taking further risks however minimal those risks might be. We quit while we are ahead, as they say. However," his carefully modulated voice hardened. "If your information concerning these three men is incorrect, you will be eliminated first. Is there anything else?"

"What about Connolly?"

"Dowling misjudged him. However, he can do nothing now that Stirlingson, Dowling and Dragonard are all dead. If I decide to invest in cycling in future I shall ensure that Mr. Connolly is taken care of at the beginning. For the time being, however, I have decided to explore other avenues. You may go."

417

As Induranna left his employer's office he reflected on the accuracy of the blonde man's word. Dowling had misjudged Connolly, only a lot.

CHAPTER FORTY-FIVE

After the tensions, dramas and uncertainties of the past
months, the dawning of a day during which the only thing at
stake would be a cycle race, seemed almost anti-climactic to
Bruce Connolly. As he lay in his bed in the team's hotel just
outside Monza, The American grinned wryly. It said much
for the events of the past two years that The Tour of
Lombardy, 'The race of the falling leaves', or as it has
recently been renamed, 'Il Lombardia', although to almost
everyone except the organisers, it was still The Tour of
Lombardy, could ever be thought of as an anti-climax. It had
always been one of his favourite races, certainly his favourite
classic, but it was also one of the most difficult to win.
Although it book-ended the classics season with the other
Italian classic, Milan - San Remo, and many riders were tired
after a long season, many of the best riders tended to ease off
towards the end of the season in order to be close to their
best for Lombardy.

Connolly marvelled again at his good fortune.
Resplendent in his Rainbow jersey as World Professional
Road champion and also winner of this year's Tour, he only
had to be fourth or better, irrespective of who won, to also
win the World Cup. Should any of his challengers fail to
score significant points he would win it anyway. To add to
his ecstasy was his love of and from Sarah. Not for the first
time did he wonder how much the new success in his cycling
was due to her. Would he have persevered with his racing if

she hadn't showed up, and in such a positive manner? He seriously doubted it.

These thoughts and many others chased each other through his mind as he dozed. Not fully light yet, there was still almost an hour before he had to get up and breakfast, ready for a race which he was now eagerly anticipating. He woke with a start half an hour later.

"C'mon blue eyes, it's time for all good cyclists to be up and about. Ah but that lets you out now doesn't it, but it's time for bad cyclists to be up as well, so shake a leg me boyo." Sean Brean had breezed in to the room. Since the kidnapping incident, Sean had made sure that his team leader had never been far from his sight, or at least with one of the totally trusted other lieutenants. Greater confidence was evident in everything Sean did these days, including of course his racing. The easy familiarity with Connolly, so different from his earlier, almost painful shyness, pleased the American enormously.

"You're getting far too big for your britches, you big Irish lummox Brean, what makes you so bright and breezy this morning?"

"Today is a day made by the good Lord for the doing of great deeds. I have the feeling in my water that I for one will indeed do those great deeds, well some of them anyway. Da Tour of Lombardy is moine dis very day, I swear it by all dat's holy." When Sean became excited, his Irish brogue became more pronounced and Bruce smiled both at the enthusiasm of the younger man, and his accent.

"You win and I'll take third how's that?" Connolly, still smiling was moving towards the shower.

"Why turd, why not secont?"

"Okay, fine by me, *you* win and I'll be runner-up it's a deal. Just don't leave it to a sprint cause if you do, I'll beat you."

"An old man loike you, I'll be foine and dandy however it finishes. I'll just be goin down an tellin the lads that our

420

Lord and master will be goin for secont today and dat he is wantin me to win."

"Get out you Irish oaf, I'll be down for breakfast in two shakes, so leave me in peace."

Half an hour later, after breakfast, the team's tactics were sorted. Although it was Bruce's position as World Cup leader that was of prime importance, the form of Brean was better than that of anyone in the team, with the possible exception of Connolly himself. It was agreed that Sean should try for the win, with three of the team helping him if a win looked a possibility, whilst the remainder of the team made sure that Connolly had all the help he needed to clinch victory in the World Cup.

The Tour of Lombardy had seen some famous victories. In many people's eyes, one of the best had been in 1965 by the Englishman Tom Simpson whilst riding in the Rainbow Jersey, beating the Italian, Gianni Motta. This was acclaimed as Simpson's finest victory and now similarly garbed in his rainbow Jersey, Bruce was feeling inspired. However, another Englishman, Roger Powell was also intending to emulate Simpson, whilst Giuseppi Vacchio desperately wanted to win the Italian classic to keep the recent Italian renaissance moving along. He also wanted to finish his season on a high as a good spring campaign for Giuseppi had been followed by an indifferent summer.

The day was glorious as the field of two hundred riders rode out of Monza. More famous for its motor racing circuit than for being the host town of this particular event, Monza was nevertheless full of visitors and the many cycling fans amongst were full of enthusiasm for their heroes. Only the most careworn riders could fail to be inspired by the scene. The sky was a deep cerulean blue and the autumnal coolness made the riders' skin tingle. Although the leaves were falling, many of the trees still shone with their copper and russet-coloured dappled cloaks and the lack of any strong wind made riding conditions almost ideal. Somewhat surprisingly for the last big race of the season, attacks started almost from the gun and those attacks contained strong riders so instant responses were always necessary. No one was going to be allowed much latitude today.

As the blue in the sky turned lighter, so the temperature rose. After a hundred and twenty kilometres or so, the significant attack of the day occurred. Ammoroso Sarro and Patrick Mertens from the Santiamo team jumped away. Americans Maynard Jones and Mark Andrews took off after them immediately, followed by Connolly, Brean, Weiss from Brooklin. Vacchio and teammate Velasquez from Bianchi and Powell, Vachot and Gilles Duclat completed the highly talented break. There was no doubt in the minds of either spectators or riders. Any rider not in this break could freewheel for the rest of the way or climb off now, the race was over for them. In a matter of five minutes, the break had 'made the difference' and had opened up a gap of almost a kilometre over the now dispirited peloton.

The break went up the Ghisallo climb and the day was now very warm. Connolly was very glad of the drink handed up to him by a fan and several of the others had water thrown over them or wet sponges passed to them by spectators. The beautiful countryside flashed by, unheeded by the riders, but the spectators were already aware that this was a classic edition of a classic race. On many occasions in the past the Tour of Lombardy has been won and lost on the climb of the Valclava climb and every member of the break was aware that final selection would probably take place on the notorious climb this year as well.

Sure enough, as soon as the group reached the bottom of the climb, Frederick Vachot, desperate to finish off a poor season on a high, launched a blistering attack. Vacchio went with him, quickly followed by all the others save two. Connolly had responded to the attack for a few seconds and then virtually instantly had felt all his strength leave him. Pete Weiss had followed Vachot but Brean had seen the instant cracking of his leader and had dropped back.

"Don't wait, Sean, I'll recover, go after them." Brean still hesitated.

"Dammit, man, go or you're sacked." It took all of Connolly's strength just to call to the Irishman, but after another angry gesture, Brean took flight. For his part, Connolly had never felt so bad. He dropped down the remaining gears very quickly but even in bottom gear on the little ring he was hardly able to keep that turning. Not only did he feel absolutely exhausted physically, he began to experience the weirdest sensations and thoughts. What on earth was happening? Dimly through a haze he caught sight of spectators' faces. He could see alarm in their eyes. The World Champion and Tour winner was clearly in desperate trouble, surely he must stop?

Still the climb ground upward. Connolly started to zig-zag across the road to try and lessen the gradient but he was aware that there was no pattern nor control in his zigzagging. Something was badly wrong with him. Then feeling as if he was dying, a scene flashed across hid befuddled mind. A vision from his childhood. There was a rider in desperate climbing a mountain, weaving all over the road and then agonisingly slowly coming to a stop, falling off his bike and then dying by the roadside.

At that moment Connolly knew that he must stop. He felt rather than saw the peloton stream by him as he stopped pedalling and fell into the arms of spectators lining the roadside. Again he remembered the eyes of the dying rider as he slipped into unconsciousness and oblivion.

Seconds later, Connolly's team car screamed to a halt alongside the stricken prostrate American. Ryan jumped out of the car and a few seconds later the Race Director and Race Doctor arrived. After a very quick but nevertheless thorough examination, the doctor administered an injection. His face told its own story. The doctor was clearly very worried. Two medical attendants lifted Connolly onto a stretcher and the doctor moved away from the crowd taking Ryan and the Race Director with him.

"He's been drugged and quite heavily I fear. We need to get him to hospital immediately."

"The helicopter is on its way, in fact I can hear it now." Sure enough, the helicopter came into sight as the Director finished speaking. In a very short space of time, Connolly was loaded onto the helicopter and was on his way to hospital.

As it disappeared Ryan turned to the doctor, anger blazing in his eyes.

"Bruce drugged, that's impossible, he's one of the riders that everyone knows is clean and always has been..." The doctor held up his hands trying to calm Ryan down.

"Hold on. I didn't say he'd taken drugs, I said he'd been drugged. It's happened before. Somebody passed him a drink I'd say."

"Bruce would've had more sense than to take a drink from somebody by the roadside. He knows the dangers." Ryan was still somewhat miffed. The doctor smiled sympathetically.

"Look, my friend, everyone knows about the problems he's had in the past. Perhaps he thought that the danger had passed and he was a little less careful than usual. It did get very hot very quickly." He patted Ryan on the arm. The Race Director, silent up this point, now spoke up.

"So what is your prognosis, doctor?" He spoke clearly afraid of the answer but having no alternative but to ask it.

"It is very difficult to say. The impossible thing to have any idea about is how hard he pushed himself before stopping. I'm afraid he may have significantly damaged his heart if he kept pushing too hard for too long. The kind of drug he's ingested basically masks the effects of the effort the athlete is making, confusing the brain so that it doesn't shut down the vital organs soon enough and they become irreparably damaged."

"Will he live?" The Director spoke as Ryan was still unable to ask the fateful question. There was a long pause before the doctor answered.

"I'm afraid that I just don't know. As soon as I hear from the hospital I will contact you on the private frequency on race radio."

The other two looked extremely downcast. Ryan spoke quietly.

"Bruce always gave everything. I hate to think how hard he would've been pushing."

"Well maybe, but a couple of spectators said that he actually stopped pedalling before he stopped and fell off the bike. That might be a good sign, but try not to be too hopeful, just in case."

"How long before you know?" Ryan again.

"If he hasn't died by the time they get him to the hospital he should make it. As far as damage is concerned, a few tests will give us a fairly accurate picture. It is a very difficult to do, but try not to worry."

Still desperately worried but still having a team to direct, Ryan had no option to get back in the car and with the usual blaring of Klaxons he sped off after the peloton. By this time the race was nearing its climax. Brean had caught the break without using up all his reserves. Another ten kilometres later the pace became too hot for first Andrews, then Velasquez and another five kilometres later Mertens. Ten kilometres remained. Powell, Vacchio, Sarro, Jones, Duclat and Velasquez all tried for a long one in the next five kilometres but all came to nothing. Now Vachot, Brean and Weiss were the only ones who had not expended any energy in trying to jump away although Weiss in particular had done a lot of the pulling back the attacks.

The crowd was now several rows deep on both sides of the road and the shouts for Vacchio and Sarro far outnumbered those for the non-Italian riders. Brean had by now recovered from his chase and nodded to Weiss.

"With no Bruce here, we've got to try to keep both Vacchio and Powell from getting better than third."

"Okay it looks like it's going to be a sprint now. Everybody's too fucked to try for another long one. I'll try and lead out Jones, he's the best sprinter but I'll go too soon. You pretend to lead out the others, 'die' too soon and then come again, we might just do it."

Three kilometres to go, still no attacks, then two kilometres, everybody still working together to keep the pace up to ensure no one broke away. Under the red kite denoting one kilometre to the finish and everybody now started to play cat and mouse. Brean and Weiss both tensed ready to go when they reached the five hundred metres marker. Unfortunately, they reckoned without the combination of Italian talent and Italian support. With still seven hundred metres left an inspired Giuseppi Vacchio launched himself from the back of the group as if rocket assisted. Powell, Brean and Jones responded as quickly as they could but the Italian had opened a very large gap. The three chasers, sprinting furiously, now began to edge closer to the Italian. Four hundred metres, three hundred. Then Brean realised that only Powell was with him. Two hundred metres. Vacchio was definitely slowing. Brean dug as deep as he could and found reserves from somewhere. Then Powell was no longer there. Sean pushed himself again. A hundred metres left. Vacchio was tying up, the build up of lactic acid making his legs scream, but Sean was tying up too. The line was so close. The Irishman threw his bike at the line in a classic sprinter's lunge and he edged out Vacchio by half a wheel!

He had won the Tour of Lombardy! Vacchio was second and Powell third. This meant that they now tied for the lead in the World Cup with Connolly in third place. For some time, the euphoria of his win, the backslapping and the general adulation of the crowd pushed everything else out of his mind. Then with a tremendous feeling of guilt he remembered Connolly! He quickly found the team bus and was relieved to see John Ryan. Rushing over to him Ryan related some of what he knew, not wanting to totally ruin the Irishman's moment of triumph, explaining that Bruce was in hospital for precautionary reasons. Sean was now able to go back to the presentation area in a far happier frame of mind and go and stand on the top step of the podium. His delight at winning his first monument, indeed his first classic was very evident. He drank literally from the champagne bottle after he had sprayed the crowd with it in the time honoured fashion, then drank metaphorically of the feeling that if only fleetingly, he was the best cyclist in the world!

CHAPTER FORTY-SIX

Although very worrying for his family, friends and team-mates and of course Sarah, who as yet didn't really fit into any of those categories, the tests carried out on Bruce Connolly at the hospital confirmed that his heart had not been damaged by the drugging incident. The bottle handed up by the spectator was still in Connolly's bottle cage and after careful analysis was confirmed as the source of the drug. The spectator in question was still being sought by the police. The only event left on Connolly's programme for the season was the classic Grand Prix de Nations time trial. For many years this had been seen as the unofficial time trial World championship. The legend that was the late Jaques Anquetil had won the 'Nations' every time he had ridden it, an incredible nine times. With the introduction of the official World Championship, the 'Nations' had gone out of favour and in fact had been discontinued for a number of years. However, in recent times there had been a huge increase in interest again it had reappeared and the world's best time triallists always tried to win it, especially those who had not quite won gold at the World Championship.

This year's event, now fast approaching, was however under something of a cloud. Bruce Connolly who had not contested the time trial at the worlds, preferring to save himself for the road race, had stated his intention of winning the 'Nations' to prove to everyone that he was not only a consummate stage race cyclist as well as a brilliant one-day winner, but also a first class time trial list as well. There had been few in the history of the sport. Jaques Anquetil, Eddy Merckx and Bernard Hinault were the three names that immediately sprang to mind, to a lesser extent, Felice Gimondi and Greg Lemond. With three days to go before the event, the favourite, Connolly was still in hospital with no chance of competing. He was philosophical when Sarah went to the hospital to take him home two days before the 'Nations'.

"Lots of cards wishing you well and commiserating about missing the 'Nations', Bruce".

"Too bad I guess, you can't have it all. Even so I sure as hell wanted to win it. If I had, I'd have won the World Cup too. Maybe next year for both."

"Try not to think about it. I've been thinking. Why don't we have a really good holiday; somewhere miles away from bikes and sport, TV reporters and newspapers. Think of somewhere you've never been and have always wanted to. I'll do the same and let's see if there's any common ground."

"Sounds good to me, I'll give it some thought."

"Promise?"

"Scout's honour."

"Were you ever a boy scout?"

"Course I was, wasn't everybody? One thing though, I want to go the watch the Nations, cheer the guys on."

"Okay by me, we could stay in one of the lovely lakeside hotels, but not, I hasten to add, one that is being used by any of the teams."

Connolly put his hands up in mock surrender.

"You're the boss."

Two days later, the two of them left their hotel and went to the H.Q. of the event, a large hotel. From outside there appeared to be even more chaos than was the norm before an event. People seemed to be milling about or talking to each in a fairly unorganised manner. As soon as they walked in and were spotted by riders and officials, people began to clap and cheer until Connolly could see no one who wasn't doing one or the other, or both. He blushed, something he couldn't remember doing in an age. The Brooklin riders were around him in seconds. Most had visited him in hospital but this was the first time they had seen him for some days.

"What's going on, shouldn't you guys be making your way to the signing-on?" Connolly asked the team members. Connolly then noticed a complete absence of all the Directeurs Sportif.

"Where's John and all the other D.Ss?" Connolly asked Joe Romain. At that moment, the tall distinguished figures of Francesco Moser, Felice Gimondi and Gianni Bugno, all previous Rainbow Jersey holders and, as the Italians called their truly great riders, 'campionissimi', came out of the adjoining conference suite, followed by all the Directeurs Sportif. Bruce noticed Ryan right behind Bugno wearing the biggest smile he had ever seen. In fact just about everybody was wearing a smile.

"What's going on?" This from Sarah. Joe started to speak but a sudden silence descended on the room as the race organiser raised his hands for quiet. He spoke first in Italian, but an English translation followed every sentence.

"Ladies and Gentlemen, this morning these three distinguished gentlemen," he waved to the three ex-champions, "came to me as representatives of the Professional Cyclists' Association, with an extraordinary request, a request supported by every one of its members. We, together with all of the Directeurs Sportif and other members of the organisers have been discussing this proposal for the past hour. I would add that this took so long, not because of any disagreement amongst us but simply because of the logistical difficulties involved in implementing the proposal. I shall now read the proposal. 'That, in view of the most unfortunate problems recently suffered by one of its members, namely Mr. Bruce Connolly, the Professional Cyclists Association proposes that the

430

Grand Prix de Nations time trial shall be postponed for one week to enable Mr. Connolly to take part.' I am pleased to announce that there was total agreement to this proposal by all the teams' representatives and that today's event is hereby postponed and will take place one week from today. Thank you for your patience." His final words were drowned by the cheering from just about everyone in the very crowded room.

Connolly was stunned and speechless. He felt his eyes filling with tears, stopped them just in time. Sarah put her arms around him and hugged him very tightly. Eventually Bruce found his voice and spoke to Ryan.

"How come, John, whose idea was this? It's, it's… they can't do this, it's ridiculous, what about all the spectators?"

"Firstly, it can be done and it has been, so there's no point in trying to do anything about it. Secondly, everybody knew that without you riding the result would have been fairly meaningless. As far as whose idea, I can honestly say I don't know and as for the fans, well the big thing about cycling is that as a spectator sport it's the best there is because it's free. Instead of one day out they'll now have an excuse for another one next week. Gianni," Ryan pointed to Bugno, "is your best bet for finding out who came up with the idea but why worry?"

Ryan was smiling.

"I need to know so I can find some way of thanking them." He moved over to the Italian. As President of the Professional Cyclists Association, Connolly knew the Italian fairly well. The two men both liked and respected each other. They shook hands and embraced.

"Bruce, my friend, you look much better than I expected. How are you?"

"I'm fine, Gianni. Look, this is an amazing thing you guys have done, but I need to know. Who came up with the idea?" Bugno shook his head and smiled.

"That I cannot tell you. I am sworn to secrecy. What I can tell you is that the idea did not come from any of your teammates. In a truly honourable gesture they all abstained from the vote. The second thing is that every other member of the association was clearly and honestly for the idea and that thirdly, you have a lot of friends in this sport of ours. Now the big question is, will you be ready for next week? We don't want to have done this for you to ride as the British say, 'like a bag of spanners' eh?" Both men laughed.

"You bet your ass I'll be ready, Gianni, you bet your ass."

Connolly marched to the end of the room and jumped up on a chair. The room quietened and everyone turned towards the American. For a few seconds there was silence.

"I've no way of saying what this means to me, so I'll just say, thanks, thank you all, especially whoever came up with the crazy notion." He then repeated his little speech in Italian and then in French. More cheers, Connolly waved, jumped down, ran to Sarah, grabbed her hand and together they ran from the building.

Seven days later, the scenario was much the same except that now there was an air of purpose and urgency about the hotel lobby. People were still smiling but in a different determined way. The gesture had been made, honour satisfied but if Connolly wanted to win he would have to fight all the way. All around the course, even more spectators had turned up than the previous week. The unheard of postponement of the event had clearly captured everyone's imagination and the selflessness of the riders' gesture to Connolly had hugely impressed everybody connected with sport. The media had loved it. The atmosphere was absolutely electric.

Unlike most races, the Nations field was always relatively small, only the really good time triallists tended to take part together with up and coming riders wanting to match themselves against the very best and a few riders who rode to help teammates by riding early on and reporting back any problems on the course. Connolly had three Brooklin boys riding today, Sean riding to repay his boss. He was number five, Sam Parker a new pro this season riding for experience, he was off at number nineteen and Joe Romain, number twenty-five who quite fancied his chances for getting on the podium. Connolly as a fancied rider, notwithstanding his recent problem was next to last man off, being followed the current World time trial champion Amoroso Sarro. Conditions were near perfect, what is referred to as a "float morning" when the rider feels that he is floating over the road. The riders started at two minute intervals and it wasn't long before the times of the early finishers indicated that the conditions were indeed as good as they had appeared, and that some riders were going very well indeed, catching the riders in front of them more quickly than would have been expected.

With half of the riders finished Sean, riding only to provide information for Connolly was next to last, Sam was lying in a very creditable fifth place, although with faster riders in the second half of the field he would be lucky to hold that position. Giuseppi Vacchio was leading with a time of sixty-eight minutes and ten seconds. At the halfway time check Mark Andrews was only two seconds down on Vacchio's corresponding time and Joe Romain a further three seconds back. That augured well for Joe as he had a reputation for finishing strongly.

As Connolly waited in the start house for his countdown he watched as his two-minute man, Felice Prosponi, a noted time-trialling specialist sped down the start ramp. Prosponi would be one of Connolly's biggest threats. He was putting everything into the start as he sped away. Connolly went up to the start line, was held in place as he clipped into his pedals, took deep breaths as he was counted down, then he was off. He started less violently than Prosponi but still with purpose and quickly settled into an excellent rhythm, his pedal cadence both smooth and quick. Riding a fairly big gear he was nevertheless riding beautifully, virtually motionless on the bike, in that state of grace almost where the rider is completely at one with his machine.

"Bruce, at the three-quarter time check, Joe was only one second down on Vacchio and Andrews is slipping slightly. Prosponi went off quickest of all but you are now holding him." Ryan voice through Connolly's earpiece confirmed Bruce's thoughts. The kilometres rolled by, the only sounds being the cheers from the crowd and the hum of his tyres with occasional comments from Ryan from the following car.

"Joe's just finished, he's beaten Vacchio by six seconds. Powell is the next threat and he was one second down on Joe at halfway. Sarro was one second up on you at five kilometres. Very good so far, you can do this." Connolly knew that he was stronger than Sarro over the last half but he couldn't afford to let the Italian gain too much time over the first half. He forced himself to let go of those thoughts and just concentrated on his smoothness, his position and his cadence. He still felt strong, relieved that the drugging incident appeared not to have weakened him.

He passed the time check at halfway and as expected Ryan's voice came in his ear again.

"You were fastest at halfway by two seconds over Joe and five over Powell who is definitely slowing. Prosponi's slowing as well, he definitely went off too fast and he's paying for it now. You should catch him." Connolly smiled to himself. The only unknown was Sarro and he would soon hear the score with him too. Sure enough two minutes later...

"Sarro's up on you by ten seconds at halfway, he certainly put in a spurt over the last five k." Ryan's voice was still calm. Ten seconds was okay, he'd need to be careful though. Bang! The noise of Connolly's back tyre blowing was a huge shock. He quickly threw up his hand and pulled over to the side of the road as his car drew alongside the mechanic out of the car before it had stopped with the new wheel in his hand. The wheel change was mercifully as smooth as silk and Connolly was racing again in less than twenty seconds. Don't panic Connolly told himself, you can still do it. Don't tense up keep smooth.

"He's twenty seconds up now but you're looking good again.

Just keep on keeping' on man."

Then another voice, female, "You look so smooth big boy you'll do this easily."

Connolly relaxed, as much as one can in such a situation, felt the tension go and the float feeling return, for two minutes there was silence in his ear.

"You should see Prosponi any second, Bruce." Seconds later the Italian came into view, still going smoothly but Bruce could see the distance closing.

"Sarro's slowing," Ryan's voice betrayed excitement for the first time, He's now only twelve seconds up and you've got five k to go."

The kilometres and the gap in seconds both counted down, four k, ten seconds, three k, eight seconds, two k, seven seconds. Bruce knew he now had to give everything for the last two kilometres as Sarro had obviously rallied a little over the last kilometre. He concentrated on keeping his shoulders still, not wasting any energy and maintaining his smoothness. He went under the red kite with a kilometre to go. He buried himself, his heart pounding and legs burning, now gasping for air. He turned into the finishing straight with four hundred metres to go and prayed for the line to come. He flashed under the finishing banner absolutely spent. He fell into the arms of his soigneur and collapsed onto the ground. He now had to wait for a little less than two minutes for the Italian to finish. He staggered to his feet looking back down the straight. Sarro came round the corner to huge cheers from the mostly Italian crowd but Bruce could tell he wasn't going to make it. He had two hundred metres to go when the two minutes were up. A huge cheer went up from the Brooklin camp and Sarah and Ryan,

435

having scrambled out of the car both threw their arms around him. Bruce Connolly's most amazing and successful season had concluded with a fairy-tale ending.

He had won the Grand Prix de Nations and Joe Romain had taken third. With the victory Bruce had won the World Cup and Brooklin had finished the season as the number one ranked team by some distance. The team's celebration that evening was to be remembered for many moons!

EPILOGUE

Sarah and Bruce lay snuggled together in the king-sized bed in Henry's biggest guest room. It was two days after the Nations and after Lombardy, Connolly's hospitalisation, his fight for fitness for the Nations, and the event itself, both were revelling in their peace. All they had to worry about now was themselves.

"Bruce, there are still a few things I don't understand."

"Hmmm?" In his rather somnambulant state, Connolly was happy to put the events of the past months behind him but Sarah was clearly not going to be denied.

"For one thing you've never explained why you were the bad guys' main target. Secondly, what was all that business about the paintings in my flat, and then, nothing? And thirdly, and it's a big thirdly, I have the very definite feeling that somewhere in all this there is some involvement by Dad. Now don't pretend to be asleep, you American lummox, I want some answers."

"Lummox! Is that any way to refer to your beloved?"

"Alright, you big dick. Is that better?"

"Oh much better." He reached for her but she slapped his hands.

"No chance lover boy until I've had some answers. Now give."

Connolly had not been looking forward to this moment. However, he knew that Sarah would not be fobbed off any longer. He sat up and leaned back against the headboard.

"How much do you know of Jason's business activities?"

"A little, why?"

"How honest would you say he is, or perhaps more importantly, was?" She was too sensible to be affronted.

"No more than averagely so. Not above pulling the occasional stroke I'm sure." Connolly now relaxed a little and smiled a little too.

"Good, that makes life a lot easier. Your first question has two answers. The first one is that Dowling had a long-standing grudge against Jason which I'll come back to that in a minute. Now God knows how, because only a handful of people knew or even know now, but Dowling found out that it was Jason who was bankrolling my team."

"Dad! Why didn't you tell me?"

"Steady, even I didn't know until I saw Jason a few weeks ago. If I had told you then you may have felt obliged to tell your group and even then I was pretty sure, there was a mole both in the team and in your group. When Jason had to pull out of racing years ago, he decided to put his support into a team without the world at large knowing about it. Strangely enough Henry has always known about it but was sworn to secrecy, and I also didn't find that out until I saw your Dad recently. Jason is also about the only one who knew that Henry was my Dad. Apparently the two of them go way back. Because of the grudge, Dowling decided to take out his beef on Jason's team whilst creating the desired diversions. The other reason was that when this all started, if you remember, I was the hard case everyone used to love to hate. Me coming cropper after cropper was only what I deserved in most uninformed eyes." Sarah nodded slowly.

"So all this time, my father has been employing my lover?"

438

"Yep! And I can tell you I'm not too ecstatic about it. I never did cotton to marrying the boss's daughter." He laughed as she slapped him again.

"Okay, wise guy, what about the other questions?"

"They're all connected. When I first saw the pictures, I was shocked. I'm not exactly an expert but I know a fair bit about art and I know valuable pictures when I see 'em and your two are really valuable. So are your two paintings." Another laugh and another slap as he gently squeezed one of her breasts.

"How valuable?"

"I thought, only hundreds of thousands of dollars, because they were fakes. Good fakes, but still fakes. I'd seen the real things in galleries."

Sarah's eyes widened.

"Good heavens! How much if they had been the real thing?"

"Exactly. Millions. Anyway, as you saw I got my friend to bring his friend. I was slightly economical with the truth there. They weren't valuing them, they were authenticating them. Here's the thing, yours are the real ones, the fakes are in the galleries and almost certainly have been for a very long time."

"Oh my God! So what are they worth?"

"One probably three million dollars, the other nearer five. Of course the big problem with selling them is they would have to be sold in secret."

Sarah put her hand over her mouth.

"Relax. Only Jason, my two pals and the two of us know and I have no fear of anybody else finding out. Jason was involved with Dowling, in the 'obtaining' of the pictures originally but I don't know how. There were four paintings in the beginning. The plan was to sell them to collectors. Then they had their row and split. Jason had two and

Dowling two. I've put my pals onto the Dowling angle and hopefully they'll make something for themselves and a bit for you and Jason as well. Jason never sold his two but he knew that Dowling still wanted his half of the money from their sale. For safety's sake Jason hung the paintings in your flat which he knew Dowling didn't know about."

"My own father! The bastard!"

"Steady. You were in no danger and by this time it was better for Dowling to use his knowledge of Jason's past to keep him quiet – blackmail without money if you like."

"Surely though what if Dowling thought that Dad might try to use me against him by putting me in the group for example?" Connolly shook his head.

"Don't forget that Dowling always had Stirlingson to tell him what was going on in your group. Your father had nothing to do with you getting involved in the group, did he?"

"Well no, I can't remember who it was now but it certainly wasn't Dad."

"And it wasn't you who suggested that I be recruited was it?"

"No that was Val Cornell, I'm certain of that. By the way, did you two have something going once upon a time?"

"Yep, great fuck, terrible temper, great girl though. Ouch!"

"No one is allowed to be a great fuck but me, so watch it buster. Anyway a gentleman does not tell tales about his former amours however great they are in bed."

"I thought everybody knew I wasn't a gentleman, anyway I was paying her a compliment. Ouch."

"Enough. Now continue."

"Okay okay! So there was no reason at all for Dowling to suspect you. I don't suppose he was ecstatic about me joining your gang but there was nothing he could do about that."

"So what happens now."

"We have a few visitors later and then we're all off to our favourite restaurant when we can thrash everything out then. In the meantime, madam, if that has settled your queries, it's high time I had some exercise."

"You mean a ride?"

"I do indeed."

"But not on a bike."

"Exactly. So let's see if you really are such a great fuck."

"I was beginning to think you were losing interest, it's almost three hours since the last time." This time the slap was administered by him on her bottom. They reached for each other. He was very hard and she was very moist.

Later that evening around the best tables in Sam's restaurant, Bruce having taken over the restaurant for the evening, Henry, Mary, John, Judith, Harry, Jessie and the whole of the Brooklin team were thoroughly enjoying themselves when Bruce stood up.

"I know everybody's hungry but we're just waiting on another couple of people to show up, in the meantime I'd just like to say thank you to everybody for all you've done in every direction this season. A toast everybody. To Brooklin." Everybody stood and responded. "Ah, here are our last two guests." Jason Curzon walked in accompanied by a ravishing looking Jessica Taylor. Kisses and handshakes followed and the Jason and Jessica sat in the chairs left vacant. Connolly remained standing.

"Before Sam, I mean Felice, and his troops descend upon us for our orders I have a few announcements to make.

Firstly, John and I have persuaded Judith to jump ship and become our chief Soigneur, or is soignéuse? Whatever. Harry and Jessie are fortunately for us, both out of work so Harry has agreed to operate as John's second D.S. but with special responsibility for scouting for new talent and starting up a youth squad. We've never had a team Secretary before and if ever we needed one it is now so Jessie has joined us.

Take a bow you guys." All three rather diffidently stood up and were greeted with huge cheers. Even Harry blushed, feeling really happy for the first time that he could that he could remember.

"My final announcement, promise. What most of you know is that Jason here is Sarah's Dad. What you don't know is that he both set up and owns," he paused, "the Brooklin team." Many jaws dropped and there was absolute silence. Only Ryan and Henry, in on the news, were smiling. Connolly also smiled at the effect of his words.

"As from this moment, he also becomes the team's General Manager. I have no doubt that he will make a far better job of it than his predecessor. He'll also fall out with John a lot less too. Welcome Jason, if that doesn't sound odd, being welcomed to your own team I mean."

Sarah stood up went round to Curzon and hugged him.

"This is fantastic, Dad."

"It was Bruce's idea and John is right there with it too. What else could I do?" She kissed his cheek and hugged him again. She then whispered in his ear.

"I think we need to talk paintings."

"Yes, I suppose we do."

They caught Bruce looking at them and all three smiled secret smiles.

"Sam, sorry, Felice, get over here, we need to eat."

"Oui, monsieur." Sam skillfully managed to gently catch Connolly around the ear with the menu as he bent over him.

"I told you she was dangerous, I always know these things."